PRINCESS
OF
SOULS

PRINCESS
OF
SOULS

ALEXANDRA CHRISTO

HOT
KEY
BOOKS

First published in Great Britain in 2022 by
HOT KEY BOOKS
4th Floor, Victoria House, Bloomsbury Square
London WC1B 4DA
Owned by Bonnier Books, Sveavägen 56, Stockholm, Sweden
www.hotkeybooks.com

A CIP catalogue record for this book is available from the British Library.

ISBN: 978-1-4714-1199-1
Also available as an ebook and in audio

1

Book design by Aurora Parlagreco
Printed and bound in Great Britain by Clays Ltd, Elcograf S.p.A.

Hot Key Books is an imprint of Bonnier Books UK
www.bonnierbooks.co.uk

For Mum & Dad,
who have always brought magic into my life

ISLES

THAVMA

FLÓGA

THE ENDLESS SEA

1

SELESTRA

I can tell someone when they're going to die. All I need is a lock of hair and their soul.

Just in case.

That's the job of a Somniatis witch, tied to the king with magic steeped in death. It's all I was ever raised to be: a servant to the kingdom, an heir to my family's power.

A witch bound to the Six Isles.

And because of it, I've never glimpsed the world beyond the Floating Mountain this castle stands on.

Not that I'm a prisoner.

I'm King Seryth's ward and one day I'll be his most trusted adviser. The right hand to royalty, free to go wherever I want and do whatever I want, without having to ask for permission first.

Just as soon as my mother dies.

I stride through the stone halls, ivory gloves snaking to my shoulders where the shimmer of my dress begins. They're meant to be a safeguard for my visions, but sometimes they feel more like a leash to stop me from going wild.

To keep my magic at bay until the time is right.

But I'm not a prisoner, I tell myself.

I'm just not supposed to touch anyone.

Outside the Grand Hall, a line of people gathers in a stretch of soon-to-be corpses. Most are dressed in rags and dirt that cakes them like a second skin, but a few are smothered in jewels. A mix of the poor, the wealthy, and those who fall in between.

All of them are desperate to cheat death.

The Festival of Predictions happens once a year, during the month of the Red Moon, where anyone from across the Six Isles can wait for a prediction from the king's witch.

The line rounds the corner opposite me, so I can't see how far it stretches, but I know how many people there are. It's the same each year: two hundred souls ready to be bargained.

I try to move past them as quickly as I can, like a shadow sweeping across the corner of their eyes. But they always see me.

Once they do, they look quickly away.

They can't stand the sight of my green hair and snake eyes. All the things that make me different from them. They stare at the floor, like the tiles are suddenly too interesting to miss.

Like I'm nothing but a witch to be feared.

I'm not sure why. It's not like I have that much magic in me yet. At sixteen, I'm still just an heir to my true power, waiting for the day I inherit my family's magic.

"Would you hang on for a second?" Irenya says.

The apprentice dressmaker—and the only friend I have in this castle—heaves in a series of quick breaths, running to catch up with me as I finally come to a stop outside the Grand Hall.

She smooths down my dress, making sure there are no wrinkles in sight. Irenya is a perfectionist when it comes to her gowns.

"Quit squirming, Selestra," she scolds.

"I'm not squirming," I say. "I'm *breathing*."

"Well, stop that too, then."

I poke out my tongue and start to fiddle with my gloves. Pulling the fingertips up and then pushing them back down so the fabric rubs against my skin.

The repetition is soothing.

It stops me from overthinking everything that's about to happen.

I should be used to all of this by now. Grateful that I've been allowed to stand by King Seryth's side for two years, gathering hair and watching as people from across the islands filter in to seal their fates.

I should be excited for the Festival and all the souls we'll reap. To watch my mother tell death's secrets, as though it's an old friend.

I should not be thinking about all the people who are going to die.

"We don't want you coming loose during the first prediction," Irenya says. She pulls the strings tighter on my dress and I just *know* that she's smiling. "Imagine, you bend down to take a lock of hair and your chest falls out."

"Trust me." I gasp out a breath. "I'm not bending anywhere in this thing."

Irenya rolls her eyes. "Oh, be quiet," she says. "You look like a princess."

I almost laugh at that.

When I was young—before my mother became a stranger— she'd read me stories of princesses. Fairy tales of demure women, powerless, locked up in towers and waiting to be rescued by a handsome prince, who would whisk them away for love and adventure.

"I'm not a princess," I say to Irenya.

I'm something far more deadly than that. And nobody is rescuing me from my tower.

I push open the heavy iron doors of the Grand Hall. The room has been emptied.

Gone are the wooden tables that cluttered the center, rich with wine and merciless laughter. The band has been dismissed and the room is drained to a hollow cavity.

To an outsider, it's impossible to tell that just a few hours ago, the wealthiest people in the kingdom celebrated the start of the Festival. I could hear the swells of music from my tower. Smell the brandy cakes and honey drifting in through the cracks of my window.

It still smells now. Cake and candle fire, charred wicks and sweet, smoky air.

I spy the king at the far end of the room on a large black throne carved from bones. A gift of love from my great-great-grandmother.

His gaze quickly meets mine, like he can sense me, and he beckons me over with a single finger.

I take in a breath and head toward him.

The cloak of my dress billows behind me.

It's a hideously sparkling thing that glitters under the candlelight like a river of plucked stars. It's a deep black blue, dark as the Endless Sea, that curls around my neck and drips down my pale skin like water. The back, tied by intricate ribbons, is covered in a long cape that flows to the floor.

It might be Irenya's creation, but it's the king's color.

When I wear it, I'm his trophy.

"My king," I say once I reach him.

"Selestra," he all but purrs. "Good of you to finally join us."

He leans back into his throne.

King Seryth is a warrior as much as a ruler, with long black hair and earrings of snake fangs. The tattooed serpents of his crest hiss across his face, and he's dressed in animal furs that break apart to reveal the ridged muscles of his chest.

All of it is meant to make him look menacing, but I've always thought his eternally youthful face was far more beautiful than frightening.

The real danger is in his eyes, darker than night, which hold only death.

"You look glorious," he says.

"Thank you."

I tuck a lock of dark green hair behind my ears.

I've never been allowed to cut it, so like my mother's it hangs well past my waist. Only unlike my mother's it curls up at the ends, where hers is as straight as a cliff edge.

Everything about her is edges and points, designed to wound.

"Good evening, Mother," I say, turning to bow to her.

Theola Somniatis, ever beautiful, sits beside the king on a throne that glitters with painted Chrim coins. A black lace gown clings to her body in a mix of swirls and skin.

She looks sharp and foreboding.

A knife the king keeps by his side.

And unlike me, she doesn't need gloves to keep her in check.

She purses her lips. "You were nearly late."

I frown. "I walked as fast as I could in these shoes," I say, lifting the hem of my dress to show the perilous heels hidden under its length.

They're already rubbing against my feet.

The king smirks at this. "Now you are here we can get started."

He raises his hand, a signal to the guards by the door.

"Let the first one in."

I take an unsteady breath.

And so it begins.

I wonder what curses death will show us today.

2

SELESTRA

The guards open the doors to the Grand Hall and I see the first woman emerge.

She approaches the throne hesitantly, two guards flanking her closely on either side as she takes slow, shuffled footsteps toward us. She's dressed in a dark red skirt that's damp with mud at the ankles.

My skin pricks on the back of my neck the closer she gets.

There's death in the air.

I can practically taste it.

Smell it on the woman's bones.

As she steps forward, skirt the color of dried blood and decaying rose petals, I know somehow that she won't last the week.

I can *feel* it.

Then my mother will snatch up her soul and King Seryth will gobble it down, like he's done for over a century. Feeding his immortality.

"Your Highnesses," the woman says, once she reaches the steps that elevate the thrones.

She curtsies, low enough that her knees touch the floor and her ankles shake with the weight.

She glances at my mother and I see the flicker of panic in her eyes before she bows her head.

They fear us. They hate us.

And they're right to.

I lift my chin up, reminding myself that I should be pleased.

This is the one time a year when I'm surrounded by magic. When I can feel the thrum of it coating the castle, as the power of my ancestors drifts through the air like sweet wine.

When I don't have to stay locked in my tower.

I grab the scissors from the table and descend the stairs.

"With these scissors, I'll take a lock of your hair and seal your place in the Festival of Predictions," I tell the woman. "Death will mark you on its list for this month of the Red Moon. It will come for you once this first week, then twice the second, and the prediction we give you today will be your only help to survive."

I recite the lines easily, as I've done since I was fourteen.

"If you die, your soul becomes forfeit to the king. But if you live through the first half of this month, you'll be rewarded with a wish of your choice and be released from your bargain."

The woman nods eagerly.

The promise of a wish makes the Festival a celebration in the realm. I've heard that the townsfolk even make bets, gambling Chrim on who might make it, throwing parties and drinking into the early hours.

People only ever enter into this bargain for the wish.

For the poor and the desperate, it's a chance to ask for gold Chrim or healing elixirs. For the rich and the arrogant, it's a chance to curse their enemies and amass more fortune.

And all of them think it's worth risking their souls for.

It's only three deaths, they probably tell themselves. *I can live through that.* And some do. Each year a handful of people get to resume their lives with a wish granted, inspiring others to try it for themselves next year.

But each year at least one hundred people don't.

It's funny how they're less remembered.

"If you choose to continue beyond this halfway point, be warned," I say, voice foreboding. "As in place of death, the king himself will have earned the right to hunt you until the month's end. For if you survive past the Red Moon, his immortality will be yours."

I feel Seryth's smile on the back of my neck.

He's not afraid.

He doesn't worry that he could ever lose his throne to any of these people.

"This bargain may kill you or bring you unrivaled glory," I say.

It will be the former. It always is.

Death has a funny habit of getting its way, and so does the king. I've seen that firsthand.

Besides, nobody who survives ever even *tries* to go past the halfway mark. Having death hunt you is one thing, but the king himself? Even before he amassed the deadliest army to ever live, the king was the most skilled warrior in all of the Six Isles. He has survived centuries, blessed by cursed magic.

It would be madness to even try to kill him.

Best to just take your wish and run home to safety.

"Do you accept this bargain?" I ask.

The woman gulps loudly.

"Yes," she says, voice trembling. "Please just take it."

With hands as unsteady as her voice, she gestures toward her hair.

I reach out with my scissors and cut a piece. The woman sucks in a breath, eyes sharpening.

I wonder if she feels something. A fragment of her taken to be stored away, so her soul is tethered to this world when she dies.

Ready for my mother to collect in her ritual.

Ready to be bound to the king.

"It's done," I say.

I turn away from her and place the hair into one of two hundred glass jars that line the steps to the thrones.

"Step forward," Theola says. "And keep your arm out."

I hear the woman's breath stutter as she ascends the first two steps. She takes a knee.

Theola extends her hand and daintily strokes the woman's palm. She closes her eyes, smile slow and damning.

Somniatis witches are like siphons. We draw in energy and let it pass through us. Energy like death that we call into our veins and let wet our lips. It's what gives us our visions and allows us to take the souls of the doomed and pour them into the king.

It's cursed magic, but it's the only magic left in the Six Isles.

My family saw to that.

Theola bites her lip as she looks into the woman's future.

There's a part of me that wants desperately to see what she sees. I want to feel the power that comes from knowing the future, from telling fate's secrets and letting my magic free from its shackles.

From *touching* someone, for the first time in years.

But then I remember Asden, my old mentor. I remember what happened the last time I touched someone.

I remember how he screamed.

The mere thought of it knocks into me as hard as a fist. I quickly right myself, swallowing the memory before the king notices the slip in my smile.

My mother withdraws her hand and looks down at the kneeling woman, whose palm is newly branded by King Seryth's crest: a blackened serpent eating its tail.

It appears on all death seekers, marking them and the deal they've made.

"In the next week, your youngest daughter will succumb to illness," Theola says.

Her voice is like ice, cold and smooth, like she's talking about the weather instead of death.

It wasn't always like that.

Once it was warm.

"She will die," Theola says. "And days later when you go to pick her favorite flowers, you will be attacked by a creature of the woods. Left to rot among the trees."

The woman gasps and even her hands stop shaking, as though terror has frozen her in place.

"No, my daughter cannot die." She shakes her head, no regard for her own life and the death my mother foresaw for her. "There must be a way. If I survive until the halfway point, then I can wish for a healing elixir and—"

"She will not last long enough for that."

With a tight jaw, my mother closes her fist and then opens it to reveal a single gold coin of Chrim that wasn't there seconds before.

She drops it into the sobbing woman's hand.

"For your troubles," she says. "Spend time with your child while you can. If you live, perhaps we'll see you again for a new wish. If you die, remember what you owe us."

The woman blinks and opens her mouth, as if to scream or cry or try to fight her future. But all that comes out is a whimper, before her eyes shift to mine.

I can see the accusation in them as the guards pull her up and drag her from the hall. The notion that I should be ashamed of my monstrous family and the evil we let seep into the world.

But she doesn't know.

She doesn't understand what it means to be a Somniatis witch, bound to the king by an ancient blood oath. Given the choice between prisoner or queen of magic, I doubt this woman would choose differently from me. She doesn't understand what could happen if I tried.

Still, once she's out of sight, I turn to my mother.

"Do you think she'll avoid the forest and forgo her daughter's flowers?" I ask.

It's a stupid question, and the moment I speak it, I wish I could take it back.

"What does it matter?" Theola's voice is scolding. "So long as we get the amount of souls we need, it's irrelevant which ones they are."

I know that she's right.

What's important is that we have at least one hundred souls by the end of the month. Enough so that the king can sustain his immortality and continue his rule forever.

"Don't you agree, Selestra?" my mother asks when I fall silent.

She looks at me with warning, telling me to nod, quickly.

"Of course," I say.

A practiced lie.

"My witches don't concern themselves with such questions."

The king stares at me tersely.

His eyes are black, black, black.

"You'll remember that, Selestra," he says. "If you ever manage to become one, rather than remain a simple heir."

I bow my head, but beneath the gesture my teeth grind together.

He calls me an heir like it's an insult, because it's all I'll be to him, to everyone, until I become the Somniatis witch.

Heirs to magic are useless until they reach their eighteenth birthday and are bound to the king by the blood oath, ready to be taught the true essence of magic and trained to take over once the old witch dies. Until then, I am irrelevant.

Sometimes I feel like a weed, pushing out from the roots of a strange garden, never quite able to blend in.

The rest of the evening goes the same way.

People are escorted in and out by the guards, kneeling as Theola recounts their new fates with little more than boredom. Betrayals from trusted friends, drowning in the local river, or stabbed in an alley outside the tavern they visit every night.

Each of them has the same horrified look as their deaths are revealed. They act as though it's a curse thrust upon them rather than something they sought out.

All the while I remain silent, only speaking to recite the rules of the Festival. I gather the hair dozens of times over, descending the stairs and watching as the king looks hungrily at each person who enters into his bargain.

Each potential new soul he'll use my family's magic to devour.

Only a handful of them will survive until the halfway point and be granted their wish.

And not a one of them could ever survive beyond that, even if they were reckless enough to try.

3
NOX

I'm good at a lot of things, but best of all is surviving.

I've got a knack for it that comes almost too easy, with barely a scar to show for years of close calls. I know how to fight, sure, but it's more than that.

The greatest skill my father taught me was how to work a room. How to get inside someone's mind and convince them I'm worth keeping around.

That I've got something special in me.

A lot of things have limits, but charm is rarely one of them. And I'm going to need that charm more than ever now.

We approach the Floating Mountain, ready to make our way to the top.

"In the list of stupid ideas you've had, this one takes the lead," Micah says.

I look to my best friend and fellow Last Army soldier with a grin. He adjusts the blade on his back and keeps an eye on the crowd of people behind us.

Micah is always suspicious of anyone and everyone who isn't me.

"You're making a list of all my bad ideas?" I ask.

We step onto the enchanted platform, a thin sheet of elaborately crafted gold that backs onto a tree tall enough to reach the stars.

It's the fastest way up the mountain, where the king's castle lies.

Micah nods. "It's a long damn list."

I shrug. He's got a point.

"This can't be at the top," I tell him. "What about that time during initiations when we decided to sneak into the sergeant's cabin and steal his—"

"Okay, okay," Micah says quickly, not wanting me to repeat *that* story out loud. "This is the second-stupidest idea you've ever had."

He's not wrong, but just because something's dangerous, it doesn't mean it's not worth it. Sometimes, the riskiest things reap the greatest rewards.

"It's not too late to change your mind, you know," Micah says.

The enchanted platform begins to ascend, the sky flicking by us as it gains traction. I look out at the world below, at the people who seem so small and barely there.

At the island of Vasiliádes the king has built his empire around.

From up here it looks peaceful, almost beautiful in a way that might rival the Southern Isle of Polemistés.

But it's a lie.

I can still hear the Endless Sea, crashing against the boats and tufts of land, like an invader trying to force its way in. The black waters swarm, refusing to freeze over even in the dead of winter when snow coats the streets. They drink the ice, burning it back to liquid. And on summer days like today when the sun beats down, the waters still ripple and swell with all the cursed magic the king placed inside them.

"If you're scared, you don't have to come," I say to Micah.

The platform docks and I step quickly off, breezing past the entry guards.

The castle grounds are beautiful, surrounded by never-ending greenery and hedges ripe with the sweetest fruit. Even the rocks are such a bright silver that people say they're carved from shooting stars.

Such beauty to house such monsters.

Micah jogs to keep step with me.

"I'm not scared," he protests. "And I'm not leaving you to the wolves."

I roll my eyes. "Seryth isn't a wolf. He's just a man."

"What about the witches?" Micah counters in a hushed voice. "They're not men and they can't be killed as easily as you or I. Their magic protects them, even from death. The witches are as endless as the king himself."

"*Witch*," I correct, lowering my voice as we navigate the path, lined by guards.

This whole place is a fortress.

For an immortal, the king sure does worry about his enemies.

"There's only really one witch," I remind Micah. "Theola's daughter won't come into her true powers for years. She won't be any trouble."

Micah's eyes dart quickly to the castle guards, to make sure none of them heard me.

"You might try keeping your voice down when you talk about treason," he says. "Stealth, Nox. *Stealth*."

I shake my head and come to a stop. "You should really stay here."

Micah's a liability when he worries and that's the last thing I need right now.

He straightens and his hand drifts to his sword. "I said I'm not letting you go in there by yourself," he says stubbornly.

It's a nice sentiment, really, but it's not necessary.

I push his hand back down. "Relax, soldier," I say, my voice light enough to let him know I'm not worried. "Soak up the sun, woo a pretty guard. Wait for me here."

Micah's eyes crease as he tries to weigh up whether or not to listen to me.

"If you're not back in ten minutes, I'm coming in after you," he says.

I smirk. "If I'm not back in ten minutes, there's nothing left of me to come after."

Walking into the king's castle is like stepping into a prison.

The walls are high and black, dark as the king's eyes and tall as clouds, with intricate threads of gold whisking across them like strokes of wind.

The marble floors resemble the Endless Sea enough so that I half expect my feet to slip through the tiles and meet water.

Instead, when I walk across them, my footsteps sound like a clock.

Like the hands of my father's pocket watch, which were just as loud.

Ticktock.

Come on, Nox! Just a bit faster!

Ticktock.

That's it! You'll be top of your class come initiation, son!

I haven't looked at that watch in years. It sits in a drawer in the barracks now, gathering dust and cobwebs, hidden behind old papers and my favorite knife.

When my footsteps echo its chimes, I don't hear my father's cheering voice anymore. I only hear the king's.

Ticktock. Ticktock.

Ready to die, are we, Nox?

I approach a group of guards outside the Grand Hall, readying to let the last seeker through.

Each year, only two hundred are allowed to enter into the bargain and risk their souls. I'm not sure why. Maybe Seryth and his witch bore if they see too many.

"I need to speak to the king," I say to the guard closest to the door.

He wears a uniform the same thunderstorm blue as mine. It hangs off him loosely, making him seem young, like he still needs to grow into it.

"Name?" he asks.

"Officer Nox Laederic," I say. "Of the Thánatos Regiment."

The moment my words register, the guard's lips part.

I guess we do have a bit of a reputation, but only part of it's my fault.

"You—you're—"

"Better looking in person, I know. Can I pass?"

"Is the king expecting you?" the guard asks, voice going up a pitch.

"Sure, I scheduled a meeting in his diary and put a little heart next to it," I say earnestly.

The guard doesn't return my grin, but instead fumbles with the large collar of his shirt. "I'm not supposed to . . ." He trails off. "We've still got one more prediction seeker left. Could you come back later?"

I can't help but laugh.

Years of preparation and all day convincing myself it's now or never, only to be turned away at the door.

If Micah were here, he'd get a kick out of it. Or think it was some kind of sign I should turn back and forget the whole thing.

But that isn't an option.

"I guess I'm that *one more*," I say to the guard.

I brush past him and place a hand on the door, pushing it open a crack.

Nobody is going to try to stop a member of the Last Army.

Especially one with a sword.

"Wish me luck," I say.

The guard blinks, mouth agape as I saunter into the Grand Hall.

I don't bother to count how many guards line the room. I'm trained to know, to always be prepared, but tonight I can only focus on one thing.

Or three things.

Seryth, king of the Six Isles, who my father served for years. Who my entire family served for generations. His lips turn up in a smile as he watches me from his stolen throne.

His witch, with her snake eyes and fingernails long enough to draw blood.

And the heir.

Selestra Somniatis.

I definitely can't help but look at her.

Her skin is so pale that it's almost aglow, with hair the color of clovers that slithers down her back and to her waist, reflecting the light of the windows outside like a river.

It almost looks long enough to climb towers with.

Her eyes, large and yellow, watch me with intrigue, and a half smile slips onto her bloodred lips.

She's truly beautiful.

It's a shame she has to die.

4

SELESTRA

When the last prediction seeker enters the Grand Hall, the first thing I notice is that he isn't being escorted by guards.

Unlike the others, he's alone as he strides toward us. He doesn't look to the floor or fiddle nervously with his hands as he prepares to bargain his soul for magic or glory.

My heart thunders in my chest as he approaches, barely even blinking.

He isn't one of the desperate or the reckless, I know that.

He's a soldier. A warrior in King Seryth's army.

And he doesn't just walk—he *struts*.

The boy is a blade of handsomeness, with light brown skin and midnight hair that curls by his ears. His eyes are the color of winter leaves. They catch mine briefly and then seem to go right through me.

Theola and the king grin as he approaches, their postures newly alert and curious.

He's dressed in the uniform of the Last Army, covered by a long black cloak threaded with blue. His sword is sheathed by his hood, glimmering in the growing moonlight.

The way he moves, so quickly and gracefully, the way he doesn't flinch when he sees my eyes: It all reminds me of someone.

Of that last person I ever touched. Of Asden and his sad, sad eyes.

I pray this boy's fate won't be as tragic.

"My king," the boy says when he reaches the steps.

He bows and turns to Theola.

"My lady. A pleasure as always."

His smile almost looks genuine as he steps up to take her hand and place a kiss below her ring.

Almost.

I have practice in perfecting smiles and I can spot a fake from a mile off. But Theola and the king either don't notice or don't care. They're both enamored with the young warrior, staring at him like he's so special.

It's been a long time since my mother looked at me that way. All the magic in the world ready to be inherited into my blood and some Last Army soldier gets the pleasure of her smile.

"Nox." Theola's voice is silk as she takes him in. "What in the name of souls are you doing here?"

"Is there word from the Southern Isle?" the king asks, sitting up straighter in his throne. "Do the rebels show signs of surrender?"

The boy—Nox—shakes his head. "Polemistés hasn't fallen, my king," he says. "The people's resolve grows as steadily as their numbers."

"They're such fools." The king is quiet, but his voice cuts through the empty hall. "Don't they know to accept me as their leader? The Six Isles are *mine*."

There is poison in his words.

He squeezes his hand slowly around a skull affixed to the black throne, and it splinters with his touch.

King Seryth has been trying to conquer the Southern Isle for as long as I've been alive. Before that. Ever since the True War, when he first deposed the witch queen of Thavma. Polemistés is the only isle left of the six that hasn't bowed to him, even after he killed their king.

I know he wants it more than he wanted the others.

Polemistés is the land he once called home, and leaving it until last, long enough to amass rebels, is his greatest anger. His desire to defeat them has only grown stronger and more destructive over the years.

"What news does my little legacy bring, then?" The king looks at Nox, waiting.

"No news," Nox says with an easy shrug. "I'm just here for a prediction."

I gape.

I can't help it.

The Festival is for *civilians*. For the desperate or the bored, but hardly ever for members of the Last Army, who are far too busy playing with their swords.

Yet the king doesn't look angry.

He has his favorites and I can see clearly that Nox is right at the top. Now that I think of it, his name does ring a small bell. A splinter of a conversation overheard at court months before embeds into my mind: *A legacy. His father served before him. His whole family. One of the king's best and brightest, I swear. The youngest soldier ever to be given his own regiment.*

I resist rolling my eyes. I'll bet Nox has got more commendations threaded into the lining of his uniform than soldiers twice his age.

What an utter tryhard.

"Are you sure about this, Nox?" the king asks him. His low voice slices across the room as he leans forward, intrigued. "There's no going back on such a bargain. You should remember who you are. How *valuable* you are to me."

Nox smiles, and something about it gives me pause.

"I know who I am," he says. He takes a knee. "And I'm ready."

"Very well." The king licks his lips. "Then we shall proceed."

He waves a hand at me, gesturing for me to take a piece of Nox's hair and seal his fate.

I grip my scissors.

It's been a long time since I've been close to a boy my own age, or anyone my age who isn't Irenya.

Children were banned from the castle when I grew up, because people can't be trusted and the king worried they'd take advantage of me. Better I stayed beside him and my mother. Better I stayed in my tower, where I was protected.

The heir to the Somniatis magic needs to be kept safe, he always said. *At all costs.*

Even now, I'm not allowed to speak to people at court. When I'm permitted—rarely—to attend celebrations, I'm always kept at a distance. Forced to stand by the thrones, surrounded by guards. Untouchable.

Like a trophy on display.

Then when it's over, I'm locked back away in my cage.

I can watch and listen in on their stories, but I'm never a part of them.

I step toward Nox.

"You're lucky," he says as I approach. "A lot of girls would love to keep my hair in a locket close to their hearts."

I raise my eyebrows. "How unfortunate for them to have lost their minds so young."

Nox's lips curve upward. "I am known to drive women crazy."

I roll my eyes.

Only a Last Army soldier could be so cavalier while selling his soul.

Seeking a prediction is all fun and games when the townsfolk toss the idea around a tavern in the bright glow of torchlight, but usually stepping into this hall and handing over a piece of hair—a piece of their soul—makes things different.

Usually, the arrogance leaves them and their fear clogs the air.

Not this soldier. Nox doesn't look scared at all.

More fool him.

"With these scissors, I'll take a lock of your hair and seal your place in the Festival of Predictions," I say, reciting the words as I always do.

They come so easily to me now that I barely have to think at all before I say them. They're as familiar as my own name.

"Do you accept this bargain?" I ask, once I've finished.

"I accept," Nox says.

Prat, I think.

He's close enough that I don't need to move to take the hair from him. I simply crouch, dress flowing down the steps like water, and slip a lock of Nox's hair through my fingers.

When I cut it, a jolt goes through me.

It pushes me back and I stumble, nearly losing my footing.

It's small at first, like tiny needles scurrying up my arms and down the back of my neck, before butting violently into my heart.

I grip the cut hair tightly and still.

I've never felt something when cutting a person's hair, but it's like the part of Nox's soul I snipped away shot through me first.

Did he feel it too?

"I guess I really can sweep women off their feet," Nox says.

I stare at him, but if he experienced the same shock, nothing on his face portrays it.

I push away the strangeness that pierces into my chest and secure the lock of his hair in the last empty jar by my feet.

"Go on, then," the king says, once I've twisted the lid closed.

"I've collected the hair," I tell him, confused.

The king laughs, and though it's a beautiful sound, I know it means something awful is to come.

"No, Selestra," he says softly. "Give the soldier his prediction."

A panic sets through me.

"You want me to do it?" I ask. "Why?"

"Consider it my gift to you," he offers.

Only I know the king never gives gifts that aren't laced in poison.

"It's just one little prediction," he promises. "Your magic should be able to handle it and it'll be good practice."

I fumble with my gloves.

The idea of taking them off in front of someone for the first time in years makes my skin itch. It makes me think of Asden's screams.

I look to my mother.

"Go ahead," she says, encouraging. "Do as the king says, Selestra."

My heart pounds.

I lick my lips.

I've both feared this moment and craved it.

It is a chance to finally let loose the magic inside me I've never been allowed to explore. To *touch* someone and feel skin on skin for the first time in over two years.

To show my mother that I'm worthy of our family's power.

I slip off a glove and let it drop to my feet.

I crouch down and my dress pools onto the marble as I reach out a hand for Nox's cheek.

He flinches when I touch him. I suppose I am a little cold. Every inch of me is.

Magic is fire and I've never let mine burn.

My heart thunders furiously against my chest as we make

contact, like a beast in a cage. All these years and I haven't touched anyone.

It's like the sudden quelling of a hunger I've always ignored.

I'm sick with it, with the feel of him. Of another person, real and in my grasp, able to feel me as much as I feel him.

Nox is warm, with skin softer than I thought. There's a scar on his face that stretches in a smooth pink line from his eyebrow to his chin, and when my hand grazes it, his eyes flicker to mine.

Usually, people flinch when they see my eyes. Eyes of snakes, that all Somniatis women bear.

Nox barely blinks.

I don't either.

I don't want to blink or do anything but savor this moment.

I know I won't get another chance for a while—maybe years— and I want to have my fill while I can, but there isn't time.

Death comes quick.

My breath catches in my chest, pushing down on me, like I'm suffocating. Then my head flings back and I know my magic isn't ready.

It feels like being hit in the head, over and over with no reprieve.

I try to pull away, tear myself from Nox, but my bones are rigid and my hand stays glued to his cheek as the images burn into me.

Flashes of dark red floors and half-painted walls.

I can't make sense of it and my head feels like it's cracking with every new image.

A crowd surrounds a moonlit Nox. Lanterns hiss like orbs around him, growing brighter and brighter until suddenly the world is on fire.

It catches across the floors and sizzles up the walls, turning everything to smoke.

I can smell the air, thick with sweat and salt. See the gaping hole in the ceiling as it crumbles down.

Nox bleeds out on the floor, surrounded by flames.

The wind howls in a mourning cry and an image sears across my mind, so painful that I scream. A handle in the ground, surrounded by broken bottles.

"This way," a voice whispers.

A hand reaches for the bloody Nox and I gasp as I catch sight of the bracelet on their wrist.

A small gold thing, with a single gem in the center. Like a watchful eye.

I know that bracelet.

I've worn it for years.

I choke in a breath and then I feel the fire on my own skin, licking up my arms and catching on the ends of my hair. It melts through my bracelet and down to the bone.

With everything I have, I wrench away from Nox, pulling myself from the vision and back into the present.

It happens so suddenly that I lose my footing and tumble to the ground, knocking over a row of jars that crash down the stairs.

They scatter glass and hair across the floor.

"What is it?" Theola asks, yellow-green eyes widening. "What happened?"

It can't be.

I tremble and clutch at my wrist as the memory of the flames seeps onto my skin.

Burning and charring.

It just can't be.

"Selestra." My mother's voice grows louder.

The king holds up a hand to silence her, and the whole room falls quiet. The guards at the door even hold their breaths at his command.

Slowly, the king descends the steps toward me.

His face dawns with the kind of look that has destroyed worlds.

"Speak," he commands.

I turn to Nox, and the deep brown of his eyes slices through me.

The brand of the serpent is on his palm and when I look down, I see it on my own too.

Quickly, I clench my hand into a fist and reach for my fallen glove, before anyone else notices.

"Well?" Nox asks.

His jaw pulses in anticipation of what I've seen.

I swallow. Look away.

I can't tell him. I can never speak it.

Because I haven't just seen Nox's death, but my own as well.

5

NOX

The witch is scared and that doesn't bode well.

"Don't tell me," I say. "I'm going to die?"

Still huddled on the floor, Selestra doesn't laugh.

She shakes her head, disbelief coating her soft features. You'd think she's never made a prediction before.

I just hope whatever she's seen in my future isn't as awful as the look on her face.

I could almost swear she wants to sob or scream, but that's impossible, because she's a Somniatis witch and they're born heartless.

Empty, right to the core.

"Aren't you supposed to tell me my future now?" I ask. "I've bargained my soul for it. Seems the least I could get is a prediction."

"I—I don't . . ." Selestra trails off.

Her eyes focus in on my hand.

I look to where Seryth's crest slithers across my palm, marking me as a prediction seeker. As someone who now belongs to him.

I clench my fist hard enough that the bones crack.

"Tell him."

The king towers over Selestra, who's still on the floor and trying to find her breath.

"Don't make me look a fool, Selestra," he warns.

His voice is cold enough for her to shiver. Selestra looks up at the king, meeting his eyes with her own. She presses her lips together and for a moment I think she might cry.

Instead she wipes the uncertainty from her face.

The shakiness and stuttered breath disappear, and Selestra tilts her chin up high enough that I can practically see her swallowing down whatever it was she felt a moment ago.

Selestra rises to her feet. Unsteady, but determined all the same.

"Death will first come for you in three days' time," she tells me. Her voice is cracked. "It's a fight of some sort. There was an angry crowd and a fire broke out. I didn't recognize the building, but it had red floors. It might have been one of the dorms in the Last Army barracks."

I wait, but when she says nothing else, I quirk a brow.

"That's it?" I ask. "Just some fight?"

So simple, so easy.

So clearly not the half of it.

I see Selestra's jaw set firm as she considers her answer carefully, like a soldier trying to strategize in battle.

"That's it," she confirms.

"Why didn't you say that to begin with?"

"It took me a while to sort through it," she says defensively. "I'm not used to making predictions."

She's not a bad liar, I'll give her that. It's almost convincing how she sweetens her voice and touches a hand to smooth out her forest hair.

The picture of innocence and confusion.

Only she hasn't had as much practice as I have in the art of pretend.

Part of being in the Last Army is knowing how to spot a liar and deciphering the tales captives tell to save their own necks.

Selestra Somniatis isn't as slick as she likes to think.

But to accuse the heir to the Somniatis magic of anything like that is treason, and that's something even I can't get away with.

"You're getting blood all over the floor, Selestra."

Theola rises slowly from her throne.

Selestra looks down to her elbow, cut open by her fall, like she hadn't realized she was injured until now.

I hadn't either. Now that I see her blood, mixed with the matted locks of hair from the jars she broke, my hand twitches by my side. I'm almost overcome with the ridiculous urge to check her wound.

I ignore it.

Selestra isn't some helpless little girl who needs to be rescued.

She's a *witch*.

I turn away from her and adjust the blade I keep strapped to my back.

My father's sword.

"Perhaps we should let her bleed," the king muses. "Such a sloppy vision should suffer consequences."

Theola stares at her daughter's bleeding arm. "Yes, but the floor shouldn't suffer," she says plainly. "I'll fix it."

She closes her eyes and takes in a long, deep breath.

I feel the change in the air, the cold creeping up through my bones as her magic slinks down the stairs and across the tiles.

Then Selestra's wound is gone, the gash on her elbow suddenly clear. Jars still litter the floor, but the heir no longer drips blood onto them.

Somniatis witches are snakes.

Shedding their skin and building themselves anew.

"So it's really just a soldier's brawl?"

King Seryth appears to consider this as he settles back down onto his throne.

"That shouldn't be any trouble for you, Nox." His lips turn upward, slow and deliberate. "You are your father's son, after all. A true legacy in my army."

He watches me closely. He wants me to react to that.

He wants to see me flinch at the mention of my father. To test me, as he's done so many other times over the years.

King Seryth always wants something from me, and it's never a thing I want to give.

I keep my voice light.

"Don't worry," I say. "I'll make my father proud."

Seryth cocks his head to one side. "Indeed."

"Thank you for the prediction," I say. "May I have my coin?"

Theola closes her hand to a fist, and when she opens it again, a piece of gold Chrim sits in the center of her palm. It glitters for a moment, until she slowly places it into the chest pocket of my uniform.

She pats the spot, right above my heart, and says, "Until we meet again, Nox Laederic."

I bow, quickly, in place of driving my sword through the king's chest. It seems the more polite option and the blow would be wasted on an immortal anyway.

I turn to walk out of the hall, but then my gaze meets Selestra's.

It's brief and fleeting, a stolen moment when her eyes focus on mine and something—a look I don't quite understand—pools inside them.

I dismiss it.

I don't need to understand the witch. All I need is to survive this month and whatever death throws at me until I get what I want.

Until I take the king's immortality and bring this family to its knees.

When that time comes, I'll kill them all.

Starting with the heir.

6

SELESTRA

That night, I dream only of Nox Laederic.

I see him die a thousand times over, flames swarming his skin like flies, as my hand reaches out toward the embers only to be met by ash and darkness.

I can't sleep without seeing it, which means I barely sleep at all.

That boy is going to get me killed.

I know it the same way I know the sky is blue and the sea is black, and the bargain is absolute. Once the hair is traded, our magic imprints itself and it's only a matter of time before death comes.

Those are the rules of my great-great-grandmother's spell.

By the time morning arrives, I've already been awake for hours, the thought of dreaming again far too horrible to try.

I dip my paintbrush into the water and glance at my hand, like there might be answers hidden inside the king's mark that is now etched into my skin.

There aren't.

Angrily, I smudge a line of black across my canvas.

Usually, painting heals my mind. Without my gloves, I feel weightless, and some days I can paint for hours—new worlds and new faces—and forget I ever have to wear them again.

This time it isn't helping.

Damn that soldier to the River of Memory and back.

"That's . . . pretty," Irenya says, staring at my painting with a look that implies the opposite.

I shove my hand back into my pocket, so she doesn't catch sight of the mark.

"What is it?" she asks.

I shrug.

I've tried to re-create the room from my vision, to narrow down where I'm supposed to die in two days' time, but everything is still a blur.

I have the red floors and the half-painted white walls, but the rest is hazy, so I've coated it in a layer of orange embers. They sprinkle from the gaping ceiling, like rain from the stars, and pool across the floor in a lake of fire.

My bracelet sits on a table in the center, melting.

"What's the huge black line across the middle?" Irenya asks.

"Therapy," I say.

And then I drag another across it in a large X.

"We should burn it," Irenya says. "Before anyone sees."

I stare at the melting bracelet, remembering how it felt to have those flames eat away at my skin.

"Throw it in," I agree, gesturing to the fireplace.

We always burn my paintings.

If the king ever saw them, he'd take away my brushes for good.

When I was eleven, I once painted a girl trapped inside a tower, with hair so long that it stretched out the window, as she looked down at flowers she'd never get to pick.

Her hair wasn't green and her eyes weren't awful, but she had all my wishes in her smile. Ideas of traveling the world, before I knew better.

My mother saw the painting just as I finished the final stroke and she held it up to the light, sighing as the sun sprinkled through the window and lit up the untouched flowers.

When she placed it back down on the easel, her eyes glistened. She looked like my mother again. Like the woman who braided my hair during lullabies and told me stories of our old goddess.

For just a stolen moment, I didn't feel second to our family's blood oath to the king. And when Theola reached down to cup my cheek, it didn't feel cold.

It felt like a mother's touch, which was something she hadn't given me in years.

"Oh, Selestra," she said.

Then the king stepped into the room and Theola tore her hand from my face, told me to practice more, and threw the canvas into the fire before he had the chance to look.

Since that day, I'm only supposed to paint for the king, but the idea of drawing nothing but clouds littered with diamonds is torture, so Irenya does it instead.

She paints what the king likes and I paint what I want. When we're done, we hand Irenya's painting to the king as if it's mine.

Then burn mine to cinders.

I like it that way.

Throw any frustrations I have onto a canvas, see them alive and in color, then watch them melt away.

I want to see this one go up in flames more than any of the others.

"Ready?" Irenya asks.

"Burn it," I say.

She throws it into the fireplace and the flames roar in response.

I watch as they grow higher, brighter, until the last vestiges of my painting turn to ash. Fire meeting fire; my predicted death erased before my eyes.

It settles my heart a little. Not much, but it's something.

The king always says that when a person dies outside of the bargain, their soul is ferried to the River of Memory, so it can flow in an endless slumber.

People become imprints, existing only as a record of all that has been. So for them, selling their souls at the Festival doesn't seem like a bad thing, when after death they'll just be asleep anyway.

But I've never believed it.

I still remember the stories my mother used to tell me of the goddess our family is descended from. Asclepina, imbued with the powers of death and immortality by ancient snakes, so she could see through death's eyes and heal her people.

My mother whispered her tales to me as a child whenever the king wasn't around. She'd tell me how Asclepina could ferry us to a true afterlife, where we would live eternal beside her. How before they were wiped out, each of the old witch families had a patron goddess who would do the same.

They're things my mother hasn't spoken of in years, but I've never forgotten. The stories circle within me.

If the king eats my soul, it's not just that I'll die. It's that I'll never get to meet our goddess or any of the witches from my bloodline.

I'll be damned.

"Come on," Irenya says to me. A look of knowing spreads across her round cheeks. "If therapy is what you need, I know just the place."

For a few seconds, I can't breathe.

I fall to the floor with a grunt as the air is knocked straight out of my lungs. It feels like I'm suffocating.

I look down to my ivory tunic with a sigh.

Irenya's boot print is in the center.

I wipe at the spot with a gloved hand and push myself back to my feet.

"You're distracted," Irenya says with a frown. "Not once have I been able to get the drop on you before."

She's right. Two years of sparring and never has she bested me.

I was taught well.

"Perhaps that's why I allowed it to happen," I tease. "I feel bad for bruising you up so often."

Irenya pushes the short blond hair from her eyes, so I have a good view when she rolls them at me.

"We don't have to spar," she says. "We can always go back to painting, or do some cooking lessons."

"No," I say quickly.

Irenya snorts. "You shouldn't be so dismissive. Punching people in the face is fun, but being able to make good pie is better."

I raise an eyebrow. "You've never taught me to make pie."

"And you've never taught me how to do one of those backflip things Asden liked to do," she says.

I bristle at the mention of my old mentor.

Asden was a Last Army soldier and trainer for palace guards. He was also the one person in the castle aside from Irenya who didn't treat me like a witch or a prisoner, despite the fact that he never spoke to me.

With the exception of Irenya and a handful of people at court, few have the privilege of *interacting with the heir*. They're also not supposed to touch me, but Asden liked to choose which rules to break and which not to.

He broke the rules when he caught me sneaking down to the gardens when I was eleven—hands full of chocolate stolen from the kitchens—and chose not to tell the king, returning to his patrol with a smirk.

He broke the rules again the very next night when I waited for him by that same spot and asked how good he really was at fighting. And if he could make me better.

For three years, Asden trained me right under the king's nose, allowing me to sneak out of my tower to find him.

And he never said a word to me.

When I gave a command, Asden nodded. When I sassed him, he swiped my legs out from under me and raised his eyebrows, like I should have seen it coming.

But never once did he speak.

I tried all manner of gibes and insults to get him to break, but it didn't matter how incredibly witty I was. Asden was a stubborn old git.

Once, Irenya even offered to sneak him three slices of rum cake if he said hello, instead of just waving me into the room. The gesture he gave her after that was far less pleasant than a wave.

Still, we didn't need words, because Asden taught me the most important lessons of all: How to be strong. How to survive.

Until the king killed him.

Irenya must notice how I stiffen, because her eyes widen.

"Oh, Selestra," she says. "I'm sorry, I—"

"It's fine," I say, shrugging it off. "*I'm* fine."

It's the biggest lie I've ever told.

I position my gloved hands into fists and adjust my stance, ready to train away all of my anger and frustrations.

I'm covered completely, with my gloves tucked under the wrists of my long sleeves, and my tunic stretching right up to the edge of my jaw. There's not an inch of skin on show, aside from my face. I'm sweating underneath it all, but I don't have a choice.

I can't risk touching Irenya.

The last thing I need is another vision.

She's covered too, with gloves on her hands so she can punch me without having to worry.

Such a nice gesture.

"I'm ready to go again," I say.

Irenya gestures to the swords at the foot of the room, where an entire wall glitters with metal of all shapes and sizes—longswords, broadswords, rapiers. Each marked by King Seryth's crest.

The same mark that's hidden beneath my gloves, thanks to Nox Laederic.

"Shall we try fencing?" she asks.

I shake my head. "I should practice how to defend myself if I don't have a weapon."

Or if I'm trapped in some fiery building with Nox Laederic, I think.

I sigh as I let the thoughts of Nox and our impending doom slip back into my mind. This training session is meant to be a distraction.

For someone who deals in death and souls, I've never had to worry about mine. In all the stories of my ancestors, tales of blood and magic, never once has a witch been marked by the bargain.

We're different from everyone else. My family created the magic, so how is it I've fallen victim to it?

Nox Laederic has cursed me.

I squeeze my hands into fists.

When he looked me in the eyes without flinching, his scar pressed under my fingertips, it threw me. I was so desperate for it—for magic and touch—that I couldn't think straight.

I let myself be distracted and maybe that made something in the magic go wrong, drawing me in.

I won't make that mistake again.

I won't be caught off guard by him.

Irenya raises her arms into fists and nods for me to do the same.

I'm more than willing to oblige. We pace in circles, daring each other to take the next jab, like it's a game.

Irenya was right: This is far better therapy than painting.

She swings first, but I twist out of the way and ram a quick punch into her gut.

Irenya lets out a groan and I smile, thinking how Asden would be pleased by my footwork.

For a moment I let that arrogance get the better of me, then Irenya shoves her elbow into the air, just as I taught her to, and I can't move out of the way fast enough.

I stumble backward from the pain.

It feels like my eye might just fall out of the socket.

I do my best to ignore it as she kicks her leg up, aiming for my stomach. I see it coming and grab her ankle, twisting hard.

Irenya spins through the air like a knife, her body whirling twice over before she lands with a thump back onto the floor.

She blinks up at me.

"If I said *ouch*, could we go back to painting?" she says wryly.

I snort and hold out a hand for her, but Irenya swipes my legs out from under me and I crash to the floor beside her.

"Damn," I curse loudly, and collapse back onto the ground, giving in to my heaving breath.

"See," she says, panting. "You're distracted."

I would nudge her in the ribs, but I'm not sure I have the energy to move from this spot.

The cold of the floor against my back is a welcome relief.

"How is your eye?" Irenya asks.

I reach out to touch it, and my fingertips barely graze the skin before pain shoots across my face.

"You're the worst," I say with a grimace. "It'll take me over an hour to heal."

Irenya shrugs by way of apology. "Oops?"

Luckily, bruises and cuts are easy to heal. A lick of magic here, a small siphon of power there, and they fade to memories. It barely requires any concentration anymore, and all I need is a good night's sleep to regain my energy after.

Bones aren't so easy.

I found that out the hard way when I left my first training session with Asden with a broken finger that took a whole week to fix.

I had to slip on my gloves each day, hiding the bruise and pretending nothing was wrong when the king asked me to pour his wine. Then at night, I'd focus my power and try to snap the bone back into place. The nosebleeds lasted well after I tried to go to sleep.

I suppose it was my magic's way of telling me to be patient and that it wasn't strong enough. But I've never been one for patience, and the pain of healing an injury got better with practice.

Besides, it's worth it.

If the king or Theola sees my injuries and finds out I've been training—that I was taught by one of their own soldiers and that I've carried on those lessons to this day with the apprentice dressmaker—their fury would tear apart the castle.

I know I risk myself and Irenya every time I go behind the king's back like this, but I can't help it. It's selfish and stupid, but this castle is lonely enough without having to actually be *alone* in it.

"You should really have breakfast before your first black eye," Irenya says.

I shake my head. "I'm not hungry."

"But *I'm* starving, and eating without you would be rude."

I laugh, but I can't stomach the thought of food. All I want is to keep distracting myself from having to think about Nox.

"Since when are you worried about being rude?" I ask. "Go wild. Eat my plate too, if you like."

Irenya snorts, standing to pull me to my feet. "*Why did the heir starve?* they'll ask me. *Because I ate all her dinners.*"

"I'm sure my mother won't be too distraught," I say. "She'll just spend some extra time in another soldier's bed to produce a new heir to the Somniatis magic."

"Souls, Selestra." A smile teeters on Irenya's lips. "You're going to have to learn to hold your tongue when you're the witch."

"When," I repeat thoughtfully.

Now it seems more like *if*.

What if Nox dies in that fire and it kills me too? What if I don't even need to be in the room with him when it happens?

Whatever cursed mistake placed the king's mark on my hand when I saw into Nox's future is unpredictable. I can't trust that hiding in my tower and staying away from him will keep me safe.

Whether I like it or not, the magic has bound us together.

Unless I do something, in two days' time we'll both die.

Irenya narrows her eyes a little. "Something's bothering you," she says. "I can't cheer you up if you don't tell me, and there's only so much I can try to beat out of you with my limited defense skills."

"It's nothing," I say.

"Liar."

Irenya looks at me with the face of a friend who knows me all too well. The face of my only friend.

She's worked in the castle as an apprentice to the dressmaker for years, but back when her mother used to work in the kitchens, she always saved me the slice of cake Theola would never let me have at the end-of-week dinner. We'd split it and stay up all night together eating and laughing.

Irenya would tell me all about the edge of the island where she grew up with her sailor father, and I'd describe the hairpin I used to pick the lock to my room and sneak out into the gardens at night.

I'd never had a friend before, or anyone to talk to my age. One taste of it and I was hooked.

When Asden died, Irenya was the one who told me I had to continue training to honor him. She offered to help me spar whenever I needed.

I *wish* I could tell her what was going on, but it's too much of a burden to keep the secret of my vision and I can't risk the king finding out.

He'd lock me up in my tower until I'm ready to become the witch and never even let me attend banquets for my own safety. He'd make me more of a prisoner than I already am, and I still want to hold on to the few freedoms I've stolen for myself.

If I want to survive this week, this month, then I need to do it alone.

I'm the heir to the Somniatis magic, after all.

If anyone can cheat death, it's me.

"One more round," I announce to Irenya. "Then we eat."

I walk over to the wall of swords.

It's summer out and the sun peeks through the ornate glass

windows, casting ripples onto the metal, bathing them in color. The weapons are all expertly crafted, some featherlight and others weighty and dense.

Each is as deadly as the next.

I lift my hand and stroke an ear dagger.

It's a small golden thing with a long black tip, stamped by a jewel above the king's crest, but what I really like is the forked pommel.

It leaves the perfect space for my thumb to grip.

With a quick glance to make sure Irenya isn't looking, I pluck the dagger from the hook and slip it under the waistband of my tunic.

Quickly, I grab two flammard swords from the wall to hide the action and turn to face Irenya.

"Get ready," I say. "I'm going to knock you on your backside."

I throw a flammard across the room in a high arc, and Irenya grabs it out of the air.

"Bring it on," she says.

I smile a wicked smile.

The king may think he's keeping me safe by having me locked away, but he's only made sure I know every inch of my prison well and exactly how to protect myself in it.

For years I've snuck out of my tower and into the grounds, sitting beside the waterfall, hidden by the shadow of the grass, and breathing in the night. I've stared at the sky and held my thumb up to the moon, marveling at how small it seems from so close up.

But now I need to go farther. I feel the ear dagger pressed against my back.

If I want to survive this month, I have to make sure Nox Laederic survives too.

In two days' time, I'm going to save his life.

7

NOX

I don't like coming to the lower towns, mostly because the lower towns don't like me being here.

When we're not at war, Last Army soldiers act as enforcers for the king, and it doesn't exactly make us popular on the streets, despite my winning personality.

I wipe a line of sweat from my forehead.

The afternoon sun is high, air warm with summer. When the soft breeze drifts by, it carries the smell of lavender trees over from the docks.

Vasiliádes is always beautiful, despite the awful things happening inside it.

"You really don't feel any different?" Micah asks as we walk along the cobbled streets.

I can sense his gaze on the serpent tattoo that smudges across my palm. He's been staring at it ever since we left the castle yesterday. So I know what Micah really wants to ask is: *How does it feel to sell your soul to a man you hate?*

I'm still not sure.

It doesn't feel like any parts of me are missing, stored away in a glass jar for safekeeping. Maybe that comes later.

Or maybe the part of myself I've given away isn't a part I needed to begin with.

"Are you sure about this guy?" Micah asks as we approach the shop. "Even the street looks crooked."

"Good," I say. "Quit being such a wet blanket about it."

"I'm being serious."

"You're always serious. It's a real personality flaw."

Micah shoots me a look.

He might have been my companion of chaos when we were kids, but things have changed and he's no longer spurring me on with each risky idea.

Apparently he's not a fan of me bargaining my soul for revenge.

"It'll be fine," I assure him. "Just trust me."

"I think we'd be safer hunting for that legendary magic in the Southern Isle than coming to this place," Micah says.

He looks over his shoulder once more at the decrepit street behind us.

"Sure," I say, shaking my head with a smile. "And then later we can hunt for sirens."

Like the sea devils, or tales of a hundred other kingdoms beyond the Six Isles, the hidden magic of Polemistés is nothing more than a fairy tale my father told me. A sword strong enough to kill anyone, even an immortal.

Fairy tales aren't going to help me now. The only way to bring down the king is to survive the month and break the bargain.

And the owner of this shop is just the help I need.

We approach the small orange door, hidden in the corner of the twisted street, and I raise my hand to knock.

Inside there's the sound of shuffling, then something smashing onto the floor, followed by a curse that makes Micah snort.

Finally, a man wrenches open the door with enough force to nearly pull the handle off.

"I knew it was you," Leo Borane says when he sees me. "Nox Laederic, too curious for your own good."

"Too willing to part with my Chrim, more like."

Leo smiles, a genuine, honest-to-souls smile. "That's my favorite kind of customer."

He opens the door wider and gestures for us to come inside, limping a little as he moves.

Leo is a strange kind of man, with a long red beard speckled by gray and hair to match, which he almost always covers with a series of caps.

If anything happens to me, my father said just a week before he died, *find Leo in the worst shop by the docks.*

Three months ago, I finally did it.

It was harder than I thought. Leo kept changing his name over the years to escape his reputation as kook inventor, and I was nearly pummeled a few times asking people if their shop was the worst one at the docks.

Apparently it's not a great conversation starter.

But I've got him now.

Someone who can help me escape Vasiliádes if my plan to kill the king goes sideways. And, most importantly, someone who can do it in a way that Seryth and his witch can't follow.

If anything goes wrong, I'll need his inventions.

"Promise me he's not going to murder us," Micah says under his breath as we step inside.

He stares at Leo's shop like it's a battleground, which I suppose it is. It's a mess of burnt metals and decapitated wood thrown about, with half-thought projects and the half-sawed materials used to make them.

"I'll only murder you if you try collecting taxes from me," Leo says. "Last Army were just here. Your king loves to demand more Chrim every month. I can't restock my shop."

"Restock it with what?" Micah asks, looking around the sparse workshop.

Leo ignores him. "Do you have the Chrim? We agreed on one hundred gold pieces."

"About that . . . ," I say.

I can see the shift in Leo already as he realizes what I'm about to ask.

"I want to renegotiate. Fifty gold Chrim now and the other fifty when I have all the riches in the Six Isles."

The Last Army may pay well in reputation, but I don't think anything would pay well enough in Chrim to keep Leo satisfied, except for the gold from Seryth's castle.

Leo simply stares at me.

He's never been one for negotiating.

He nods to my tattoo. "I want my Chrim before you die."

"I'm not planning on dying."

Leo huffs and walks toward the center of the room. "Yes, yes." He waves his hand about. "Last Army soldiers think they're invincible."

Leo sweeps a row of dusty nails off the benches by a small table.

"Sit down," he says.

We oblige, watching as he wipes his hands on a small rag, staining it with oil grease.

"What if you don't succeed and get your wish for riches?" Leo asks. "What if I never get my Chrim? I'm losing sleep worrying I won't be paid."

It's nice that he even gets to sleep.

It's a luxury I haven't had in years, since the day my father died. Each night, I only ever snatch a few hours of broken rest at a time.

"Let me worry about cheating death," I say, easing back into the chair. Letting him know I'm confident.

There is no option of failure.

No scenario where I won't get my vengeance.

"Just have the transport ready for me."

Once the king realizes I'm after his immortality and not some magical reward, I'll need all the help I can to leave.

He'll never let anyone get close enough to surviving the month.

"I entertain these interactions out of respect for your father," Leo says. "But I am no charity. If you need more money, do what every other fool on this island does. Visit the After Dusk Inn and make a bet on your death."

I blow out a breath.

It isn't a bad idea. The Last Army loves visiting the tavern and gambling on the lives of townsfolk, to secure extra money for ale or the latest sword from the blacksmith.

"You're really stubborn in negotiations, aren't you?" I say to Leo.

"I learned that from your father," he shoots back. "He also died before he could pay me."

I shift. My back goes rigid and I can't help but sit up a little straighter, as though my father himself just walked into the room.

Leo shakes his head and then looks at me with a sigh.

"He was far too headstrong," Leo says. "But a good friend. His death was tragic." He sighs again and throws the rag down, hard enough that it slaps against the counter. "Unexpected."

Only one of those things is true.

My father's death was tragic, but it wasn't unexpected.

I remember the last time I saw him more clearly than any memory I have. I was fourteen when he came home with blood on his hands and a look in his eyes like nothing I'd ever seen.

"Nox," he said, voice stiff and quiet. "I'm going to tell you a story and I want you to remember every detail."

So I nodded and sat beside him.

"There is a weapon, made from magic," he said. "From the last breaths of the witches of Thavma. Over a century ago, before Isolda Somniatis and the king drained their power and left them to die in the start of the True War. Before they conquered the Six Isles."

"But you already have a weapon," I said, pointing to the sword on his hip.

He shook his head. "This weapon can kill anything," he said. "It's the reason Seryth fears the Southern Isle so much. It's what's kept them safe all these years. The king won't stop until he has it. And he'll sacrifice anything and anyone to get what he wants."

He looked down to his hands. The blood had crusted between his knuckles.

"It's just a story though," I said. "Isn't it, Father?"

His face was plain. "Stories have great power. They should never be destroyed."

I didn't know what to say to that, but I knew I hated the look in his eyes, so I hugged him. He stiffened, and when he wrapped his arms around me in return, it was almost desperate.

The next day he was gone and a soldier came to my door and told me he was dead. Drowned while taking a morning swim.

Only my father didn't know how to swim, and there was no reason he'd try to learn by himself in the depths of winter.

I remembered his last words.

The king will sacrifice anything. Anyone.

After that, I moved into the soldiers' barracks and trained day and night, sparring alongside the other Last Army recruits so I'd be nothing but perfect.

I practiced to be the best.

To live up to my father's legacy. To ace the entrance exams into the Last Army and convince the king I was a loyal soldier. And it's been easy, because I've been training toward something.

A hope. A *need*.

Every day I think of my father—who valued loyalty above all else—making sure the last words he spoke to me were of a fairy tale to kill the king.

The fact that he died the very next day only makes me certain it wasn't an accident. He was killed, for knowing something he shouldn't. For believing in a story and wanting it to be true.

In the distance, the sound of the waterfalls from the Floating Mountain crash through the windows of Leo's shop, like the first wave of a battle. They sense the fight growing within me and are eager to see it spill out.

And it will.

I'll survive this month and steal the king's immortality. And once I do, I'll finally be able to rid the Six Isles of monsters once and for all.

I'll avenge my father, not through fairy tales, but through blood.

8

SELESTRA

I pull my hood tighter over my face and try my best to blend in.

The grounds are a maze of hedges and wildflowers. For anyone else it would be impossible to navigate in the dark. Luckily, I'm not anyone else.

I've had the patrol schedules memorized for years, and picking the lock of my bedroom and sneaking down to the grounds is almost too easy for me now.

I've always known it's my destiny to spend my life inside this castle, bound to the king until the next witch takes over, but since my vision of Nox there's been a gnawing in my chest.

With my death on the horizon, now more than ever the walls feel taller and the rooms feel smaller.

I can't stomach the thought of dying before I've ever really lived.

If tomorrow is when death will come for me, then I have to leave the grounds to find the place where Nox and I are supposed to be killed.

I must make sure he never steps foot anywhere near it, for both our sakes.

I'll lock him up in my tower with me if I have to. After all I've gone through, I'm not about to let some reckless soldier risk *my* life.

I catch sight of the platform and slip behind a rosebush that's taller than most trees.

I watch the guard blow out a puff of smoke from his pink lips.

He leans back and yawns.

I wish I had the power to send him to sleep, or fling him out of my way with a flick of my wrist. But I don't, and even if I did, it would alert people that I'm here.

So I wait.

I don't know much about the myths of other witches who came before, or the great powers they may have had. Maybe they could have sent the guard flying through the air. The only thing I know for sure about the witch island of Thavma is what my mother told me about the swirls of magic that lit up the skies in pink and orange, like the inside of a grapefruit.

A land of witches, until Isolda Somniatis teamed up with Seryth to depose their queen and siphon the life and magic from all her subjects.

Now my family is all that's left.

The guard checks his pocket watch, sighs, then heads toward the lake to continue his patrol.

Like clockwork.

I slip out from behind the rosebush and approach the platform.

"Hello," I greet an old friend. "Long time no see."

From behind the ropes, a Lamperós bird's bronze head peers.

It's as beautiful as ever, the size of a horse with a metallic gray beak and eyes radiating with white light. Its golden wings ripple as it turns toward me, sharp enough to cut through anything, except for its chains.

What a beautiful thing it is.

What an awful life my family has condemned it to.

Most people think the platform is enchanted and rarely ever see the creature hidden in the hollowed-out tree trunk it rests against, ferrying them up and down the mountain.

I pull a handful of berries and mint flowers from my pocket. Its favorite. I bring them for the bird whenever I sneak out of my room.

I'm not the only one in this place who needs a reprieve every now and again.

"I brought you a gift," I say.

The Lamperós shuffles forward and sniffs the berries in my palm. Then snatches them up, ravenous, like it hasn't eaten in days.

It's a prisoner just as much as I am, trapped in this place until the king commands otherwise. Even if I can sneak from my tower, or this mountain, there is no way off this island for either of us.

I reach out a hand and my fingers sweep over the smooth feathers of the bird's head. I wonder where it would go if I had the power to free it. If I had the magic to dissolve the chains my great-great-grandmother conjured.

Maybe when I'm the witch, I'll get my answer.

I step onto the platform.

"Just this once," I say. "Will you take me to the ground?"

The Lamperós ruffles its feathers in response, as eager as I am at the thought.

It leaps down.

I bite my lip as the platform descends, sky rushing by in blurs.

The wind whips against my face and excitement rises in me, above the fear. In just a few moments, I'm going to set foot on the true ground for the first time.

Vasiliádes is not a prison, even if it's home to one.

It's a wonder of boldly colored shop fronts and streetlamps tall as buildings, which hold fire bright enough to light the streets in small blobs of daylight.

I am breaking every rule I have ever known just by being here, and for once I don't think to care.

I feel dizzy, the rush of stepping through the streets making my head spin. My feet, tapping against cobblestones. My lungs, breathing in sea air. And the clouds that surround the Floating Mountain where my tower stands, so far away for the first time.

I practically run along the harbor edge, taking in the sight of the large boats tied to docks. They wave back and forth against it, tugging at their bindings in a bid for freedom. The birds flock around them, flapping their great white wings, singing and screaming for joy as they fly up and over the sails.

There is a whole ocean out there. A whole world. I grip the stone barrier and lean out, wondering what it would be like to see it.

To be like those birds, flying over the ocean.

I look back to Vasiliádes, my breath catching as I hear the distant thrum of music.

A street performer perhaps?

Or entertainment from a nearby tavern?

I wish I could find out, but I don't have the time even if my heart so desperately wants it. I would love to see this place in the light, when the bakeries open and the pastry displays glisten in the shop fronts. I want to walk the streets with Irenya and hum along to the street musicians.

I feel as though I've cheated the town somewhat, by only seeing it in darkness. But there isn't time to wallow.

I have to find Nox.

I walk through the streets of Vasiliádes for an hour, over to the wet sands of the docks and then weaving through cobblestones lined with empty tea shops and closed storefronts.

Think, Selestra, I tell myself urgently. *Forget about the bird songs and flying, and think about where a soldier might be in the middle of the night during the Festival month.*

The answer comes to me quicker than I thought.

Ahead, I spy a knobble of a building that smells of peanuts and honey, with a thatched roof and a sign outside that screeches in the wind like a warning not to enter.

A sign that says *Last Army welcome.*

I wonder which kind of places would dare to turn them away. The king's soldiers aren't exactly known for their charming personalities.

I step inside.

I've never been to a tavern, and the After Dusk Inn is . . . damp. Each table drips and the floors are sticky enough that my boots squelch into the wood.

I look around, and when I see there are no red floors and most of the walls are covered by black curtain, I'm caught between relief and disappointment.

This isn't where we're supposed to die tomorrow, but that means I still don't know where to warn Nox away from. Or how to find him in the first place.

I adjust my mask to make sure my disguise is still in place.

The women at court love to adorn their faces with them, giving me the perfect way to hide in plain sight. But the real trick is my eyes, no longer hissing yellow. I've disguised them with a dye stolen from one of the court ladies, who love changing their eyes to whatever's fashionable.

I've learned a lot, watching from afar.

Though I don't exactly fit right in, I'd rather the tavern people think I'm some lost court lady than a witch. And Irenya's dress—which

I had no choice but to steal from her trunk, unless I wanted to wear a ballgown—is simple enough that it draws the least attention.

When I catch myself in the mirror, brown eyes and hair hidden by my cloak, even I have trouble recognizing myself.

I walk over to the bar and slide onto an empty stool, far too tired already.

"What's your poison?" the barkeep asks.

I clear my throat and try to look casual. "Whatever's cheapest," I say.

He snorts and moments later pushes a frothy jug and a large round glass over to me.

"Honey juice," he says. "Two pieces of silver Chrim."

I slide them over. Chrim is easy to come by in a castle.

"It's rather busy," I say, looking around at the crowded tables, desperate to make some kind of conversation.

"Always is during Festival," the barkeep says. "Everyone uses this place as their own betting ground for changing their futures. Only works half the time, but they like to try."

Poor fools, I think. So willing to risk their souls for the paper dreams the king and my mother whisper.

I pour the honey juice into my glass, and the sweet froth bubbles up over the rim. When I bring it to my lips, it's like nothing I've ever tasted before. Far from the bitter squeezed grapefruit juice in the castle. This is like warm syrup, a nectar from the gods that feels like silk going down my throat.

I savor the indulgent taste with a grin, closing my eyes as a group of men playing a game of cards in the corner of the room lets out a series of loud curses.

"That's a serpent's straight!" one of them declares. "I think you just made me rich."

I freeze, glass hovering by my lips at the familiarity of that voice.

I turn slowly to see Nox Laederic slam his cards down, to the outrage of the other eight players. He drags a heap of gold and silver Chrim toward him, a roguish smile on his lips as he basks in his winnings.

He's actually here.

I dip my head low, afraid he'll see me, before I remember that he won't recognize me even if he does.

Besides, didn't I *want* to find him?

The whole point of me venturing out here was to convince him to stay home for the next few days. To describe the place he's going to die in more vivid detail so it's as burned into his mind as it is mine.

I bite my lip under my mask and summon the courage to turn back, watching Nox pour his Chrim into a small hip pouch.

"Care for a rematch?" he asks.

"Bite me," one of the men says, glaring like he wants to kill him.

I understand the urge, but Nox doesn't seem to care.

I should have expected as much.

Even if I've only ever met him once before, it's easy to spot the air of recklessness around him. Nox has the feel of someone who never seems content to let life run smoothly. The king's untouchable prize.

"Come on," Nox says. "I'll go easy on you."

He smiles casually, unbothered by the glaring men. I guess the thought of them picking a fight with him is amusing.

If these men knew who he was, they wouldn't challenge him.

I narrow my eyes.

So maybe they don't know.

Nox isn't wearing his uniform, he has no weapons, and there's a relaxed smile as he reaches for his drink.

His new tattoo is clear on his palm, but I'd bet at least half a dozen people in the After Dusk Inn also have that mark.

Including me.

For once I'm grateful for my gloves, keeping my secrets tucked away.

I stare at Nox, unable to stop myself. He isn't the polished soldier who walked into the Grand Hall just two days ago.

Nox's hair is tousled and unkempt, curls scattered in every direction, bringing a new innocence to his face. Stripped back from his uniform and prestige, with only the echo of night on him, he doesn't look so much like a warrior of the Last Army.

He just looks like a boy.

A boy who's going to get me killed.

Suddenly, being this close to him feels like tempting fate.

Maybe it was a mistake to come here after all. What if I'm just making it easier for death to find us both?

What if Nox doesn't listen to my warnings and instead runs to tell the king I've left my tower without permission?

I can feel myself losing nerve by the second, when suddenly Nox turns.

My eyes widen and I swivel quickly back to the bar, hoping he didn't see me staring.

No such luck.

Nox's boots are heavy on the floor as he approaches, and when he pulls out the chair beside me and sits down, I can smell the sea air on his skin.

I adjust my mask, sweating beneath my disguise.

"Do I know you?" Nox asks.

"What?" I'm surprised by the lightness in his voice. "No."

I keep my eyes on my drink.

"From court?" he tries again, noting my mask.

Just tell him, Selestra, I think to myself. *Now's your chance to save both your lives, you fool.*

"Do you play?" Nox gestures back to the card table.

I shake my head.

"I can teach you," he offers. "It's really not that hard."

"Clearly not, if you can do it," I shoot back before I can help myself.

I curse inwardly.

At the castle I'm always best at keeping my thoughts to myself and nodding along to whatever the king and my mother say, like a good little heir.

Yet something about Nox leaves me unable to bite my tongue.

His smile is slow and dangerous. "You'd be the perfect opponent."

"I'll pass." I nod to his hip pouch. "If you win any more Chrim, you might just topple over."

Nox laughs. "Could I lessen the weight and buy you another drink?"

"It would have to be a dozen drinks to make a dent in that thing," I say.

Nox's brown eyes twinkle under the lantern fire. "A dozen drinks it is. If you wouldn't mind me joining you?"

He waits patiently, kindly, for my answer.

Nox has never looked at me kindly before.

Nobody has, except for Irenya and Asden.

I'm the heir to the Somniatis magic and I'm meant to be feared above all else. And if someone isn't scared of me, they're scared of my mother, or of the king and what he'll do to them for one wrong gesture.

"Do you usually offer drinks to any stranger you meet?"

"No," Nox says. "I guess you're that special."

"Oh?"

I breathe a short laugh.

He must think he's so charming. The beautiful soldier, so used to men and women falling at his knees.

"I'm special?" I repeat with a scoff. "Why is that?"

Nox shrugs. "You've got kind eyes."

My smile fades instantly, though Nox doesn't notice under the shield of my mask.

No, I haven't, I think.

And if Nox could really see my eyes, he'd think the same.

He holds out his hand for me to shake, the king's serpent creased inside his palm.

"I'm Nox, by the way."

I suck in a quiet breath.

I have my gloves on, my own mark hidden beneath them, but the thought of a handshake still makes me uneasy.

Nox is the first person I've touched since Asden, and that didn't work out so well. Even so, part of me craves it.

The only contact I ever get is from Irenya straightening out my dresses, or trying to punch me in the face.

"It's just a handshake," Nox says, noting my hesitation. "It won't kill you."

"Actually," I say. "It might."

Even so, I reach out for his hand.

Not quite skin on skin, but the touch sparks through me all the same.

I feel wild with it. Rebellious.

I know I should tell Nox who I really am and why I'm here, but I can't help but want to enjoy this new anonymity for a few moments more. There's nothing stronger than a dream that wants to live, and I've been dreaming of touch, of conversation, my whole life.

"Nice to meet you," I say.

"Likewise."

I look down at our hands, gripped together.

It's a strange greeting, to grab someone and shake their arm about. I hope I'm doing it right.

Is there a way to do it wrong?

"Your bracelet," Nox says. He focuses in on my wrist, where my gold bangle hangs. "Where did you get that?"

I pull away, tucking the bracelet quickly under the sleeve of my cloak.

I curse myself for not removing it.

It's easily recognizable as a royal jewel, but it belonged to my great-great-grandmother and is the only heirloom, the only puzzle piece of my family and a possible life before the king, that I have ever owned. Besides, King Seryth is furious whenever I take it off, so it's become like a second skin.

One I didn't think to shed in my disguise.

"It's just an antique," I say dismissively.

Nox narrows his eyes, gaze still fixed on my hands.

"You're wearing gloves," he says, nodding to the black fabric that slips across my hands. I'd thought they were discreet enough to go unnoticed, but Nox's voice gets low. "That's a strange thing to do when it's so hot out."

I swallow.

I see the moment his face changes. The ease slipping away, his smile turning flat and his jaw tensing as the realization sets in.

"What are *you* doing here?"

His voice is jagged.

"Are you spying on me?"

"Keep your voice down," I urge.

I don't need the whole tavern hearing this.

"I know who you are." He says it like an accusation. "What twisted little game is Seryth playing, having you come here?"

I stare in disbelief. "You can't refer to him by name like that. He's the king. You'll get in trouble."

Nox's lips press together, like he's trying to hold back a smirk. A hint of lightness makes its way back onto his face. "Are you saying that you're going to tell on me, princess?"

I narrow my eyes at him. "That's not why I'm here," I assure him. "I came to warn you."

"Warn me," he repeats.

"About your death tomorrow," I say, lowering my voice as much as I can. "You have to remember every detail, so you never go to any place like it. The floors were red and the walls were half-painted white. There were lanterns on them and some kind of handle in the ground where you tried to escape and—"

"Why are you here?" Nox asks again.

"I just told you," I say, confused. "I'm trying to help."

Nox looks almost amused by the idea. "The king doesn't help people survive the Festival of Predictions. So come on, why are you really here, princess?"

I glare. "Stop calling me that. I'm not a princess."

I was raised to know that.

I'm not royalty or the daughter of the king. I'm born from a man my mother borrowed for the night, whose name she never knew and who was killed in secret shortly after, so he could never lay claim to me.

I swallow and Nox cocks his head to the side, like he's trying to work out what's taking so long for me to try to kill him.

He doesn't believe for a second I want to save him.

I wonder how he'd react if I told him the real truth.

If I explained that he somehow sealed his fate to mine, would he brush it off and vow only to care for himself? Or run and tell the king, hoping he might be able to trade the information for his soul back?

Or maybe he'd want to work together to figure it out.

I wish I knew for sure.

"Hey!" a voice says, breaking through the quiet between us. "I want my Chrim back!"

One of the men from the earlier card game stumbles toward Nox. He points his finger accusingly.

"That gold should be mine and you know it."

Nox slips from the stool. "I already offered you a rematch," he says calmly. "But this lady has caught my attention for the night. Perhaps tomorrow instead?"

If we're not both dead by then, I think.

"You're a cheat!" the man yells, staggering closer. I can smell the alcohol on his breath. "I've thought about it and there's no way you won that many in a row. You were palming cards!"

"I wouldn't dream of insulting your honor like that," Nox says, voice smooth as the honey juice. "You were one of the most challenging opponents I've ever faced, I assure you."

I blink.

Is he really trying to charm his way out of a bar fight?

"Give me my Chrim," the man demands again, unconvinced.

Around us, a crowd begins to gather, watching restlessly. They're eager for a fight, I can tell. A place like this must see blood often.

"Just give it to him," I urge in a fierce whisper.

Calmly, Nox says, "Not a chance."

I throw my hands up. "What is it with you and death wishes?"

The drunk man glowers and snaps his hand out to grab my wrist. His fingers squeeze against the fabric of my gloves.

"Give it to me, before I hurt your girl."

I gape.

The nerve of him, grabbing me like I'm a bargaining chip instead of a person. If this man thinks he can threaten me to get to Nox, then he's mistaken. Least of all because this soldier couldn't care less what happens to me.

I'm tempted to throw down my hood and let my green hair tumble out, just to see the look on this man's face when he realizes who I am, but revealing myself means the king and my mother finding out I've left the castle and, worse, that I came to warn one of their prediction seekers.

They'd think I was a traitor.

So I settle for the next best thing.

I prepare to twist out of the man's grip, aim a knee to his groin, and cast an elbow into the bridge of his nose, just like Asden taught me.

This man doesn't know who he's dealing with.

I only just have the time to angle my body for a fight when Nox's hand shoots out.

He strikes the man in the throat, causing him to fall backward and gasp for breath.

I whirl around to him and glare. "What was that?" I ask, outraged. "I don't need you to save me!"

"I know. You're not a princess." Nox rolls his eyes. "But in some circles, it's still polite to say *thank you*." He turns back to the drunken man. "Really, I'd like to settle this without a fight. I don't want to hurt you."

The drunk lets out a loud laugh. "I don't think that's going to be a problem."

The seven other men from the card table glare.

They slam their drinks down one by one on the sticky table and rise to stand beside their injured friend.

"You'll die tonight," the first man says, still a little breathless. He nods to the king's mark on Nox's hand. "I wonder if this is what the witch predicted for you?"

I step back just as one of the men smashes a glass against a nearby table and holds the shattered piece out like a sword.

"We're going to gut you."

Nox raises an eyebrow. "This seems like an overreaction, don't you think?"

In a blink, the men spring forward.

Nox evades them easily and smacks one man in the nose with his elbow so hard that he falls to the floor and doesn't get back up. When the man with the broken glass launches at him, Nox kicks the shard from him, with enough force that I hear the man's fingers break.

He moves quicker than I thought possible, like a storm bursting from the skies and puncturing the Endless Sea. Watching him fight is nothing like watching Asden fight.

Where Asden was fast, Nox is faster.

Where Asden was fierce, Nox is unparalleled.

Even without a sword, he's unmatched, pushing his way through the crowd like they're nothing. His movements are graceful and merciless.

Though none of the blows are deadly.

It almost seems like Nox is holding back, which doesn't make sense. Last Army soldiers are supposed to revel in destruction. It's why the king was able to win the True War and conquer the Six Isles over a century ago. So why is a Last Army soldier like Nox trying so hard *not* to kill anyone?

The first man pulls out a knife, and I gasp as he tries to plunge it into Nox's back.

"Watch out!" I yell.

Nox spins out of the way, so quick it's like a blur.

He grabs the knife from the man and slices it across his chest.

It's not a killing blow, but it's brutal enough that the crowd screams and runs for the door, suddenly shocked at the mere thought of death.

Then someone stumbles in their escape, ripping one of the black curtains from beside the door and revealing the walls beneath.

Bare brick, licks of forgotten white paint peeling from them.

I look again to the floor, now red with our attacker's blood.

I gasp.

Red floors, white walls. This *is* the place from my vision.

And it's all happening a day early.

"Are you okay?" Nox asks, breaking from the fight for a moment to check in on me.

No, I think. *I'm not.*

It was stupid to come here and leave the safety of my tower to warn him. Stupid to think I could cheat a thing as smart as death. Or overcome the curse of a witch as powerful as my great-great-grandmother. I'm an heir, nothing more.

As I think it, an incredibly large man comes up behind Nox, taking advantage of his splintered attention, and rams his fist into the base of Nox's spine.

Nox stumbles to his knees and I run for the door, following the crowd.

I'll escape before they come for me.

I won't die in this place.

Maybe my and Nox's souls aren't connected and if I can just leave, just get back to the castle, then I'll be safe.

I push through the fleeing crowd and I'm nearly out the door when I hear Nox cry out.

The sound freezes me in place.

Half a dozen men stand over him.

One of them laughs, then kicks Nox in the ribs so hard I hear a crack.

I wince as he is kicked again.

In the back.

The knees.

They're brutal as they hunch over him, showing none of the mercy Nox had shown them.

It doesn't matter, I tell myself. *Run for your life.*

But it does matter.

However hard I try to ignore it, however much I remember the king's words that caring is weakness and people are never to be trusted, it always matters.

Who am I, if I flee this place and let Nox die?

What does it make me, if I leave him to his fate?

I know the answer. It screams inside me like a curse as I see a flash of Asden's face. Hear him screaming out for a mercy that would never come.

If you leave, it truly makes you the king's witch, the voice tells me.

It makes you your mother.

"Damn it," I say.

And then I run toward Nox.

9

SELESTRA

I slip across the floor, my boots gliding over the blood.

My stomach rolls.

I steady my footing and swallow down the bile, shoving a few of the men aside as I try to pull Nox out.

I'm not strong enough.

Burdened by Nox's weight, it only takes one of the men to swing his arm back before I'm thrown to the floor. They laugh and a horrible fury burns inside me.

The lanterns on the tavern walls are a dark amber, and when I look at them, the flames dance.

I can feel my magic, begging me to do something. To not be powerless.

From the floor, Nox glances up at me.

Though his face is bloody, I'm sure he can see the fire breaking into my eyes.

Someone kicks him again and Nox's head falls back.

My breath stops.

It's like watching Asden be killed before me all over again. But this time I can do something to stop it. I'm not a child, hiding behind my mother.

I tear a glove from my hand and set my sights on the man who started all this. The one who accused Nox of cheating and grabbed my arm.

I cannot fight this many people at once, even with Asden's training, but if I can scare this man with a vision of his future, maybe he'll stop his attack.

Without considering the pain that hit me the last time, I reach up and clasp my bare hand around his arm.

Skin on skin.

Flesh against flesh.

The man goes rigid, but the vision doesn't come.

I focus, letting my fear and anger grow, thinking maybe that's the key. I let it all seep out of me.

I picture the king's black eyes and the sound of my room locking every night, sealing me in. Of my mother's smile disappearing and being replaced by something cold and distant.

The sound of her lullabies disappearing to silence.

The man convulses.

Then I feel strange threads, grasping and tugging inside me.

Inside the man.

It's *invigorating*.

"What are you doing?" someone yells. "Stop her!"

Nobody does.

They don't dare touch me, too afraid as the man shakes beneath my grasp.

I can feel his energy funneling into me. His life. I drink it in like I'm dying of thirst. I can see the torchlight of the tavern becoming stronger, bolder, around me. Their flames growing and growing with my strength.

"Selestra." Nox's voice sounds far away and throaty. "You'll kill him."

Kill him.

The words knock into me and the room hurtles back into focus at startling speed.

I don't want to kill anyone.

I focus on my hand, still gripping the dying man.

I don't know how I'm doing it, but I'm sucking the life from him. Just like my mother siphons souls from the dead and feeds them to the king. Just like my great-great-grandmother siphoned the life and magic from all the old witch families.

I rip my hand away, terrified, and the man collapses to the floor, pale as the night stars.

The room sharpens.

What's left of the crowd screams.

There's horror on their faces as they see me. No serpent eyes, but my mask has slipped and so has my cloak, revealing the green of my hair.

"Witch!" someone calls out.

"She'll kill us all!" another cries.

I swallow.

No. No. No.

If they know who I am, that means the king will know I've been here. I can practically hear the sound of more padlocks being fixed to my tower.

New bars on my windows.

He'll make sure I never see the light of day again.

The crowd backs away as I rise to my feet, dizzy.

The dozen people who remain in the tavern watch me carefully, unsure of what I'll do next.

The room spins, the energy I've siphoned from the man catching in my throat. I feel drunk with it. I feel like I might be sick.

"If any of you speak of this night, then my mother and I will punish you," I threaten, trying to hide my own desperation. "I'm the heir to the Somniatis magic and you'll suffer at the hands of my family's power."

My voice is bolder than I feel and I hope they won't see through it and spot how terrified I am. I have to convince them to stay silent, for all our sakes.

The king and Theola will kill every person in this room for even looking at me wrong.

"Run!" I say to the crowd. "Run home and never speak of this again."

To my surprise, they do.

People rush like a stampede of animals, fleeing from the big bad witch, knocking lanterns from the walls as they shove each other in a desperate bid to escape first.

A small group lifts the man I drained from the floor and I'm relieved to see his breath—shallow, but still there—as they drag him to the door.

One of the lanterns smashes against the floor and catches the edge of a fallen curtain. Flame pools quickly across it, like the rivers on the Floating Mountain, burning through the fabric.

I squeeze my eyes shut and try to settle myself, but the room is still wobbling inside my mind and the sound of the flames is deafening.

I reach up a hand to wipe the blood from my nose, but nothing comes.

Using large amounts of my power has always come at a cost. A nosebleed here, a splintering headache there when I heal the injuries from sparring with Irenya. Not this time.

Instead of feeling drained, I feel energized, like I might faint with the power of that man's energy swirling inside me.

Is this how the king feels whenever he feeds on a soul?

Is this how he always feels, made immortal, invincible, by the power my family gives him?

I swallow.

Whatever this feeling is, I hate it.

Across the room, the tavern burns.

The room has emptied of everyone but Nox, and now the fire that minutes ago was licking up the curtains seems to shoot like stars across the walls and over the floors.

It moves so quickly.

The smoke thickens and my skin grows hot.

This is my vision.

Quickly, I bend down to Nox, who's lying on the blood-soaked floor. I'm not sure when he lost consciousness.

With my gloved hand, I touch his cheek, coaxing him awake.

"We have to get out of here," I say.

He stirs, but when his eyes don't open, I shake him at the shoulders.

"Wake up!" I yell more urgently.

Nox grunts and sucks in a hard breath. "Are you trying to kill me or save me?" he asks hoarsely.

"I'm not sure yet."

I pull Nox to his feet, slinging his arm over my shoulder.

His face is red with blood, and by the way he moves, I know some of his ribs are cracked.

We turn toward the exit, but the room is filled with smoke and all I can see is fire.

Across the walls.

Over the door.

"I don't suppose you foresaw a way out?" Nox asks. He coughs and waves his arm to clear away the smoke.

I study the room, but I don't know any other way out. The windows have smashed open, but the fire around them is crackling fiercely, leaving no way to get past.

Then I remember.

My vision.

The image that carved itself into my mind with enough force to make sure I never forgot.

A handle in the floor, surrounded by broken glass.

A trapdoor.

I turn. I did foresee a way out.

"This way."

I stagger over a small ribbon of fire and drag Nox behind the bar. On the floor, among a litter of bottles, is the door.

I crouch down.

"How did you know about this?" Nox yells over the roar of the flames.

He kneels beside me, wincing as the pain of his injuries takes hold.

"I can predict the future," I say. "Remember?"

Above us, the ceiling quakes, spitting dust.

I know it's going to fall at any moment.

"We have to hurry."

I twist the handle and flip open the small hatch to reveal a narrow tunnel.

"Any idea where this leads?" Nox asks.

"Away from here," I say, and jump down.

Nox follows quickly, landing with a thump beside me.

I reach up and pull the hatch closed behind us, hoping it'll keep the fire at bay.

My eyes squint to adjust to the darkness.

The tunnel is only just tall enough for us to crawl farther in. A single light hangs from the ceiling of the door, casting a glow down the tunnel and illuminating the dirt of the walls.

"Go," I urge, pushing Nox forward.

With a sharp breath, every movement looking painful, Nox crawls ahead.

Everything is mud-slicked, weeds clinging to the walls and ceiling. As we move forward, dirt falls onto my shoulders.

Nox holds up a hand crusted with mud.

"This seems unsanitary. When was the last time they cleaned their escape hatch, do you think?"

"Would you just hurry up?" I press.

"Not enjoying your view?" Nox says dryly.

I roll my eyes.

I wish I hadn't let him go in front.

"Just move."

The tunnel is filling quickly with smoke, burning my throat dry, and coughing only makes it worse. My chest aches, like the smoke is inside me and trying to push its way out through my skin.

My eyes sting with it.

"I see a light!" Nox announces.

He crawls quicker.

Moonlight seeps through the cracks of the opening, boarded hastily over with wooden slats.

Nox slams his elbow against them, hard enough for me to flinch.

It sounds like it hurts, but he must be used to pain or it doesn't compare to the injuries he already has, because Nox doesn't stop. He hits the wood, over and over until his elbow pushes through and he can rip the rest away.

We crawl from the hole.

The dry summer grass crunches beneath my palms. I heave in a gasp of the fresh night air and pull myself to my feet.

My hands are blackened with mud and soot, and I cough out breath after breath, pushing the smoke from my lungs.

Nox clambers to his feet beside me. He stumbles a bit, but manages not to topple over. I feel like collapsing too, back onto the grass, where I can sleep for days.

The initial high from absorbing the energy of that man is gone and there's a weight on my chest as my magic whimpers over how much of it I've used.

Whatever I did, it doesn't feel right.

About half a mile from where we stand the crumbled remnants of the After Dusk Inn are engulfed in flames. I watch as it burns to nothing.

"Looks like I'm going to have to find a new place to play cards," Nox says. "At least I got my Chrim though."

He reaches up his sleeve and tosses two crown cards onto the grass.

"You really did cheat?" I ask, aghast.

Nox raises a mocking brow. "I didn't realize you had such a strict moral code, princess. Besides, I needed the Chrim."

"A few pieces of gold was worth risking your life for?"

"Spoken like someone who's never had to worry about not having it."

I roll my eyes and walk toward the nearest alley. Nox knows nothing of my life. He may think it's all diamonds and ballgowns, but at least he can go wherever he wants and do whatever he wants.

I may have Chrim, but he has freedom.

I walk faster. I need to get back to the castle and clean myself up before anyone notices I'm gone.

"I thought you said I was going to die tomorrow," Nox says. He limps after me, struggling to keep pace. "Bad time to get your dates wrong, don't you think?"

Tell me about it.

I nearly got myself killed with my own carelessness.

I wouldn't have ventured out into the lower towns or a tavern, of all places, if I'd known. What use am I as a witch when I can't even predict my own death right?

"I made a mistake," I tell him.

"And then you saved me," Nox says. His eyebrows pinch in confusion. "Which one was the mistake?"

I shake my head.

Truthfully, I'm not sure.

Saving him meant saving my own life, but it also means I've betrayed the king. If he were ever to find that out . . .

I bite my lip and keep walking.

Nox clutches at his ribs, trying to keep step with me as I speed up.

"You could have let those people in the tavern beat me to death," he says. "But you came back."

He looks at me curiously, like I'm a puzzle in place of a person.

"Why did you come back?"

"I don't know," I say, at the same time as the voice in my head whispers, *Because it was the right thing to do.*

Because you damned me too, the day you sought that prediction.

And because maybe I don't want to be exactly like my mother.

"I won't do it again," I say.

Nox pushes the hair from his face. It's wet with blood and ash. "But we make such a good team."

I stare in disbelief.

We nearly died, and if the king finds out that we were together tonight—if anyone who escaped ignores my threats and spills that secret—we'll both be punished.

The king will think I'm conspiring against him to deny him a soul and he won't suffer an insolent heir. He can't afford to let anyone live who isn't loyal only to him.

Even witches.

Especially witches.

"Next time, you're on your own," I say to Nox.

We both are.

And with that, I walk away from him and head back toward the castle.

10
NOX

I can't stop thinking about Selestra Somniatis.

I'm only half listening as Micah and I walk past the army docks, where the black waters of the Endless Sea push gruffly against the boats.

Maybe not even half listening.

I can't get Selestra's face out of my mind.

I picture her leaning over me, eyes like small sunrises as her fingers graze my scar.

Every time I close my eyes, I see her, lighting up the night with her magic. And when my eyes are open, I hear her telling me she wants to help me. Calling out my name as I'm attacked.

Like it mattered.

Like I'm not just some soldier whose soul she wants for her king.

It's been days since she saved me, and that night repeats on a loop. Even now as we head to the castle to answer a mysterious summons from the king, my every thought is of Selestra Somniatis.

The girl with fire in her eyes.

"Look out!" Micah yells.

In a second, I'm pushed roughly to the ground, and the loud shattering of roof tiles falls around us.

By my feet a mountain of broken clay builds, the dust from its fall fogging the air. I look up and see the masons on the growing building, gaping down at me in horror.

"Are you okay down there?" one of them yells.

"Is he dead?" another asks.

"Not yet," I mumble under my breath, wincing as the pain from my ribs takes over.

Even with the various healing salves Micah bought me from the market, I still haven't recovered from the fight at the tavern. Luckily, this latest attack of death has only left me with a small scrape on my elbow.

"He's moving!" one of the masons yells. "Get that mess cleaned up!"

I survey the mess in question. Broken tile coats the cobbled streets, some pieces crushed so badly by the fall that they've turned to dust.

Good thing it wasn't my skull.

"I guess it's my lucky day," I say, taking it in.

"*Lucky?*" Micah lies breathless beside me, from where he flung us both out of danger's path.

He leans his head back to the ground and lets out a long groan.

"I'm locking you away in a room of cushions," he says.

I push myself painfully to my feet and then hold out a hand for Micah. He looks less than impressed.

"You have to be more careful," he chides as I pull him up. "This is the start of the second week, Nox. That means two deaths before you reach the halfway point. And it looks like the first one is nice and prompt in coming for you."

I wave him off as I wipe the dust from my jacket. "You worry too much."

"You don't worry enough," he counters. "This bargain is dangerous. There's a reason only a handful of people ever make it to the point of having a wish granted and a better reason nobody ever goes beyond that."

"But none of those people have you looking out for them." I sling an arm over my friend's shoulder. "Why do I need to worry when I've got you around to be my hero?"

Micah nudges me off, exasperated. "You could die any day now, with no vision to give you warning. Remember that."

"I appreciate the confidence boost."

"You want confidence when you're standing next to me covered in bruises like an overripe banana?"

"It looks worse than it is."

"Really?"

Micah reaches over to jab me in the ribs and I jerk back, nearly breathless with the pain.

"What was that for?" I growl.

"For being a bad liar," he says. "You cracked a rib."

"Two, actually," I tell him, rubbing the spot gingerly.

I've got a right mind to get my money back from those healing salves.

"Do you really think this is what your father wanted?" Micah asks, his voice growing suddenly somber. "Don't you think he'd be angry, seeing you like this?"

I know he would. He would've bought up all the remedies and ointments the traders had, and brought warm soup to my bedside, not letting me up again until the very last bruise disappeared. He always worried far too much.

If he were still alive, he'd tell me to just survive until the halfway point, make a nice wish, and then put an end to my bargain.

Don't try for the king's immortality.

Don't attempt to defeat him.

Just let it go.

But I can't.

If I don't kill the king, he'll only grow more powerful and feast on as many souls as he wants, stealing people's futures forever.

I won't let that happen.

Nobody else will have to lose their family like I did.

"Death can come for me all it wants," I say to Micah. "But no matter what this month throws at me, I'll make sure the king meets his end."

It's a promise to both Micah and myself. A vow to my father's memory. Whatever the cost.

"I know," Micah says with a sigh. He relents to my stubbornness. "We'll do it together."

He places a warm hand on my shoulder, his way of telling me I'm not alone.

It's not your fight, I once said to him.

All your fights are mine, he said back.

I don't have a father anymore, but thanks to Micah I know that I still have family. The king can't say the same. When I take his immortality and drive my father's sword through his chest, nobody will plant a tree in his honor and bring flowers to rest against its trunk.

They'll wish for it to wither, so he can be forgotten.

On the day that happens, maybe my father's soul will finally find peace.

And maybe I will too.

I stand at the foot of Seryth's throne, the skulls of the dead men that make up the seat staring back at me with hollow eyes.

"Congratulations on your survival," Theola says, seated beside the king. "Not that I'm surprised."

"Was that fire in the lower towns your doing?" Seryth asks with piqued interest.

He watches me closely, cocking his head to the side as he studies my slightly disheveled appearance. I don't think he's ever seen me with a real bruise before, let alone a black eye that marks half my face.

It's new to me too.

I was careless in the After Dusk Inn. Wrong to not assess the situation more clearly and see the man I was cheating had seven friends willing to kill me for the transgression.

I won't be that stupid again.

I stare back at the king, casual as I can muster.

"I might have made an appearance."

"A very memorable one. How did they manage to bruise you so badly?"

"Eight against one," I say. "It caught me off guard, what with it being the wrong day."

I think of Micah, waiting outside the doors, wanting to lock me in that room of pillows again.

The king's smile twitches. "It seems my heir cannot even make a simple vision without a fuss."

Beside him, Theola's yellow-green eyes flicker. "Nox is alive and well," she says, voice soft as a melody. "Her vision was help enough to him."

More than just her vision, I think. She pulled me from that fire with her own hands, saving my life when she could've just as easily left me to burn.

Stop thinking about the witch, I scold myself.

Letting her occupy my thoughts and distract me this morning nearly got me killed.

"Yes," the king says in a low rumble. "I suppose Selestra was somewhat useful."

He eases back into his throne.

There's not a hint on his face that he knows Selestra was in the tavern with me that night, but the king has centuries of practice in hiding, honing his anger and secrets until it's most painful to strike.

I can't trust that he isn't suspicious.

"I'm glad you're still alive," Seryth says. "Truth be told, I need my best soldiers ready, Nox."

"Did something happen?" I ask, playing the part of the dutiful soldier.

"It's much of the same." Theola waves her hand as though the conversation bores her. "The Southern Isle refuses to relent."

She means they refuse to die, I think.

The Southern Isle of Polemistés is the only place to withstand nearly a century of Seryth's reign.

It's not just that it's the birthplace of the best warriors in the Six Isles, but it's also nearly impossible to dock there. They're surrounded by sea blockades and whirlpools with as many arms as the branches of a tree. Not to mention the great barricade. Even when the Last Army brought down one of its walls and swept into the island, killing their king, it didn't matter. Polemistés drove them back out and built new walls, each taller than the next.

As for the island itself, everyone knows the stories of their haunted forest. A place where the spirits of their warriors go to rest before they attain paradise, filled with the most treacherous trials and challenges, so their spirits can prove their worth.

Monsters live there.

The rivers can reach out an arm to drown you.

The ground can swallow you whole.

It's not a place for the living.

Really, it isn't just the people on Polemistés who won't relent to Seryth—it's the island itself. Maybe that's why my father chose it for the location of his fairy tale about a sword that could kill any being.

Such a mythical thing could only exist in a place like that.

"Never mind that," the king says, dismissing the idea of war in a moment. "I summoned you here because of the bargain, Nox. Of course, you'll be giving it up if you survive until the wish ceremony, as everyone does."

It isn't a question. Nobody would dare try to go for his immortality and he wants me to know it.

"I know you wouldn't want to lose your soul if it could join your father's in the River of Memory years from now," the king says. "He would want to see you again."

Beneath my skin, my blood boils. Red hot, charring my veins with an indestructible anger. My father's soul isn't in the River of Memory.

We both know that.

"Because of that, because I am a just king who would never want to get in the way of such a reunion, I want to offer you a chance." Seryth leans forward, the whites of his eyes aglow. "Another vision, to help you survive."

I stiffen.

I've heard rumors of the king granting second visions to people he favors, but they've only ever been rumors. And in those stories the people were always wealthy merchants, who were far more useful to him alive.

What use does he have of me, beyond being a soldier?

Unless, of course, he's worried that I might just go further, and this bribe—this reminder of my father—is a way to keep me satiated.

"It's why we summoned you here," the king says, as Theola stands from her throne and descends the steps toward me. "I look after my own, Nox."

That's what he thinks I am. What he wants me to be: his.

I flinch backward.

Theola's hand pauses midair, just moments from my cheek.

"No," I say.

The king's face twitches.

I know I've failed whatever test this is, but I can't stomach the thought of letting that witch touch me, knowing it would give the king ownership of me. The soldier in me is yelling to take this chance, but it would betray my father's memory to be indebted to them like that.

And what's to say they won't use this vision to look into other parts of my future and see a glimpse of my plans for their destruction? A vision from them could take away my advantage as easily as it could give it.

"It would be an unfair favor," I say, recovering quickly. I will my voice to steady. "You trained me to be the best and I want to prove to you that's exactly what I am. If a simple townsperson can survive until the halfway mark, then a soldier in your army can make it easily, without extra help."

"Are you sure?" the king asks. "Pride may be the death of you, Nox."

"If it is, then I wasn't worthy of the bargain to begin with."

The king smiles and reclines back into his throne, satisfied for the moment.

"A true soldier to the end," he says. "Very well."

If he's slighted, he's careful not to show me.

"You may leave and prepare for your next death however you see fit," the king says. "I'll see you soon, Nox."

I bow, quickly, and push open the doors to the Grand Hall.

It takes barely a second of the doors closing behind me before someone smacks me around the back of the head.

"What were you thinking?" Micah says, outraged.

I knew he'd be eavesdropping right outside.

"That my next death might be a head injury," I say, rubbing the back of my head.

Micah isn't impressed. "You just turned down a chance of surviving," he says. "Are you crazy?"

"Maybe he's just stupid."

Selestra's voice echoes from behind us.

I turn to see her perched on a ledge to the side of the large doors, with a girl beside her who I don't recognize.

Suddenly, my frustration turns to intrigue.

"Oh, right," Micah says. "She was listening too."

I watch Selestra rise to standing.

She isn't wearing a sparkling ballgown or hiding her face with a mask like she was at the tavern.

She's strangely unelaborate.

Relaxed, in a way I haven't seen before.

Wearing all black—a shirt that buttons up to her neck, long cuffed trousers and plain gloves—she looks a little bit like a soldier. She could almost blend in, if not for the deep green of her hair that drips down her back like moss.

Witch, I remind myself. *She's a witch.*

"We meet again," I say, stepping toward her. "This is becoming a habit."

"A very bad habit." Selestra folds her arms across her chest, like a barrier between us. "So you're still alive, then."

"Looks like it," I say. "Though I could have used your help again this morning."

Any chance of a smile on Selestra's face quickly dissipates and she looks around at the empty hall, to see if anyone is listening in.

She's worried.

It takes me by surprise, because I didn't think witches had fears, not even death. And if a person doesn't fear death, what's left to be scared of?

Selestra presses her lips tightly together and glances at the doors to the Grand Hall, and suddenly I know the answer.

Her mother. The king.

Selestra doesn't want them ever finding out what happened at the tavern. She's happy for them to think I made it this far alone.

It's a reckless hope.

She may have threatened the people in the tavern to silence, but that'll only last so long. They don't fear her as much as they fear her mother or the king.

And secrets have a habit of never keeping to themselves.

"You know it's my job to be your hero, not hers," Micah says, filling the silence.

He steps forward, makes to shake Selestra's hand and then awkwardly clears his throat when his eyes meet her gloves.

"We didn't really introduce ourselves during our spying," he says. "My name's Micah. I'm the person who saves Nox's life all the time."

Selestra arches an eyebrow. "You say that like it's something to be proud of."

"Never," he says, laughing nervously. "Who's your friend?"

Selestra turns to the girl beside her, who seems equally unimpressed.

She's not one of the rich court ladies. I can tell that much by the muddy blond hair ending at her chin that's free from any intricate style. And judging by the way her dark brown eyes glare at me, she doesn't give a damn if we're in the Last Army or not. She isn't intimidated.

Why would she be? She spends all her time with a witch.

"This is Irenya," Selestra says. "She's an apprentice to the dressmaker."

"Irenya," Micah repeats. "Ever wanted to date a soldier?"

"You're not my type," she tells him plainly.

Micah frowns, like that might just be impossible. "What did your last partner have that I don't?"

"Breasts."

I clear my throat to stop myself from laughing.

"Ah," he says. "Maybe in the next life, then."

"Assuming all of the Last Army soldiers aren't reborn as cockroaches," Selestra says.

She looks at me with a rogue smile, beyond what I've known from the brief glimpses of her before all this started. I always thought the heir was rigid and uncompromising, carved from obedience.

Now I know I was wrong.

She's a wild and reckless thing, hiding under the guise of pretense and duty. I can see it in her, threatening to break through and destroy anything in its wake. Maybe that's why she disguises herself and frequents taverns in the night.

"What are witches reborn as?" I ask.

"Queens," Selestra says, not missing a beat.

I watch her, keeping a close eye on that spark in her eyes that could erupt into flame. "Even insects have queens," I say.

Selestra's lips toy with the idea of laughing, but she decides against it. Her eyes flit to the serpent crest on my palm and a new seriousness takes over her face.

"You really should have taken the king's offer," she says. "Another prediction could be all the help you need to survive and be released from this bargain. You could go back to your life before all this."

"What if I don't want to go back?" I challenge.

Whatever she expected me to say, it isn't that.

Selestra frowns, wondering why a Last Army soldier who has worked his whole life to be the best and achieved just that might not want the life he has so carefully selected.

For someone who predicts the future, she doesn't know as much as she thinks.

"Death has a habit of getting its way," Selestra finally says, clearing the silence between us. "You're not safe, Nox. Nobody is. Be careful."

I blink when she speaks.

Be careful?

I'm not sure if it's supposed to be a threat or a warning, but Selestra turns quickly on her heel before I can reply, making her way down the corridor at record speed. Irenya practically runs to keep step with her.

I watch them leave and I don't look away until Selestra has turned the corner and is completely out of sight.

Micah claps a hand on my shoulder. "You're getting rusty with the girls."

"She isn't a girl," I remind him and myself. "She's a witch."

"Good point," he says. "And speaking of witches, do you have a plan for how to survive the next death now that you've turned down the king's offer?"

I shrug.

Plans have never been my strong point. Micah should know that.

Plans and routine are how you become predictable, and predictability gets people killed in the Last Army. The king likes his soldiers to intrigue him, to adjust and adapt, and souls forbid he ever thought we were *boring*.

My life has always been about thinking on my feet.

"Once you reach the halfway point and choose to continue rather than make a wish, the king will be allowed to hunt you down," Micah reminds me.

"Let him try," I say.

Micah sighs. "You really should've taken that vision," he groans.

I press my fingers to my temples, feeling a growing headache.

Maybe he's right, but I entered into this bargain to try to cheat death, hoping to break the king's immortality and avenge my father. If I want to win, I can't keep following the rules that man sets.

Doing everything—even dying, even living—on his timeline.

"We're going to need a miracle for this to work out," Micah says.

I turn and look down the corridor Selestra disappeared into.

I think back to her, pulling me from the burning tavern, so unaware of the consequences.

"We don't need a miracle," I tell him. "We just need a witch."

11

SELESTRA

"It's a bit of a shame you won't be able to touch him again," Irenya says, running a brush through my hair.

I look at her reflection in the mirror, confused.

"Who?" I ask.

"Nox," she says, as though it's obvious. "Bruises aside, I'm starting to think he's quite pretty."

"Have you bumped your head?" I ask, outraged at the thought. "Where did that come from?"

"From my eyes. Looking deep into his."

I shoot Irenya a look. "You know, he doesn't have breasts either."

Though Irenya has never cared much either way.

She's dated both women and men and always said she cares more about people than their bodies. I envy her a little. She's free to be close to whoever she likes. Talking and touching.

All the things I can only dream of.

"I'm sure Nox has other fine attributes," Irenya continues, somewhat dreamily.

"And worse ones too."

Irenya laughs. "Admit it, Selestra, he's got a nice face."

"Shame he has to ruin it by talking."

Nox might be pretty, but it's his personality that's the problem.

I've never met anyone so sure of themselves. He laughs his way through life—and death—like none of it can touch him. He even gambled his soul away because he was so confident he has the strength to survive.

I don't know what it's like to be that certain. Everything I want is in conflict and sometimes I feel like a mess of clashing thoughts and faraway hopes.

To be the witch and use my powers freely, but not to be under the king's hold.

To want my mother back, but to want her gone at the same time.

"So why did you tell him to be careful?" Irenya asks.

Her smile is teasing. She's too focused on Nox's face to think that perhaps I might have ulterior motives for wanting him safe.

Like the fact that if he dies, I might just die too.

I'm still not sure how I'm going to help him survive this month if he is set on doing everything he can to die, like turning away visions from the king.

Just what was he thinking?

I can't believe my soul is tied to a reckless soldier with a death wish.

"Everyone needs to be careful when it comes to this month," I answer. "And my mother."

I lower my voice into a silky drawl.

"Seeing people's death takes its toll, and what a shame it'll be to take their souls. It's so hard being the king's witch, maybe that's why I'm such a—"

"Selestra!" Irenya yells out, though she's laughing.

Seeing the look of disbelief on her face, I start laughing too. It feels like a relief, the weight of death lifted from my shoulders.

Then someone clears their throat.

We turn to see a young castle guard standing with his hands behind his back, teeth scraping his bottom lip.

"I'm sorry to interrupt," he says. "The king requests your presence."

"Is that so?" I sigh and reach for my night robe. "And where might my presence be required?"

The guard shuffles. "The crypts, my lady."

My smile disappears, as quick as the light when a cloud swoops across the sun.

"He and the Lady Theola are conducting the first extractions," he says. "They'd like for you to be present."

Rather than race, my heart starts to slow.

To nearly stop.

"The extractions," I repeat.

Beside me, Irenya stiffens.

For the first time in my life, I'm about to see what it really means to be the king's witch.

I descend the staircase alone.

Nobody is supposed to enter the crypts but the king, my mother, and the keeper of the dead.

Tonight is different.

I think of all the bodies waiting at the end of the steps.

The soul extractions happen whenever there are a few dozen dead to reap. Enough people who haven't survived their predictions.

The smell hits me first, like rot and damp, and when I breathe in, it gets stuck somewhere, the smell embedding itself inside me.

The crypts are a windowless cavity, built beneath the castle, deep into the Floating Mountain. The rock walls are wet and the ceiling shakes with the force of the waterfalls outside.

It's like at any moment it might crumble inward and bury me down here with the dead.

"You're here," the king says. "Finally."

He's wearing a long cloak open at the chest, the hood hiding his eyes enough so half of his face looks like unyielding darkness.

My mother is also wearing black, and standing together they nearly blend into the shadows.

I squeeze my hands together.

The bodies of the dead are not in boxes.

They're lined up across the floor in rows of two each that stretch back into the cavern of the room, beyond where the faint torchlight can find them.

More than a dozen.

I've never seen a dead body before. I try not to gag.

Some look peaceful, but on others there's blood and the things that lie beyond the blood: organs and bone and yellow fluid that seeps from their open wounds.

I look away.

I could have been down here, if I hadn't survived the After Dusk Inn.

Lined up beside Nox.

"She shouldn't be here," Theola says to the king.

She looks at me fiercely with yellow-green eyes, broken only by a black slit in the center.

"She's not yet eighteen," my mother says. "She doesn't have the blood oath inside her, and—"

"She has to learn," the king interrupts, voice low and absolute.

They talk about me like I'm not here.

For once, I wish it was true.

"Better we teach her about her duties early," he continues. "I still remember how nervous you were the first time, Theola."

My mother blinks, as though the memory of herself as a child, as a girl my age, is almost painful.

"Perhaps when she's eighteen," she says. "It's tradition for the heir to—"

"Enough." The king's command echoes through the tomb. "She watches and she learns and that's all there is to it."

His tone is final. His word is as good as law.

Theola nods and places a hand on his shoulder, delicate and calming. "Of course," she says.

She doesn't want to make him angry.

When he's angry, the world shakes.

"You always know what's best for the kingdom."

She turns to me, hand still stroking the king's arm, like a woman taming a wolf.

"A witch must be strong," Theola says, taking in the new paleness to my face. "Only the strong ever survive."

"What do I have to do?" I ask.

"Watch," my mother says. "And learn."

Theola walks toward a body in the first row.

A woman who doesn't look much younger than her, and whose body is frail enough to seem like it's made of bones and skin and little else.

Theola kneels, her robes slicking across the soiled ground.

She presses a hand to the woman's heart, until her fingers are coated in blood. The smell of it salts the air.

Then she draws a symbol: a sword wrapped in a serpent. The crest of the Somniatis family.

Next, my mother places a lock of hair on the women's chest. The piece of her that was taken during the prediction, helping tether her to this world.

"In the name of the first witches, I call you out," Theola says.

Her voice skips through the room and sinks into the walls.

"In the name of the last magic, I call you out."

The woman's body jolts and a guttural moan creaks through the room.

I stumble back a step.

The moan climbs, churning through the room like a trapped echo, before the body takes a sudden breath.

The dead woman lurches upward. Her chest heaves as she gasps in the stale, putrid air. For a moment she is alive again.

She blinks and a single tear, black as my mother's cloak, slips down her blood-ridden cheek. The woman's mouth forms the shape of a word.

No.

Theola presses a hand against the symbol on her chest.

"I call you out," she says.

The woman's mouth stretches open like it's being pulled apart and her eyes grow to large black disks. Her body flings back to the floor with a crack and she screams, an inhuman sound.

I want to run back to my room, lock myself in the place I've always yearned to escape.

Run and forget.

Run and forget.

I am still.

I have seen this part before, I realize. With Asden crying out and begging for mercy that night.

I never wanted to see it again. I never wanted to remember it in any detail, past his eyes. I only wanted to think of the good memories and never, ever that one.

From the woman's gaping mouth, a gray shadow slithers out.

It's smoke and air and nothing else. The gray thing crawls across the woman's lips and down to her chest, until it reaches my mother's open hands.

Theola stands and turns to present it to the king.

I can't see his eyes, but his smile is clear as daybreak. He licks his lips and I go back to holding my breath.

The soul swirls in my mother's hands.

The king strokes her cheek in response. "My beautiful thing," he says. He turns to look at me just as fondly. "My Somniatis girls."

The words rip through me.

They are the same he used the day Asden died.

This whole evening is like a repeat of that night.

Forget, I beg myself. *He wouldn't want you to remember that.*

My mother smiles back at the king, but when his head dips low to look at the dead woman's soul, I see her face change.

Her lips curl, and from where I stand, just feet away, I could swear I hear her breath hitch.

She remembers too.

The king doesn't notice. He ogles his meal and slowly reaches down to press his mouth to the soul.

At first I think it'll seep into him, that he'll draw it in with his breath and it'll be over quickly.

Then I hear the sound of him slurping.

Of him gobbling and *chewing*, like the soul is filled with bones and grit.

I press my back against the wall of the staircase, but no matter how hard I try to tear my eyes from it, I can't look away.

I watch him feast.

This is my future, I think.

This is what the blood oath of my great-great-grandmother truly means. The promise she made, binding us to him for eternity once we turn eighteen, so we can't help but remain loyal to him.

It doesn't mean getting to leave my tower whenever I want, or removing my gloves and giving harmless predictions to those who ask for it.

It's ripping souls from the world and ensuring they never meet the River of Memory.

This, of all the wonderful magic that must have once existed, is all that's left.

King Seryth wipes his hand across his mouth and breathes out a dreaded sigh.

"Another," he says.

His voice is ragged. Ravenous.

My mother turns back to the bodies that remain.

And another she chooses.

12

SELESTRA

After the extraction, I retreat quickly to my room.

I shower, desperate to scrub the death from my skin. It makes me feel dirty and *wrong*. Even after, when I'm about to climb into bed, I still don't feel quite clean enough. The memory of it lingers on me.

"Your hair is getting too long."

I pause by the foot of my bed as my mother enters the room.

"What are you doing here?" I ask.

She never drops by for a visit.

Witches have more important duties than that.

"The king and I have noticed differences in you lately," Theola says. She looks over to my unmade bed with a pinched brow. "You seem distracted. Hesitant."

I swallow. "I'm not. I'm just . . ."

Just realizing what kind of a monster I'll have to become to survive this place, I think. *Realizing that if I don't live through this month, it could be me on one of those tables in the crypt.*

Asden's training will only get me so far. It only got *him* so far.

I want so desperately to tell my mother the truth about my vision of Nox and all that's happened, but I know it'll only end in disaster. The blood oath won't let her keep such a secret. Any love she may have left for me doesn't compare with her fealty to the king.

Maybe it'll happen to me too.

When I turn eighteen, I'll have no control over my destiny and I won't be able to resist the king's commands.

I'll truly become a monster.

"Do you love the king?" I ask my mother suddenly.

"We all love the king," Theola says automatically. In the vein of a call and response. "It is our duty and our promise."

I bite my lip.

I'd never tell her this, but I don't think love is meant to be a duty, and if it's a promise, then it isn't one that I made.

"I didn't come here to talk about love," Theola says firmly. "I came here to tell you to be careful. Displeasing the king won't end well."

Her voice is gruff in warning.

It's the only thing my mother gives me anymore: warnings upon warnings and never anything as tender as hope.

"He wishes for you to be confined here for the rest of the month," she proclaims. "As punishment for giving the wrong death day to Nox and your odd behavior, the door to your room will be magically sealed. You won't be able to leave for any reason, even to attend the banquet in two days or the wish ceremony at the end of the week. And you'll use this time to think about your future."

I stare at her.

"To think about all our futures," she says.

Long gone is the woman who told me about our goddess and whose soft fingers brushed out my hair at night.

I miss the way she used to look at me, back when I was too young to savor it. Now whenever her eyes meet mine, they're only ever uncertain.

Grave.

"I know I have a lot to learn before I'm like you," I say.

Theola steps backward and shakes her head, like I'm speaking of impossible things.

"You can't learn to be something that you're not." Her voice is a sigh. "And you've never been like me, Selestra."

She looks at me with a flicker of what I could swear passes for grief. Then she turns, dress swooping like black wings behind her, flying from the room so quickly it's as though she's worried staying any longer will make her a prisoner too.

Like it's the castle that traps people, rather than the man who built it.

Theola doesn't close the door when she leaves, and it feels like a taunt. A wide-open door, with nowhere for me to go.

Her magic, our family's magic, trapping me inside.

I don't bother to close it before I climb into bed and squeeze my eyes shut, desperate for sleep to come so this day can be over.

I'm not sure how long passes with me lying there, but eventually, the world slips away.

Eventually, I dream of horrors.

Of memories.

I am fourteen years old and the moon is covered in blood.

The Grand Hall is constant, boundless, immeasurable. It towers above me, closes in around me, wrapping huge arms across my chest.

The jewels on the thrones smile like teeth. The mouth of a great beast that wants to eat me whole, bones and skin and all.

"You killed them," Asden says.

The first words I have ever heard him speak.

I want to treasure them, lock them away inside my heart, but they are so awful that my hands shake.

Asden's eyes are brown and sad, and though his voice is soft, I know it aches to roar.

It reminds me of something torn and broken: A ripped dress. A shattered vase. Something that was destroyed and made meaningless.

"They were innocent," he says. "They just wanted to be free."

There is so much authority in him. In this shattered vase of a man.

The way he stands in his great uniform with his shiny medals and his head tilted high so he can look the king straight in the eyes.

Not just a soldier, or a trainer for palace guards. But a General.

Fearless.

Commanding.

Broken, but not destroyed.

I hide behind my mother, hands gripping tightly onto the fabric of her ballgown.

I am scared. Not of Asden, but of how much the king might shatter him more.

The king taps his fingers on his dead throne.

"Nobody is innocent," he says. "Nobody will ever be free."

My mother tenses. She pushes me farther behind her.

"Can the sword really be worth all of this, Seryth?" Asden asks.

My mother swallows at the use of his name.

Treason.

It is treason to call the king anything but a king.

The king's smile crawls up one side of his face. "It is worth everything," he says. "Even your life, old friend."

Asden doesn't blink or move to run, though he must sense what is coming.

I want to scream for him to escape. To take his sad eyes and his shattered voice and just run.

But I don't scream and he doesn't move.

"Selestra," the king says.

My mother's breath breaks. Snaps clean in half the moment he calls my name.

He holds an arm out.

I make to move, but my mother's hand presses firmly against my shoulder, keeping me rooted behind her.

"Selestra," the king says again.

But he is not looking at me. He is looking at my mother.

She swallows and releases me.

The king points to Asden. For a moment I think maybe he has discovered how we've been training in secret and wants to punish me too, but the king's face is calm.

This isn't about me or our training. It's about something else.

A treachery far deeper.

"See. Touch. Learn," the king says.

And though my mother pleads and her eyes glisten, I step forward.

"This isn't the Festival," she says. "Seeing into his future won't link his soul to yours."

"I don't care about his soul," the king says.

My heart pounds when Asden looks at me.

I take off a glove and he holds out his hand so I can thread it through mine. He squeezes softly, letting me know it's okay. He isn't mad.

He doesn't fight. He doesn't beg.

Neither of us do.

This is our fate and we have come to accept it.

When the vision comes, it's cloudy and dark. A wind cold enough to bite into my flesh rushes through my mind.

I see us as we are in that moment. In that room. In that second.

Then Asden screams inside my mind and a tear slips from his eyes. That tear carries into the air and turns to smoke.

To a soul. Gray and slivering.

I drop Asden's hand and nearly fall to the floor, but my mother swoops me up in her arms and wraps herself around me so tight, hand pressed against my thumping heart.

"It's okay," she says, kneeling so we are level. I stare at Asden, at my friend and mentor, as my mother buries her face in my neck, whispering, whispering words only for me. "It's okay," she says again.

Asden's eyes meet mine. Kind and brown and resigned.

You should have run, *I think.* Or fought like you taught me to.

"Today," I say, even though he knows. My voice is a tiny thing. "You're going to die today."

I want to cry.

Asden looks to my mother.

"Promise you won't let my son pay for this," he says. "Protect him, like you wish to protect her."

The king rises from his throne and moves forward.

"Your son will make a fine soldier," my mother says.

She speaks quickly, before the king has the chance, rising to stand like a mighty tower. "If he is loyal, he will remain."

"Yes," the king says slowly.

His voice is made of shadows. His fingers curl around my mother's shoulder.

"He will remain. But you will not."

Asden touches a hand to his sword and I hold my breath, waiting for him to draw it and fight. Fight hard and determined, like he showed me how to.

But he doesn't.

He knows it is useless.

There is no ritual when my mother takes this soul. No bargain, or choice. Just her power, rising around us as she tears Asden's soul from his body and the light from his eyes.

His screams clamp over my heart, squeezing and squeezing until I can't breathe.

This is not for the Festival or the king's immortality.

This is for nothing. This is for a lesson.

I don't want to see this, *I think.* I don't want to know this.

Forget. Forget. Forget.

"There," the king says, after Asden slumps to the floor.

My mentor, vanished in a moment. A solace in this castle torn from me.

Asden blinks, just once, his mouth agape, before a final sigh escapes his pale, pale lips.

Then he is gone. He is nothing.

The king reaches over and strokes my head. His fingers feel like insects in my hair.

"My beautiful thing," he says. He looks down at me, lips stretching to a thin smile. "My Somniatis girls."

He turns to my mother and there is nothing in her eyes when she looks back. Not fear or regret and not that bright, bright spark I'd always seen before.

She is empty and she won't look at me any longer.

"Yes," she says. "We are yours."

My eyes shoot open.

In the depths of the night, with my heart racing, a small noise pulls me from the dream.

A creak.

A footstep.

It's soft and light, and I wonder if my mother has returned to punish me further. I grind my teeth together, steel my breath, and then shoot up from under the covers.

The flame beside my bed crackles.

And then I see him.

Asden's face above mine.

No, not Asden, I realize all too quickly.

But the boy who looks so much like his father.

The boy I can't believe I didn't recognize before now.

Nox Laederic, standing over me with a knife.

13

SELESTRA

I was a fool not to see the similarities between them until now.

Asden never spoke to me to tell me anything about his life or his family, and I've never been allowed to talk to anyone myself to glean anything, even after his death. I only learned his first name when I overheard someone at court say it a few months after we began training.

To realize all this time it was Asden Laederic sends me spinning. Nox, the king's best and brightest soldier, is the son of the man who taught me to be strong.

The son, who tied his fate to mine.

I swallow as Nox clutches his knife tighter.

"Evening, princess," he says.

"Isn't this past your bedtime?" I ask, feeling a fierce bravery in my stomach.

I'm not scared.

There's a Last Army soldier standing in the dark at the foot of my bed with a blade that glistens like moonlight. It should scare me, but it doesn't.

"I don't sleep," Nox says. He moves beside my window, swift as a breeze. "Aren't you going to scream?"

"Aren't you going to stab me?"

"Maybe," he says.

The wind from the open window ruffles the curtains against the floor by his feet.

"I'm taking my time. Murder is a tricky business."

Liar, I think.

If Nox wanted to kill me, he'd have done it by now.

I sit up farther, pushing my pillow against my headboard and leaning back to call his bluff.

He truly does look the spitting image of his father. How had I not seen that before? How had I pushed so many details of that night down into the very pits of myself?

What would Asden say if he could see us both now?

"Take your time," I say to Nox.

He is like a shadow, part of his face lit up by the candle but the other part coated in night, so I can only see half of him.

Just one side to Nox Laederic, but I suspect there are so many more.

Nox clutches his knife and it shimmers under the light. It's a weapon Asden would have been proud to display on the rack in our old training room. The handle is as red as rose flowers, dripping on to a pure black blade.

I wonder if it was a gift, from father to son.

"Why are you really here?" I ask.

"I'm here to talk about my future."

Nox glances briefly outside the window, to the sky that beckons below.

"I want a second prediction."

I'm torn between laughter and disbelief. "Did you forget that the king and my mother already offered you one and you turned it down?"

"I don't want it from them," he says. "I want it from you."

Why he wants such a thing is beyond me. If it's a vision Nox is after, then the real witch is the best one to give it.

Just a few hours ago, Theola stood in this very room and warned me not to step out of line. Giving Nox a prediction behind her back would be doing just that and then some.

Nox moves into the light, knife still tight in his hands. "You helped me before," he says. "You can do it again."

I scowl, but Nox is undeterred.

"If you don't," he says, "I'll tell the king you're the one who rescued me in the tavern the other night, denying him my soul."

My mouth drops open.

I can't believe the nerve of him, using the fact that I saved his life to blackmail me.

I pull my bedcovers back and step onto the floor.

The wood is cold under my feet as I walk over to Nox. I look at him, dead in the eyes. He's close enough that I can see the scar on his face up close.

I swallow, remembering what it was like to touch him.

"You should watch who you threaten," I warn.

Nox simply stares at me. "What is it you're going to do exactly?"

Without warning, I make to elbow him in the stomach, just like his father once showed me. Only Nox dodges it just in time and so I twist and go for his blade.

I manage to graze the handle before he moves it swiftly out of the way and slices open my palm.

I recoil, bringing my bleeding hand to my chest.

A blink later, his knife is at my throat.

"Impressive," Nox says. "But not too smart."

I keep my gaze steady. "Are you talking to me or yourself?"

His blade presses harder against my skin. "I didn't realize witches needed to know combat."

"You'd be surprised how much you don't know about me."

Nox smiles, quickly, like he can't help it.

"I'll bet."

He lowers his knife and looks to my hand.

It stings, but it's nothing compared with wounds I've gotten in training. I'll be able to heal it within a few minutes. I'm more concerned about the blood dripping onto the floor. I'll need to clean that up before anyone notices.

"You saved my life at the tavern," Nox says.

I wave my bleeding hand in his face. "And this is the thanks I get for it. Forgive me if I don't jump at the chance to do it again."

I stare into the tree bark of his eyes and I can see Nox is torn between apologizing and just slitting my throat now to get it over with.

"I'm trying to convince myself that you're not evil," he says. "But you're making it difficult."

"All witches are evil," I remind him, because it's true.

It's what my mother taught me best. And if Nox truly knew what happened to his father, he wouldn't even be debating it.

"Yet, I'm somehow not killing you," Nox says.

To him, everything is as simple as kill or be killed. He doesn't understand what it's like not to punch his way through every problem or to have no solutions to something at all. To have to just *bear it*. Forever.

He's never had to accept his enemies, because he's always been given permission to fight them. Even now, standing in the bedroom of a Somniatis witch, he thinks there are only two choices to be made.

How lucky for him to have a choice at all, after he has taken away mine.

"Selestra," he says.

My name is strange on his lips. Melodic, in a way it's never been when my mother says it or the king growls it.

"You're going to give me this vision."

I roll my eyes and try to shove Nox away. It's a last act of defiance before I know I'll relent. After all, if helping Nox survive helps me survive, I'd be a fool to refuse. Only when I push him, it's like pushing a statue. He doesn't move, except to brush the front of his shirt, as though I've wiped death all over it.

"You really need to work on your manners." He wags his knife in the air. "I'm a guest, after all."

Souls, he's infuriating.

I curse death for trying to glue our fates together like tree sap.

"I'm not afraid of you," I tell him. "If you think you can threaten me into helping you, then you're wrong. What you need to do is say *please*."

I go to push him again.

Such a small, meaningless thing.

Except this time Nox catches my wrists, and by the time I realize I'm not wearing my gloves and see the satisfied raise of his eyebrows, it's too late.

My pulse thumps against his fingertips.

Nox's skin burns into mine.

Then death comes.

We're in the castle and the rumble of thunder shakes my bones enough that my legs feel unsteady beneath me.

Outside, the sky is an angry black.

Nox holds on tight to my gloved hand and pulls me through the halls of the castle. I try to keep pace, but he's running too fast and I trip.

Nox's hand slips from mine.

I fall to the stone.

He yanks me back up, but as he does, lightning explodes against the window beside us, smashing glass across the marble.

The king and Theola step from the shadows. "I know what you have done. There is nowhere you can hide," the king says.

I back away, but suddenly the corridor is a tiny room and we're boxed in. All I can see is the moon, darkening in the distance.

"You're so much like your father." The king turns to Nox, a beat of disappointment mixed into his disgust. "Him and that forsaken sword, you and this damn month."

Nox pushes me behind him.

"Kill them," the king says. His voice pounds inside my head. "Kill them both like the filthy traitors they are."

Theola advances toward us, yellow-green eyes growing large as a forked tongue slithers between her teeth.

"You can't kill me," I call out. "I'm the Somniatis heir."

The king pulls his thin lips into a smile, desperate for destruction. "You don't have to be," he says. "Theola can make me a new one."

He presses a hand to my mother's stomach, mocking me with my own irrelevance.

"Goodbye, Selestra," my mother says.

And then Nox is shaking me, jolting me back into the real world so swiftly that my neck almost clicks.

His hands are wrapped around my wrists, eyes searching mine, desperate to know what I've seen.

I open my mouth to speak, but the words get stuck inside me.

The serpent crest aches against my palm.

"What is it?" Nox asks.

I look at the young soldier and see my future swimming in his eyes.

If he dies, I die. Every time.

It's an anomaly. A trick of fate. The thread of destiny a fine chain that binds us together. A part of me thought that maybe if I stayed away from Nox, rather than seek him out again, I could escape. But it's clear that fate won't let us stay separate.

As long as Nox is part of this bargain, then I am too.

It dawns on me then that I'm not safe in this castle I've called home, or in the walls the king said he built to keep me protected.

I'm not protected at all. I'm *replaceable*.

And when the king eats Nox's soul, he'll eat mine without a second thought.

I can't wait for that to happen.

If Nox wants help to survive the month and cheat death, then fine.

But first he has to get me out of this castle.

14
NOX

"How am I going to die?"

I know that she's seen it.

Selestra has the same look in her eyes that she did the first time she saw my death. It is one of fear I don't think I'll ever get used to.

"Let me guess," I say. "You kill me with your dazzling personality?"

Selestra breaks away from me, and it's only then that I realize I was still holding on to her wrists.

Suddenly I feel colder.

"That's not funny," she says.

"You're right." I shove my hands into my pockets. "Your personality really isn't all that dazzling."

"You're going to die at the end of the week." Her words drip with resentment. "During the wish ceremony."

Just like that.

"How?" I ask.

"My mother."

Selestra flinches when she says it and I wish I knew why.

Just once I want to know all the things that go through Selestra Somniatis's mind and why, for a girl who's supposed to revel in death, she seems to hate it so much.

It destroys every notion of a witch I've ever had, twisting up all my plans and all the things I think my father would want until they don't make sense anymore.

Selestra pushes her hair violently out of her face.

The moonlight grazes her cheek.

Witch, I remind myself again, to steady my racing pulse.

Witch. Witch. Witch.

"You should never have asked for a prediction in the first place," Selestra says. "And I shouldn't have been able to see—"

She breaks off to glare at me.

"You've ruined everything."

"It's a bit late for that. Where does it happen?"

Selestra sighs. "You were running through the halls of the castle. The moon wasn't too high, so it must be before the wish ceremony begins."

I laugh a little.

I know I shouldn't look so pleased in front of the girl whose family I'm going to bring to its knees, but if the king and his witch are conspiring to murder me in this very castle, right before the halfway point of the month, then that doesn't just mean he knows what I'm really after.

It means he thinks I stand a chance at getting it.

And he's scared.

Selestra takes in my grin with wide eyes.

She doesn't understand that this is what I've been waiting for: a chance to make the great immortal Seryth of the Six Isles fear death.

"You really are like your father," she says.

My smile disappears at that.

Outside, the moonlight hides behind a small cloud and Selestra's room darkens with my scowl.

"What did you just say?"

I don't want my father's name anywhere near her bloodred lips.

Selestra lifts her chin up, indifferent to my anger. "It's what the king said in my vision," she says quickly, a hint of something else in her frown. "That you're just like your father. Him and some sword that made him a traitor."

"What sword?"

I step closer to her once more and Selestra backs away, shoving her hands behind her like she's afraid we might touch again.

"I don't know," she says. "Don't you all have swords?"

Yes, we all have swords.

But there's only one sword my father ever spoke of.

A sword of fairy tales, strong enough to kill an immortal. One forged by the witches of Thavma before the king and Selestra's great-great-grandmother wiped them out in the True War.

A last hope held tightly by the Southern Isle of Polemistés. The reason, according to my father, that the king has never stopped trying to conquer them.

"Was it a sword of magic?" I ask, desperate to know.

"A magic sword," Selestra repeats. "Are you a child?"

When she sees I'm serious, she frowns, a dimple appearing between her brows, just as deep as the ones that puncture her cheeks.

"There's no magic anywhere but in my blood," she tells me. "Isolda Somniatis saw to that."

What if she's wrong?

What if my father was right and the king fears the Southern Isle because they have the power to kill him? Why else would the king mention it in her vision?

If that's true, then maybe it means I don't have to wait for death to find me, holding out until the month is over. Micah said I needed another plan and this could be it.

My chance to change the game and kill the king before he has time to thwart me.

"Say there is a sword," Selestra says, eyeing me uncertainly. "What does it do?"

"It's a sword," I say. "It stabs things."

Thinking that, I grip my knife again and ready to bring it back to Selestra's throat. Though I'm not sure what I'll do after that.

"Are you going to tell your mother and the king that I got a second prediction from you?" I ask.

Selestra looks at my knife.

"Oh, please," she says, unafraid. "You're not going to kill me. You need me, remember?"

I drop the knife back to my side, resigned.

"Then where does this leave us?"

Selestra turns from me and walks over to her nightstand. She pulls a pair of gloves from the drawer, a little too late.

"You have to leave Vasiliádes."

"Is that an order, princess?"

"Yes."

Selestra bites her lip and when her eyes flick back over to mine, I can tell that she really doesn't want to say whatever she's about to next.

"And you're taking me with you."

I blink, trying to hide my surprise.

"When you leave to escape the king or find your magic sword, I'm coming too."

I lean back against the wall and fold my arms slowly over my chest.

"Is that so?" I ask, enjoying the look of desperation she's trying so hard to hide. "You've snuck out of the castle by yourself just fine before, princess. Why do you need me?"

"I've never left the island," she says. "You're going to take me away from Vasiliádes."

I kick my leg back up against the wall, reclining farther into the stance. The more at ease I look, the more worried she seems to become.

"What else did you see in that vision?" I ask.

"It doesn't matter."

"It does to me."

Selestra's jaw tightens. "I don't care what matters to you."

She looks down at her bracelet, the very piece of jewelry that led me to suspect her disguise in the After Dusk Inn.

I narrow my eyes, as if it'll help me figure out anything about her.

She's like a puzzle made from other people's pieces. I wonder if she even knows who she is outside of what she's expected to be.

"Let's just say that the king is going to find out that I helped you," she says. "In my vision, he threatened me. I can't live as a prisoner any more than I already am, so I want to leave."

It's the closest thing to the truth she's ever said, but close isn't the whole thing and I don't like how quiet her voice gets when she speaks about the king.

It's small in a way that makes me feel bad for her. And why should *I* feel bad for the poor princess, locked in her castle, given everything she could dream of, including the power to harness death?

Selestra can look at me with those troubled eyes all she wants, but there's no way for me to know which parts of her are real. From her stories to her sadness, it could all be part of a bigger plan to betray me.

"Why should I trust you?"

"Because you don't have a choice," she says. "People rarely escape death. If you want to get out of this alive, then you need a witch."

She's right.

It's why I came here in the first place.

If I want to be the first person in the Six Isles to survive the entire month of the Red Moon, then I need her predictions.

Besides, magic calls to magic. So if that sword does exist, then maybe Selestra is the way to find it. It could be the reason my father never did. The heir might be the key to ending this.

Find the magic, kill the king, and avenge my father's memory.

"Do we have a deal?" Selestra asks. "I give you my word that I'll help you live if you help me leave."

I hook the knife into my belt loop, knowing I don't have another choice.

Winning is all that matters now, and if I have to align with a few monsters along the way to victory, then so be it.

"We'll head to Polemistés," I say. "Legend says that's where the sword the king mentioned is. And it's the one place he can't follow."

"What is your family's obsession with this sword?" Selestra asks.

"It's the key to killing him," I tell her simply. "Just like my father wanted."

I wait to see how she'll react.

"Your father?" she asks, voice almost timid.

She frowns with that dimple again, then narrows her eyes. I can't tell whether any of it is intrigue or anger.

"Just meet me in the central maze, an hour before moonrise on the night of the banquet," I say. "Everyone should be too distracted to notice you leave."

"Not the maze," Selestra says, shaking her head. "You can't come anywhere near the castle or my mother. It's too risky."

"I didn't realize you were so concerned with my safety, princess."

"I'm concerned with my escort getting killed before he can get me off this island," she counters.

At this, I smirk. "Can you get out of the castle on your own?"

"I've been sneaking my way around this place since I was a child."

"Then I'll meet you at the base of the mountain," I agree. "But just so we're clear, if this turns out to be a trap, I'll kill you. And if you're even a minute late, I'm leaving."

It's half a bluff, since leaving without Selestra and her visions gives me no way to find the sword or survive any more brushes with death.

But the less she thinks I need her, the better.

"I'll be there," Selestra says. She holds out her newly gloved hand in a promise. "I swear it."

I take her hand, closing my fingers around her palm. Her magic sparks between us, like a match readying to be lit.

With the heir on my side, together we'll bring down a kingdom.

15

NOX

It's dark out and that's when Vasiliádes is at its best.

Away from the watchful castle that floats above like an all-seeing eye, when even the soldiers get a little merry and the smell of fish and salt from the Endless Sea reaches through the streets.

The night is when this island can relax, because it knows that nobody is watching.

"I thought your plan was to stay alive," Micah says as we walk down the narrow passageway.

"Don't be so green," I scold. "You're not afraid of the dark, are you?"

The moon is at its peak, but the lantern lights on the street are dim, the fires inside them barely aglow.

The buildings to either side of us act like walls, dank and crooked as they reach up into the night. The ground is damp, though I don't remember it raining, and most of the shop windows are too black to see inside.

Only a few have names scratched into the wooden doors, or painted onto small signs, but most have nothing to tell passersby what they are or what they sell.

If you know, you know.

If you don't, it's best to keep walking before anyone finds out.

We approach the door, where Leo is already waiting.

I don't even get the chance to knock. The moment I raise my

hand, the door swings open and Leo is standing there, looking at me like I'm late for an appointment we didn't make.

His deep red hair reminds me of the foxes that hide in the gardens of the soldiers' barracks and I'm almost positive he's wearing the same shirt and overalls that he was the last time we were here.

"Finally," Leo says. "In you get. Quick, quick. I've just given her a makeover. She looks more beautiful than before."

Leo is nothing if not always pleased with himself.

"In, in," Leo says, hurrying us into the far back of the shop.

When we first walk in, we're surrounded by darkness and it takes a moment for Leo to relight the oil trough that encircles the room.

The flame practically jumps from his match and spreads like a ring of fire, banishing every shadow in a matter of seconds.

Then I see it, in the center of the room.

Our way off this forsaken island and to Polemistés.

"No," Micah says, backing away. "No way in souls are we getting on that thing."

He stares at the contraption, shaking his head adamantly.

"I knew there was a reason why you wouldn't tell me what it was! *A surprise*, you said. Is the surprise that we're going to die?"

He turns to me in an accusation, but I only smile back.

"It's beautiful," I say, because it is.

"It's a death trap," Micah splutters. "There's a reason those things never passed inspections, Nox. They're kook inventions."

"My baby fails no tests," Leo argues. "She passes every time."

"And what's life without a little risk?" I ask.

"Living," Micah answers.

He puts a hand on my shoulder, like it might keep me grounded. With this invention, that's the last thing that's going to happen.

"You ask me to help you stay alive," Micah says. "You ask me to help you escape Vasiliádes. But now you're asking me to get on *that* thing? I have to draw the line somewhere."

"Draw the line up your backside," Leo shouts, waving his hand behind him. He crouches down beside his creation and picks up a paintbrush to resume his work. "Silly little soldiers afraid of heights."

Leo laughs to himself and Micah turns to me with raised eyebrows. There's disbelief on every inch of his face.

Micah always needs a little bit of a push to risk his life.

"It's the perfect plan," I say. "We can fly right over the whirlpools that guard Polemistés."

"I don't think this thing will get us across the street."

"She is sturdy!" Leo yells over to us. "My girl is like a bird."

"She looks more like a chicken," Micah says.

Leo dips his paintbrush back into the pot. "Chickens don't fly."

"Exactly!"

I ignore them and look up at the marvelous thing in front of me.

It doesn't have a proper name.

Back when they were first being tested—and then promptly regulated to the rubbish bins when none of them could sustain a proper journey—the king called them flightless birds.

"What's the name of this thing?" I ask Leo.

"She is *Anna-Maria*," he says. "After my wife. But she called it our little butterfly."

A butterfly.

It's perfect.

The balloon stretches tall enough to touch the very edges of the roof, in a large raindrop that's the same black blue as the Endless Sea, dotted by specks of silver stars that look like a reflection.

A perfect camouflage, as we hide among the clouds.

I touch a hand to the basket secured below.

It's made from woven trees, dark oak willow and reeds, stitched together like a blanket. It's big enough to fit at least half a dozen people, with room to rest and store supplies. There's even a small cabin hosting the outhouse in the very corner. Four large flames burn above the basket, like a ceiling, breathing an inferno of air into the balloon above.

This is the only way out of Vasiliádes that the king can't follow. A way to the Southern Isle that could bypass all their barricades and whirlpools.

I pull out the pouch of Chrim I nearly died protecting in the After Dusk Inn. "Can you have it ready by tomorrow?" I ask.

Leo stands and brushes the wood dust from his knees. "She's ready now," he says.

"Then you've got yourself a deal."

I hold out my hand for him to shake, and when he does, I grin.

Tomorrow night, we're going to leave Vasiliádes once and for all to find the sword my father spoke of. The key to destroying the king.

Me, Micah, and a princess of death and magic.

16

SELESTRA

I push open my bedroom window.

The sun is drifting into sleep, hazed the color of tulips and apricots. Soon, the moon will rise against the darkness and night will hang over my room like a shadow.

I won't be here for that.

My mother may have magically sealed the door to this room, but she didn't think about the windows.

The bag on my shoulder feels light and I wonder if I should quickly throw some more clothes inside, or an extra dagger just in case.

Asden would have recommended an extra dagger.

I only hope Nox has thought to bring food, because I haven't been able to sneak down into the kitchens and it's been nearly a whole day since any food was brought up.

My stomach rumbles just thinking of the wasted chocolate cake with almond frosting that Theola loves to have at banquets. Half of it will end up in the bins without Irenya and me there to sneak slices.

Thinking of Irenya, I almost don't want to leave.

I haven't seen her since I was confined to my tower and so I haven't had the chance to say goodbye or tell her about the deal Nox and I struck.

I can only hope she'll understand. If I could take her with me, then I would.

"This is it," I say to myself.

I shift the bag higher onto my shoulder and peer down at the courtyard below, to see if anyone might be watching.

It's more or less empty.

Everyone is too busy preparing for the banquet and swapping stories on what deaths they might have seen in the streets so far.

I slide my leg out of the window and hold on tightly to the frame, until my foot finds the small ledge below.

The wind picks up, whipping across my bare ankles and my face.

The ledge below is only ten or so feet and if I make that, then I just need to hop the roofs for a couple of floors until I can shimmy to the staircase window.

It's just ten feet.

I count inside my head to prepare.

One. I shift my foot to the side to make room.

Two. I hold my breath, readying to swing my leg over.

Thr—

"Be careful, dear. You might just fall and break your neck."

My mother's voice cuts through the night, like a shard of glass.

She watches from the door, head angled as she takes in what she sees: me halfway out of a window, with a bag slung over my shoulder and a look of horror on my face.

The king is there too, a whole two heads taller than my mother, his broad chest heaving with measured breaths. The action makes the snakes on his skin hiss at me in his place.

"Don't be in such a hurry, Selestra," he says. "We have a lot to discuss."

He moves aside and a guard steps forward, pushing a ragged girl into the room.

The king grabs her before she can fall to the floor, seizing her by the neck so that his nails draw blood across her throat. A throat already bruised.

Just like her face, which is covered in marks the color of an angry sunset.

I gasp. "Irenya."

She shivers under the king's grip.

"I know what happened at the tavern," the king says.

Just those words alone leave me breathless in horror.

"The people from that night came to your mother and me."

"They wanted help in surviving death," Theola says tightly. "To make a deal in exchange for information on you."

"What did you do?" I ask, but I already know the answer.

"I did what every good mother would."

She reaches over and runs a perfectly pointed fingernail down Irenya's cheek.

"I cleaned up your mess."

I close my eyes for a brief moment.

"People can't think they have power over me," the king says.

My throat is too dry to swallow.

I warned those people in the tavern not to say anything. I *told* them to keep quiet and now they're dead because of me.

I don't even know how many.

"You're hiding so many secrets, Selestra. I'd like to know them all."

The king squeezes Irenya's neck, and at her choked whimper, I grip tighter on to the window frame.

"I don't have any secrets," I lie.

The king looks pointedly to the bag slung over my shoulder.

"You can't leave Vasiliádes," he says. "There is no escape, Selestra."

I slide my leg back over the ledge and slip slowly inside the room, not taking my eyes off the king or his grip on Irenya.

He'd kill her just to prove a point.

"Please," I say, glancing briefly to my mother.

I try desperately to reach out to a part of her that isn't loyal only to the king. Somewhere under there must still exist the woman who used to tell me I was beautiful and special. Who spoke of our goddess and the afterlife she could give us.

The woman who flinched when she fed that soul to the king.

"Don't let him do this," I beg her.

Theola shakes her head, warning me not to bother.

I don't have a mother anymore. There's just the king's witch and nothing else.

"I thought talking to your friend would give us more information," the king says. "But even she doesn't know your secrets. You're very good at keeping them all to yourself."

He throws Irenya to the ground and she hits the floorboards with enough force to make her yelp.

I want desperately to run toward her and pull her to safety, but I don't dare move.

"You're going to tell us why you saved Nox Laederic and what the two of you are planning," the king says. Commands. "If you don't, you and your friend will die tonight."

I turn back to the window.

I think of Nox, waiting for me so we can make our escape.

If you're even a minute late, I'm leaving, he warned.

"Tell him, Selestra," my mother says. Her tone is almost pleading. "Tell him before it's too late."

It's already too late.

I thought death wouldn't be here for days, but just like at the tavern, it's come early. It's almost like I can't escape my fate. Any action I take to avoid it only makes it come faster.

I wonder if Nox is gone already, escaped to the Southern Isle without me. He'd be a fool to risk his life and wait.

Just like I was a fool for ever thinking I could get out of this castle alive.

17

SELESTRA

"You can't kill me," I say. "I'm the Somniatis heir."

Though it isn't true and we all know it.

I've *seen* it.

King Seryth drags his lips to a smile, the handsome edges of his face growing darker still.

He touches a hand to my mother's stomach, just as I foresaw.

"Heirs can be replaced." He speaks the words I already know. "Only I am forever."

To him, my family are nothing more than animals to breed.

Creatures to conquer worlds with.

All this time I've wanted to be the Somniatis witch and for what? I convinced myself it would mean freedom, when really I knew that I'd just be making myself a willing prisoner of a cruel man.

"You're not special, Selestra," my mother says. "I've always told you that."

Her voice falters a little. It's enough to remind me that it isn't her fault the curse of our family has left her hollow. It has done the same thing to every witch who came before, and if I ever lived to truly serve the king, it would do the same to me too.

"I hope the new heir burns your kingdom to the ground," I spit.

The king just smiles. "Only if I tell her to."

He is a shadow, looming over me. So tall that if I look straight ahead, I can only see his jugular. His battle-scarred neck.

I press my lips together.

The king looks to Theola and she nods. She's known for a while this is how things would end.

My fingertips spark with fear as she approaches.

My eyes meet hers. Snake to snake, witch to witch.

I feel the energy of my magic inside me, just like in the After Dusk Inn when I nearly siphoned the life out of that man.

"I told you to be careful," Theola says. "You should have listened to me."

I nod. "I know, Mother."

Then I punch her in the mouth.

As hard as I can, just like Asden taught me. For his death and for Irenya's injuries and for every person whose soul they've stolen and especially for *me*.

For my mother too.

For the person she used to be, who is as dead as those people in the tavern are now.

She falls backward, her head thumping against the floor, and whether it's from the force of my punch or the mere shock, I don't care. I don't waste time.

I grab Irenya and drag her toward the window.

The king's laughter bellows through the room, almost impressed.

"Drop down to the roof ledge!" I yell, practically shoving Irenya out of the window. "Go, now!"

Irenya doesn't argue, shaking as she twists her bruised body around and lowers herself down.

When she drops, she closes her eyes, and I breathe a sigh of relief when she lands safely.

Before I can follow, I'm being pulled back. My mother's fingers tangle into my hair, ripping and clawing. She tears me from the window and throws me to the floor, between her and the king.

"Enough!" she screams. "Do you have any idea what you're doing?"

Her voice is shaken and acrid.

"I told you that you can't escape this, Selestra." The king wags his finger from side to side.

I squeeze my hands into fists, refusing to let him see my fear.

The king's smile crawls across his face at the small defiance. "Everyone has to die sometime," he says. "Unless you're me, of course."

Then he lets out a cry.

I hear it before my mother does.

I see the blade before she has time to gasp.

The sword goes straight through his back. Through his old, wretched heart and out of his chest.

King Seryth looks down at the black blade, stutters a breath, and then collapses to the floor.

"You have no idea how long I've been waiting to do that," Nox says.

"Traitor!" Theola screams.

"You're quick to catch on."

He throws a blade toward her.

From his hand it flows straight into Theola's neck.

Suddenly she isn't screaming anymore.

She collapses to her knees, clutching at her wound as the blood weeps like tears from her throat.

My eyes go wide at the sight of it.

"Come on," another soldier says, appearing from the hall. Nox's friend. *Micah*. "We have to go before they get back up! Immortals don't stay down for long."

Quickly, I leap over my mother's blood that pools across the floor and toward the window. A part of me wants to run to her side, but it would be a useless gesture. I can already feel her power sparking into the air, healing her injuries. It swarms around her.

"This way!" Nox holds out an urgent hand for me, gesturing to the door of my room.

I blink. His knuckles are bloody and his breath is punctured.

He fought his way into this castle, through dozens of guards.

For me.

Why did he come here?

He could have died returning to this place.

I told him he would.

But I don't have the time to ask.

"Not that way," I say, already flinging my leg over the window ledge. "The door is magically sealed. You can get in, but you can't get back out. Unless you're my mother."

At the edge of the room, the king stirs, his eyes starting to flicker back open, and Theola, choking on her blood, lets out a gasp.

She reaches a shaking hand toward us, eyes glowing in the night. From the floor, her blood begins to seep back into her.

Nox makes for the window, Micah following.

"You'll die for this," the king utters throatily. "Just like your father."

We turn to him.

His hands shake as he grips the blade, ready to tear it from his heart and puncture it through ours.

His wounds will disappear soon, immortality pulling him back together the way it has done for a century. He looks straight at Nox.

"I know what you're after and you'll never find it."

Nox tenses, fists squeezed by his sides.

"Let's go" is all he says to me.

My mother crawls toward us, the hole in her neck fading fast. She opens her mouth to speak, but all that comes is a gurgle of breath and blood.

I take one last look at her and then I jump.

18

NOX

We jump from roof ledge to roof ledge, like we're hopping across stones in a shallow lake.

"Through that window!" Selestra says, pointing to the patterned glass on our right. "It'll lead to the servants' staircase."

"Back into the castle?" Micah asks. "I thought we wanted to escape."

But it's a good idea.

We're sixty feet in the air and running out of rooftop. We can't exactly scale down the castle walls without rope.

Selestra grabs Irenya with a gloved hand, pulling her injured friend toward the window.

Irenya limps and I see the way she grits her teeth, swallowing down the pain like I've done so many times after a rough training session at the soldiers' barracks.

Whatever Seryth and his witch did to her, she's lucky to be alive.

Selestra pushes the window open with enough force that it almost shatters against the wall on the other side.

We clamber through, one at a time. I wonder if the king's immortality has already begun to stitch his skin back together like a fine quilt.

The staircase is dark, barely any light afforded to the black steps. It isn't a route the wealthy take to navigate the castle, but one for people who need to be invisible.

The spiraled steps seem almost never-ending.

"You couldn't have a bedroom on the ground floor?" I ask.

Selestra's eyes shoot to mine, bright and angry.

"Why did you come back here?" she snaps. "I said you'd die."

"You said I'd die days from now," I say pointedly. "Besides, you were late. I only came to see if you needed a hand with your bags."

Selestra rolls her eyes and brushes past me, her shoulder gliding against mine as she runs down the steps.

"I believe you said you'd leave if I was even *a minute late*," she reminds me, calling over her shoulder.

I shrug, following her down the steps. "Lucky for you, I'm not a man of my word."

I know it was risky for me to come, but I can't find a mythical sword on an island of deadly warriors without the use of her visions. Especially if Seryth and his witch are onto me. It made sense to go back for her.

Besides, I owed her a life debt for the tavern.

Now it's repaid, I can breathe easy knowing that I don't owe her a thing. This partnership is strictly business.

I follow Selestra farther down the winding staircase, Micah and Irenya in tow.

The walls are high, barely broken by the light from an occasional window. When we finally reach the end of the staircase, the door is dark and narrow. It's at the edge of the shadows, jutting from the chasm of the stairwell, barely as tall as I am.

"Where does it lead?"

"Out into the gardens," Selestra says.

"The guards will be waiting for us there," Micah says. "As soon as we open that door, they'll have their swords at our throats."

"Maybe." I take out my own blade. "But our swords will be at their throats too."

The familiar weight of the weapon in my hands is a small comfort. I'm glad I didn't use it to stab Seryth.

Not yet.

I'm glad I stole the sword from one of the guards instead. This is my father's blade and it'll meet the king again, when he doesn't have his immortality to protect him.

I kick open the splintered door and charge out, Micah beside me with his own weapon raised.

The gardens are empty.

Deathly quiet, save for the roaring of the waterfalls.

"Maybe the king hasn't had time to alert them yet," Irenya suggests. "You injured him quite badly. It could be he's still healing."

I doubt it.

With all their power, the king and his witch would have recovered quicker than this.

"I don't care about the reason," Selestra says. "Just get me off this mountain."

I raise my hand in a salute. "As you wish, princess."

We head to the maze formation. The hedges are high enough to hide buildings, entwined with purple flowers that reach out like hands toward the sky, beckoning us inward.

"If we follow the outer maze, it'll take us to the platform," I say. "From there, we can blend in with those coming for the banquet."

Selestra nods, pulling her hood up and dipping her head low to hide her eyes. She'll be recognized in an instant otherwise.

We walk slowly, careful not to draw attention to ourselves, as though we're meandering through the gardens, admiring the sapphire waterfalls and the way the strong mountain winds blow flower petals across our feet and into the air like butterflies.

"Keep your head down," I whisper as we approach the platform.

I count the guards.

Twenty. Far more than usual.

"Let me do the talking."

"It's what you're best at," Selestra mumbles under her breath as the four of us approach the platform.

"Names?" the guard asks.

"Kell Rain," I lie, giving the name of a soldier in my regiment. Hopefully he won't pay the price for that. "Corporal in the Last Army."

"Sebastien Hart," Micah announces, following my lead.

"And you?" The guard gestures to Selestra.

"She's my date for the evening," I say, pushing Selestra behind me. "Lady Sophia."

Selestra snorts in disbelief.

"And that's her handmaid." I gesture to Irenya. "Lady Sophia is feeling unwell, so we'll have to miss the banquet."

"Fine," the guard says, with a roll of his eyes. "We just need her to remove her hood so we can check her over."

"My hood?" Selestra keeps her head dipped low. "I'd really rather not. It's about to rain."

The guard sighs, tired of us already.

I'd be tired too if I spent all day dealing with the wealthy elite of Vasiliádes.

"We're checking everyone," he says plainly. "New measures from the king. No hoods or cloaks." He looks to Selestra with a glare. "And no exceptions."

Which means there's no way for her to leave this mountain without being noticed. One look at her eyes and her hair and they'll scream for help.

The king has prepared for the chance of her escape.

Somehow, he knew something was wrong and made sure that even if Selestra left the castle, she wouldn't be able to leave the mountain.

That's why there's no alert.

Why would the king panic people and put a damper on his celebrations with news of a missing heir, when there was no chance of her escaping?

I lean over to whisper into Selestra's ear. "How good are you in a fight?"

She blinks. "What?"

"You take the ten on the left and I take the ten on the right?"

"Are you serious?" she hisses. "No."

The guard narrows his eyes. "What are you two whispering about?"

"Just a lover's tiff," I say. I look to Micah. "Plan B."

He nods.

I elbow the guard in the face.

Micah follows suit, punching the man beside him.

I swing my knee into another guard's stomach and then throw him to the floor, pushing my way through the new gap in the line of guards.

Quickly, Micah and I shove Selestra and Irenya onto the platform, then turn to hold out our swords, keeping the other guards at bay.

They glare at us, their own weapons drawn.

"You're going to pay for that," one says. "You can't take us on just the two of you."

"He's got a point," Micah tells me. "We're looking a little outnumbered here, Nox. Need a plan C?"

"We've already got one," I say.

I look over to Selestra.

"Take off your hood."

"What?" she asks.

The panic is clear on her face, far more than it was a moment ago when we attacked.

"Why?"

"So they know who they're dealing with."

Selestra sighs and throws it off.

Her leafy hair tumbles down her shoulders.

The guards' eyes widen at the sight of it and her serpent eyes glaring across to them. A real witch, ready to kill them and drain their blood along with their souls.

They back away, swords still out but not daring to attack.

"That's right," I say, all bluster. "She's the heir and if you come any closer, she'll turn you to dust."

I can practically hear Selestra roll her eyes as we step backward to join them on the platform. I keep my focus on the guards as I fumble around with the chains, trying to find some sort of an *on* button.

"How do we get this thing to go?"

"You really are ridiculous," Selestra scolds.

She pushes me aside and leans over to reach behind the stone wall.

The shadows move and Selestra's hand curls around something.

A head.

There's some kind of creature peeking out from behind there. It's a bird I've never noticed before but that's more beautiful than anything I've ever seen.

"Ready for one more adventure, old friend?" Selestra asks.

From the shadows, the bird nods.

Then it jumps.

I nearly fall as the platform descends, quicker than it ever has.

"You're friends with a magic bird?" I ask as the sky flicks by.

"It's one more friend than you have," Selestra says.

I pretend to laugh.

The platform is heading to the ground at record speed.

We shoot past the central waterfall, its waters gleaming blue, clear as the sky on a summer's day.

Micah peers over the edge and whistles.

We can see the ground below.

Just a little bit farther and we'll be free.

The platform jolts.

I barely keep my footing as it comes to a sudden stop, just feet from the ground.

It starts to move back up.

Selestra looks up to the echoes of the Floating Mountain. "It's my mother," she says in horror. "She must be calling the Lamperós back to her."

"Can you stop it?" I ask.

Selestra shakes her head. "The bird is compelled by our family's power. It can't fight her magic and neither can I."

I curse under my breath as the platform gains traction, ferrying us back up the mountain and toward the king.

"Let down your hair." I gesture to Selestra's braid. "We can use it as rope."

She's unamused.

"Did we have a plan D?" Micah asks with a groan.

I peer over the edge, to the pool of water below. "We have to jump."

Selestra gapes at me. "It must be forty feet! What if we die?"

I shrug. "We die if we don't."

"That's comforting," Micah says. "I'm so glad I decided to come with you."

Thunder rumbles above us as the sky itself loses patience with our uncertainty.

"Nox is right," Irenya says. "We don't have a choice."

She squeezes Selestra's arm, but when the heir looks down at her hand, pressed against the long sleeves of her tunic that don't end until they meet her gloves, she barely offers Irenya a weak smile in return.

Selestra can't be touched.

She can't be properly comforted.

"Trust me," I say to her. "We'll make it to the pool below."

We're not supposed to die jumping off a mountain, after all. Selestra would have seen it when she predicted my death in her bedroom.

Unless jumping off the mountain is your next death, a voice in my mind taunts.

I ignore it.

Selestra clenches her gloved hands and turns to me. Her bright eyes twinkle with fear.

"I really hate you," she says.

I grab her hand. "Fair enough."

Then together, we jump.

19

NOX

For a few seconds, I'm weightless.

Then the wind hits my stomach like a fist, like the commanders who pushed me to the floor and pounded me until I puked during training.

It feels like being punched.

I hear the rushing water behind me as my body spins. Then see the rocks, the clouds, the sky.

Selestra, with the wind blowing her hair wildly into her face.

And the ground.

The small lake we careen toward.

I kick my legs out, pushing my body into an arrow.

Then we stop.

About ten feet from the lake where the central waterfall ends, the wind stills. It's sudden enough for my stomach to jolt up into my chest.

We're floating, midair.

"Are we dead yet?" Selestra asks, her eyes squeezed closed like she can't bear to look.

"I wish," Micah says. "I think I'm going to puke."

His dark cheeks look tinged gray and I'd bet anything I look the same. I swallow down the bile rising inside me.

I'm not sure how she's doing it, but Selestra is keeping us in the air, using her magic to stop us from crashing into the water.

"Open your eyes," I tell her. I'm surprised to find my voice isn't hoarse with the wind. "Focus and let us down slowly."

"Right," Selestra says. "Slow."

She opens one eye reluctantly, then the other, and squints in concentration—

Without any warning, we plummet into the lake below.

I hit the water hard and sink to the bottom like a star shooting for the ground. A thousand needles prick my skin as the cold takes over. The pricking turns to agony as my arm slices against my father's sword.

I open my mouth to yell out, but swallow a mouthful of lake water instead. It tastes like mud and salt.

I give myself a second to feel the pain, letting my blood mix with the water. Then I kick off from the ground and propel myself up toward the surface.

I break through with a gasping breath and spit out a mouthful of lake water.

Micah, Selestra, and Irenya are treading water beside me, alive and unharmed. Though Micah still looks a little bit like he wants to be sick.

I cough to clear my throat of the lake.

"That was a stupid plan," Selestra says.

"It worked, didn't it? Luckily I'm a good swimmer."

"Not from where I'm standing."

A line of blood drips from her nose, but I can't see how she would have injured herself.

Selestra wipes it away quickly and swims toward the muddy bank.

Micah grins over at me. "You're really charming her, aren't you?"

"Shut up," I say, and swim for the edge.

My clothes feel endlessly heavy in the water. They slow me down, as does my father's sword, wet with my blood.

There are only a handful of guards at the bottom and they don't seem to know what to do as we emerge from the water. They gawk at the heir, Selestra's damp green hair falling to her waist as she struggles to wring out her cloak.

Word of her escape—or *kidnap*—must not have reached them yet.

The king didn't think we'd make it off the castle to need to warn them. So now they just look at her, wondering what to do and if they should get to their knees and bow, or run instead.

The crowd parts to let us through and I notice Selestra stiffen as they watch her with fear and surprise. Some of them have never seen a witch before and the others have definitely never seen one fall from the sky.

They're terrified of her and she doesn't seem to be enjoying it.

"Follow me," I say. "We don't have much time."

I grab Selestra's hand without thinking and we take off in a run, Micah and Irenya following behind.

The wind feels pleasant as it brushes against my damp skin, pulling the water from my clothes.

Selestra's fingers tighten around mine, the warmth of her pressing through the gloves. She feels like fire in my hands.

"Slow down!" she yells as we wind through the alleys.

She's panting, and when I look back, she almost winces as she runs.

She's hurt somehow, somewhere.

I clutch her hand tighter, keeping the wet fabric of her gloves, the only barrier between us, from slipping away.

"Speed up!" I call back.

We don't have time to stop and tend to any wounds.

I almost swear I hear her mutter a curse under her breath as we turn onto a new, narrow street.

I spot Leo's door instantly, the orange wood like a beacon.

"Leo!" I yell, pounding my fist against it. "Open up!"

"You don't have a key?" Selestra asks, gathering her breath.

"Welcome to the world of Nox and his foolproof plans," Micah says.

I knock again, hard enough that it feels like the door might splinter.

"Who is this man?" Irenya asks.

She looks at Leo's shop front like she doubts anything of any use could be hidden inside.

"Oh, just you wait," Micah says. "You're going to wish we'd stayed on the mountain when you see what Nox has planned."

I ignore him and continue knocking on the door with enough force that my fists start to ache. I almost consider kicking it down, but once the thought crosses my mind, the door swings open.

"You break my door, I break your nose," Leo says, as if he knew just what I was thinking.

"Nice to see you too." I brush past him. "Having a good day?"

We hurry inside before the guards catch up to us.

They don't know about Leo, but if they trace us to this alley, it won't be long before they find out.

"Yes, yes, welcome," Leo says as Selestra, Micah, and Irenya follow me in. "Come right through, no invitation. Wait . . . is that a *witch*?"

I ignore him. "Is everything good to go?"

Leo struggles to tear his eyes away from Selestra. "I told you, she's always ready," he says. He pulls a set of keys from his pocket. "Fires are lit. Don't look so serious."

"What fires?" Selestra asks.

Leo opens the door to the back.

The room is already illuminated, our ride out of Vasiliádes in full view. Leo's butterfly is more beautiful than the last time I saw her.

"Is that a *balloon*?" Selestra asks.

She looks a little too outraged for someone getting a free ride off this island.

"It is a butterfly," Leo says.

I nod over to him. "A *butterfly*," I repeat. "Not a balloon."

"You're unbelievable."

"You say that a lot. I might just start taking it as a compliment."

I can sense her resolve only growing stronger.

"We're going to die in that."

"No dying in my *Anna-Maria*," Leo scolds her. "You'll get blood on her and she is freshly clean."

He leans over to take hold of a nearby handle secured to the floor and starts to wind it slowly to the right. There's a small click and then the sound of thunder follows as the roof above us begins to part.

I start throwing in the bags of supplies I brought to Leo's earlier that day. Weapons, a few bags of clothes, and army rations as well as some fresh bread and fruit.

It's enough to get us across the Endless Sea and to the island of Armonía, where we can restock and refuel.

I jump into the basket, and the flame beneath the balloon sizzles like an inferno, as if it senses my presence and the notion of its first real journey into the skies.

"Are you ready to fly?" Leo asks. "Ready to see stars up close?"

I hold out a hand for Selestra. "Get in," I say. "It's a long way to Armonía."

She folds her arms across her chest, staring at my hand like it's some kind of a weapon. "You mean this thing won't take us all the way to your magic sword?"

"I doubt it'll even take us across the street," Micah says as I pass him a few blankets to load inside.

Selestra's face falls.

Thanks, Micah.

He helps Irenya inside, ignoring my glare.

I hold out my hand to Selestra again.

"We need to stop at Armonía to refuel," I tell her. "But you can always stay here. Go back to the castle and your tower, if you like."

Selestra swallows and looks back to Leo.

He gives her an encouraging thumbs-up.

She lets out a sigh, turns back to me, and says, "We were safer jumping off the mountain."

She brushes my hand out of the way and hoists herself up into the balloon, like she doesn't want to owe me anything. Even something as simple as a helping hand.

"Hold on to something," Leo calls up to us.

He reaches over for a large blade and begins to cut the rope that tethers us to the ground.

"I'm holding on to my common sense," Selestra says to Irenya.

Her friend snorts a laugh.

"I tried that once," Micah says. "Doesn't really work when you spend time with Nox."

I tune them out and watch as Leo cuts the last thread of string. The balloon jolts as it's finally set free. I grab the edge of the basket for support as the balloon rises, but Selestra forgets to do the same.

She gasps a little as the balloon sweeps upward and then stumbles straight into me.

I clasp my hands around her arms to steady her, glad that she's wearing long sleeves. The last thing I need tonight is another death prediction.

Selestra blinks up at me, her yellow eyes like their own sun in the night.

They're strange, but I've always found strange things to be the most intriguing. And Selestra Somniatis is nothing if not that.

I hold on tightly to her, feeling her shiver. Her clothes are still damp with lake water.

"You know," I say, clearing my throat. "When Leo told you to hold on to something, he didn't mean me."

Selestra's eyes widen and she pushes me quickly away.

"Next time, let me fall," she says, grabbing on to one of the dangling ropes that secure the basket to the balloon.

I laugh and look down to the ground as we float up higher, the balloon ascending like a real butterfly into the sky. The wind is strong and icy against the back of my neck.

"Fly safe!" Leo yells, his voice like a fading whisper in the wind. "No dying!"

I smirk and keep looking until Leo becomes a dot, then a smudge on the ground, and then until I can't see him at all.

The clouds swallow him and the rest of the island whole as we float higher and higher. Me and my stolen princess, drifting away from Vasiliádes and into the night.

20
SELESTRA

The wind is soft against my cheeks, cold but gentle. As I tend to Irenya's wounds in the narrow basket of the balloon, night drifting over us, the world seems still.

Quiet.

The only sounds are the voices of Nox and Micah as they debate what to do when we land. They pause every now and again so that Micah can throw up.

"For the love of souls," Nox says, wincing as his friend retches over the side. "I hope that doesn't land on anyone."

Micah groans and presses a hand to his stomach. "I think I'm going to pass out."

"You're so delicate," Nox says. "How would you have made it through initiations without me?"

"I always have a better chance of surviving when I'm *not* with you," Micah shoots back.

Nox's cheeks line with laughter.

It's strange seeing him with a friend and looking so relaxed. It's different from the uppity soldier at the Festival, pandering to the king and holding on to his sword like it's some kind of trophy.

It's also different from the boy who barged into my room in the dead of night and demanded a vision to save his life.

Nox adapts and changes himself to whoever he needs to be in the moment. I can relate to that. I've spent a lifetime making myself small so others can feel big. I've molded myself into what they want me to be so well that I'm not sure who I am outside the walls of my tower.

"Ouch!"

Under my touch, Irenya sucks in a sharp breath, and I tear my eyes from Nox to look down at her ankle.

"Oh," I say, cringing. "Sorry. I've never healed anyone else before."

"I can see why," Irenya teases. "You're not very good at it."

I poke out my tongue and I would jab her in the ribs if I didn't know they were broken.

Every part of her looks broken and I've spent the last hour trying to put back together the pieces that I can. I feel weak and my eyes threaten to flutter closed, but I can't stop. Not with Irenya still in pain and not when I know it's all my fault.

I press my hand softly back to her ankle, then move the other to the tender skin over her ribs and close my eyes, so as not to be distracted again.

I feel the magic of my ancestors sweeping through me, trying to find the wounds that need healing. I gather that power up and let it seep out of my fingers and into Irenya.

Hoping, praying to Asclepina, that it obeys.

Our goddess was said to use her magic to heal villages, but I've only ever used it for myself. My mother and the king never considered training me on how to help others.

Why would they?

The sooner someone dies, the sooner we get their soul.

"Rest," I tell Irenya, once I feel my magic recoil.

Depleted almost entirely.

Her skin is no longer bruised purple and she doesn't flinch as much when she moves, so it must mean I've done something right. Put the bones back together.

I wipe the blood away from my nose, before it drips down onto the blanket that I've pulled across her.

"It'll be better tomorrow," I promise, smoothing my friend's hair across the pillow with a gloved hand. "Just rest."

Irenya nods, and when she closes her eyes, her breath shakes with the weight of her tiredness.

I stand and step to the edge of the basket that keeps us floating across the sky.

"How is she?" Nox asks.

He's at my side, gesturing to where Irenya lies on the wicker floor.

"She'll be fine," I tell him. "How's he?"

I look to the other side of the balloon, where Micah is still retching.

"Dramatic," Nox says.

He watches me press my hand to my nose again. The blood is heavier than ever before, soaking through my gloves.

Healing Irenya has drained me in a way that healing myself never has. It's as though I've siphoned all the energy from inside myself and poured it into her.

"You're hurt," Nox says.

"I'm fine," I lie. The tiredness seeps even into my voice and I know he can hear it.

"You were bleeding back in Vasiliádes too," Nox says. "After we jumped off the mountain."

There's a note of concern in his voice that throws me off guard, even though I know that it's only because he needs me to keep him alive until he finds his precious make-believe sword.

"One nosebleed doesn't compare to what's ahead," I say.

Or to the injuries I used to get during training with Asden.

Just thinking his name makes my heart ache.

I look over to Nox, their faces such a perfect echo of each other.

"The king will be coming for us," I say, lowering my voice to a whisper so we don't wake Irenya with all this talking.

Nox leans against the basket, looking out at the tiny world below with a sigh. All we can see for miles is ocean and darkness.

If not for the balloon's navigational system directing us to Armonía, telling us which way to steer the small wheel so the propeller can fight against the winds, we'd be lost to the night.

"He knows I want the sword," Nox says. "Do you think he'll use your mother's visions to follow us to Armonía?"

He throws a pouch into the balloon's furnace. The flames turn blue and the balloon rises, picking up speed with the higher winds.

Irenya stirs but doesn't wake.

"My mother can't see our future if we're not there to touch," I say.

"What about the king's future?"

I shake my head, gripping tighter on to the rough branches of the basket. "The king doesn't have a future."

Nox looks puzzled, which is to be expected. The king has spent lifetimes making sure the only thing people know about him is that he's all-powerful.

"King Seryth eats souls, which means he's full of other people's destinies," I explain. "Every soul he's taken is muddled inside of him. He's a patchwork person, with no future of his own."

It's a weakness and a strength.

The king can never know what's in store for him, but nobody else can either. It means they can never use it against him to their advantage.

He's a shadow in this world, ever present, and with my mother by his side there will never be enough light to cast him out.

"The king doesn't just kill people," Nox says, taking in my words. "He destroys them too. Takes everything they are and keeps it for himself."

His voice is cold and distant, much like the wind, which fights against the roaring fire.

He's thinking of someone, I can see it in his eyes.

Of Asden. The General. *His father.*

I swallow, the cold bite of the wind seeping down my throat. I wish I didn't remember that day so clearly.

My whole life I've been raised to be the king's witch, just like my mother and her mother before her. Isolda Somniatis made it our destiny to serve him. To keep him in power, whatever the cost.

Even if that cost was people like Asden Laederic, a man who taught me how to protect myself. Whose love for his son wasn't weaved in a web of deceit and intricate betrayals. It was simple and true. The kind of thing I've always wished for: someone to care without motive and without agenda.

Asden loved Nox more than he loved himself. That was clear in his voice when he pleaded for his son to be kept safe.

Would knowing that bring Nox comfort or make his pain worse?

Would knowing that I also cared for his father make a difference?

"You're bleeding too," I say.

I gesture to Nox's arm, where his wound has soaked through. The tear in his shirt gives me a glimpse at just how deep it truly is.

Nox grabs a washcloth from one of the bags of supplies.

"I cut myself when we jumped from the mountain," he says, like he's only just remembering.

"I can heal it if you want," I offer. "It'll scar otherwise."

"No." Nox presses the cloth to his arm. "Scars aren't a bad thing. They show that you've lived, and who wants to die without living?"

"People who can't afford to keep buying new shirts?"

Nox laughs and those lines press into his cheeks again. He puts a hand to his mouth to muffle it, careful not to wake Irenya. Then he clears his throat, as if to clear the laughter away, but I still see hints of it on his lips. Tugging his mouth to the side.

Nox looks young when he laughs, unburdened.

"How did you stop us from falling, earlier?" he asks, breaking the quiet between us. "Before you dropped me onto my own sword, that is."

The question makes me nervous because I don't have a real answer. There's a lot about my magic and my family that I don't know and I've never been allowed to explore.

You'll find out soon enough what it means to be the witch, my mother always said. *The king will make sure of that.*

"I've only ever had visions or healed before now," I tell Nox. "The true power of the Somniatis witch doesn't come into force until . . ."

I trail off.

Until the previous witch dies.

Until my mother dies.

I think about her bleeding on the floor, reaching out a hand to me. For comfort? To kill me? I can't be sure which.

"So this is all new to you?" Nox asks. "Floating in midair and whatever you did in the tavern?"

Souls, I wish he hadn't brought that up.

I've got enough guilt on my shoulders to last a lifetime without remembering that.

"You mean when I saved your life?" I ask. "You're welcome, by the way."

"I think we're even now."

"You're keeping score?"

Nox raises an eyebrow. "You're not?"

I press my lips together, because he's right. I am. How many tallies will we have to put on the board in our bid to outmaneuver the king?

"This magic sword," I say to Nox. "You can't really be thinking of going after it, can you? Now we've left Vasiliádes, surely the most important thing is to focus on surviving until the Red Moon."

"That sword is how I survive," Nox says. "It's how everyone does."

"It's a fool's mission," I argue. "Polemistés is too dangerous."

I can feel the bite of the king's serpent on my palm. If I have any chance of living through this, then I have to convince Nox to give up on this hunt.

"I don't mind a bit of danger," Nox says in a shrug. "So long as it gets me my revenge."

"That's not what's important right now."

"It's the only thing that's *ever* been important to me," he corrects.

He finishes wiping the blood from his arm and tosses the rag into a nearby bucket. The light from the torches of the balloon flickers across his face like tiny bursts of lightning.

"The king needs to die, and my father thought the sword in Polemistés was the way to do it," Nox says. His voice is sharp-edged, like the point of his blade. "I owe it to him to try."

I would scoff and tell him to stop believing in fairy tales, if not for the mention of Asden. Nox may think he owes his father something, but in truth it's me who is in his debt.

"You don't need magic to kill the king," I say instead. "He's nothing without his witch."

"You want me to kill your mother?" Nox asks, unconvinced.

I bite my lip.

I want him to kill the thing she's become and save the person she was. Kill the monster and bring back my mother. Deep down there must be sparks of the person she used to be inside.

"You nearly killed her back at the castle," I say.

"Nearly isn't the same thing." Nox's sigh is loud enough to make the fire blink. "I know the stories about witches."

"Stories?"

"A witch can only be killed by beheading, drowning, or fire." He recites the lines as if it's a play.

"That would kill anyone," I say.

"But anyone else would also die from being stabbed, especially in the neck," Nox says. "Not your mother. Not you."

"You're wrong." The flames crackle behind me like a warning. "I'm not the witch yet."

I've spent years being reminded of that.

Nox pauses then, studying me. His eyes narrow, just a little, as if he's deciding something. Calculating.

"So you'd be easy to kill, then," he says.

"Not as easy as you."

Nox's eyes relax, but I can still see the intention behind them. The plan formulating, for what he'll do if I betray him.

Nox doesn't trust me, and regardless of how much I cared for his father, I don't trust him either.

I wish there was a way I could escape from this bargain.

I wish I knew more about our goddess and our powers, so I could use them to unbind our fates.

And most of all, I wish death hadn't tied me to the most reckless soldier in all of the Six Isles.

I seem to be the only one out of the two of us concerned with not dying. Rather than focus on shutting ourselves away to survive this month, Nox wants to infiltrate an army of deadly warriors on an even deadlier island to try to kill an immortal king. It's madness.

He's not trying to escape death, he's seeking it out.

And the moment he finds it, we're both damned.

21

NOX

It's barely past sunrise when the balloon jolts with the force of Micah scampering to the edge like an excited child.

I swear he nearly flings himself overboard.

Around us the sky is painted in yellow and pink, the sun almost close enough to touch as it rises from the ocean. I've traveled a lot in the Last Army, but I've never seen the world this way. It looks milky, the waters behind us streaked in a mirror of clouds.

My father wanted to make this journey, taking Leo's butterfly to the Southern Isle himself. Being up here makes me feel closer to him, crisp air biting my cheeks and howling promises of his vengeance.

"I can see it!" Micah yells. "Land!"

The color returns to his face at the sight of the mass of buildings and thick grassland below. Three days on Leo's butterfly is clearly too much for Micah to handle.

"We're there?" Selestra asks. "Truly?"

She leans over the side and follows Micah's gaze, marveling at the market stalls and tiny dots of people.

The wind seems to pick up speed with her smile.

I stare at the island below us, watching the light catch across the treetops, shimmering against the leaves so it looks like they're alight in yellow.

"Armonía," I say in a breath.

Once the land of harmony and now the land of the forgotten.

It was the second in the Six Isles to fall to the king in the True War, after Thavma, and now it sits quietly on the edge of our circle of islands, like the tip of a teardrop.

It's a place where nature once sang and people worked together to build homes and plant forests. Where for every day of rain there was a day of sun and nothing was without balance.

Each of the Six Isles used to have something like that in the old days. A trait, a story.

Vasiliádes was home to kings of thought and philosophy, who built a floating mountain to try to reach the gods. Nekrós, the land of bones, with a city built from the dead, so they could forever remain a part of the land and help it grow. Flóga was a place of fire and light, where the next rulers were chosen by the one child not burned in the phoenix's breath. Thavma, the land of witches and magic, where Selestra's ancestors must have once been born.

And Polemistés, the land of warriors. Where strength still rules above all else. The land that birthed Seryth, who left it to search for enough magic to conquer the world. It's the land that stayed while the others crumbled, that kept its traditions and magics while the rest were stripped of theirs.

The land that holds the key to my father's dying wish.

"How do we get down?" Selestra asks.

I pick up the bag of ice dust that Leo left us, examining it carefully. It's a small brown thing the color of burnt straw, and when I open it, a whiff of lavender soaks the air.

"Leo said to throw this into the fire. As the flames cool, the propeller should slow and we can begin to land."

I throw the contents of the bag over the flames. The tiny shards of ice are a bright silver white as they fall, like snowflakes. This bag holds winter.

The flames splutter beneath it and I grip the wheel, trying to keep it steady as the balloon descends.

We get lower and lower, the propeller slowing enough so the wind moves us away from the town and into a large field of wild-flowers and long grass.

The flames flicker and subside as the ground approaches, turning from blue to warm orange, then to a breath of yellow that struggles against the wind.

The descent gets faster and I realize too late that there isn't much to cushion our fall.

Leo taught me how to prepare to land, but not how to actually *land*.

"Hold on!" I yell.

The balloon knocks into the ground and skids across the grass, skipping over the soil and then crashing back down, like it's hopping.

I brace myself as it trips over the dirt, but it's no use. We're all thrown to the floor, sliding around the basket like we're pieces of loose fruit until finally we're flung from the balloon entirely.

I hit the dirt hard and roll across the muddy ground. The earth thumps against my injured shoulder and I feel the sting of mud press into the open wound.

Every piece of me feels bruised, but by some miracle nothing feels broken.

I lift myself from the ground and look across the empty field we landed in.

"I'm starting to get really tired of falling out of the sky," I say, rolling my shoulder back as I feel a new bruise forming.

Just another one for the collection.

Micah picks himself up from the weed patch he was thrown into. "This is worse than Last Army training," he says.

He retrieves his shoe, a good ten feet from where he landed.

"Did I mention I hate you?" Selestra asks.

I turn to see she's somehow managed to stay inside the balloon and is working to untangle herself from the basket, foot caught in the rope. She curses as she rips her ankle free.

"You might have mentioned it once or twice," I say.

Selestra glares at me, wiping the dirt from her dark blue gloves and onto her trousers.

"Good."

She blows out a huff of air, swiping her leafy hair from her face, and helps Irenya to her feet. I'm not sure what the big fuss is.

Aside from a few scrapes, we're all okay.

It would have really put a dampener on the quest if we'd died before we could complete it.

"Luckily I didn't break my ankle for a second time," Irenya says. She's covered in as much mud as the rest of us. "You'd have to carry me to Polemistés."

I survey the damage to the balloon. Twigs and wood protrude from the basket in our wake and the great balloon itself has sputtered and collapsed into a heap on the grass, torn from the fall.

"Be thankful it's not your neck," Selestra says, stepping beside me to eye the broken balloon. "Do you have another plan?"

"A plan," I repeat. "I wouldn't exactly call it that."

I've spent my life reacting, without needing to overthink it, so I hadn't really *planned* much past taking this balloon to Polemistés and killing the king.

"We'll head into town and find a way to repair the balloon," I announce, turning away from the new holes in Leo's butterfly. "It's the only safe way to Polemistés. We can't just abandon it."

I dig through the collapsed fabric to find our supplies and throw a backpack to Micah.

"You too," I say, throwing one in Selestra's direction.

She catches it with a grunt and glares in a way that I'm starting to think is reserved only for me. At least the glares I can get used to.

They're far less unsettling than when I see sparks of something else inside her. A lost and hopeless look, like the one she gave me back on the balloon, when she spoke of destroying her mother. It's the kind of look that makes me have to constantly remind myself what she truly is.

Witch. Witch. Witch.

"Help me fold this up." I gesture to what's left of our balloon.

When we reach Armonía's main town, our first step will be to find a fabric weaver who can help stitch our safe passage back together, before death—or the king—comes for me again.

The four of us gather at the edge of the fabric and begin to tightly roll it, squashing all the air out. We keep going until it starts to look like a comically long sausage that fits snugly into the large bag Leo provided. It'll take at least two of us to carry it.

"Is it this way into town?" Selestra asks, pointing excitedly into the distance. She hitches the backpack on her shoulder.

She's more desperate to get to town than I am.

I suppose that since she doesn't care about the sword, the disappointment of losing our travel to Polemistés isn't nearly as important as the novelty of being able to explore somewhere new.

"Once we get to town, nobody will know who you are," I remind her. "They won't be bowing at your feet. It might not be to your liking."

"*You're* not to my liking," Selestra says simply, and begins walking across the field. "I'll lead the way."

I smirk. "Town is in the other direction, princess."

Selestra stops and swivels back around, not missing a beat. She strides back past the balloon basket and knocks her shoulder into mine as she passes.

"I've told you I'm not a princess," she says, for what feels like the hundredth time.

She seems to hate the word, which only makes me want to say it more.

"So you've mentioned." I eye the bracelet on her wrist. "But you should remove those royal jewels if you want to convince everyone else."

Selestra pauses to touch a hand to the gem on her wrist and a look of grief passes across her delicate features, quick enough that I almost miss it.

Everything about her is rushed and fleeting, like she can't bring herself to linger on any kind of emotion for long. It could be that it's too painful, but part of me thinks she's just not used to emotions at all.

Everything I've heard about witches points to them being creatures of death and curses. Their kind helped the king conquer islands and Selestra's family has kept him in power for lifetimes.

I can't let myself think she's different.

Selestra's right: She isn't a princess, or some innocent girl who needed to be rescued.

She's made from dark magic and I can't ever forget it. There's a fire inside of her—if she lets it, it'll burn through the world.

I pick up my sword from the rubble, steady my breath, and lead the way into town.

22

SELESTRA

The main town in Armonía is nothing like I thought it'd be.

From the stories I've heard at court, I imagined scattered markets of old wares. Not the endless stalls of thick chocolate cake and freshly caught fish in front of us.

They stretch into the far reaches of the sun, each filled with a different brightly colored fruit, or loaves of freshly baked bread. The smell of garlic and cream from the pots of simmering soup soak the air, and between the masses of marketgoers there are wildflowers that spring up from the street. Their petals are unfettered by the treading crowds, ever bright and swaying in the wind.

I take it all in, my heart pounding with every new discovery.

A new world, beyond my castle and beyond Vasiliádes.

Beyond my tower.

"It's beautiful," I say.

From the thatched dome buildings, striped in brown wood, to the floors that are a mosaic of cobblestone in a rainbow of colors that look like shattered glass. When we step on them, they illuminate. The sound our boots make against them is like rain falling through tree leaves. The cobbles shimmer and ripple in response, as though they're absorbing the sound and becoming fluid.

This isn't some quaint and unassuming town on the edge of the Six Isles, like the court snobs made it out to be. Perhaps it's not refined and glamorous, but it's grand and brimming to the teeth with traders and the throngs of people who barter with them.

I'm in awe of it.

"Don't you think it's pretty?" I ask, looking back over my shoulder to Nox.

He blinks at me, frowning a shade, as if he's noticing something for the first time.

Then he swallows, gripping tighter on to the balloon bag.

"Your hood" is all he says.

For a moment I'm confused, but then I realize the problem. I'd thought we were almost unnoticeable in the crowds, but with the summer green of my hair, people are stopping to stare and whisper as we walk by.

A witch in Armonía.

A Somniatis woman, outside of the Floating Mountain.

They look at us with such hatred that we may as well have a target on our backs.

I swallow and bring my hood quickly up to hide my face from this bustling town.

Then something curious happens.

A woman passes by, her hair the same shade as mine.

We stop to stare. For a moment I think the king and Theola have found us. I see the panic in Nox's eyes too, as he mistakes the stranger for my mother.

Then another woman crosses the market square, hair a darker gray green.

Then another.

Armonía is full of them—women with green hair cut short above their ears or swaying by their collarbones.

"They look just like you," Irenya says, blinking as if her eyes could be deceiving her.

With a smile, I realize it must be the fashion in Armonía to emulate the Somniatis witches. I wonder why Nox didn't mention it, but then I see how surprised he looks.

I'm not the only one who didn't expect this.

In Vasiliádes, it's common to wear green masks to show allegiance to the crown, but that's nothing like this. The people in Vasiliádes fear us, and their masks pander to the king, but on these streets it's not about him at all. They've colored their hair to be like us.

Like *me*.

I tuck my hair behind my ears.

They don't think I'm some kind of evil creature. For the first time, I'm one of them.

I pause as a few of the townspeople stop again to cast disgruntled looks at us. I see now that their focus isn't actually on me at all, but on Nox and Micah, dressed in their Last Army uniforms.

Nox sets the bag down and fixes his collar, taking in a breath as he realizes it too.

He's the outsider here and I blend right in. The thought makes me grin.

Emboldened, I hurry farther into the town, unable to take my eyes off the wonders it holds.

"How much Chrim do you have?" I ask Nox as he trails after me, staggering with Micah at the balloon bag's weight.

Nox ushers me farther into the markets, away from the people who might have already seen him.

"Out of the two of us, which one is royalty?" he asks. "Shouldn't you be supplying the gold, princess?"

I ignore him and point to a nearby market stall. "I've never seen that kind of fruit before." I gesture to a large round piece the same color as my hair, veined in pink. "Buy it, won't you? Oh, and that bread over there!"

I point to another stall. It's filled with sweet rolls, sprinkled in sugar, and long crusty loaves with sprigs of rosemary and coarse sea salt.

"I wasn't aware I was your royal Chrim keeper," Nox says.

I roll my eyes and walk toward the stall, only to hear Nox sigh before he eventually follows.

"Two of those, please," I say to the trader, pointing at the large sweet buns. "And three of those!" I gesture to a square loaf with sun-soaked tomatoes.

"Now I'm getting hungry," Micah says. He drops the bag and holds on to his stomach, causing Nox to stumble a little.

"That's because you threw up everything you ate," Nox reminds him.

"All the more reason to fill me back up." He moves to my side. "Can we get some of the butter-fried bread too? With those little crispy onions?"

"Don't forget the cheese sticks," Irenya says. She clasps my gloved arm, suddenly intensely serious. "We *must* have cheese sticks."

Nox looks at us all in disbelief.

"Anyone would think we'd been starving on that balloon," he says. "I packed food."

Micah waves off the incredulous look on his face.

"Nobody wants your sand crackers and canned cheese, Nox," he says. "Pay the man, won't you?"

Reluctantly, Nox reaches for the pouch of Chrim coins hidden in the lining of his jacket. I can tell by the way he glares that it costs a good chunk of what we have to satisfy the trader. It's worth it. I've never smelled such delicious food in my life. Even the castle cooks can't compare to the freshness of these stalls.

The trader takes a handful of Nox's silver Chrim, and with it he takes in our disheveled appearances. My muddied gloves and Nox's torn shirt. Then my eyes.

I notice his stare immediately and it sends a wave of panic through me. I've been enjoying my anonymity far too much to let it end so soon.

"It's dye," I say quickly. "This color is very fashionable right now."

"Honestly, you lot are unbelievable," the trader says, shaking his head.

He accepts the lie easily enough. It must be a common practice in Armonía, just as it is back in Vasiliádes. Though the women there prefer browns and bright-set blues to yellow.

"Everyone's so desperate to look like a witch these days," the trader says. "You should embrace who you really are."

"You're right," I say, pressing my lips together to hide a smile. "I'll be sure to do that."

I take a mouthful of fresh bread as we move away from the stall. I can't help but moan as I bite into it, not caring when the people beside us stop to cast me funny looks.

Nox gawks at me. "Do you and that bread need some alone time?" he asks. "We could give you a minute."

"A minute would never be enough." I take a larger bite and grin at him as the crusts tumble to the ground.

Nox shakes his head, but I can hear his stomach growling. Though he's hungry too, I know he's far too stubborn to take a piece of the butter loaf Micah holds out to him.

"Where do we go now?" I ask.

"We need to find a fabric weaver to help us fix the tears in the balloon," Nox says. "One that won't ask questions."

We turn onto a second street and the light darkens a little. A group of people dressed all in black huddle on the cobblestones beside a small gray door, filled with scribbles. They sob, and the cries bounce from the street windows and across the lamps, dampening the flames.

One of them steps forward and dips a feather tip in a pot of ink. He writes something onto the door face in tiny letters I can't make out from this far away.

"What is this?" I ask, swallowing down the last gulp of bread.

The street is empty save for us, and though it's only early afternoon, something eerie coats the street, usually reserved for night.

"It's a mourning street," Nox says, voice low and tight. His hands clench at the sides of the balloon bag. "It's where people who have lost someone to the king's bargain come to pray for their souls. They inscribe the names of their loved ones across the doors."

I watch as the man dips the feather into the ink again and begins writing something else. Another name.

My heart fills with dread as I think about how many he might list. There are at least a dozen mourners surrounding him, and if each of them has lost someone to the bargain, then that door will be overtaken by their names.

"What about the people who live in those houses?" I ask, lowering my voice to a gentle whisper. "Don't they mind?"

"They're empty," Nox explains. "To house the dead, should they be unable to find the River of Memory."

It breaks my heart to hear it.

Entire streets devoted to the dead and the souls my family have stolen. Despite what these people may want to believe, those souls aren't struggling to find the River of Memory, but are feeding the king and his immortality.

They only wanted a better life—to escape death for long enough to reap the magical reward of a healing potion or enough Chrim to feed their families.

Instead, they've been cursed to an eternity of nothingness.

It's such a contrast to the thrumming market just around the corner, and I realize this is what's hidden behind the curtain of every smile and summer's day. Endless mourning and grief, overtaking half the streets.

Does Vasiliádes have mourning streets too?

Do all the Six Isles?

I swallow.

It's my family who have sentenced these people to such pain. I wish there was a way I could help make it right.

As we pass the mourners and my heart wrenches at their cries, a row of town guards turns onto the street. Their swords rest over the top of their shoulders, hands by their hearts as they clasp them.

"The king wants us to keep an eye out," one of them says. His voice is hushed as he nears us. "The heir could be on our very streets."

My eyes widen and Irenya moves closer to my side, ever the protective friend. Nox and Micah drop the bag beside a nearby shadowed doorway.

"Don't be ridiculous," the other guard says. "What would a Somniatis witch be doing in Armonía?"

"Well, it isn't by choice, is it? She was kidnapped, I heard! Right before the king's banquet."

At their words, I turn to veer from the path, but Nox grabs out for my arm and keeps me pressed close to him.

"Keep walking," he says with clenched teeth.

"But—"

"We don't want to draw attention to ourselves."

I look to Irenya and Micah, who nod and continue moving forward, as if the guards are no bother to them. We're just four people, out for a walk in the early afternoon.

I stiffen as we near the guards and their eyes cross over us briefly.

They shouldn't be able to tell me apart from any of the other women here, but I dip my face low to the ground all the same, keeping my eyes from their view. Fooling a trader may be easy, but I can't gamble with a lie about yellow dye in my eyes when it comes to town guards.

I won't risk being dragged back to Vasiliádes.

I *can't* go back to being locked in that tower.

The guards pause a step before they pass us, eyes drifting over my green hair. I don't look at them or raise my stare to meet theirs, but I sense them lingering on me. Immediately, I worry that our deception has failed and we've been caught.

Should I run?

Punch one of them in the nose and make a getaway?

"Afternoon," Nox addresses the guards, nodding in greeting. His voice is casual, and if he's as panicked as I am, he doesn't show it.

The guards take in his Last Army uniform and any sign of apprehension on their faces relaxes.

"Afternoon," they reply back in unison.

The vague recognition disappears as they brush past us.

Only a brazen fool would greet the town guards they were on the run from, and so the guards suspect nothing as we walk onward, only stopping once they've turned the corner and are out of sight.

I breathe out a loud sigh of relief, my heart practically bursting.

"That was too close," Micah says.

"I thought for sure they recognized Selestra," Irenya agrees. "Thank the souls for the witch wannabes in this town."

I'm grateful too.

If it wasn't for the fashion sentiments in this town and Nox keeping his uniform, then we would have been caught. I wondered why he didn't change when we left Vasiliádes, but it's clear to me now: People respect and fear the Last Army.

The king may have told people that I was kidnapped, but Nox knew he'd never tell them that one of his own soldiers was responsible for my leaving the castle.

It would make him look a fool. As though he was easily lied to and easily betrayed.

He'd much rather spin some kind of story about a rogue assassin or a lone traitor than put the reputation of his whole army on the line.

Nox's and Micah's uniforms will allow us to move through the Six Isles without much suspicion.

"Over there," Nox says. "Let's lie low for a bit so we don't run into any more of the Last Army."

He points to a small tavern at the edge of the marketplace, beyond a crooked row of stalls. The Soul's Keep. It's a fitting name for a building that juts out from the side, like a tear in the world. The lantern above is covered in enough cobwebs that it's clear it's never been used. The kind of place that thrives on darkness is the perfect place to hide while we pull ourselves together and let the guards tire themselves searching a town of lookalikes.

"What about the bag?" I ask, gesturing back to where we discarded the balloon.

"Leave it," Nox says. "Nobody would ever steal from a mourning street. Let's head inside."

"In there?" Micah asks.

His voice drips with uncertainty and I don't blame him. It doesn't exactly look welcoming. Besides, the last time I was in a tavern with Nox, it didn't work out so well for the two of us.

"We're going to need a place to be inconspicuous," Nox explains. "Somewhere we can figure out a strategy."

"A strategy for what?" I ask.

He wrenches open the door to the Soul's Keep and the hinges scream in response.

"For saving my life."

23

NOX

The Soul's Keep doesn't have windows.

It's a cavern that curls around us in a wall of black, with floors as bright as clouds. A harmony of light and dark, as is the Armonían way.

Cigar smoke swirls into the air, a mix of blues and bright reds, from whatever flavors have been infused inside. It coats the black, and the sparks of flame that ignite them give light where there was none before.

We settle at a table in the farthest corner, where a small torch flickers on the wall in place of a window, like a blinking sun.

It's quiet, bar the sound of occasional laughter and the slap of a deck of cards across the splintered tables.

I used to dream of drinking in a place like this, beside my father.

A small nook in the world, where we could laugh and talk about the day's training. Strategize together, as I was so sure he'd done with his father before him.

A barkeep crosses the floor and over to us, his long blond hair tied in a ribbon at his neck. "What can I get you?" he asks.

His eyes only briefly dart to Selestra before he shakes his head and dismisses her green hair.

"Rum," I tell him. "Four glasses."

He nods and holds out a hand. "Eight pieces of silver Chrim."

I nearly topple out of my chair at the thought.

I should have known to bring more Chrim, but I thought the

supplies I'd brought would last. I didn't realize I was traveling with wolves, who'd go ravenous at the first sign of bread.

I hand the barkeep the eight silver Chrim and look dismally down to the handful I have left.

If we have any luck, there will be no need to barter once we reach Polemistés.

"I thought we were stopping to think of a plan," Selestra says. "Not to become drunkards."

I don't miss the way her eyes spring to the door, like she's nervous the guards might break it down at any moment to capture her.

"I can do both," I say, settling farther into the cushion of the log chair. "Besides, I'm dying of thirst."

"If only," Selestra mutters under her breath.

The barkeep returns with our drinks, sliding the tray into the center of the table with enough force that the rum sloshes over the shallow rims of the glasses.

I take a long and generous sip from my glass.

It burns going down.

Selestra eyes the rum with mistrust.

"It's not poison," I tell her.

"Don't be so sure," Micah says, wincing as he takes a slow drink.

Irenya doesn't have such hesitation and practically downs her glass in one swig.

Selestra lets out a sigh as she presses it to her lips, then gasps out in horror after swallowing her first taste.

"That's *disgusting*," she says, outraged.

"That's rum." I raise my glass in a toast.

"I can have yours if you like." Irenya reaches for Selestra's drink.

"Help yourself," Selestra says, pushing it toward her friend. "But I'm not carrying you out of here."

Irenya snorts a laugh into the glass, just as the door to the Soul's Keep opens to let in another round of patrons.

Each of them looks to Selestra as they walk in. They're drawn to her somehow. Even with so many women coloring their hair to match hers, Selestra doesn't blend in.

I think it would be impossible.

Some people are made to puncture through the world and something about her shines a little brighter, stabs a little sharper. Even I'm not blind to it.

"We need to cut your hair," I say.

Selestra looks over to me, surprise coating her face.

"What?"

"It's too recognizable."

"Everyone here has green hair," she protests.

"But none as long as yours," I say. "It makes you look far too much like your mother."

Selestra grimaces, the thought of it clearly not something she's ever wanted. I almost want to apologize for the slight. I've lived for years trying to match my father's legacy, but it seems Selestra would much prefer to escape any legacy of her mother.

"I thought we were safe here for now," she says.

"We're not safe anywhere," I tell her. "But that's the price to pay for adventure."

"Adventure?"

Selestra's eyes flash when she scowls, like orbs of light. Under the close torch flame, I can see for the first time that she has freckles. Just a handful, dotted across her cheeks, one toward the tip of her nose.

I'm not sure why I focus on that.

"If we're truly not safe anywhere, then I don't want to waste any more time on mythical swords or wetting our lips with rum all evening," Selestra says. She stands suddenly and gestures for Irenya to do the same. "I'm going to find us an inn and we're going to stay there until this month is over."

She turns toward the door. Without thinking, I reach out for Selestra's arm, holding her in place before they can go.

Selestra jolts with the shock of it. She isn't used to people touching her. Even if my hands only wrap around her gloves, I know it must still feel strange.

It feels strange to me too.

The last time we touched—the last two times—death shortly followed. It's like she carries it around with her. The shadow of death, in her skin.

I think then that her gloves aren't really gloves at all, but chains, keeping death at bay.

Either way, I can't let her out of my sight.

I need Selestra to find the magic my father spoke of. Her power is the key to destroying the king and to keeping me alive. I'm not going to have her wandering around Armonía without me.

"Seryth will find us wherever we go," I remind her. "The only place he can't follow is Polemistés, which just so happens to be where the key to killing him lies. In this little game, we're not hiding. We're seeking."

"So no matter what," Selestra says, "we'll never be safe?"

"You're safe right now," I promise. "With me."

Selestra's eyes fix on my hand, still closed around her wrist.

Slowly, she pulls her arm from me. "Am I?"

Her voice is throaty.

"I swear it."

Selestra blinks at the vow. She glances back at the door again, then, resigned, settles into her chair.

"If you truly are determined to go on this suicide mission to Polemistés, then why can't we find a ship to take us the rest of the way?" she asks. "Surely it would be safer to go somewhere the king can't follow, rather than waste time fixing the balloon."

"We need the balloon to bypass the whirlpools," I explain. "A ship won't do. Too many have been lost to them before."

"How many?" Selestra asks, looking uncertain.

"A lot."

"I heard the one by the Southern Isle is as big as a city," Irenya says in a hushed whisper. Her eyes are wide and rum soaked. "That it has arms and mouths, like a great beast of the sea. Sirens used to make their home there until Isolda and the king banished them all outside the Six Isles."

Selestra turns to her friend with wide eyes. "*What?*"

"And then there's the Polemistés Forest of the Damned too," Irenya says. "I've heard such stories about that!"

Micah groans.

He looks like he might throw up again.

"I hate ghosts," he says.

"Ghosts?" Selestra says the word like it's a curse.

Like there's one right behind me.

"It's another one of the Polemistés barriers to the outside world," I explain. A place where monsters lurk behind every tree, and in every breath of wind is the soul of a warrior, ready to cut down those who dare venture inside. "It's a place for the damned, not the living."

"How can you expect to fight ghosts?" Selestra asks.

"I don't," I say. "Leo's butterfly is our way to bypass every defense Polemistés has. We can fly over their walls and haunted forests."

The entire reason I hunted Leo down and risked my life to pay him so much gold Chrim was to have a way of escape that would keep us safe.

"Then if we truly need the balloon fixed, I think there's a better way than to risk trusting the town fabric weaver," Selestra says. She turns to Irenya.

"Me?" her friend asks, shocked.

"You," Selestra confirms with a nod.

Irenya looks thoroughly panicked. "I couldn't," she says. "I wouldn't know where to start. That fabric is different from any we've had at the castle. What if I make a mistake?"

"You won't," Selestra assures her. "You might be an apprentice, but we both know you surpass the dressmaker herself." Selestra turns to me, looking surer than I've seen her before. "You've seen how intricate the gowns we wear are. Many are Irenya's designs, or things she's stitched without help."

I have to admit, the idea is intriguing and one I hadn't thought of before.

"You know fabrics better than anything or anyone," Selestra says to her friend. "I *know* you can do this."

Irenya smiles at her, relaxing somewhat. I can see how emboldened the princess's approval makes her feel. Selestra's right: I've seen the gowns at court, and if Irenya is responsible for any of those intricacies, then patching up a balloon should be quick work.

Irenya downs Selestra's rum for courage. She slams it onto the table and lets out a breath. "Okay," she says. "I mean, yes. I can do it. I think."

"What supplies would you need?" I ask.

"The most important would be the right fire-resistant fabric to patch the holes."

I nod. "Then that's our next step. We find the fabric, let Irenya work her skills, and then we fly across the whirlpools and into Polemistés before the king can find us."

"I really hope your magic sword is worth risking our lives for," Selestra says. "What if you get to Polemistés and it doesn't even exist?"

"It exists," I say firmly. "It has to."

Selestra might think that magic is gone, that there's nothing left but what lives inside her, but it isn't true. There are still sprinkles of it across the Six Isles. Small glimpses of magic that have escaped the king. Things like Leo's butterfly or the mosaic cobblestone that glitters across the town.

Or whatever forces are keeping Polemistés from falling.

Maybe Selestra doesn't believe in the stories—I didn't either—but she can't deny the island's survival. She can't chalk it all up to them being good warriors.

There's something there that's protecting them and I need to take it so I can protect the world.

"If Irenya fixes the balloon, then we only have one worry left," I say.

"One big worry," Micah corrects him.

Selestra looks between us. "What?"

"My death," I say simply. "The greatest worry of all."

"Your death," she repeats.

"The halfway point of the month is tomorrow and after that the king himself can hunt me. If I'm going to escape, I'll need another vision."

Selestra pales the moment I say it.

Her hands tighten around the arms of her chair and I feel her desire to spring back up from it and run toward the door, rather than give me what I need.

Unlike her mother, she hasn't made quick friends with death.

"We made a deal," I remind her. "Your escape from the castle in exchange for helping me survive this month. You gave me your word."

"I know," Selestra starts. "But it isn't that simple."

"I've gotten you this far, princess," I say. "Now it's time you held up your end of the bargain."

24

SELESTRA

After the last breath of sunset, Nox leads me back to the mourning streets, which empty out when the town bell chimes.

"So the dead can return, unseen and undisturbed," he explains. "The tavern is too busy to risk exposing you having a vision. Nobody will see us here. They don't come after dark."

It's not comforting.

I don't want to see myself die alongside Nox, while we huddle together in a ghost street, even though I know it must be done.

Nox approaches a black door with the least names scribbled on it.

Micah and Irenya stand by the door opposite, their hoods drawn up, ready to keep watch as they stand by the balloon bag. Any passing guards would think them straggling mourners and a simple sob, or loud cry of grief from them, will alert us to the Last Army's presence.

The door Nox chose creaks as we enter.

Inside is an empty room, mottled in gray with all the life seemingly carved from it. There are a few basic pieces of furniture: a chalky-white sofa and a cracked wood table cobwebbed at the legs, but aside from that, our footsteps echo in the emptiness.

Nox holds out a hand for mine. "Whenever you're ready," he says.

"I'm never ready for this."

Nox pauses and I see a note of regret soften his usually sharpened features.

I know that he's right and we need to be prepared. The king and my mother will do whatever it takes to stop him from surviving until the Red Moon.

Even without the sword, Nox poses a risk to the king's immortality. If he survives until the Red Moon, it could destroy the bargain and the power the king holds. It could mean that these mourning streets no longer need to exist, without the king stealing souls and trapping death in a hunt.

Saving Nox could save the Six Isles from a tyranny I'd resigned myself to my whole life. It could help get justice for Asden.

Still, Nox doesn't understand what he's asking of me and I can't tell him.

How do I trust him enough with the knowledge that our deaths are linked and that with every vision I have to see myself die alongside him?

I slip the glove from my left hand, keeping the snake's crest hidden in my right. The moment I feel the breeze from the cracked window wash over my skin, I let out a breath of relief.

My hand twitches in anticipation of what's to come.

The desire for touch almost overrules my fear and I would be hungry for it, if not for the prospect of death in the back of my mind.

Nox steps toward me, and my breath catches with his closeness.

The notion of skin on skin creates a yearning inside me.

I'm overcome with the urge to do something I've been forbidden to do my entire life: to *feel*. To touch and know the warmth of someone else instead of the cold constant of nothing.

I want to do what others do so easily, without thinking or taking the time to bask in it.

"Ready?" Nox asks again.

He holds out his hand again, fingertips close enough to graze mine.

I glide my palm slowly across his, bringing my fingers to clasp around his wrist. He does the same to me, thumb pressing firmly against my pulse.

My chest tightens and the immense rush of relief rolls through me, as though I've satisfied a deep and unyielding craving.

By the time death comes, my heart is already pounding.

The first thing I see is the flash of a pirate's ship, shaped like a dragon, hissing out onto the sea.

Swords clash, sparking like fires as they catch each other in the night. Then Nox is on the floor with a soldier looming over him. I scream his name, but it's too late.

Lightning bursts from the sky as he is pitched overboard.

I hear my feet thump against the deck as I run toward him.

Then suddenly I'm thrust overboard too, discarded to the cold depths of the Endless Sea.

Its black waters choke me, pushing into my throat and filling my lungs. I try to kick back up, but something is holding me down, pushing me beneath the surface until I can't struggle anymore.

A flash of green flicks across the water's edge as I splutter my last breath.

My mother.

I gasp and stumble back from Nox in the present, breaking the connection between us. I'm brought instantly to my knees, heaving up the dredges of the Endless Sea that aren't there.

I'm gagging on the memory of water in my throat.

"What is it?" Nox asks, kneeling down beside me.

He reaches out for me, but I skitter back, like a scared animal.

I don't want to see it again.

Souls, I couldn't bear it.

"Selestra, what happened?" Nox asks, voice growing urgent as I clutch at my throat.

It feels like I'm drowning right here in this hollow of a house.

"Let me help you," he says. And then, so soft I almost don't hear, "Please."

I look up at him and try to steady my breath. The concern in his face catches me off guard.

Nox's brows knit tightly together. "What did you see?"

I swallow down the dryness caught in my throat. "I saw you drown."

My voice sounds far away and cracked.

"In three days' time, you get thrown from a pirate ship shaped like some kind of a dragon."

"A dragon," Nox repeats. A look of familiarity descends upon him, but I'm too terrified to pay much mind to it. "Are you sure?"

I nod.

You drown. I drown. We drown.

"I think—" I stumble on the words, trying to make sense of the vision. "I think my mother was there. She held you under."

I bite my lip.

She held *me* under, pushing me into the cold and watching as I gasped for life. How can the blood oath be so strong that she would be able to shove aside any love she once had for me like this?

"They know we're here in Armonía, then," Nox says, considering this. "Or at least they will soon enough."

"What do we do?"

"We make sure Irenya has everything she needs to fix the balloon in the next three days," he says simply. "And then we run."

It'll be tight. Irenya is the most skilled seamstress I know, but making sure she can complete such a task in so little time is going to be difficult. And until she does, we're sitting ducks waiting to be found.

"Cut my hair," I say to Nox.

He raises his eyebrows. "*Now?*"

I nod briskly. "You said I was too recognizable and if we're going to have to stay in Armonía, then we need to make sure I look just like every other person playing dress-up. The king and my mother can't discover us sooner."

I set my jaw, determined.

"Are you sure?"

He sounds uncertain, but he's already drawing his blade.

"I'm no castle stylist."

"And here I was thinking you were unmatched with a blade," I say, quirking a brow.

Nox grins and twirls his blade. "As you wish, princess."

I squeeze my eyes shut as he gathers my hair into his hands. There's a moment of hesitation in him that I can sense, even though this was his idea to begin with.

The seconds dangle between us and the longer they drag on, the more aware I am of the sound of Nox's breathing and the syrupy scent of rum that lingers on him.

It's intoxicating.

His blade slashes.

My hair falls to the floor.

I open my eyes in a blink to see a bundle of it at my feet. Quickly, I reach up a hand and feel the ends of my hair swooping just beside my chin.

I feel lighter. Like a weight has gone not just from my body, but my soul too.

"How do I look?"

Nox stares at me for a moment, seemingly at a loss for words.

"Is it that bad?" I ask, worried by his silence.

I reach up to fiddle with the ends again. They must look so ragged.

"No," Nox says, sounding caught off guard. He clears his throat. "You just look . . . like you, I guess."

"Did I look like someone else before?"

Nox only shrugs and then hands me his blade, so I can see my reflection. The sword is dirty and smeared, but I'm able to catch a glimpse of myself somewhere in it. When I do, the first thing I think is *he's right*.

I do look like me. Not my mother or the king's pristine trophy.

The cut is rough and uneven, but Irenya can fix that later with some fabric scissors. Despite it all, I can't help but grin.

My hair was always kept just how the king liked it. How my mother and all my ancestors before her wore it. It made me look exactly like a Somniatis witch was supposed to, showing the world I was the person they expected me to be.

Now it's gone, I can be something else.

A person of my own, not hidden by their shadows.

We search for the fabric shop that the barkeep in the tavern told us was the best—and only—in town. The streets are alight as we cross them, the new day's sun reflecting from the mosaic floors, and the sound of soft music coming from a single violinist set up in the middle of the square.

People dance when they pass him, throwing Chrim into his hat and then spinning each other around in circles.

It doesn't take us long to find Marigold.

As we approach, I see the name in bright gold letters, like rays of sunlight. The shop itself is covered in white glitter that looks like rain falling from the sky-blue walls.

The bell sings behind us as we enter, filling the room with a symphony of birdsong.

I'm still struck by how Armonía is so different from Vasiliádes. It may not actually *be* magic, but it feels like it in a way the castle never did, despite being home to witches.

Is this what Thavma felt like before the king conquered it and killed anyone else with magic? Did their doors sing and their walls glitter and their people dance on sunlit streets?

I take a moment to admire the fabrics and gowns that line the walls of Marigold, each as bright and breathtaking as the next.

They don't quite compare to Irenya's in design, but in color they're a wonder. Irenya had to keep her creations dark, dressing me only in the king's color, so that I could play the part of his trophy well. But these dresses are alight in pinks and oranges, like the inside of a hearth. They are grass green and summer yellow, and some an unimaginable mix of rainbow that glides from the hangers.

I'd love nothing more than to try one on and see myself in color for once. If we get out of this, I hope Polemistés has equally wonderful fabrics so Irenya can weave wonders as bright as these.

"Good morning!"

A woman in a pink velvet suit that cuts in a deep V across her chest steps out from the back of the shop.

"So nice to have customers this early on a summer's day," she says. Her smile is bright, stretching her flower-pink lips. "My name is Edlyn Marigold. How can I help you?"

"We're looking for some fabric," Nox says.

"I wasn't expecting you to be looking for much else," Edlyn says with a cheerful wink.

"It's a special kind of fabric," Irenya tells her. "It has to be completely fire-resistant, strong enough to help carry heavy loads without the risk of tearing, but also very lightweight."

"How specific! May I ask what it's for? That could help me recommend something."

"I'm afraid that'll have to remain a mystery," Nox says.

Edlyn doesn't seem to mind. She brings her finger to her chin and sucks in a breath. "I do like a challenge. And a mystery. Very well then!"

She swivels on her matching velvet shoes and then disappears abruptly into the back of the shop. Moments later, she returns holding up a roll of material the color of a buttercup.

"Norcad," she announces. "Entirely lightweight, yet untearable and able to withstand great force. Plus, it could withstand the heat of a dragon, if one should ever exist."

"You're sure?" Nox asks.

"About the dragons?"

"About everything."

"I never lie about fabrics, young man," Edlyn says, very seriously. "If you want something indestructible but weightless, then you'll get no better."

"It won't be as inconspicuous as Leo's original design," I say, remembering how the balloon reflected the night sky so well, keeping us invisible during the dark, at least.

"I don't believe in being inconspicuous," Edlyn tells us.

"We'll take it." Nox holds out a handful of silver Chrim. "How much?"

"Oh, dear boy," Edlyn says regrettably. "I'm afraid that wouldn't nearly cover it. Material such as this would cost at least ten gold coins for a hundred yards."

"We'd need twice that to cover the patches," Irenya says.

Nox's face contorts into a grimace. "We don't have that much," he says. "We'd pay you more if we could, but if you'd be willing to make a deal, then—"

"I'm afraid not." Edlyn pulls back the fabric abruptly.

Disappointment slicks over Nox's features.

I'm not used to seeing him without a plan, or at least the bravado of faking one, and it leaves me unsettled.

At least one of us has to have some certainty in this quest.

"How much would this fetch us?" I ask, holding out my arm to show the bracelet the king long ago gifted me.

Edlyn gawks at the mere sight of it. "Souls," she says. "Is that pure gold?"

"With a ruby eye."

Edlyn's eyes grow wide and I see her fingers twitch as she tries to restrain from reaching out to touch it.

Such a gem is rare and it's exactly why the king gifted it to me.

A rare stone for a rare creature. A prize for his prize.

"Wherever did you get such a thing?" Edlyn asks.

"It's a family heirloom."

"If it's sentimental, I'd be reluctant to trade for it. Are you sure you want to part with such a thing?"

I can't help but hesitate.

I've worn this every day of my life for as long as I can remember. The fact that it was a gift from the king has made it feel like a chain often enough, but the knowing that it once belonged to my great-great-grandmother has always made me feel connected to our family's magic.

To part with it feels a little bit like parting with a piece of myself.

With a piece of my mother too. It is the last piece of her I took with me when I left the castle.

"Would it take care of the fabric?" I say, unclipping it from my wrist and holding it out to Edlyn.

She takes it with a series of enthusiastic nods. "Yes, yes, of course!" she exclaims. "More than so! You could have the fabric and the pick of any outfits from the store. At least a dozen!"

"I'm not sure we need a dozen," I tell her with a smile. I touch the bare spot on my wrist. It feels cold. "A change of clothes would be nice though."

I look around at her shop, once again taking in the array of color and silks.

"Do you have anything less extravagant?" Nox asks, following my eye.

"Let me guess," Edlyn says in a laugh. "Black?"

Nox must see the way my nose wrinkles at the thought, because he says, "Maybe just nothing that glows in the dark."

Edlyn laughs again. "I'm sure I can find you something."

She heads back into the far stretches of the shop to dig out the more muted outfits she doesn't keep on display.

Once she's gone, Nox turns to me.

I reach up to tuck my hair behind my ears. It still feels strange to have it so short, no barrier between me and the world to hide behind.

"You didn't have to do that," Nox says, gesturing to my wrist.

"I am the one who spent most of your money on bread and cakes," I say with a quick smile.

Nox's jaw quirks slightly. "Your appetite has robbed me blind," he admits.

"Here we are!" Edlyn says. She heaps a colorful array of dresses and shirts onto the counter in front of us. "One of these must be more endearing to you than your current attire."

I look down at my black shirt and matching black boots and pants with a grimace. Between that and Irenya's unassuming brown skirt, we do look a little somber.

"Thank you," I say gratefully.

Irenya's fingers are already dancing between the fabrics, exploring all the colors she has never been allowed to work with before.

"This one!" she says, holding up a bright orange sweater.

I recoil a little.

"Not for you," she says, sensing my hesitation. "I meant for *me*."

She puts it down and then holds up a long burgundy dress, embroidered with rose petals.

"This one is for you," she announces.

Though the dress is beautiful, I can't help but laugh. "I don't think a ballgown is the right outfit for our plans," I remind her.

"Oh, you can pick something else out for travel," Irenya says dismissively. "Please, Selestra, the only time I've ever seen color on you is when you're painting. You simply *must* try this on."

I sigh, taking the dress from her with a shake of my head. She has been as robbed of variety as I have, forced to mute her creations in the king's colors.

"I'll be quick," I say to Nox.

"I'm glad to know that a ballgown means more to you than my life," he retorts, though there is a glint of humor in his eyes.

"Irenya's new orange sweater means more to me than your life," I say, twisting on my heel to head into the back room.

It doesn't take long for me to slip the dress Irenya chose over my head, letting it fall down my waist and swing to a rest at my ankles.

It's beautiful. Nothing as intricate as Irenya's designs, but the rose petals catch the light, just so, almost making it look like they're dancing with my movements.

And the *color*. Actual color against my skin, the same red as the cherries that sat on top of the cakes Irenya and I used to sneak.

Even with my green hair swinging by my chin, I no longer look like a witch, bound to the king. I look almost normal. How I imagine any other girl who walks these streets might look when they attend a ball or a celebration.

"Come out, then!" Irenya says. "I'm going to die of curiosity."

I step cautiously from the back room and Irenya squeals in delight when she sees me.

"You look like a strawberry!" she says.

I blink. "That is not a compliment."

"Strawberries are delicious."

"I'm going to get changed now," I say pointedly.

But Irenya pulls me farther into the room, circling me like a vulture as she examines the dress.

"How do you get the tulle to fall like that?" she asks Edlyn.

I sigh as the two of them begin talking fabrics, and turn my attention to Nox. He's staring at me, lips pressed together, and a flicker of uncertainty passes across his face.

"Don't tell me I've rendered you speechless," I tease.

"Hardly," he says. The frown smooths out and he gives me a knowing smile. "I'm just trying to think of the right words."

"Let me guess, I look like *me* again," I say to him, mocking his words from after we'd cut my hair. "Really, soldier, you must work on your compliments."

Nox runs a hand through his dark hair. It falls back over his eyes disobediently. "You look like a princess is all," he finally says.

I huff out a breath, irritated at the nickname.

"I told you, I'm not—"

"I know," Nox says firmly. He clears his throat, skin flushed. "But you look like one."

The earnestness in his voice catches me off guard and for once I can't find a retort. Suddenly, I feel far too warm in this dress. Nox's stare intensifies and my breath turns newly ragged with every moment our eyes are fixed to each other.

"I'm going to go get changed," I finally say, shocked by the quiet in my voice.

Nox only nods and then turns quickly away, finally breaking his stare from mine. I swallow and head into the back room, but his words linger, following me.

You look like a princess.

I can't help but smile.

25

NOX

I curse as I prick my finger yet again, trying to mend this damn balloon.

We barely have a day left until the death Selestra predicted comes. Until the king comes.

And our transport isn't finished.

"I told you, go slow," Irenya says to me.

"I don't think he could go any slower," Micah says, his needle threading easily through the fabric.

I scowl at him, then look over to where Irenya has worked her section of the balloon.

I knew she was skilled, but even I had underestimated her. Within just a single day she weaved nearly half the rips and tears our crash caused in the balloon fabric, stitching them back together with remarkable speed and delicacy.

I, on the other hand, have not been anywhere near as fast or delicate.

We work on the floor in one of the empty houses in the mourning street, where we have been staying for the past couple of days, leaving only for the rare food run and to gather any more necessary supplies for Irenya.

With the Last Army patrolling the streets, we can't risk being seen too often. Even with so many women made up to look like witches, Selestra stands out.

She could be recognized easily by the wrong person.

I thread the needle through the fabric and then sigh when my carefully tied knot unties and the thread falls onto my lap.

"This is impossible," I say.

I'm appalled at how Irenya could ever manage to weave dresses as perplexing as Selestra's when I can't even stitch in a straight line.

I'd thought fixing the balloon might take a few hours, but we're on the third morning when Irenya finally holds up the last stitch with a satisfied grin.

"Fabric weavers across the Six Isles, bow down to me," she announces grandly.

"It's done?" I ask Irenya, a little too eagerly.

Not that anyone could blame me, when the next dawning of my death is only hours away.

"I present to you the gift of flight," Irenya says, sweeping her hands over the last patch of fabric.

"Let's hope Nox doesn't crash this time," Selestra says.

"You're welcome to fly it yourself, princess."

"And surrender the chance to see you fall on your backside again?" she says. "I wouldn't deprive myself of it."

"Enjoy looking at my backside, do you?"

Selestra gapes and I see the blush creep onto her cheeks, the red patching over her delicate freckles. It sends a rush through me.

How can she be so beautiful and yet so deadly?

I know I should focus less on the *beautiful* part and more on the *deadly*, but something in her seems to override all my sense. When she saw my latest future and fell to the floor, choking on my death, I wanted nothing more than to rush to her side. I was overcome with the urge to comfort and protect her when I know it should be the other way around.

After all, I'm the one on death's list.

Yet when she blushes, tucking her newly cut hair behind her ears—when I saw her in that red gown—it set off a small fire inside me, catching me unawares.

She's good at that: throwing me off-kilter and tilting the world so that things look different from how I've always known them.

She's a witch. I repeat the mantra, but then another thought slips into my head.

Perhaps she wants to be more.

Not the evil witch who rules by the king's side, stealing souls for him. Nor the princess who stays in her enchanted castle, enjoying life at court. I think she might want something else beyond all that.

I know because I want it too: freedom.

The chance to be more than the sum of our family's pasts.

"With the balloon fixed, can we be off the island before nightfall?" Selestra presses.

Before the vision comes true.

I don't nod, because something in me doesn't want to lie to her.

The truth is, I can't guarantee anyone's safety. Not even my own.

Until we find the sword and kill the king, nobody in the Six Isles will ever truly be safe.

I'm quick to roll the repaired balloon into the large bag Leo provided and ready everyone to begin the walk back to the field where we crashed. The basket is still hidden there, far from any Last Army patrols looking for the king's missing heir.

The walk is quicker than it was before. We're all eager to leave Armonía before we're caught. Selestra practically jogs halfway and even I struggle to keep up with her.

If I didn't know better, I'd say she's more desperate than I am to get out of town and far from the clutches of my next death.

Her visions must be scarring.

I picture her again and how pained she seemed after seeing into my future. I'm not sure why the visions have such an effect on her. I've seen Theola recount countless people's fates without even blinking, but with every death Selestra sees, it's like she's experiencing it for herself.

I haven't quite worked out if it's because her magic is still young or if maybe it's because she actually cares.

It's late afternoon by the time we reach the grassland and I nearly step into the back of Selestra when she stops abruptly at its edge.

"Is this it?" she asks, looking around the empty field.

I can see the skids and mud marks stretching for yards, marking our crash.

The tracks are there.

But now I see that the basket isn't. I should have expected death wouldn't let me escape this easily.

"Did it . . . move?" Selestra asks. She looks around the empty field, as puzzled as I am. "Where did it go?"

"Good question," I say, narrowing my eyes. "Though I think the better one is who took it."

An empty basket in an empty field isn't exactly a popular prize in Armonía. Without the balloon, it's useless.

"Who could carry something that heavy?" Micah asks. "It would take a dozen people. That's why we left the damn thing here."

"And what kind of person would want an empty basket to begin with?" Irenya asks.

Another good question and I can only think of one answer.

One type of person who'd take whatever they found and claim it for themselves.

Scavengers.

More specifically, pirates. And if Selestra's vision of a dragon ship is anything to go by, I know exactly which one.

26

SELESTRA

The harbor of Armonía isn't like the brief glimpses I've had of the boat docks in Vasiliádes. There aren't any patrol guards, nor are there army boats and soldiers with swords as big as horses.

The piers stretch out like the rays of the sun, scattering from the semicircle of sand in wooden beams of bright yellow. The boats tied to them are an array of colors, with names inked in cursive. Some are as big as houses, others no larger than I am, with oars hooked over their sides.

"This is going to be a breeze compared to Vasiliádes," Nox says smugly. "Not a Last Army ship in sight. It's just leisure boats and pirates."

"Are you forgetting that I saw you *die* on a pirate ship?" I ask.

"I guess I'm an optimist," he says. "Besides, we need that balloon to get off this island and if it's on one of these boats, we don't have a choice."

I sigh, frustrated at his flippancy.

I know we have to do this, but he could at least pretend to be worried. Nox doesn't fear death as much as he should. I've told him it's coming and how and that only makes him more confident that he can defeat it.

The only thing he seems to be wary of is the unknown, and without that he flourishes.

"Is it that one?"

He points to a boat.

No, not a boat, or even a ship. It's a creature of the sea, exactly like the one I saw in my vision.

A great beast with sails like wings that are a translucent green curving upward to the sky in a flurry. The wood and rope holding them together are like bones and veins. Its wide, curved body is a deep jade and sharply forked like a hissing tongue down the center.

"That's it," I confirm.

"I knew it," Nox says. He smiles like it only makes things more interesting. "If anyone in Armonía was to scavenge something useless to them, merely because it's of value to someone else, then it's the owner of that ship."

"Who is it?" I ask.

"An old friend." Nox's brown eyes glisten with mischief, reflecting the waters of the crystal harbor beyond.

Micah snorts a laugh. "He's going to be pleased to see you."

"I bet," Nox says, drawing his sword. "And that'll make it even more fun when we steal the basket back."

My jaw nearly drops at that. "Steal?"

Nox turns to me. "Would you prefer commandeer?"

I cross my arms over my chest. "Can't we just ask for it back?"

"Did you forget he was a pirate?"

"Did you forget that you just said he was an old friend?"

"Oh." Nox nods, as though he's only just realizing the lie. Then he shrugs. "He's more of an enemy actually."

"Is there anyone on the Six Isles who actually likes you?" I ask, because I'm not sure how it's possible.

Nox nods over to Micah. "He likes me."

"Anyone who isn't an idiot?"

"Hey!" Micah says, at the same time that Irenya cackles a laugh.

"Look," Nox says, holding his sword up to the light. He studies it for a brief moment—checking for blemishes—and then when he's satisfied at its perfection, he continues. "If we want to survive, we need to get our transport back. I didn't come this far to lose it all to a pirate."

I'm all but jogging to keep step with him as he walks toward the ship.

"So we're just going to steal this thing while nobody's watching?"

"Don't be silly," Nox says. He looks at me with a roguish smile. "There will be plenty of people watching."

I swallow and for some reason my mind draws back to the moment in the Grand Hall, when we first met. When I cut a piece of Nox's hair—a piece of his soul—and a shock pierced through me.

Something like that courses through me now as he smiles.

Not a jolt, but a buzzing. A murmur deep inside, as the wind breezes ripples into the harbor.

A rogue sense of excitement, mixed with my fear.

Adventure.

I can't believe I'm even considering it, but I think of the painting I drew when I was a child, of the girl locked in her tower with hair stretching out the window and toward the ground she never got to walk on.

The picture my mother burned, searing the king's hold on me.

But she can't burn this.

She can set a painting alight, but not a moment. Not an idea.

"How do we steal it?" I ask.

"Easily," Nox says.

We come to a stop by the foot of a long plank that leads up to the boat.

"You and Irenya make sure the harbor guards at the patrol

station are taken care of," Nox tells Micah. "We can't risk them getting help from the town guards if they notice what we're doing. There should only be two or three and they're almost always asleep at this time in the afternoon."

Micah hesitates. "I don't want to leave you alone."

"I'm not alone, I have a witch," Nox reminds him. "And in Selestra's vision, it wasn't a pirate who killed me. It was her mother. Look around, do you see the Somniatis witch anywhere?"

"Fine," Micah relents. "But if you die, I'm going to be pissed."

"I appreciate that," Nox says.

"Will you be okay without me?" Irenya asks.

"Of course," I assure her.

It's sweet that she's concerned for me, but I'm the one who should be worrying after her. I've put her in so much danger already.

I couldn't imagine losing her like I lost Asden.

"Be careful," I say. "And if anything happens, don't be afraid to sacrifice Micah's life to save your own."

"Oh, I will use him as a human shield in a heartbeat," she says earnestly.

"You guys are so sweet," Micah says. "I'm glad we've become such good friends."

Irenya only laughs and nudges him in the shoulder. "Come on. Let's leave the heroes to their quest."

"No dying," Micah warns again, pointing to Nox. "I'm serious."

Irenya rolls her eyes and pulls the reluctant Micah away.

He sighs and lets her lead him toward the harbor guard.

"Here," Nox says.

He hands me a dagger.

I recognize it as the one he brought to my room when he asked for a second vision. The blade is as black as the Endless Sea, the handle bright enough to be carved from the Red Moon itself. A single thread of gold weaves delicately across its body.

It's beautiful.

And it easily replaces the ear dagger I'd stolen before, which I'd been forced to return before anyone noticed.

"Risky business giving me this," I tell Nox, holding back a smile. "I could use it to stab you in the back and take Leo's butterfly for myself."

Nox blinks. "Are you flirting with me?"

I roll my eyes. "I'm threatening to kill you."

A lazy smile spreads across his lips. "Sometimes it's hard to tell the difference with you."

I shake my head and twist the knife in my hand, unable to help but be dazzled at the sight of it.

A true fighter's blade.

"Come on, princess," Nox says. "Let's go steal ourselves a butterfly."

The ship looks even more like a dragon once we're aboard. The floors of its forked body are awash with green, the same color of its winged sails, and ripple with blues and pinks, so each mark of the wood looks like scales.

The wheel deck sits elevated to the rear, and I spy Leo's butterfly in its center, like a prize on display.

Beside it, a man sits with a lit cigar.

"Nox Laederic," he says.

He spits the cigar into the water and slides down a long pole, bringing him to the main deck.

"What in the name of souls are you doing on my boat?"

He's a good few years older than us, with black hair streaked silver and a beard that pulls across his throat. A scar slashes down his right eye and curves around his cheek, leaving his eye stained bloody.

"Meet Dray Garrick," Nox says to me, sweeping an arm out to the man by way of introduction. "One of the richest thieves in Armonía. He makes his Chrim stealing jewels from the crumbled towers of the old royal families. And murdering anyone who gets in his way, of course."

"That's quite the introduction," I say.

"He's quite the criminal," Nox admits. "Too greedy for a real crew."

Garrick narrows his one good eye. "I asked what you were doing on my boat."

"I considered bargaining with you, but I'm all out of gold and we've already resorted to selling our jewelry," Nox says.

He nods up to the balloon basket.

"You have something of mine and I'd like it back. I'm assuming I'll have to use force, but let me know if you're feeling charitable."

Garrick is too incredulous to laugh fully, and so what comes out of his mouth is a large breathy sound that flares his nostrils.

"And who's this?" he asks, looking at me. His stare lingers. "Your partner in chaos?"

Despite my eyes, surely he can't suspect that I'm a witch. Not with so many women in Armonía sharing the color of my hair. Perhaps they even mimic the glow of my eyes too. With my hair cut to no longer resemble my mother or our ancestors, Garrick must think I'm one of them.

It's freeing to have someone look straight at me and have no expectations or preconceptions.

He doesn't know who I am and so I can be whoever I want for once.

"A partner in chaos," Nox muses. "That's fairly accurate, don't you agree?"

I nod as casually as I can muster. "I like the sound of it."

Garrick sneers. "Whatever you two are up to, do it somewhere else. I don't want to have to hurt you, *Regiment Leader*."

He practically spits those last two words, mocking Nox's position in the Last Army and, it seems, his apparent allegiance to the king. Nox doesn't look the slightest bit ruffled.

"You and your three deckhands are going to take us on?" Nox asks, looking around at the men dotted sparsely across the ship. "I'm insulted."

A smile cracks across Garrick's face, like a splinter. "You're just like your father," he says. "He was an arrogant git too."

As quickly as the smile appeared on Garrick's face, it disappears from Nox's. I see the flicker in his eyes and the way his hands clench quickly at his sides, as if on reflex.

Not bracing himself for an attack, but absorbing one.

The mention of Asden clearly sends him reeling, as it does me.

Who is this man to dare to speak of him that way?

"How do you two know each other?" I ask, breaking the silence and with it the fragile look in Nox's eyes.

"I told you," Nox says. "We're enemies."

"The Last Army is enemies to everyone," Garrick says. "Especially Nox and his little Thánatos Regiment."

"You're not still angry we confiscated those jewels, are you?" Nox asks, recovering quickly. "You couldn't really think you'd get away with pilfering from the old Thavma royal family. You know the king likes to keep all the islands' riches for himself."

"Finders keepers," Garrick says.

"Well, in that case."

Nox holds out his sword, pointing it directly at Garrick's throat.

"We found your ship, so I guess that means we get to keep that and everything on it. Including what we came for."

The deckhands stand up.

Nox's eyes move to them. "Careful," he says. He gestures quickly to me. "She's just as deadly as I am."

I feel that thrum in my heart again with his words.

That buzzing of adventure.

"Over my dead body is this happening," Garrick spits. He draws his own sword. "You're a fool, Nox. That cargo belongs to the king," he says. "He's set a bounty on such transport. More than you could ever imagine. Apparently it was used to kidnap his heir. You wouldn't happen to know anything about that, would you?"

His eyes twist over to mine and my heartbeat thumps.

He can't know. He couldn't possibly.

"I don't have a clue what you're talking about," Nox says.

And then his sword clashes against Garrick's.

"Fetch the harbor guards!" Garrick yells, just as Nox pushes him into the side of the boat. "Tell them I've found the heir!"

One of the deckhands makes for Nox, who swivels out of the way and slashes his blade across their arm.

"Selestra, don't let anyone get by!" he yells.

I widen my eyes as one of the deckhands charges toward me.

He's large, at least a foot taller than me and a great deal wider too. But I remember Asden's training and I know that power is no match for speed.

I won't let him reveal our location to the guards and to the king.

I crouch low and sweep my leg out, tripping the man to the floor. His head hits the deck just as the third deckhand grabs me from behind.

His arms crush around my waist.

I don't try to pry them off.

I know I'm not strong enough.

But strength is no match for quick thinking, I tell myself.

I fling my head back, cracking it into the man's nose. His hold loosens and I turn, kicking him square in the stomach.

He falls to his knees, bleeding on the deck with a groan.

"Thanks for the practice," I say, bringing my arm into the air. "I've been worried I'd get rusty."

I punch him, hard enough that I hear a loud crack before he falls to the floor.

Asden would be proud.

I turn to check on Nox, just as he slams the butt of his sword into Garrick's mouth, knocking one of his teeth clean out.

Garrick stumbles, back pressed against the edge of the ship.

"You won't get away with this!" he yells as Nox approaches. "The king will kill you and your entire family!"

He raises his sword to slice across Nox's chest, but Nox blocks it easily. Effortlessly. He knocks the sword from Garrick's hands and grabs ahold of his collar.

"The king already did that," Nox says darkly.

My breath catches.

Then he pushes Garrick from the ship and into the harbor waters below.

"What did you just do?" I ask, shocked.

"Relax," Nox says. "He can swim."

I look around the ship. "Where's the third deckhand?"

"Down there too somewhere."

Nox gestures to where Garrick curses below.

I don't feel any sympathy for him or his men: *Murderer*, Nox had called him. And pilferer of dead kings and queens, including those of the witches my family descended from.

Better he be thrown overboard than us.

I laugh in relief before I can help myself and Nox looks just as surprised as I am. It's the laugh of a girl, not caged by a centuries-old blood oath, or trapped by a king of souls.

And Nox is the reason for it.

This soldier, who took me from the castle, saving me from my own mother. He flew me to a land where I don't have to hide.

The ship sways against the harbor waters.

I take in a breath.

He's dangerous, I remind myself. *He's marked by death.*

The king's crest burns against my hand, reminding me of what could happen if I let my guard down for even a moment. It's because of Nox and that odd curse of fate tangled between us that I've nearly died so many times.

So why is it that I feel safest when I'm with him?

"Nox!"

I whirl to see Micah and Irenya running breathlessly onto the boat.

"Let's go!" Micah says hurriedly.

He notices the two deckhands unconscious on the floor and begins dragging them from the boat.

"They're coming for us," Irenya says, running to my side.

In the distance a flurry of guards run toward Garrick's ship, their pounding boots like thunder.

"I told you to take care of them," Nox says. He climbs the rickety ladder up to another deck, which houses the ship's wheel.

"You told me to take care of two sleeping guards," Micah argues, dragging the last deckhand away. "Not the Last Army!"

"The king knows we're here," I say in a gasp.

Which means my mother is here.

Above, thunder rumbles behind the clouds as the sun finally finishes setting. I watch in horror as the sky turns black.

"Damn," Nox curses, as realization sets in.

My eyes widen and I turn back to look at the guards again.

They're not guards at all. They're soldiers.

The uniform coats their broad shoulders, the king's insignia clear on their chests as they approach, swords drawn, screaming at us to *stop right there*.

"We don't have time to inflate the balloon before they get to us!" Nox yells. "We'll have to take the ship and launch it later once we're clear from attack."

"Irenya, untie the docking line!" he commands. "Micah, lift the anchor! Selestra, take the wheel so I can ready the sails!"

I don't hesitate to run toward the ladder and climb up to the wheel, readying the boat just as we begin to drift away from the harbor.

I keep the ship steady and straight as I can, while Nox yells orders and Micah and Irenya run from one end of the ship to another.

I'm shocked that Irenya doesn't question it, or stop to ask Nox what he means when he talks about *mainsails* and *port side*. Then I remember that she grew up right by the docks of Vasiliádes. Her father was a sailor before he met her mother, and he must have taught her a thing or two.

But before we're a safe enough distance away from the harbor, two Last Army soldiers manage to jump onto the ship.

"Get the heir!" one yells.

"Don't let them take her!"

They claw their way up onto the deck, and both Nox and Micah grab their swords to fight them off.

Then I see a third. A fourth. Then two more.

As we sail away from Armonía, we take half a dozen of the Last Army with us. The clang of their swords rattles the ship.

"We're outnumbered!" Micah yells.

"Thanks for the update," Nox says, driving his sword through one soldier's stomach.

The blood splatters onto the dragon-scale deck.

"The king will kill you for stealing his witch!" one of the soldiers sneers. "Your father would be disgraced by this."

"Actually, I think he'd be proud," Nox says, not realizing just how true that is.

He cuts the man down in a heartbeat.

He turns to take on another, but he and Micah are still outnumbered and the Last Army are just as brutal.

A sudden gloom settles over me and I'm drawn to look back toward the dock.

To my horror, I see my mother standing, staring back at me.

Her green hair sways in the breeze and her wild eyes lock onto mine in a promise of death.

I see her lips move and I hear the call of my name on the wind.

Selestra.

I gasp and Nox must hear it because he turns from battle to look up at me.

"I won't let them take you!" he calls to me in a promise.

My eyes meet his and that relief—that feeling of safety—returns in an instant.

I watch him fight off the soldiers, acting as a barrier between them and the ladder that leads to me. I realize then that he's not just fighting for his life, but for mine too.

He's *protecting* me.

"What should we do?" Irenya asks, climbing up the ladder and to my side.

"Take the wheel," I tell her.

Too many people have died while I just stood there and watched.

If Nox is going to try to save me, the least I can do is save him right back.

Without thinking, I slide down the pole, racing into the fight.

I might not be Last Army, but Asden taught me enough fencing to hold my own.

I grab Garrick's sword from where Nox had knocked it to the floor and slash it across the air, meeting the blade of a soldier. Then I twist and elbow him straight in the cheek. Before he has time to recover, I slam my foot into his knee and bring my blade across his back.

It's not a mortal wound, but it's enough to stop him from getting back up for a while.

I turn to see Micah just about to kill another of our attackers, but my eyes search the ship for Nox, who has disappeared from beside the ladder.

I spot him quickly by the ship's edge, nearly hidden behind a wing of sails. He struggles as one of the soldiers pins him to the side of the ship.

Nox's blade is the only thing between the sword of the Last Army and his throat.

He heaves the soldier off just in time and slashes his sword across his neck. Then Nox collapses to the floor, a little breathless.

Another soldier comes from behind, but I know Nox doesn't see him.

This is the moment I foresaw.

He's about to be thrown overboard, and if I run to him, I'll follow.

Once we're in those waters, my mother will seize the opportunity to drown us both. She'll siphon all the power she has into keeping us under, so the king can be satisfied that his immortality will never be challenged.

I only have moments, seconds, to do something.

I feel the wind on my cheeks and the breeze brushing my hair from my face as I reach inside myself, looking for the power I've always pushed down out of fear it might turn me into my mother.

I call for it to come to the surface and feel the spark of it abiding.

Just small, just for a moment. But it's enough.

I thrust my arm out and the magic breaks into the world.

It's as though a gasp of wind bursts from my heart and rams into the soldier who's about to attack Nox.

It hits him with enough force to knock him clear over the edge of the ship and into the crystal waters below.

Then it dissipates.

There and gone in an instant.

My heart pounds ferociously.

I channeled the *wind*, just like my mother. I siphoned power from it.

I bring a hand quickly to my nose, but just like in the tavern, there's no blood. No pain.

The king always said I wouldn't come into my true powers until my mother died. That they weren't mine to have.

You're just an heir, Selestra, he always told me. *You have no real power yet.*

But I felt it. I still do.

I run to Nox's side.

He looks up at me. "I thought I told you to steer," he says, panting a little for breath.

I hold out a gloved hand to him.

"That's three times I've saved your life now."

I pull Nox to his feet, but he keeps ahold of my hand. Not letting go as he rises.

"Looks like I owe you one again," he says.

His fingers stay interlaced tightly with mine. The mark of the king like a magnet between us, stitching our palms together.

Nox's eyes flare with something bright and new, as our hands hold steady. It's a look that makes my body hum.

Some people have adventure in their bones. Nox is one of those people, and when I'm with him, it feels like I might too.

He makes me want to seek out challenges and be curious, when life has only ever taught me to be indifferent and obedient to the world.

Nox squeezes my hand, just a little, and my stomach shifts. His touch ignites me. I wish, harder and more desperately than any wish before, that I could feel him without the barrier of my gloves.

"Come on, princess," Nox says. "We have a sword to find."

27

SELESTRA

Dray Garrick is a painter.

Or at least, he's stolen from a fair few of them.

As Nox loads supplies into the basket, waiting for the balloon to inflate, I slip belowdecks and see an array of blank canvases and brushes. Some nearly as intricate as the ones back in my tower.

I'm supposed to be checking if Garrick has anything of use we could bring with us on the last leg of our journey to Polemistés, but I'm too distracted to search through his pilfered goods properly.

All I can think about is how I somehow managed to siphon power from the wind during the attack.

I stare at the largest of Garrick's paintbrushes, sprawled across a small, chipped table, and will it to move. Just like the Last Army soldier flew from the deck of this ship and like we flew from the Floating Mountain.

I call to my power.

The warmth of it simmers within me and the brush starts to tremble.

I narrow my eyes, focusing harder. I've never known I can move things before. So much of what's inside me is hidden and I've rarely been given the chance to seek it out.

I didn't even know about my healing until I was ten and fell over in the salad gardens, scraping my knee across the rough dirt. I nearly fainted at the sight of the blood, having never seen my own before.

It can be undone, my mother's soft voice cooed. She'd bent down, stroking my hair from my face. *You can undo it, Selestra. You can fix it all.*

She told me to focus, to look at the small scrape on my knee and imagine the skin stitching together. The blood fading to nothing.

Imagine it gone, she'd said. *Like it was never there in the first place.*

And so I did it and when I was done imagining, I saw it was true.

I healed myself and my mother smiled and patted my head and told me I was powerful and I should never forget it.

I shouldn't cry when I had the power to change things.

I look down at the paintbrush now and it lifts from the table and flicks across the canvas.

My heart pounds.

"What are you doing?" Nox asks.

I jump a little and the brush smudges across the paper and then drops quickly to the floor.

Nox is always so quiet when he approaches, with featherlight footsteps and whispered breaths. Only unlike his father, he's not at all quiet after that.

"Acrobatics," I say teasingly. "What does it look like?"

Nox picks up an unused paintbrush and fans the bristles. "Like you're stealing."

"Paint supplies from a thief," I say. "Hardly the worst crime."

"Not as bad as stealing a ship, I suppose."

"I thought you said it was *commandeering*."

Nox tilts his head, offering me a smile.

Sometimes I think that smile is the most dangerous thing about him. The sight of it presses strangely against my heart.

Irenya always told me stories about the men and women who caught her fancy back in the castle. The people she thought were beautiful and admired from afar, and the people who thought she was beautiful right back. She told me what it felt like to hold their hand, which was especially torturous since I knew it wasn't something I ever thought I could do.

Until Nox.

I've held his hand and felt his touch, warm against mine.

"Show me," he says.

"Show you what?" I ask, puzzled.

Nox gestures to the fallen paintbrush. "Your magic."

I don't ask why he wants to see because I don't really care. I want to practice. I'm desperate to feel my power, to use it even for something small and stupid. Without it, I feel lost and cold.

I've lived years being taught I'm just an heir and not a witch. The king always said my powers were limited and I wouldn't be able to do half the things my mother could until she died and passed on our family's true magic. It was the rule I grew up with: There could only ever be one true Somniatis witch.

What if that was all a lie?

What if I've been squashing down everything great inside me because other people weren't ready for it? Because they didn't want me to see how powerful I could be?

I cast an eye to the floor where the paintbrush landed and this time it lifts easily up to the canvas. It glides across, swiping gray paint back and forth.

I concentrate harder, trying to steady it and see if maybe I can paint something more controlled. A tree or a sunset. Not just wild strokes, but something deliberate. Purposeful.

I stare so hard at it that it quivers, and with it, my mind does too.

I get dizzy as I press harder into this new magic, forcing it out. Commanding it to move as I wish.

My breath shallows and the room starts to narrow.

Before I know what's happening, my body gives way. The paintbrush slams to the floor and I'm about to follow when the next thing I know I'm in Nox's arms.

Suddenly he's wrapped around me.

I look up at him and the room sharpens back into focus.

"You're hurt," he says.

We're close enough that I feel his breath tickling my cheeks.

He reaches out a hand, as if to touch my face, and then stops inches from me. When he remembers himself and who I am—*what* I am—he withdraws.

Nox clears his throat and steadies me back to standing, then moves a few paces back.

I press a gloved hand to my nose, trying to stopper the blood.

I don't understand.

I did it back on the ship deck with no pain. What's so different this time?

"You keep getting hurt around me," Nox says, watching my gloves turn red at the tips.

"I'm fine," I say. I can already feel the blood stopping, readying to crust and dry. "It happens sometimes when I use my power too much, or do things I haven't practiced."

Nox frowns. "It hurts you to do magic?"

His voice is rough with concern.

"It would hurt me more not to," I say honestly.

I turn and rip the ruined paper from its stand.

"Where are Micah and Irenya?"

I try to steady my voice, which for some reason feels rickety and unstable.

"They're preparing the balloon for flight," Nox says. "We'll be approaching the Polemistés whirlpools soon, so we need to get up in the air before they swallow this ship whole."

"How long?"

"Three days at most."

He won't need me for much longer, then. After we arrive and Nox finds his magical weapon, I'll be of no use to him. What if he wants to part ways after that, never to see each other again? No more adventure, no more fire at the brush of his touch.

The thought is sour in my mind.

"Soon you'll have your sword," I say, unable to help but let the bitterness seep into my voice.

"I'll have the thing to free the Six Isles," Nox corrects me. "To kill Seryth and his—"

He stops himself before he can say it, but I already know the end to that sentence. *His witch.*

My mother.

I'd almost forgotten that Nox's quest could end in her death.

"She's not evil, you know," I say.

Nox casts me a strange look. "You saw her trying to kill us."

"It's not her fault. The blood oath does things to our family."

I want him to understand. It's important that he knows me and where I come from, beyond what stories the king would have everyone believe.

"Somniatis witches have to be loyal to the king," I say. "We don't have a choice."

And my mother was kind once, I think. She braided my hair and sang me lullabies and promised she'd keep me safe.

She was kind until the day Asden walked into the Grand Hall and the king gave his order.

Thinking about Nox's father sends pangs of guilt rippling

through me. He may suspect what the king did, but he doesn't know for sure and a part of me never wants to tell him. I don't want him to suffer with that same knowledge I have of the horrors of that day. And, perhaps more selfishly, I don't want him to blame me.

I don't want to lose the way he looks at me now.

"Have you ever heard about our goddess?" I ask.

"I make it a habit not to listen to horror stories," Nox says.

Still, he takes a seat, leaning on a nearby desk as if readying to hear the tale.

"It's not a horror story," I promise. "It's a fairy tale. Just like your sword."

A legend, really.

"Long ago people used to hunt snakes for sport," I explain. "And they'd use their skin for clothing, their bodies for meat, and their teeth to fashion weapons."

Nox grimaces.

Snakes have been revered across the Six Isles since the king came to the throne. Butchering them is unimaginable to most.

"One day, while out hunting with her father, a young girl fell into a snake pit," I say, retelling the story my mother once told me. "But the girl didn't cry for help. She thought the snakes were beautiful and she knew that if she called for her father or the other villagers, the snakes would be killed. Sensing her pure soul, they bit the young girl as thanks, imbuing her with their powers of life and immortality. And so she was able to heal the people in her village and see through death's eyes to protect their futures. She was able to siphon good into the world."

"Quite the story," Nox says. "But what does that have to do with anything?"

"That's the story of Asclepina," I tell him. "The patron goddess of the Somniatis family. We're descended from a healer."

Nox's eyebrows rise, and I can see the smirk threatening to spill onto his lips. "So you're not just a princess, but a goddess too?"

"Every witch family is descended from some kind of goddess," I say.

I wish I knew any of their legends to tell him. Things to make Nox understand that witches aren't just monsters in a world of men. We were once so much more and part of me hopes there's a way we can be again.

Nox wants the sword to defeat the king and create a better world from his vengeance, and now I know I want something similar. I want to create a better world from my magic, if only I knew how.

"What happened to all those goddesses when the witches died?" Nox asks.

I shrug because my mother never told me any of that when I was younger, and by the time I was old enough to wonder, I knew better than to ask.

"Maybe they died too," I say. "Maybe the stories were all that kept them alive."

Nox bites down on the corner of his lip, like he's considering something. He's always considering things. He jumps from daring and reckless—from flying across oceans and stealing from thieves—to calculating his every movement.

He's wild when it comes to decisions and adventure, but cautious when it comes to giving anything of himself away.

Even a look. Even a moment.

"My father always said stories had the greatest power of all," Nox tells me. "He said they could never truly be destroyed."

I bite down on the edge of my lip, to keep my memories of Asden from spilling out. My own stories of him teeter on my tongue.

"I'm not proud of what my family has become and all the pain we've caused," I confess. "I don't feel good about the souls we feed to the king. But we don't have a choice and the people who come to us do."

Nox takes a long pause, his dark eyes creasing at the corners. Finally, he looks over to me and says, "You might not feel good, but there's always time for you to do good."

He looks at me like maybe he believes I could be more than I am, if only I tried.

"Do you really think that?" I ask. "That I can redeem my family's magic?"

He nods. "It's in your eyes."

"My eyes?" I ask, startled.

"I told you before, back in the After Dusk Inn. They're kind."

I blink back my surprise.

Nobody has ever said that.

People flinch when they see me. They stop and stare, or bow as I walk past so they don't have to look at me. Even the women in Armonía who color their hair to match mine don't do it because they think I'm beautiful or because they want to be like me.

They do it because I'm strange. Something *other*. They think I'm a costume and not a person.

"Look, you can't change the past or other people," Nox says. "But you can change yourself. Who you are now, today. If that's what you really want."

I've never been sure of what I want before now, but I know I can't accept things as they are anymore. Now I've seen the world outside Vasiliádes, I can't go back to pretending. To letting those around me suffer.

If I can help spare people like those on the mourning streets more pain, shouldn't I try? Maybe I'm meant to do more with my family's power than just survive. Asclepina was a healer, a warrior. Why can't I be that too?

"I want things to be better for the Six Isles," I answer truthfully.

Nox pushes himself to standing and approaches me with his fists in the air.

"First things first, we need to work on your punches," he says.

"What's wrong with my punches?" I place my hands on my hips. "My mentor taught me well."

Your father taught me well, I ache to say.

"I don't doubt your teacher was great," Nox says a little hesitantly. "It's just that in the heat of the moment, you pull a little to your left. Don't worry, it's nothing some training from the best fighter in the Six Isles couldn't fix."

I arch my neck to look behind him. "Will they be joining us anytime soon?"

Nox shoots me a look. "As though anyone could best me."

"You're so modest."

He grins. "It's part of my charm."

"You say that about all your bad traits."

Nox reaches over to pull my arms into a defensive stance.

My eyes widen in surprise at how fearlessly he reaches out for me, unafraid of my touch.

He notices me stiffen, and though his eyes soften, he doesn't let go. He brings my gloved hands slowly up in front of my face.

"Trust me," he says, as though it's the easiest thing in the world to do.

It's never been before.

But I want to trust Nox.

I already do trust him, I realize.

He slides his hands on top of mine, closing them into fists. Outside the window, the wind whistles and hums.

"Ready?" he asks.

I nod, but suddenly all I'm thinking about is how I wish I could feel the smoothness of his palms across my hands again or how warm his fingers are as they rest on top of mine.

Now more than ever I want to touch someone and experience all the things Irenya speaks of that I know aren't mine to have.

It would almost be worth seeing death again, just to have that.

I look at Nox's hand, wrapped around my now-closed fist.

"First step is to never give your enemy an opening," he says.

He throws a deliberately slow punch in my direction and I move out of the way, letting my hands fall to my sides.

Nox pulls my arms firmly back in front of my face.

"Keep your guard up," he says.

"I will," I tell him.

But though I try, I know it's already fallen.

28

SELESTRA

The balloon teeters against the moonlight as we cross the black waves of the Endless Sea.

The world up here is calm and quiet, no sign of the war below. Of all the souls, vying to cling to their mortality and escape the clutches of the king and his witch.

Soon we will arrive in Polemistés, where the fiercest warriors in the Six Isles will descend upon us. As the only people to have ever held out against the king, I don't imagine they'll be too welcoming, but Nox is determined that Polemistés holds the key to his salvation.

He believes that the sword his father spoke of, *died for*, is there and so there will be no turning around or thinking of another destination.

Where Nox goes, I go.

Staying together is the only reason we've survived this long.

"You should rest," Nox tells me, leaning over the edge of the balloon beside me. "Take note from Micah and Irenya."

He gestures to our sleeping friends, wrapped in blankets at the edge of the balloon, not at all bothered by the way the wind blows the contraption to and fro through the clouds.

"I'll sleep when you do."

"I don't sleep," Nox says with a sigh. "Not really."

"Too busy trying to save the world?" I ask.

He laughs at that, the sound carrying through the whistle of the wind so that he almost becomes a part of it. That's the thing I've noticed with Nox. Where I've just existed in this world, shut away from all the things that make it special, Nox has lived in it and become a part of it. He exists in the wind and every promise of adventure. Floating up here, where the stars make their home and the moon is a kiss away, he doesn't look out of place. He is at home in the sky.

You look like a princess.

I wrap my arms around myself, to keep away the shiver that overtakes me at the memory of his words.

"Polemistés isn't far," he says. "I can hardly believe we're so close to finding the magical weapon my father spoke of."

I pause slightly at the notion of vengeance in his voice.

It surprises me, the calm in him parting as sudden as an ocean wave to reveal something far more fatal and unyielding beneath.

"What will you do when you find it?" I ask him.

Nox squares his shoulders and draws in a steadying breath.

"Whatever it takes to bring the king to his knees," he answers.

Though he doesn't say it, I hear the unspoken words. *Even die.* Nox is willing to lay down his life for this and I'm the only thing stopping that.

Protect my son, Asden said before he died. *Don't let him pay for this.*

I don't think he realized that the person Nox would need protecting from most was himself. That despite his wishes, Nox has been paying for Asden's choices every day since.

In a way, I feel like I have too.

It's strange, but the day Asden died wasn't just the day I lost my mentor. It was the last time I ever saw a glimpse of caring in my mother, or felt the relief of her touch. Over the years, the pieces of her faded as the blood oath forced her to relent to the king. It stole her more and more over time, but still there were always parts of her, small pieces, that I could find and put back together. After that day, they disappeared completely.

Every glimpse gone.

Every light extinguished.

She never spoke of Asclepina after that, or sang me to sleep when I cried. Now she's even willing to kill me if that's what it takes.

Nox may have lost his father that day, but I think I lost my mother too.

"I'm sorry for what happened to him," I say.

"Who?" Nox asks.

"Your father."

Nox grows still. His hair tumbles into his face, but this time Nox doesn't push it away. He lets it stay there, shielding a part of him away from me.

"I miss him," he says. "And a part of me hates him too."

His voice is low and tired, as though he has ached to say this for so long.

"I hate him for giving me the burden of this grief," Nox says. "The burden of trying to end the king's reign so nobody else will ever have to go through what I have." He looks to me, brown eyes meeting mine, just as sad as his father's were. "Does that sound awful?"

I shake my head. "No."

"It seems impossible to love and hate someone so equally," he says.

I nod, running a finger across the space where my bracelet used to be. "I understand how that feels."

"I know you do," Nox says. He raises a brow. "I've met your mother."

I snort out a laugh, unable to help myself.

"I wish I knew what happened to him." Nox leans farther over the edge of the balloon, to the world that beckons below. "I know the king killed him and made it look like an accident, but if I knew what my father's final moments were truly like, how it happened and what he was thinking, then maybe it would . . . I think maybe it would give me . . ."

He pauses, searching for the right word.

"Solace?" I offer.

"Closure," he says. "For years, my every thought has been of my father. Even if we find the sword and kill the king, I'm not sure I'll ever be able to free him from my mind. How can I move on if I don't know what I'm supposed to be moving on from?"

A shard of sorrow gets lodged inside me, sharp enough that I want to wince and cry out.

If Nox discovers that I was there when his father died—worse, that I was the one who foresaw his death—he'd abandon me to the king. He wouldn't care that Asden was my friend and my teacher. He'd think all magic, including mine—*especially mine*—was evil and would never trust me again.

I want so desperately for Nox to trust me, I realize. Whatever bond tied us together to begin with has been replaced by something else, not dictated by fate, but by choice.

I don't want to lose that.

"I'm sorry I can't help you find out what happened," I say.

The betrayal slips easily from my lips.

Nox's hand shifts, moving just a moment across the balloon's edge, a fraction closer to mine. My hand aches beneath my gloves.

"You help me in other ways," Nox says.

I look at his hand, so close to mine. At his arm, his neck, his dimpled chin, until I reach his eyes.

They aren't cautious and demanding like my mother's, or dark and angry like the king's. They aren't fearful or expectant like everyone else's have always been.

They're just brown and staring straight back at me.

"I should give you another vision," I say quickly, swallowing the unsteady feeling in my chest.

Nox blinks back his surprise. It is the first time I've ever offered in place of being asked.

"Are you sure?" The concern in his voice makes my heart pound. "I know how much they affect you."

I nod. "We have to be ready for what may happen on Polemistés."

Between the island of warriors and the immortal king, it makes the most sense to be prepared. Though it isn't just that. There is a more selfish part of me that wants to give Nox a vision because I don't want to push down this craving for his touch any longer.

I pull my glove from my hand and place it into my pocket.

Nox swallows and the sound is louder than even Micah's snoring.

"Ready?" I ask him.

Nox smiles at the familiarity of the words that he has always been the first to ask. "Ready, princess," he says.

He slips his hand over the top of mine, cool with the touch of night. My heart races, every inch of me humming as his fingers slide down my hand and press against my wrist.

Wrapping around me, securing me to him.

It is the safest I have ever felt.

This time when death comes, I am ready.

We are standing on a beach, with legions before us.

The sky above roars with thunder and the clouds gather, turning a bright crimson. The Red Moon.

My mother holds out a clenched fist and I am caught in the net of her power, my arms raised in the air, frozen, like an icicle dripping from the rooftop. The wind wraps around me as she siphons its power into me, turning it from flowing breeze to chains.

"If you will not bow, you will die," she says. "You both will."

She turns to Nox and I see him on his knees, gasping out for breath. Above him, Seryth towers like a mighty statue.

"I'll give you what you crave," he says. "I'll let you meet your father again."

Then without ceremony, he picks up Nox's sword—Asden's sword—and slices it through the air.

Wordless, almost casual.

The blade cuts clean into Nox's heart.

My mother unclenches her fist and I fall to my knees.

Across the beach, Nox's eyes find mine.

Run, he mouths.

The light fades from his eyes before he hits the ground.

My breath dies in my throat.

Seryth turns to me, his eyes such a pure, bottomless black.

"Now it's your turn," he says.

"Selestra," Nox calls to me now.

This time, he doesn't rip his hand from mine to pull me from the vision.

His voice alone is enough to do that and his fingers stay laced in mine, pulse pressing steadily on my own as he coaxes me to the present.

From the worst moment I have ever seen.

"There will be a battle on the shores of Polemistés," I say, gathering my breath. "And—"

"Later," Nox says, pushing the words away as if they don't matter to him anymore. The concern in his eyes grows. "Are you all right?"

I shake my head.

His father's sword. The king is going to kill Nox with Asden's own sword and I will be powerless to stop it.

"I won't let it happen," I promise Nox.

Though he doesn't yet know what I'm talking about, his face softens. "Why do you keep saving me?" he asks.

Because we're connected by fate, I think.

But the moment I think it, everything in me screams that it's a lie.

Nox and I are connected, but it isn't the only reason I've saved his life. It isn't what drove me to search for him in the battle on the pirate ship, or what called my magic from deep inside to save him. Nor is it what makes my heart feel like it might explode at the thought of him dying on that beach.

It's because I've already seen so many people's lives ruined during the Festival of Predictions.

Because Nox reminds me of his father.

And because there is something about him, this wild boy who steals adventure from the clouds, that calls to me. It punctures through me more fiercely than any blade.

The king can't take that.

I won't let him.

29
NOX

It takes three days on Leo's butterfly before Polemistés appears over the horizon.

The island is bathed in sunlight, as if it comes straight from the golden tufts of sand that scatter around the island's border. Even with dusk ready to sweep across the world, Polemistés isn't touched by night. The fortresses of the great barricade are a shining wall of silver, made from a thousand sparks of lightning caught in their strike and tethered to the earth to create an unconquerable wall.

It's a surviving thread of wonder in a world where the king tried to stamp out any that's supposed to exist.

"Down below!" Micah yells.

I break away from the skyline to look at where he's pointing.

The waters curl and surge in a way that makes it look as though the ocean is dancing.

The whirlpools spring out from the sea like they've sensed our arrival. Six giant mouths ready to devour us.

"What are those?" Selestra asks.

Her fingernails turn white as she grips the edge of the basket.

"Those would be the whirlpools I warned you about," I say. "But don't worry, we're safe up here in Leo's butterfly."

The balloon rocks in the sky, mocking my words. I feel the shift in an instant, watching as the skyline gets higher and we only seem to get lower.

We're descending.

The whirlpools are sucking us straight from the sky.

"You just had to say it, didn't you?" Micah chides. "*We're safe up here.*" He repeats the words back to me with a scowl.

I pick up one of the many inferno pouches Leo supplied and throw it into the fires, trying to fan the flames and lift us higher into the air.

They spit blue, but rather than the balloon picking up speed and height, it continues to be dragged down.

The whirlpools are too strong.

I spin around to face Selestra, who stares down at the waters with dread in her eyes.

"You have to do something."

She jerks her focus to me. "Do what?"

"Siphon the energy from the pools, or manipulate their currents somehow," I suggest, gripping on tightly to the edge of the balloon.

Selestra shakes her head. "I can't do that, Nox."

"I bet your mother could."

Selestra scowls. "She's the *witch*," she reminds me, as though I've forgotten.

"Well, you might want to try."

We are dragged faster toward the whirlpools.

Selestra looks truly panicked.

"I've seen what you can do," I remind her.

"You saw me float a paintbrush," she says dismissively.

"You saved us from falling from the Floating Mountain." I hold my gaze steady against hers. "You saved me from those people in the tavern. And you threw that Last Army soldier from Garrick's ship."

Selestra still looks uncertain.

"We're not supposed to die here, remember?"

I rest my hand against the ship's rails, just inches from hers. A spark of warmth fills the air between us, tickling at my fingertips.

Souls, I wish I could touch her for real. No visions, no death.

"You have power," I say, firmer this time. "I've seen it. I trust it. Now you have to trust in it as well."

Selestra's breath is shaky as she turns toward the whirlpools.

She clenches her jaw, determination set firmly on her face. Her hands clench at her sides, steadying herself and her nerves too.

She closes her eyes, taking in a long and slow breath. The gusts of the sea air grow more ragged as we descend, but Selestra is unmoved.

When she opens her eyes, the balloon shudders and starts to climb.

The wind whips more fiercely around us now and Selestra barely blinks, keeping her gaze on the balloon steady as we rise.

I catch sight of her eyes and they are so bright, almost golden, like their own little fires. She pulls us up from the whirlpools' grip, higher into the air and closer toward the safety of Polemistés.

As soon as we're clear of the deadly seas, she blinks and lets out a punctured sigh.

"I did it," she says, breathless.

She presses a hand to her nose like she's expecting blood. I am too, but I don't see any, and when she pulls her arm back, it comes away clean.

Selestra told me that using her magic without practice hurt, but she doesn't look injured or weakened.

She looks strong.

"Nox, move!"

I'm pushed to my knees as Micah shoves me out of the way of a rogue arrow.

Its point misses me by mere inches and then sails through the air and into the sea.

"Can death give you a bit of a break?" Micah says.

"This isn't death," I tell him. "It's our welcome party."

A bevy of yet more arrows follows, shooting up from the island below and aiming right for us.

The Polemistés warriors are here. And they're trying to shoot us out of the air.

"Selestra, get down!" I say sharply, pulling her from sight and to the floor beside me as another arrow sails past.

Their points are deadly sharp, gleaming gold and sparking off the sunlight.

"Throw another pouch into the fire!" I command. "We have to get higher and out of their scope."

I've survived far too much to die here at the hands of a few arrows.

Micah nods and reaches for one of the last of the fire pouches on the floor, but just as he's about to throw it in, the balloon jolts sharply.

I look up and see a large tear rip its way through Irenya's mended fabric.

An arrow hangs from the broken threads.

We careen toward the land, the winds flapping through the new hole in Leo's butterfly.

"Now this would have been handy to foresee," I say.

"This is hardly my fault!" Selestra protests.

"Relax, princess. I was just trying to get the last word in before we die."

Selestra glares at me and then clenches her hands again. She closes her eyes and I can see her trying to use her powers to siphon the wind once more and save us.

But it's no use.

The balloon only picks up speed the closer we get to the ground. Selestra curses.

"Brace yourselves!" I yell, wrapping an arm around the balloon ropes.

We hit a cluster of small forestry by the beach land and I'm nearly thrown from the basket as the balloon fabric knots in the arms of a large tree.

It suspends us in the air.

"Everyone okay?" I ask.

"That's three times now," Selestra says. "Three times you've made me drop from the sky."

I shrug by way of apology. "At least we're still alive."

"Speak for yourself," Micah growls, pushing himself up to standing.

He helps Irenya to her feet and she peers over the edge of the basket. "How do we get down from here?"

"We climb," I say.

I use my sword to sever the edge from one of the balloon's many ropes. I tug it, to be sure it's steady, and am relieved when we don't move.

The balloon is well and truly jammed in this tree.

I sling the rope over the side. It doesn't quite touch the ground, but it'll bring us close enough.

I hurl a few of our bags over the edge, letting them fall onto the soft tufts of sand below. Then I hitch myself over the side.

"Come on," I say to the others. "We have to climb down before the warriors that shot us from the sky find where we've landed. I don't fancy getting one of those arrows to the face."

"Can it take our weight?" Selestra eyes the rope cautiously.

"It'll be fine," I say. "Now hurry."

She follows my lead and slips over the edge of the basket, gripping on tightly to the rope.

"If this rope snaps, I'm using you to break my fall," Selestra says through gritted teeth.

"If we hadn't cut your hair, we could've used it to climb down," I tease her.

"Don't make me push you off."

I laugh, and when I'm close enough to the ground, I let go of the rope to jump down.

I land on the blush of pink sand the color of unripened cherries. As the sun slips from the sky, the light scatters a glow of oranges into the calm waters of the nearby shore, making it seem like I'm standing by a pool of sunlight and burnt coral, on a beach of petals.

I'm energized with the beauty of this place and the knowledge that my father once wanted to walk these shores. It might be stupid to think, but I feel like the sand holds the potential of him, the idea of his footprints buried somewhere deep inside.

"We actually made it," Selestra says, coming to my side.

Her voice is filled with warmth and wonder.

Neither of us pays any mind to the shipwrecks on the far edge of the shore; bones of the vessels that came before us who couldn't penetrate the whirlpools from above like we did.

Irenya jumps down onto the sand. "Impressive," she says as Micah follows. "Not sure it's quite beautiful enough to risk our lives for though."

Micah picks up one of the bags I threw down from the butterfly. "Only I fit into that category," he tells her.

I point over to a small mass of trees. "We should make camp somewhere before nightfall truly hits. We'll head in that direction, far enough from the crash site to keep us safe until morning. Then we can think of a plan to find the sword."

I'm about to pick up one of our bags, containing some of our food supplies, when I hear the crunch of leaves underfoot. The tree branches behind are brushed aside.

Before I can draw my sword, we're surrounded.

Over two dozen Polemistés warriors rise up from the island. From the trees and from the sand and from the waters we've just soared above.

From nowhere and from everywhere.

They're dressed in suits of slim gray-white armor, covering their chests and arms. Gold markings break at the joints, a bronze arrowhead in the center of their hearts and a large set of metallic wings on the backs of their shoulders. An ashen cape ties loosely around their necks.

"Last Army," one of them sneers.

His voice is low and wolflike.

He looks to Selestra, taking in her hair and then her eyes, still alight with magic. Something in him shifts as he recognizes who she is.

"A Somniatis witch," he whispers.

It's not an accusation or an insult.

He speaks as though it's a miracle.

Selestra looks to me in panic. I can see the fear inside her threatening to spill out onto the surface. Her hand goes to the blade I gifted her, which is hooked to her belt.

"We're not here to fight," I say quickly.

Polemistés warriors are unmatched. Near unkillable. I may be good, but I don't want to risk starting a fight when we're so unprepared. And especially when we don't need to. We're on the same side, after all.

If I choose to ignore the part where they shot us out from the sky, that is.

"I'm not your enemy," I say.

The laughter courses through them and surrounds us. The birds fly from the trees and the waves crash against the shore and then quickly retreat, dragging the mottled pink sand back into its waters and away from the warriors.

"Last Army are everyone's enemy," the warrior who spoke first says.

I can tell he is the leader of this pack.

He must be in his midtwenties with a square face and muscles that bulge against the fabric of his sleeves. With a large metallic breastplate and a gleaming sword, he looks every bit the warrior as he stalks toward us.

"I'm not with the Last Army." I raise my hands in the air as a sign of peace. "Not anymore."

"We'll see about that." He turns to his warriors. "Escort them to the Forgotten Forge."

"Lucian," one of them says, eyes wide. "Are you sure that's wise? We can't trust them."

"We know what we've been told," the lead warrior—Lucian—says, nodding to Selestra. "What must come to pass is now beginning."

"What are you talking about?" I ask, stepping protectively in front of Selestra. "What must come to pass?"

"That doesn't concern you, soldier," Lucian growls, pointing his sword at my throat.

I have half a mind to rebound the hilt back into his nose.

"You're not taking her anywhere," I say.

I draw my sword, but in a flash the dozen Polemistés warriors who didn't seem to think we were worth threatening with weapons moments ago now whip their blades and daggers from their belt loops in response.

They advance closer, their eyes narrowing to vicious glares.

"Nox," Selestra says. She places a soft hand on my wrist, lowering my sword. "Stop. We didn't come all this way to die."

Her voice disarms me quicker than any of these warriors could, bringing me back to my senses and reminding me of why we're here. It isn't to fight the king's enemies: It's to help them by getting the sword and using it to defeat him once and for all.

Selestra moves in front of me, putting herself between me and Lucian's sword. His eyes widen and he lowers his weapon quickly.

They all do.

I watch them curiously.

Selestra squares her shoulders and tilts her chin up, steadying her breath as she meets the warrior's gaze.

"If we must go, let's get it over with," she says.

I smile at her bravery, facing off a dozen Polemistés warriors without blinking.

The warriors lead us onward, away from the beach and into the shallows of the trees. Lucian leads the way, but the others linger behind us and to our side, making sure we have no exit if we change our minds and choose to run.

Or at least that's what they think.

Escape is my specialty.

It doesn't take long for us to reach the Forgotten Forge Lucian spoke of. The trees soon part, the ground turning from sand, to mud, to tufts of evergreen grass with bulbous pink flowers and large circles of fruit that drip from them like brightly colored raindrops.

As we approach, I ignore the dozens of other warriors who turn to watch us with suspicion and curiosity. I focus instead on the figure, hidden partially by the shadows, standing at the archway of the forge.

A woman, cloaked in a dark hood and surrounded by soldiers.

I can't see her face fully, but I can see the soft glow of her smile.

"Your Highness."

Lucian kneels devoutly before her and the other warriors follow.

"Your Highness?" I repeat, confused.

"I thought the Southern King was dead," Micah says.

I stare at the woman before us.

"He is dead."

The lady smiles. "But I am not a king."

Her voice is dulcet and raspy.

"He had no spouse." My eyes narrow, discerning. "Who are you?"

The lady takes off her hood and I see her green hair fall across her collarbones. She steps closer toward us and into the fading sunlight.

Her eyes are aglow.

Yellow, just like Selestra's.

"I am the Lady Eldara," she says. "The Once Queen of Thavma and ward to these great lands."

That can't be.

"The Queen of Thavma is dead," Selestra says in a whisper.

I turn to her, because if this woman is telling the truth, then that means—

"Hello, niece," the old queen says, smiling. "I've been longing to meet you."

30
SELESTRA

Niece.

The woman in front of me smiles softly. There is a warmth to her that reminds me so much of my mother.

They look alike, even though this woman is far older, the beautiful creases of her face like the wrinkles of a rose petal.

I can see my mother in her.

I can see myself in her.

My great-great-grandaunt.

Her yellow eyes shift to focus in on Nox and she pulls up her sleeve to reveal a small insignia on her wrist. A sword wrapped in a serpent. I recognize it as our family's crest, the same one my mother draws on those who die in the Festival before she siphons their souls into the king.

"I hear you've been looking for me," Lady Eldara says to Nox. "You and your father too."

Nox's breath catches in his throat, like a fish caught on a hook.

"It was you," he says.

His voice is heavy with something like hope, or excitement. Silly things only a fool would feel with death on the horizon.

I don't care who she says she is, there's an army ready to kill us at this woman's command.

"You're the sword of the Southern Isle," Nox says.

"Wait, *she's* the sword?" Micah says, voicing all of our confusion. "How does that make sense?"

"The magical weapon I've been looking for isn't a thing," Nox says. It's like a light brightens in his eyes. He gestures toward the sword on Eldara's wrist. "It's a person."

I don't like the way he looks at her.

It's dangerous, showing every vulnerability he's always worked so hard to hide before. Everything I know of my family says they're not to be trusted, so if this woman is telling the truth, that only makes it worse.

"You're supposed to be dead," I say. "Isolda Somniatis killed you."

Her sister. My great-great-grandmother.

"And yet here I survive," Lady Eldara says. "Using the last sparks of magic my sister couldn't take, so I can empower Polemistés and fight against a king of souls."

"We were told that Isolda drained your magic," Irenya says. "It's the story all of us hear as children."

Irenya moves to my side and I can tell she's trying to gauge how I feel, but truthfully I don't know. The only family I've ever known is my mother. We were supposed to be the last of our line.

Everything about my life has been made of lies.

"Isolda took most of my power," Lady Eldara says. "But I still have enough in me to do some good."

I wince at the word *good*.

Eldara has stayed hidden safely here, protecting Polemistés from the king, but she did nothing to protect our family from him.

To protect me.

A sad smile makes its way onto Eldara's rosy lips. It's as though she knows just what I'm thinking.

"Come," she says gently. "We have much to discuss."

She heads inside the forge and gestures for us to follow. She glides as she walks, feet slipping across the stone floors as she leads us to a small room away from the furnaces and metal workers.

If it were up to me, we wouldn't follow her anywhere, but Nox is practically racing after her. He can see the end of his battle for vengeance in whatever she has to say, and I'm not going to leave him alone with her.

I don't trust her enough for that.

The room we settle in is bare, the walls made of brown stone with nothing but a handful of wicker chairs inside, and a circular table that sits across from a small fire. There is a teapot brewing beside it.

"You're right to be cautious," Eldara says as she sits down on the chair closest to the fire.

Lucian hovers by the door, keeping a watch on us.

He's protective of his queen.

"What do you know of me, niece?" she asks.

I wish she'd stop calling me that.

"I know the same story everyone in the Six Isles does," I say. I don't take a seat with the others. "King Seryth was a warrior who fell in love with Isolda Somniatis, and together they decided the rulers of the Six Isles were unjust and unworthy. So they killed them. First the queen of Thavma. Then the rest, siphoning their powers and their souls."

Condemning the world, though the king likes to speak as though he was righteous.

"As you can see, they did not manage to kill me," Eldara says. She pours herself some tea. "But do you believe that if they had, it was because I was unjust?"

I cross my arms over my chest. "I don't know what to believe."

"That's smart," she says. "All the world is a lie. It is only ever what we wish it to be."

I stiffen as Eldara holds out a cup to me. I squeeze my fists together and Nox must notice, because he stands and his hand moves closely beside mine. Not touching, but letting me know he's there. Making me feel safe again.

"What really happened during the True War?" he asks.

Eldara places her cup carefully down and sighs. "Years ago, the king of Polemistés was chosen by who was the strongest warrior," she explains. "One of those warriors, Seryth, was mighty and powerful, but even he couldn't defeat the king. So he left in search of magic to bolster his strength and make him worthy of the crown."

It's not the story I've heard, of the noble warrior who set out to save the Six Isles from the terror of the witch queen, but it is far more believable.

"He came to Thavma and there he found my sister."

Eldara's voice turns mournful.

"Isolda felt she would be better placed as ruler and that with all the power our land had, we should have conquered every island there was. She couldn't understand why our people used our powers self-lessly or why I taught peace. Isolda wanted more. She was hungry for it. So she and Seryth made a deal to combine their strengths and conquer all."

I take this in.

Her sister betrayed her, stole her throne, and burned it to ash, and yet she looks sad instead of angry, as though the thing she regrets most is that she couldn't save Isolda from herself.

Did I have the same look when I jumped from the castle window and left my mother behind?

"Seryth and Isolda tore through Thavma," Eldara explains. "She siphoned the life and magic from every witch on our lands, into her-self and Seryth, until they were bursting with power."

Until they made sure that Isolda was the only witch left in the king-doms, I think.

Our family. Our blood.

Leaving us alone with the power to rule.

My family's past is steeped in death and betrayal. Isolda turned on her sister, just like my mother turned on me.

That's my legacy: greed and deceit.

How do I fight against a past as powerful as that?

"But when they attacked Vasiliádes, Seryth and Isolda were drained in the battle. Weakened, Seryth pleaded with my sister for a way to have truly everlasting life. With all the magic of Thavma lost and her own power dwindling, there was only one way. My sister siphoned the power of the Red Moon itself," Eldara says. "That is how her spell survives after her death. The magic feeds from the moon and with that the souls are bound to Seryth for eternity."

Eldara shakes her head, like she wishes she could talk her sister out of it, even now.

"In order to remain immortal, Seryth must devour one hundred souls each year," Eldara says. "He can only do so during the month of the Red Moon, when Isolda's spell is renewed. The souls must be tied to him, and so you collect hair. It's also why he allows people who survive the halfway mark to escape the bargain; because one hun-dred souls are all he requires for immortality. He acts as though he is generous in letting them go, but it is all simply a ploy to make people think they stand a chance at survival and encourage more to come to the next Festival, so he will always have souls at the ready."

"What about stealing his immortality?" Nox asks. "The bargain states that whoever survives the month can take his power for them-selves. Is it true?"

"Yes," Eldara says. "It's not just that you are bound to Seryth, but that he is bound to you. If he does not devour a soul tied to him, then the bargain is broken and Isolda's spell will transfer to you. That is the weakness of my sister's magic. And the arrogance of Seryth that he would reveal it, believing it could never be possible."

"So if Nox survives the Red Moon, the king dies?" Micah asks.

"Indeed. The Festival is Seryth's salvation, but it can be his undoing," Eldara says. "We must keep Nox alive until the Red Moon, whatever the cost, so that Seryth's immortality will be stripped."

I cross my arms defiantly over my chest. "I was doing that long before you asked me to."

Eldara nods. "Because you have a gift that none who came before took advantage of," she says. "The magic my sister used was a pollution of Asclepina's powers. It started to drain her own life force, and so she vowed that when she died each generation of her bloodline would continue to draw souls to preserve Seryth's immortality once they turned eighteen."

Though her voice is soft and delicate, Eldara's words are a cutting reminder that I'm cursed.

"She bound us to him," I say, my heart heavy. "What gift is that?"

Eldara's face softens, as though she's sorry she can't share my fate.

"You are not yet eighteen," she says. "You are not bound. You are free and that is the greatest gift."

I hate how sure she sounds when she says it, because I have never been truly free until these past weeks with Nox. My life until then was a prison under the pretense of destiny.

"My magic is old and tired," Eldara explains. "I'm not long for this world and so it falls to you to take my place and help Polemistés fight, Selestra. Like mine, your magic has no allegiance to him. So you must be the one to destroy him."

"*Me?*" I ask, stunned.

Though I want to help Nox's quest, years spent in hiding must have truly addled Eldara's brain if she thinks I'm capable of taking on the king and his armies.

I came to Polemistés to escape a war, not lead one.

"You will rule in my place as queen," Eldara declares. "You were always destined to be my heir, not Seryth's. After you defeat him, you will take the throne and—"

"Wait, stop," I interrupt, shaking my head. "I came here to find freedom, whatever that means, but you can't just task me with destroying my home and killing a king who has imprisoned the world for a century. I'm sixteen years old," I remind her. "I don't know the first thing about war or being a *queen*."

Eldara's smile doesn't slip from her face. "It is your destiny," she says. She looks to Nox. "Both of you."

"You want me to be your queen too?" he asks, raising an eyebrow.

"Aren't you here to fight?" Eldara asks, growing impatient. "To battle for vengeance and free the Six Isles in the name of your father?"

Nox eyes her with mistrust. "How do you know that?"

"Visions run in the family," Eldara says. "Now we have much to do before the battle comes. The trials, for one, will be a great challenge when you're so unprepared, but I'm sure that—"

"What trials?" I ask, cutting her off.

"The trials you must face in order to earn the true wisdom of our goddess, Asclepina," Eldara announces. "Every past queen has taken them. I shouldn't be surprised your mother wouldn't have mentioned them, but they will help you unlock your true power and inherit the essence of our goddess. It will aid you in the fight against Seryth."

"Wait, slow down," I snap, holding up a hand. "I can't even float a paintbrush without getting a nosebleed, let alone face magical trials."

"That's only because you aren't practiced," Eldara tells me. "You have not been taught the right way. I suspect you've been siphoning power from yourself, when really you should have been siphoning from the world around you, like your mother surely does."

"From the world?" I repeat.

I blink as I take in what she's saying. Suddenly it all makes sense.

That's the reason I could throw the soldier from Garrick's ship and how I managed to float the butterfly away from the whirlpools: I siphoned power from the wind. But when I tried to float the paintbrush, I was drawing from inside myself.

That's why it weakened me and why I've been getting nosebleeds and why healing Irenya took so much out of me.

I was siphoning off my own strength for her.

Why would my mother hide this from me? Why wouldn't she want me to know the truth about what my power could do?

I know the answer as soon as I think it: the king.

He didn't want to be outnumbered. Heirs are so much easier to control than true witches.

"We don't have long," Eldara tells us. "Nox's time is ticking away and death is impatient."

"So no pressure, then," Nox says.

He gives me a teasing smile and I want to laugh, but inside I am shaking. I am withering with the weight of this new responsibility.

"There is little more than a week until the month is over," Eldara says, unamused. "If you survive past then, it will undo my sister's magic. Seryth cannot risk that and so he will attack us with all he has. If Selestra faces the trials, she'll be given enough power to stop him before he can kill you."

My head spins with the weight of what she is saying.

I meant it when I told Nox I wanted to help change things, but having an entirely new destiny thrust upon me isn't what I had in mind. Just a few weeks ago I thought I was destined to steal souls at the king's side and help trap the Six Isles in death. Now I'm on an island of warriors with a runaway soldier, being told that it's my job to lead them all into battle and destroy the kingdom I was once supposed to preserve.

"I need time to think about this," I say.

"Very well." Eldara nods. "But we don't have long and you must complete the trials before Seryth attacks. Take comfort in knowing that this is your birthright, Selestra."

It's no comfort at all.

I want to ask Eldara how she can be so sure that I'm worthy of such a destiny, without even knowing me. If the king has taught me anything, it's that someone should earn the right to rule, rather than having it handed to them, stealing it through lies and brutality. The last thing the Six Isles needs is another leader who doesn't deserve it.

Even if I could lead, why would they want to follow?

Eldara's frown grows deep, as though she can sense all my doubt and hesitation.

"Please, Selestra," she says. "Without you, Polemistés will fall."

31

NOX

I can't sleep.

I'm not sure how late it is, but Micah has been snoring beside me for hours.

I'm used to not sleeping. I haven't been able to get more than a couple of hours at a time since my father died, but I'm not used to being too excited to sleep.

With the end of this quest so close, all I can think about is that I stand a real chance of finally fulfilling my father's dying wish.

And Selestra holds the key.

If she agrees to do the trials Lady Eldara proposed and become queen, then we could have all the power we need to kill Seryth and rescue the Six Isles.

I get out of bed.

Micah shifts in his bunk and mumbles something to himself. I shake my head, treading lightly as I leave the room so that I don't wake him.

Selestra's room is only a few doors down the narrow hallway. I hesitate before knocking, wondering if maybe she's asleep already. I don't want to wake her, but we have to talk. If I don't say what I need to say, then I'll be up staring at my ceiling until the sun rises.

Thankfully, the door creaks open and Selestra pokes her head out from the other side.

"What are you doing here?" she asks in a whisper.

She's wearing a long white nightgown that brushes to the floor, and her green hair swings by her chin, catching the moonlight that streams in through the open window. She is so beautiful it catches me off guard.

For a moment I just blink and stare at her.

Then I remember to actually *speak*.

"Do you want to go for a walk?" I ask.

Selestra leans back into the room and I see a sleeping Irenya hug the covers closer as the breeze from the open door wafts in.

"Hang on," Selestra whispers to me.

She grabs a nearby blanket and wraps it around her shoulders, then steps out, closing the door softly behind her.

"Is Micah snoring again?" she asks.

She was subjected to it just as often on Leo's butterfly.

"He sounds like a blow horn," I say. "I should stuff a sock in his mouth."

"And put a peg on his nose," she suggests.

"I'll bear that in mind for the next time."

We walk down the narrow hall of the sleeping quarters and out into the moonlight. The stars are brighter than I've ever seen them in Vasiliádes.

We take a seat on the steps by the forge and I waste no time in asking what's been on my mind.

"Have you thought about what Lady Eldara said?"

"Not you too," Selestra says in a sigh.

I laugh. "Oh, come on, princess. I had to ask."

"I wish you'd stop calling me that," she says in a frown.

"Would you prefer queen?"

Selestra shoots me a look. "That's not funny, Nox."

"No, it's not," I admit.

She wraps the blanket tighter around herself and breathes in a shaky breath.

"I know that you're scared," I say carefully. "I am too."

Selestra raises her eyebrows, not believing that for a moment. "*You're* scared?"

"Okay, not scared," I relent. "I'm far too manly for that."

Selestra scoffs.

"But I understand you're worried," I say, turning serious. "You have every right to be."

"I just don't know what to do," she admits.

"Do what's right," I say simply. "This could be the way to change things for the better, like you said you wanted to. Use your magic for something good."

"I meant helping you find a sword, not becoming queen," she protests.

"Well, technically we did find the sword," I say. "It just happened to be your aunt."

Selestra groans. She looks down at her gloved hands and a note of anguish passes across her face. "My whole life, I feel like I've been crafted from other people's stories. From their wants and expectations," she says. "Everything has been about pretend and threats from people trying desperately to cling to power."

That takes me by surprise.

Surely Selestra doesn't think Eldara is anything like the king.

"I don't know who I am," she says, sounding more tired than I've ever heard her. "I was the king's heir. My mother's heir. And now I'm supposed to be Eldara's heir?" Her voice wavers. "I just feel caught up between who everyone else wants me to be."

The lost look in her eyes makes me shift.

"I know who you are," I say firmly, surprised by the surety in my own voice. "You're Selestra Somniatis. Descended from queens and goddesses. You don't have to be anyone that you don't want to."

"You really believe that?" Selestra asks, sounding every bit like she doesn't.

"What I believe doesn't matter. It's about what you believe."

Selestra squeezes her hands together. "What if I let everyone down?"

"Then we all die," I say with a shrug. "Personally, I vote for you to succeed."

Selestra smiles in spite of herself. "That really takes the pressure off," she says. "Thank you."

"I just want to make sure you know the stakes," I tell her, voice as earnest as can be. "The stakes being my life, of course. Which is extremely important to me."

Selestra shakes her head, but I can see the daring easing its way back into her eyes, replacing the doubt that was there before.

"I think you place far too much importance on yourself."

"Not possible," I say. "I'm the most important person in my life. And if you're not, then you're doing it wrong."

Selestra's laughter blows across to me. "You're unbelievable."

"And you're a queen," I remind her. "If you want to be."

Selestra bristles, but she doesn't look away. Her eyes lock onto mine.

"I believe in you," I tell her, and I truly mean it. "Even if you don't believe in yourself yet."

"You do?" Selestra looks uncertain.

I'm a little surprised by my words too. I started this quest with every intention of killing Selestra once I killed the king, but somewhere along the way I found myself wanting to protect her instead.

Selestra isn't just a witch. She isn't just a girl, but a maze. A never-ending pathway of possibility, and I can feel myself getting lost in her.

With each day that goes on, every guard I try to keep up tumbles. Even now, when I'm supposed to be convincing her to take this crown so I can get what I want and avenge my father, I find myself wanting her to have faith in herself instead. She has saved my life again and again. Though she may think she is a product of what everyone wants her to be—her mother, Seryth, even Eldara—I've seen firsthand that she is nothing like any of them. I've seen the fire inside her.

"I believe in you," I say again.

Selestra brushes her hair from her face in a sigh.

"There's something I've been hiding from you," she says.

She looks cautiously at me.

"Oh?" I ask. "What's that, then?"

I don't expect her to slip off a glove and hold her palm up to the moon. Or to see the king's mark imprinted on her skin. My eyes go wide and I shuffle closer to her, to make sure I'm seeing right.

"How did you get that?"

The mark of the Festival.

"It appeared the first time I saw your death," she says. Then she shakes her head and shrugs off the blanket, like she's shrugging off a weight. "The first time I saw *our* deaths," she corrects herself.

"Ours?"

I'm not prepared for what she says next.

"I saw myself die that day too," Selestra confesses. "At the tavern, in the fire. We were both meant to perish. I thought that by saving you I'd somehow save myself."

I look back down at the snake on her palm, twinned to mine.

"So that's why you've been helping me?" I ask. I can't help but be a little disappointed. "To keep your own life safe?"

"That was why at first," she answers honestly, quickly. "But eventually I started saving you because I wanted to. I care about you, Nox," she says. "And I'm not a monster. I'm not heartless."

I'm not my mother, I hear her say.

"I know," I tell her.

Selestra is nothing like Theola or any notions I ever had of a witch.

"It happened again the night you came to my room," she says. "I saw myself die alongside you in the castle."

I can't help but laugh and Selestra blinks in surprise.

"What's so funny?"

"Nothing," I say, sobering up my voice. "It just makes a lot more sense now why you wanted me to take you along for the ride."

"I drowned beside you after being thrown from Garrick's ship too," she says. "Every vision I have of your death shows me mine too."

Suddenly a lot of things start to make sense. Especially why Selestra always had such a visceral reaction to the futures she saw in me. I can't imagine what it must have been like for her to have to see her own deaths, especially by her own mother's hand.

Despite all that, she still tried to save my life.

Again and again, even though it risked hers.

"There's nobody quite like you," I tell her honestly.

"That's the problem," she says in a bitter laugh. "I don't want to be strange, Nox. I want to fit into the jigsaw of the world and not worry about being the right shape or color. I want to be part of something."

"You are part of something."

Selestra takes in a breath and blinks up at me. "Will you stay by my side if I do the trials?"

I nod. "I will."

She holds my gaze, tethering me to the moment. I'm struck with the sudden urge to reach out and touch her.

I want to feel her without it bringing about some stupid death vision.

"We should head back inside," she says in a delicate whisper. "Get some sleep before I make my decision."

It's the last thing I want to do.

"I don't sleep," I remind her.

She bites her lip. "Everyone sleeps, Nox."

"Not me."

I look into her eyes, where I once stupidly thought there was only ever cold and dark. Now all I can see is brightness and fire.

I swallow and lean toward her. Her breath brushes my lips and my heart is like thunder in my chest as I reach out a hand for her cheek.

Then she pulls back.

She looks down at the mark on her palm.

"Are you worried about the visions?" I ask, shifting back.

She shakes her head. "No," she says. "I mean, yes. But that's not it. It's *you* who shouldn't want to do this."

"Why not?"

I can't imagine anything she'd say could make this hunger for her disappear.

I want this.

I want *her*.

Selestra's hands tremble and when she takes in her next breath, it's almost like she chokes on it.

"Nox, about your father—"

"Don't," I say, stopping her.

The last thing I want to think of right now is vengeance, or what Selestra's mother and the king did.

For the first time in years, I want to forget about that.

"Can we not be who we are tonight?" I ask her. "Not a soldier out for vengeance, or the king's heir. Let's just be us, without the past weighing us down."

I can see the hesitance in her eyes.

Maybe I'm a fool for thinking we can do something as complicated as starting fresh, but I find myself thinking a lot of foolish things around her lately.

I take Selestra's hand in mine and plant a kiss on her gloved fingers.

"You were right," I say, not wanting to push her. "We should go inside and rest."

Souls knows we're going to need it. The king's army can't be more than a few days behind us, and with Theola by his side, it won't be long before he's able to bypass the whirlpools and infiltrate Polemistés.

This sanctuary we've found won't last.

Sooner or later, the death Selestra predicted will come for us.

32

SELESTRA

"I want you to tell me exactly what the trials entail."

We're sitting in a small glass tea room in the middle of a large garden with sunflowers the height of trees. The sun is just pushing itself off the horizon, casting a pink glow across the fields of Polemistés.

"Nobody can say for certain," Eldara tells me. "The trials are tailored to the witch and the skills and lessons she needs to learn."

"You can't even tell me whether or not it's going to be rivers of fire or deadly forest creatures?" I ask, disbelieving. "What trials did you face before you ascended to queen?"

Eldara laughs, more to herself than me. My lost aunt reaches over the small table to pour me a cup of peppermint tea.

"My trials were my own," she says. "As will yours be."

I sigh and blow on my cup.

"What made you decide you were ready?" Eldara asks. She sips slowly on her tea, a look of quiet mischief in her eyes. "If you're questioning what the trials are, I assume that means you are willing to take them on. Why the change of heart?"

Nox, I think, though I don't say it.

I may have spent all of yesterday learning more about my great-aunt and her warriors, who have outsmarted the king for lifetimes, and then debating the pros and cons of ruling a kingdom with Irenya into the early hours of morning, while eating what might have been the best almond cake I've ever tasted—but none of it compared to my talk with Nox.

He had so much trust in his eyes when he came to me the other night. I've never had someone believe so openly in what I could be capable of. My mother and the king spent a lifetime lying to me and convincing me I was weak and would be worthless until I became the true witch.

Nox thinks I can be a queen. He has faith in me, for better or worse, and that makes me want to have faith in myself.

If I want to change this kingdom for the better, I can't keep letting my doubts overrule me.

I have to believe in my power. The Six Isles depends on it.

"You must be certain, if we are to proceed," Lady Eldara says.

"I am."

My jaw hardens in determination as I think back to what Nox said about not holding on to our pasts.

"I want to fix what our family has broken."

Eldara's face dawns in understanding. After what her sister did, she knows better than anyone how important it is to make amends. It's up to us to ensure that the Somniatis line can stop being used for evil.

"Just to be clear, this doesn't mean I'm agreeing to be anyone's queen," I clarify quickly. "But I know we need more power and these trials will give us that."

"Indeed," Eldara says. "If you succeed, they will allow you to truly be one with Asclepina and earn your right to the crown. What you decide to do with it afterward is up to you."

"Assuming I don't die."

Eldara scowls at me, as if to tell me not to even joke about things like that.

"Fate has brought you to me so we can save the future of our lands," she says softly. "It's all part of the goddess's plan."

Eldara nods to my palm, to the king's mark, which I finally revealed to her this morning.

I feel it tingle.

"You think my visions and the shared fate with Nox are a message from Asclepina?" I ask.

Eldara nods.

"Is she what led you here too?"

At this, Eldara sets her cup firmly down, her face turning severe. "I was not led by destiny," she says. "But by cowardice."

I haven't known her long, but even I can tell this firm and unforgiving tone isn't normal.

Eldara is soft and gentle, but now her voice turns to something else.

"My sister was not the only one in our family who fell for a Polemistés warrior," she explains. "When the attacks started on Thavma, I fled here, to my love. And here we stayed, while my sister and Seryth laid waste to Thavma's witches and conquered the islands. I helped Polemistés fight against it the best I could. I placed whirlpools around this island to protect it, but when Seryth killed my love years ago, I knew my time was limited too."

It dawns on me in that moment that Eldara is ashamed, not only of her sister but of how she fled and left her kingdom to be destroyed.

"What was Thavma like?" I ask her, desperate to know more about where my family once came from. "What were our people like?"

All the stories my mother once told me were about the magic and how it lit up the sky like bursts of fire, but she never spoke of the people.

Eldara's face softens at the memory. "They were peaceful," she says. "We used our powers to help others escape danger and heal their injuries. All the witches on Thavma used magic for good, from the fire starters who warmed the lands to those with nature magic who nurtured our crops. We had an accord with many kingdoms beyond the Endless Sea, including those with great ice mountains and princes whose blood runs with gold Chrim. The sirens steered clear of our island and never attacked, for our veins both shared magic. When the king and Isolda cursed our waters, they shut us away from the rest of the world and all its creatures, so he could keep the magic of our lands for himself."

This shocks me.

I've only ever known the Six Isles. To imagine a wider world out there makes my heart leap. To imagine *sirens* and other magical creatures.

What more has the king been hiding to keep us all prisoners?

"If the king is powerful enough to do that, are you sure we can defeat him?" I ask. "What if the magic the trials gives me isn't enough?"

"You're stronger than you know," Eldara tells me, unwavering. "It's clear you were having visions before Nox. So what age did you come into your magic?"

"Fourteen," I say.

I shrink at the memory of that day with Asden, but Eldara looks proud.

"A vision that young is rare, Selestra. Witches do not usually come into their powers until at least sixteen. Is that not proof of how special you are?"

The words aren't a comfort. She doesn't know what a horror it was for me. The last thing I want is to be reminded of the day that I lost so much.

"It is impressive," a voice says.

I turn to see Nox and Micah step into Eldara's tea room, sweaty from their morning training.

My heart jumps at the sight of Nox.

I can't help but think how he kissed my hand the other night and tried to kiss me. I wanted it more than I've wanted anything in a long time.

I wish I would've let him.

"What was the vision?" Nox asks, brushing the dirt from his arms. "Did you foresee me kicking Micah's ass in training this morning? Because that really was a sight to behold."

Nox gives me a teasing smile as Micah rolls his eyes and mutters "Hah-hah-hah" as sarcastically as he can.

I want to laugh alongside them, but inside I'm shaking. I'm withering at the thought of that day.

"What visions was the king trying to get out of you at fourteen?" Nox asks, resting his sword in the gravel. "Souls, that man is a monster."

I don't answer. I don't know how.

"Selestra?" Nox asks, taking in my nerves.

He stares at me, and I wonder if my silence alone conveys all the things I want to hide from him the most.

I look quickly away from him, unable to bear the sudden scrutiny of his gaze.

"What was the vision?" he presses.

I don't answer. I don't know how.

Not now, I think.

Not after he's started to see me as more than a witch.

Not after he kissed my hand and looked into my eyes without flinching.

I will myself to look back at him. "I've wanted to tell you for a while," I say. "The other night, I tried. But I just couldn't find the words."

"The other night?"

Nox frowns, and I swallow loudly at the thought of causing him more pain by dredging up the past.

"The other night?" Micah looks between us. "What happened the other night?"

"Your father," I say to Nox. I hate the feeling of disgust that sinks into me as I force myself to finally reveal the truth. "I want to tell you what really happened that day."

A sudden gloom twitches onto Nox's face.

"Wait," he says. "This is about my father?"

I nod.

The realization washes over him like a storm. "You know how he died."

It isn't a question, but when I push my lips together to keep from crying, he can see he has his answer. A curtain pulls across his face, and where a moment ago there was laughter, there is now shock.

His eyes are full of betrayal.

"You lied to me," he says.

I recoil at the truth of it.

I should have told him two nights ago during our talk, or back on the balloon when he told me how much it pained him not to know about his father, but I was too selfish to risk losing him.

I stand and Nox's hand twitches by his sword—by Asden's sword. I wouldn't blame him if he tried to press that blade against my throat and make me feel the pain that my family has caused him.

But he doesn't.

"Tell me what happened," Nox says. Practically pleads.

I steel my breath. He has been waiting years to know this.

"Your father trained me in secret behind the king's back," I explain, the truth finally spilling out of me after all this time. "He was my mentor."

Nox remains silent, his breath shallow.

"Two years ago, the king called him to the throne room. I thought he wanted to punish him because he knew what we'd been doing," I say. "But it was something else. The king discovered Asden was planning to look for a magic that could hurt him. He made me look into your father's future and I saw him dying right there in the throne room."

The words are like acid in my throat. The memory is just as awful to relive for a second time.

"Before I knew it, my mother was siphoning out his soul," I finish.

"He was still alive?"

Nox looks pained.

I blink.

"When they took his soul," Nox says slowly, sounding broken at the thought. "Was my father still alive?"

I nod, and I see every nightmare in his eyes suddenly coming true.

Nox must have imagined the moment his father died a thousand times over the years, but to know that his last moments were this terrible must break him.

How could he ever find his solace now?

"You knew my father," he says in disbelief. "When I told you how much it meant for me to know his final moments, did you not think I deserved that? I thought we were . . ."

He breaks off and my heart aches to ask: *Thought we were what?*

"I trusted you," he says, like an accusation.

"You can still trust me," I promise him. "We can defeat the king, just like you planned."

"My plan was to kill you," Nox admits, not cruelly but as though it's a simple fact. "When we first met, I thought all witches were evil and you deserved to die alongside your mother. But you changed my mind. You made me think there was such a thing as a good witch."

I step toward him, but Nox holds up a hand to stop me from getting any closer.

He has never looked at me the way he does now.

"I was wrong," he says.

I press my lips together to keep from shattering.

"You must not fight," Eldara says.

She moves toward us like water, gliding across the floor. Her voice is so serene it chafes against the grief ravaging the air.

"You must stay by each other's side," she says to Nox. "Selestra must protect you and you must support her rule."

"I no longer trust her enough for that," Nox says. "We can defeat the king, but it won't be by each other's side."

Around us, the sunlight sways and flashes through the windows, the breeze from the open arch knocking it back and forth. It turns the tea room from dark to light and then back again, the rising sun still unable to reach its crevices.

The shadows dance across Nox's face as he stares at me.

"You'll never be my queen," he says.

He casts one last look at me and I see the conviction in his eyes. The grief, so similar to the look Asden had that day.

Then Nox turns and leaves me to the shadows.

33

NOX

It's been a long time since I've been stabbed. Or surprised.

Over the years I've perfected the art of staying alive and knowing when the blows were going to come. My father trained me every morning to always be my best and do my best. There was no other option.

The Six Isles are not a place for people to be average or forgotten, he used to tell me. *The king doesn't let the unworthy live.*

He taught me to be an expert swordsman, so I would always be prepared for a fight, but he never taught me how to prepare for betrayal.

The sound of metal screaming against metal ricochets through the small amphitheater of the Polemistés training grounds, encircled by grassy steps where a crowd gathers.

"This is a bad idea," Micah says. "At least wear some armor or something. That Polemistés soldier looks like a tin can."

I shake my head. "I'm not used to it. It'll weigh me down."

"It'll keep you alive," Micah says in a huff.

I eye the man in the center of the amphitheater.

Lucian Crowe. My opponent.

The very first warrior to threaten my life when we arrived five days previous.

We were pitted against each other just moments ago. Me as the Last Army traitor and him as one of five reigning Polemistés champions. It's supposed to be a simple sparring match, but Lucian's sword is at the ready, a zealous gleam in his eyes as he points it at me.

We both agreed to sharp iron instead of blunted fencing gear, as is the Polemistés way. The training ground is at the border of their forest and it seems the warriors make it a point to look tough in the face of the ghosts that roam there.

Staring at me now, Lucian smirks.

No doubt, he's eager to show some Last Army soldier what it means to be a true champion. Or maybe he just wants to beat one of the king's men. Either way, he looks eager and arrogant.

And those are two things I can use.

Eager men are too quick to think, and arrogant men don't think much at all.

"You don't need to do this," Micah says.

But I do.

It's not just that I have something to prove, but I have something to get out of me. After what happened with Selestra, I've spent the last three days alone with my anger. I *need* this fight.

This release.

Micah holds out my sword to me. "You know, if you're that bothered about Selestra, you could kill her instead of getting yourself killed," he says.

I snatch the sword from him, not appreciating the bad attempt at a joke.

Just hearing her name sets me on edge.

"She lied to me."

Micah only rolls his eyes. "You both make a habit of lying to each other every chance you get. You were planning to kill her."

"That stopped being my plan a long time ago," I say.

I hadn't thought about betraying Selestra since we left the castle. Yet she looked me in the eye when I spoke of my father and told me that she knew nothing.

I step into the center of the ring.

The training grounds are filled with a handful of other warriors. I scan them briefly and it only takes a moment before I find what I'm looking for.

On the low steps, above where the other warriors stand to watch, Lady Eldara is perched. She looks down at me, smiling ever so slightly.

Beside her is Selestra.

She's easy to spot. It's not just her hair or her eyes making her stand out. It's more than that.

Sometimes I almost feel like I can sense her.

I grit my teeth.

She's dressed in a white tunic that goes right up to her chin and I watch as she fidgets nervously with her gloves.

I don't meet her eyes.

I can't.

I know it'll throw me off balance.

"I don't remember." Lucian paces in circles around me. "Do Last Army soldiers bleed easily?"

I bite back a smile when I look at him. "I really couldn't say. Nobody's managed it in a while."

"When I cut you, all the warriors of the island will cheer." Lucian licks his lips. "They'll be glad to see Seryth's precious soldier bleed. A failed warrior with a failed army."

"It's possible," I say.

I stick my sword into the orange sand and lean an elbow on the hilt.

I like hearing him talking about the king like he's a failed peer, rather than a royal. In Polemistés they don't see Seryth as someone to be feared. To them, he is weak. He couldn't win their crown and so he tried to take the world instead.

They pity him.

"Don't worry, little soldier." Lucian continues circling me. "I won't spill too much of that precious blood. The Lady Eldara still thinks you have some use left in you."

"I appreciate that."

Lucian juts his sword out toward me without warning and I only just slide out of the way in time, rolling onto the sand.

I pick up my own sword and crash it against his, but Lucian blocks it easily.

"Too slow," he says.

I hit him again by way of response and he stumbles slightly, but easily gets his sword back in the air.

I make to hit him again, slowly and clumsily, but he swerves out of the way.

He grins at me.

Good, I think. *Let him smile.*

If I pull back enough, he'll get cocky.

It's easier sometimes, to let someone think they have the upper hand or to wait until they wear themselves out.

Though Lucian doesn't look like there's a possibility of him being worn out any time soon.

The old-fashioned way, then, I think. *I'll beat him by simply being better.*

"Again?" asks Lucian.

"Sure." My voice is breezy. "Whenever you've got a minute."

He lunges toward me, sword aimed for my shoulder, sudden as a rock slide. But what Lucian doesn't realize—what nobody in this crowd does—is that I'm faster.

I trained every day to be.

Quickly, I bring my sword over my head in a graceful loop, blocking Lucian's blow.

Furious, he swings again, harder, but I hold my ground, refusing to fall back. I take a step forward and cut my blade through the air, narrowly missing Lucian's cheek.

I have him on the defense.

Lucian darts backward. His footwork is impressive, but I'm unforgiving, surging forward two steps for every one of his. With a determined breath, Lucian blocks my sword and then uses his free hand to punch me square in the face.

I stumble back a few steps, surprised, and touch my lip.

No blood, thankfully.

The warriors cheer, their expressions joyous. They are savoring each moment, and the more violent and dishonorable things become, the more they smile.

I catch Selestra's gaze on the steps.

Her eyes are narrowed and I could almost swear there is a look of fury in her eyes.

Fire.

Lady Eldara places a hand on her shoulder.

"Ready for more?" asks Lucian.

I meet his smirk with one of my own.

So he's playing dirty, then.

Dirty, I can do. I have ample practice in that.

When the champion's sword meets mine again, I use my left hand to grab his wrist and yank his guard down. I twist it, hard, and Lucian yelps in pain.

Then, with little grace, I slam the hilt of my sword into his nose.

His hand flies up to his face as blood gushes from his nostrils.

"Well," I tell him. "I didn't promise not to spill any of *your* blood."

"Just like a Last Army soldier to play dirty," Lucian says.

"Not to sound like a child, but you started it."

Lucian wipes the blood onto his sleeve. "Are you trying to impress Lady Selestra with those moves?"

I grip my father's sword tighter, letting it tether me to the world. Without it, I feel like I might just keel over at the sound of her name.

"I'm not trying to impress anyone," I say.

"Then what is it you want?" Lucian asks. He's goading me, I know it. "I'm sure it isn't to help us in this fight."

I don't know the answer.

For two years my only goal has been to avenge my father. I've thought of nothing else and dreamed of nothing else. The only certainty I've had in my life is that I won't find peace until I kill the king.

It has been my everything.

Then Selestra came along and I found that every now and again I forgot. For a few moments out of the day, I let the very thing that consumed me for years fade.

Or at least, I wanted it to.

She made me consider that when this was all over I could be more than just a soldier with a mission.

"She watches you now," Lucian says.

He cocks his head up to where Selestra is sat. It takes everything I have not to look at her.

"Her warrior," Lucian says.

"I'm not hers." I grit my teeth together. "Witches can't be trusted."

"Can you?" he asks.

I try to respond, but the words stick in the back of my throat.

No. I can't be trusted either. That's the nature of the Six Isles: betrayal and selfishness. Everyone wants what they want and will screw over whoever they can to get it.

"Let's go again," I say to Lucian.

He doesn't hesitate.

He charges forward, sword in the air. The sound of our metal meeting reverberates through the stadium, above the deafening cries of the other warriors.

But there's nothing Lucian can do now.

He set the rules by making sure there were none. He allowed me to fight like I would if I weren't dueling an ally.

Like a Last Army soldier.

When Lucian raises his sword once more, I use my own to knock it to the ground. With no mercy I raise my knee and kick him in the chest.

The champion stumbles back, breathless and gasping, then falls to the floor. I walk slowly toward him and bring the tip of my father's sword to his throat.

"Do you yield?"

Lucian glares up at me. At least, it looks like a glare. It can just as easily be a wince, since moments later he begins coughing and grasping at his chest.

"Really, Lucian." I roll my eyes. "I can't let you up until you say you're done. As you pointed out, people can't be trusted."

He coughs again. "Yes."

"Yes, what?"

This time, he does glare. Louder, Lucian says, "I yield."

I sheathe my sword. "Perfect." I hold out a hand to pull him up.

Once Lucian is back on his feet, the warriors around us grow silent, watching me with what I can only hope is a look of respect and not one where they're planning to kill me in my sleep.

Above them, Lady Eldara remains tight-lipped, nothing but an unsurprised smile on her face.

And Selestra.

She bites her lip as she stares over at me, letting her gloved hands fall to her sides as though she can finally relax.

"How did you do that?" asks Lucian between breaths, drawing my attention from Selestra.

The absence of her leaves me cold.

"I've never known anyone to move so fast," Lucian says.

I regard him for a moment. Lucian doesn't look bitter at the loss. He simply looks curious.

A true champion to the end.

"My father taught me."

Lucian claps me on the arm, his hand clasping around me. "He would be proud," he says. "Even if you are Last Army scum."

I snort a laugh.

"Come," he insists. "I will introduce you to the other champions. No doubt they will want to test you next."

He leads me toward where a relieved-looking Micah stands. But before he's able to give me an earful, someone steps into our path.

"Robin!" Lucian says to the warrior, as tall as an ancient oak tree. "Come join us to see the others. We must celebrate my great whooping."

The warrior shakes his head. "Another time, Lucian." He looks at me, face severe. "The Lady Eldara and her niece wish to see you."

"Her niece," I say.

I turn quickly back to the stadium and see that while the rest of the warriors stand, waiting for the next duel to begin, Selestra has disappeared.

The steps that housed her and Eldara are now empty.

"By all means," I say. "Lead me to them."

34

SELESTRA

Nox arrives at the small outpost on the forest's edge, looking every bit the victor.

He's dressed in a loose white shirt, cuffed in black lace up to his elbows and parted by his chest. A long belt is wrapped around his waist three times over—securing knives and what looks like a small whip—only to stretch across his shoulder and act as a hold for his sword. A jacket is slung over his shoulder, the same color as his tree-bark eyes.

His dark hair is ruffled every which way from the fight, but there is a smile on his face, almost hidden to anyone who isn't looking.

I can never help but look.

It's as if the fight has revived him. I can see the glint in his eyes, fresh from the battle. The pride of victory and adventure.

You'll never be my queen.

Nox's words come rushing back to me and I turn away, dismissing any thoughts of him.

"That was a fine battle," Eldara compliments him. "I was thrilled until the very end. Please, take a seat."

She hands Nox a wooden goblet of nectarine juice and gestures for him to sit on the small log set outside the forest's edge.

Nox shakes his head and doesn't sit.

At first I think it's because he can't stand to be near me, but when I look harder, I see that it's not about me at all.

Nox is animated.

His hands linger by his sides, and I can tell the last thing he wants is to be trapped in this clearing, or even this conversation. The spirit of the battle is still on his skin, sweat licking across his chest.

He wants to be out in the open, away from the forest and the seriousness I know has seeped into my stare. To drink and laugh and let the fire in his belly fade slowly, purposefully, into the night air.

Quite the battle, Eldara said, after Nox threw the Polemistés champion to the ground.

Nox is quite the fighter, I told her.

Even I couldn't deny that. Or the fact that my heart raced whenever Nox got knocked down. Eldara could see me holding my breath all the way to the end, when she finally took my arm and guided me to this place.

The king would have used such a thing against me. Made it a weapon to strike me with: my every emotion a weakness and a failure to him. My mother would have scolded me and hissed that I should know better than to be so transparent.

Eldara only smiled.

She offered me sweet nectarine juice while we waited for Nox to arrive. She talked about the weather and asked if I liked to swim in the summer months, ignoring the cries of the haunted forest beyond us.

She didn't speak of anything she thought I might not want to.

I can see why she was queen to a magical island and how she'd won the heart of the fiercest warrior in the Six Isles. It's clear why his people followed her after his death.

She's a leader, because she's kind.

"What are we doing at this place?" Nox asks. "Why did you call me here?"

He looks briefly at me when he says it.

"You are here because we must begin the trials," Eldara says.

"I've received word that Seryth is nearing our borders. We cannot wait any longer."

My blood freezes at the thought.

"But I haven't *practiced*," I protest, turning toward her. "My nosebleeds—"

Nox's eyes snap toward mine and he frowns. If I didn't know better, I could almost think he was checking to make sure I'm not bleeding right now.

He clears his throat and looks away.

"I've told you, those only happen when you siphon power from yourself," Eldara reminds me. "Draw from around you, Selestra. From life. That is the key."

She places a warm hand on my lap. A motherly touch, unlike any I've felt in years.

"You must be strong. The Six Isles need you to usher us into freedom when I pass."

"Can she really do that?" Nox asks Eldara.

He doubts me.

He doesn't think I'm powerful enough.

"She can," Eldara says with confidence.

I shake my head. "Maybe soon, if I had a couple more days to prepare—"

"Sooner or later, we all run out of tomorrows," Eldara says, unease slipping into her delicate voice. "We cannot afford to wait. Your quest must begin now."

There is a finality to her voice that I've never heard before.

"Begin where?" Nox asks.

Eldara smiles up at him. She gestures to the forest that looms behind us. "Where all warriors are made."

My eyes grow wide.

I remember everything Nox told me about the forest when we were back in Armonía, sitting on the cushioned chairs in the Soul's Keep.

He said it was a place of nightmares, where the dead came to play and their ghosts could be heard screaming through the rivers, battling the monsters that lay beneath. I've been ignoring its growls for the last few minutes, avoiding even glancing at the gnarled trunks, safe in the knowledge that the ghosts can't possibly pass the barriers of the trees.

It's a place for the damned, Nox had said. *Not the living.*

"Use this compass to guide your way." Eldara slips it into my hands as she pulls me to my feet. "Stay north," she says. "That's where both of you will find what you need."

A dozen Polemistés warriors appear beside her, stepping forward to usher us into the forest.

I barely have time to frown before they're forcing us backward and toward the trees.

"Wait—" Nox says, looking as startled as I feel. "What do you mean *both of us?*"

But he's too late.

I feel the sudden brush of soil beneath my feet and then a tree branch curls around my waist, jerking me inward.

I scream as I hit the ground, and when I scramble to my feet, I see the world has shifted.

Around us new trees loom, their spindly branches curling like nooses, their skeletal trunks entwined with bone. The air is a mix of fog and distant moonlight.

A howl sounds in the darkness.

The crunch of leaves under feet that aren't ours.

There is no sign of the entrance—of the edge of the forest we were just standing before. It is as though the trees have closed in, swallowing us from the world.

I gulp down a cold, dry breath and Nox draws his sword.

"This is it," he says. "The Forest of the Damned."

35

SELESTRA

At first I think the forest is dying.

Its leaves are decayed and cracked, petals from the wildflowers wilting across the floor and turning to mulch. Then I notice the way the trees sway on our arrival, as if to warn us of the dangers ahead.

Their leaves crinkle in continuous song and the great loom of the trunks cast shadows on the mossy ground, dancing to the squeals of whatever creatures are in the distance.

I quickly realize that I'm wrong. The forest isn't dying.

Great swells birth from the ground beside the biggest trees, rising up and down with the wind. It's like the hills are inhaling and exhaling beneath our feet.

The forest is *alive* and it's breathing.

I slip back a step, unsteadied by the movement.

Nox catches my arm. "Stay close to me," he says.

I swallow. "I don't like it here."

"I don't think we're meant to. It wouldn't be much of a trial if we did. Not that *I'm* the one meant to be on trial," he adds.

I can't help but shoot him a sour look. "I thought you'd jump at the chance to see me in a life-or-death situation. It would save you having to kill me yourself."

Nox's sword is tight in his hand. "I'd prefer to watch from afar," he says. "Why do you think I'm here?"

"I don't know," I answer honestly. "Maybe it's because of the mark."

I hold my gloved hand up, reminding him of the king's crest beneath that we share. If my death and destiny are tied to Nox's, then perhaps his are also tied to mine.

"What does the compass say?" he asks.

I look down at the small bronze object Eldara gave me.

The inner ring is a bright green, the tiny needle flickering between the swirls of north and east.

I squint and see that underneath the elaborately drawn *N* is a small inscription: *Magic is never lost to be found*.

"That way."

I point up ahead, to a wide expanse of mossy hills, shadowed enough by trees that the sky above them doesn't seem visible for miles.

"You're sure?"

I wiggle the compass. "Stay north, right? It's what Eldara said."

Nox walks onward without waiting for me.

He's so fast that I nearly trip over my own feet trying to follow. The tree roots stick up from the soil like hands reaching out for my ankles, so I have to watch each step.

It's dark here.

Night, when I remember it being barely sunset just moments ago as we spoke to Eldara. I can see the moon, peeking through a line of dark clouds, which hide any chance of stars.

The forest soil is thick and sticky under my feet, coating my boots, but there isn't any path to speak of. And it smells. There's the musty odor of damp and rotten flower heads, but beneath is something worse.

It smells like blood.

We walk for a while, long enough for the night to turn to something darker. The moon is dim and smudged overhead.

"Are we going far?" I ask.

I can't stand the silence. It makes way for the cries of the forest.

When Nox doesn't reply, I press again. "What kind of trials do you think will be ahead?"

"Having to put up with you *is* a trial," he mutters under his breath.

I glower at him and come to a stop beside a nearby bush.

It's covered in sickly-looking thorns, held together by the thread of cobwebs and mold, but beside its graying leaves are bright red berries shaped like stars.

"How strange," I say, and reach out a hand for one.

Nox wrenches me back.

"They could be poisonous," he warns.

"I wasn't going to eat them," I protest.

Though just the mention of food brings a gnawing of hunger to my stomach. I haven't eaten since this morning.

"Did you bring any food?"

"Lady Eldara didn't exactly give me a chance to pack before she shoved me into this place."

I groan. "I'm hungry."

"Eat your arm, then."

"Maybe I should cook and eat you," I say, narrowing my eyes. "Boil your bones to make my bread."

"Be quiet," Nox hushes me.

I raise an eyebrow. "I was joking."

"Shh."

His voice turns serious.

I scoff in disbelief. "You can't tell me to—"

Nox brings my own hand quickly across my mouth. He gestures to the bush of star-shaped fruit.

It rustles.

My eyes widen in horror and I step backward.

"Is it a ghost?" I ask in a small whisper.

"As far as I can tell, it's a bush."

I elbow him in the side and he grunts.

The rustling grows louder and I'm about to run for my life when a bird bursts out from the thorns, nearly the size of me.

It stares at us for a moment, cocking its bronze head. Its beak is muted gray and its eyes are like sparks of white fire.

At first I think it's going to attack us, but it quickly opens up its golden wings and sails past us and up into the trees.

A Lamperós bird.

Just like the one the king keeps in chains back on the Floating Mountain. I thought it was the last of its kind. A lonely, dying thing.

But I was wrong because here it is. Another one, even bigger and more beautiful, its feathers unsnarled and silken.

I marvel as the great creature sweeps through the sky, weaving in and out of the stars.

"Selestra," Nox says. "I think we should go."

His voice is unsteady and I laugh at him.

How can the big, strong soldier be so scared of something so beautiful?

"It's just a bird," I say, staring up at the sky until it starts to make me dizzy.

"I'm not talking about the bird."

A cold creeps along the lines of my spine, prickling my skin as I turn.

Sitting on one of the breathing mounds before us is a figure.

Its face is as torn as its clothes, slashes every which way, with blood crusting across its cheeks like salt. It bubbles from its mouth too, then dribbles down its chin as it watches us with blank eyes.

Its fingernails dig into the grass and the soil slithers up its arm like ants.

"How do we kill it?" I whisper to Nox.

He studies the ashen figure. "I think someone already did."

At the sound of our voices, the figure stands.

"Run!" Nox declares.

We turn and flee in the other direction, the heavy thump of our footsteps as fast as my own heartbeat.

We don't get far.

Neither of us sees the maze of tree-root hands, reaching up for us, until it's too late.

We fall, tumbling down the slope of a large hill.

I roll, my head jolting back and forth until we finally splash to the bottom in a pool of mud.

It smells of the forest.

Of blood and decay.

"This is disgusting," I say, grimacing.

I bring my hands up and they drip with rot.

Nox looks to the top of the hill, unfazed. "At least we're not being followed by that thing," he says. "I can't see it anymore."

"He probably didn't want to roll around in the muck." I pull myself up from the puddle. "I don't think I'll ever be clean again."

Nox smirks as he tries to clean his blade on the front of his marred shirt. "I'd think your hands have been far dirtier than this before."

I stop to stare at him. I don't miss the pointed tone in his voice.

I climb from the puddle and wring out my hair. The murky water has turned it from green to a muddled brown.

Nox proceeds to nonchalantly pick up the compass from where it fell into the mud, ignoring my clear annoyance.

It only makes me angrier.

Over this past month, I started to think he was a noble soldier with more to him than arrogance and bravado. I started to trust him, more than I'd trusted even his father.

Now I see how wrong I was to be so foolish when he has so easily turned his back on me.

"You know what," I say, having had enough. "I think I'm going to go prove my worth all by myself. So how about I go this way." I gesture behind us. "And you go that way."

I point a muddied hand in the opposite direction.

"Perfect," Nox says. He holds the compass up and shows the pointer set hard on north. "My way is the right way."

I glare. "Good luck lasting an hour without me."

Nox raises his eyebrows. "I didn't realize you had so much experience navigating haunted forests."

I roll my eyes and take a step forward, away from Nox.

It takes me a moment to realize something is wrong.

When I go to take another step, my foot doesn't move.

I look down and see I'm being swallowed into the ground.

The soil has turned to a gaping mouth, folding in on itself and dragging me down with it.

The forest, this living and breathing beast, is trying to devour me.

I panic and wrestle to dislodge my foot, but it only makes me sink faster. Like it enjoys my struggle, my fear whetting its appetite.

"Help me out!" I yell.

Nox stands on the edge of the unstable ground, eyeing me with an uncertain look. "I thought you were better off without me."

"This isn't funny," I sneer. "Pull me up!"

"What if I get stuck too?" he says, looking far too calm in the face of my doom.

I grit my teeth. "Nox—"

"Okay, okay," he says, and kneels on the edge of the forest mouth.

He reaches out a hand for mine and I grab it desperately.

The weight of the soil dragging me down is crushing.

It's like I can't breathe.

"Pull me up!" I say, frantic. "Please."

"I'm trying," Nox says tightly.

He lurches forward a bit and I see the moment he realizes that his grip isn't strong enough.

"Damn it," he curses loudly.

His hands are clasped through mine, but I can feel his hold slipping. We both can. His scowl is as prominent as the scar across his face as he tries to haul me out, but I'm already chest deep.

Our hands slip away.

Nox falls backward with a thump, my glove in his hand.

He discards it quickly and reaches for me again.

"Don't!" I say, whipping my hand away in horror.

I can't let him touch me.

I don't want to see that horrible death on the beach again.

"I have to pull you out," Nox says. He holds out his hand for mine. "Come on, Selestra."

I shake my head. "Not like that."

"You must give me your hand," he presses.

I hold firm and Nox sighs, leaning back onto the soil.

"Help yourself out, then," he says.

At first I think he's joking, but Nox simply stares at me, waiting.

"Are you trying to be funny?" I ask. "I'm sinking!"

This forest is going to eat me whole and he's just going to watch.

"Maybe this is part of the trial," he says. "Try using your magic."

"How?"

"You floated a paintbrush, didn't you?"

I'm starting to think he's mocking me again.

"You floated us when we jumped from the mountain, so just . . . float yourself out. Siphon the wind or something."

"This is not the time for jokes!" I yell.

I'm falling deeper and deeper into this pit. The soil is licking at my stomach and up to my throat. Its teeth nip at my toes.

"I can't save you if you won't let me touch you," Nox says. "You need to save yourself."

I swallow, the crushing in my chest deepening with every moment.

The soil presses against my neck and I know within moments I'm going to disappear into the darkness.

I close my eyes.

Focus, I tell myself.

On the dirt, crumbling in, and on the shallowness of my breath.

On the feel of it all, pressing into me.

Focus.

"Come on," Nox urges. "You can do this, Selestra. Trust yourself."

That's something I've never been able to do.

I grew up trusting Irenya and Asden, and as these weeks have drawn on, I've even started to put my faith in Nox. Trusting other people is so much easier than trusting myself.

I want to change that. I want to trust myself first, most.

Not last. Not least.

I search deep down for the power that Eldara claims has always been inside me. Magic that isn't waiting for my mother to die, but waiting for me to find it.

My mother said my powers weren't to be explored. The king said only the true Somniatis witch could have free rein of magic.

Hide it.

Push it down deep.

Be a witch, but also a shell.

Have magic, but never own it.

Don't do what you're not told.

Don't learn or hope or create or wish.

Not anymore, I think to myself, and a spark bursts out from me. A flicker from inside my chest, pushing itself into the world.

I open my eyes and find that I'm free.

I hover a few steps from the mouth of the forest floor. It seems to sigh once it sees me, and when I drop down to the ground in a thump, the hole closes over, waiting for its next victim.

"You did it," Nox says as I catch my breath.

He looks me over, eyes roaming the soil that coats my arms and legs, and then to my face, which I imagine is also covered in dirt.

His eyes crinkle in a frown.

"You're not bleeding."

I bring my hand to my nose, and when it comes away dry, I see that it's true. There's no blood.

Eldara was right: When I channel from the world, rather than myself, my magic doesn't hurt. I'm just now realizing that it's the opposite. I feel the wake of it thrumming through me like a series of lights blinking brighter and brighter inside me.

"Are you okay?" Nox asks.

"I'm fine."

I'm better than fine. I feel *alive*, and not in the awful, tainted way I did back at the After Dusk Inn, when I nearly siphoned that man's life.

This is different. It feels right.

"I'm glad," Nox says.

I arch an eyebrow. "Are you?"

He shrugs. "Lady Eldara would be pretty angry if I let her niece get killed so soon."

"You're an idiot."

"Says the girl who nearly got eaten by a puddle."

I laugh before I can help myself.

The tingle of magic still nips at my heart, the breeze of the wind on my bare fingers rejuvenating something deep inside me. I see my glove discarded on the ground, and I feel so free without it.

So light.

The notion of a smile creases around the corners of Nox's mouth. I wonder if he can see it in me: the sense of a shackle being broken.

It's as if for that moment we forget all the reasons we should be angry. We don't think about kingdoms falling or the weight of worlds in our hands, and in that moment of forgetting we're each someone different.

Someone impossible.

We're who we want to be, instead of who someone else decided.

I wish it would last, but Nox jerks back and I'm lost to reality all too fast.

I sigh at him. "Are you ever going to trust me again?"

Nox's jaw twitches at the question.

He pauses, studying me intently. I can see the debate in his eyes and it breaks me in two, cleaving me like a promise lost.

I shouldn't care so much, but I do.

He once said he trusted me to be his queen.

"We should make camp," Nox finally says. "Let's look for somewhere safe to rest for the night."

But it's not an answer and he knows it.

He looks to the forest floor, then at the large expanse that surrounds us.

To anywhere but me.

I nod, wordless, and pick up my glove from the dirt, clenching it tightly in my hands. I trail after Nox, watching as he scours the forest for some kind of safe shelter.

I don't take my eyes off him, even as the moon dulls and the stars begin to blink out, making way for the promise of dawn.

Will you trust me?

I want to ask again, but I don't because I'm afraid of what the answer might be.

36
NOX

We make camp by a small rock face, clustered in thorn trees.

"Are you sure this is safe?" Selestra asks.

"As safe as we can be in a haunted forest."

At the very least there's no unsteady ground that might try to eat us in our sleep, or ghosts swarming. The sharp blades of the trees surrounding us give some protection, and with our backs to the rock face, we can keep an eye on the one entry point to this small cove.

Besides, the nearby stream will give us some much-needed drinking water. Assuming it isn't poisonous.

Selestra slumps onto the gravel and throws a stick of wood onto the small fire I've started.

It sizzles and flickers, spitting embers up into the air.

I wish Lady Eldara let us pack supplies before whisking us off to this place. No bedrolls, no food, and no kind of map. If it wasn't for the small stream we'd stumbled across while making camp, we probably would've died of thirst already.

If this is her idea of a trial for allies and queens, I'd hate to see how she treats real prisoners.

"I'll go and see if I can gather berries for us," I tell Selestra. "We've had training on wild fruit species in the Last Army, in case we were ever stranded during a mission. I'm sure I can find something."

"As long as you do the first taste test," she says.

"These are your trials," I remind her. "Shouldn't you lead by example? You're the future queen."

"I never said I was anyone's queen." Selestra settles against a large log. "But if I was, I'd delegate this responsibility to you."

"How kind."

"I'm a benevolent leader."

She smiles nonchalantly.

"We can't stay long," I tell her. "We'll rest until sunrise and then we have to keep going."

Selestra looks uncertainly up to the sky, marred by night.

"Are we sure this place even has a sunrise?"

"No matter where you are, the sun always has to rise," I say. "Not even the darkest of days are permanent."

They were words my father always used to echo to me. I'm not sure why I speak them now, but Selestra blinks over to me, her eyes as bright as the fire that flickers between us. I wonder if he spoke those words to her once before too.

I hear the sound of her swallowing over the howls of the forest monsters.

"Be glad that nothing is permanent," she finally tells me. "Or you'd be stuck with that haircut forever."

I reach up a hand to touch my hair, but then I see that she's grinning.

I pick up my sword. "Try not to die while I'm out collecting food."

I dust myself off and head back into the forest.

"You try not to die either!" Selestra calls after me. "I need someone to keep the fire going while I sleep."

It only takes an hour or so for me to find enough berries that don't look like they'll kill us and should fill our empty stomachs. I return to our makeshift campsite to see Selestra curled up on the ground beside the fire, already fast asleep.

"So much for being hungry enough to boil my bones," I mutter.

I set the fruit—which I've gathered up in the waist of my shirt—in a small pile on the floor. It's stained my clothing a mix of purples and reds.

I take a handful, and though it's sour and a little grainy, it doesn't kill me, so I consider it a success.

I stoke the fire and Selestra stirs on the ground by my feet.

I'm tempted to wake her so she can eat, but something in me is reluctant to disturb her. For someone stuck in a haunted forest, she looks so peaceful. Covered in mud and forest dirt, her hair pulled up and away from her face, she's a far cry from the Somniatis heir, wrapped in ballgowns like some kind of trophy.

I turn to the fire with a sigh.

"You're back," Selestra mumbles.

I glance down at her, sleep coating her face in the firelight.

"It's freezing," she says in a shiver.

She's clearly not used to the cold. Vasiliádes never experiences true winters compared with the other islands, and I'd bet that up in Selestra's tower she is surrounded by thick blankets and large, roaring fires.

She gets closer to the fire and to me, shaking as the breeze takes hold. Summer seems unable to reach this forest, the chill like a permanent breath on the backs of our necks, tingeing even Selestra's lips blue.

"Maybe Eldara is trying to test how long it takes for us to lose a finger to the cold," I say.

I pull off my jacket and hold it out to Selestra.

"Here."

She takes it with a grateful smile and I ignore the chill that settles into my bones.

"You should sleep," I tell her.

"You should sleep too," she says.

I keep stoking the fire, trying not to look at her again. Things always seem so much more complicated when I do.

"I'm fine."

"Oh, I forgot." Her voice is quiet. "You don't sleep."

I hate that she knows that about me.

It feels like a weakness has been uncovered and laid bare for her to see.

I clear my throat and then settle stubbornly into the ground beside her, reclining where Selestra does, as though it proves something.

I can sleep if I want to, I lie to myself. *You don't know me that well, princess.*

Wordlessly, I pull a corner of the jacket from her so the edges cover my chest too. My arm grazes hers, pressed against her side as I nudge closer to share the heat. Being this close to her is like being close to a volcano, waiting for it to erupt and burn me whole.

I brush off the gnawing in my stomach.

"Nox," she says.

I stiffen as Selestra's voice tickles at my ear.

I wish she'd stop saying my name so softly. I hate how it jars everything inside me.

"Do you think things will change after the trials?" she asks.

"Change how?"

"I thought Lady Eldara was different, but it's all the same," she says, sighing into my jacket. "Constantly trying to prove that I'm good and worthy. Never having it be enough for anyone."

The world goes quiet for a moment.

"It's like I never even left the castle. I feel the same as I did in my tower, trapped by expectation."

The grief in her tone takes me by surprise.

I thought these trials were a way for Selestra to gain more magic and take on the king without needing to be afraid. To boost her power.

I never thought she'd think they were a way for her to feel worthy. Proof that she was good enough.

I don't answer. I'm not sure what I can say to make her feel better, or if I'd even want to. I'm supposed to be angry at her, aren't I?

Selestra sighs, and as the night draws on, her breathing turns deep and soft. The firelight flickers across her pale skin, embers dancing over her lips.

My father trained her, just as he trained me. He may have hated the king, but he thought Selestra worthy. He wanted her to know how to defend herself against someone like Seryth.

Did he sense how different she was from the king and her mother?

I breathe in the night.

Selestra was just a child when she saw my father die. I wonder how much that helped shape who she is today. The responsibilities put on her then were as grave as those my father put on me. He wanted me to save the world while her family wanted her to destroy it.

Why are the sins of our parents something we have to bear?

Selestra turns a little, the dirt and leaves rustling underneath her. I hold my breath, just in case she wakes.

I keep hold of it for far too long.

Selestra wakes me at the crack of dawn.

I didn't realize I'd fallen asleep until she kicks me in the shin and says, "Rise and shine!"

To my surprise, it's daylight when I open my eyes. Turns out the forest really isn't coated in endless night.

I can't believe I slept for so long and that I actually feel rested. Years of sleepless nights and now, despite being in a haunted forest filled with an old queen's sadistic trials, I didn't wake up once during the night.

How can it be that beside the heir to my greatest enemy, I was able to so completely relax?

"For someone who says they don't sleep, you were like a dead man," Selestra says. "Not to mention the *snoring*."

I still.

"I don't snore." I slip my jacket back on. It smells like her. "And I wasn't sleeping. I merely rested my eyes for a brief moment."

Selestra snorts, seeing easily through the lie.

I don't even bother trying to convince her further.

Across from me, she's busy putting out the fire, and I notice that her hair is once again a bright green. There's not a speck of mud left on her.

She notices me staring.

"I washed up in the stream," she explains. "I couldn't stand the smell of myself any longer. You should do the same."

She grabs a handful of fruit and holds it out to me.

I shake my head.

"I nearly ate it all while you were asleep," she says. "I woke up ready to start trying to cook the tree bark." She sighs wistfully. "I miss the fresh buns dipped in cherry sauce that Irenya and I used to steal from the kitchens. Oh, and *potatoes*. With garlic butter and garden herbs, crispy on the outside and fluffy enough to melt in your mouth."

I could swear she drools.

I stretch into a yawn, shaking off the long sleep. It's not something I'm used to.

"Who needs potatoes when you have forest dirt and berries?" I say.

Selestra takes another reluctant mouthful of fruit, wincing at the bitter taste. "Which way do we go today?"

I lean over to grab the compass from the ground beside me.

"Looks like north is that way."

Selestra sweeps her hair back away from her face. "Let the trials begin," she says, but the way she sighs tells me that she'd much rather stay here and eat sour berries than face whatever else the forest and Eldara have in store.

We walk for several long hours without the sight of ghosts or much else before we finally come across a large canyon.

The forest pauses, cleaving in two like a walnut shell. The drop is large enough that I can't see to the bottom. Holding the two sides together is a rickety bridge, with ropes that look fit to crumble to dust.

"I don't suppose there's another way across?" Selestra asks.

I hold up the compass. "This is north. Looks like your aunt is trying her best to kill us."

Selestra grimaces at the use of the word *aunt*, like she hasn't fully accepted that Lady Eldara is her family.

"Technically she's my great-great-*grand*aunt," she says, eyeing the bridge with disdain.

"I'm starting to think she doesn't like you very much."

"You think this will hold our weight?" she asks.

I pocket the compass. "Only one way to find out."

I step onto the bridge and hear a crack, like a splinter. I wait a moment, and when it doesn't snap, I take another step.

The bridge sways but holds my weight.

I clutch the ropes and look over my shoulder to Selestra.

"Whenever you're ready."

She groans but follows me onward.

With each step we take, the bridge creaks and rattles. The wood is disturbingly soft underneath my feet and the rope we cling to is thin and frayed.

We barely make it halfway across when my foot slips through the rotten wood. The force of it brings me to my knees, slamming me across the bridge floor.

My leg dangles, the wind gnawing at my ankles, trying to pull me down into the pit below.

Selestra rushes to my side. "Souls," she says. "Can you be careful?"

She tries to pull me up, but it's no use.

"My foot is stuck," I say.

"We could chop it off?" Selestra offers.

I glower at her and grab on tighter to her gloved hands. "Just pull a little harder."

"Maybe you should save yourself," she says, mimicking my own words back to me. "Float yourself out like a paintbrush."

Her tone is wry as she continues to try to pull me up, ignoring the way I glare up at her. Really it would serve me right if she left me here.

I wiggle my leg and see it's starting to get free when Selestra suddenly stops pulling. She pales, eyes focusing on something behind me.

At the edge of the bridge where we just came from is a dead man.

I recognize him as the ghost from yesterday, who watched us in the forest and chased us down that damn hill.

He is stained in blood, skin dripping from his face like candle wax. He wears the same armor that Lucian wore during our fight, sword drawn and ready for battle.

This is a forest of fallen warriors and we are trespassers.

"It's back," Selestra says.

The dead man charges toward us.

"Go!" I yell.

I slip one hand from her grip and free my sword from its fast.

"Take it and run."

I push my father's sword into her hands. I will not let the savior of the Six Isles die because of me.

Selestra gapes, like she can't quite believe what I'm saying. But the surprise quickly turns to a frown that's all too familiar to me now.

Souls forbid she does what she's told for a change.

"Don't try to be noble," Selestra scolds, dropping the blade to her side. "It doesn't suit you."

She grips tighter on to me and leans back, putting all her weight into helping me out of the hole. To my surprise, it works, and within moments I'm freed.

I slump to the floor just as the dead man reaches us, its sword ready to swipe across my neck.

Selestra blocks it.

Before I have time to reach for my blade, I see it's already in her hands and she is thwarting blow after blow from the fallen warrior.

She brings the blade back and stabs into its stomach, but the metal passes through the man like smoke.

Still, she keeps him on the defense, never letting down her guard. She is an adept fencer. My father taught her well.

"How do I kill it?" she asks me, breathless.

The warrior is unrelenting.

"The jewel on its neck!" I say, spying a green gem around his throat. It looks far more solid than he does. "Smash the jewel."

Selestra nods and whips around to smash the sword across the warrior's necklace.

The creature begins to fade, its legs turning to wisps.

But before it goes, it lifts its arm in one final blow.

The blade tears across Selestra's stomach.

37

SELESTRA

During my fencing lessons with Nox's father, I'd gotten used to being kicked, punched, and even sliced across the arm with a rapier.

I've healed black eyes and, once, a cut on my arm that stretched from my shoulder right down to my wrist. Still, the wounds were harmless and most of the bleeding came from my nose as I tried to heal myself during the night. They were painful, but surface level.

Asden knew how to teach me a lesson without ever *really* hurting me, which is more than I can say for anyone else.

When the ghost's blade rips into my skin, it's nothing like that.

The blood is instant, soaking into my shirt, and the pain is searing. White hot, like I'm being burned from the inside out.

It doesn't feel like a blade, it feels like fire.

My knees buckle and I slump, expecting to hit the ground, but instead I find myself in Nox's arms. His warm hands wrap around me.

He presses a hand against my bloody shirt and I see the unmistakable grimace on his face.

"I'm fine," I manage to choke out.

"For someone who keeps so many secrets, you're an awful liar," he says, voice stretched thin.

"I'm not lying."

The air feels chill.

"See?" Nox says, shaking his head. "Awful."

He presses his hand harder to my stomach.

I will myself to get up, to do something other than just lie here on this broken bridge, in the middle of a devouring forest.

If Asden were here, he wouldn't let me do nothing.

Get up, he'd say, with no words but a raised brow and a nod that I could easily translate. *You're stronger than this. Fight.*

"Can you heal yourself?" Nox asks.

"I'm not sure I have the energy," I admit.

Using magic takes so much focus and strength. When I was younger, it would exhaust me for days. I know now that's because I was drawing from myself, but as I close my eyes and try to draw from the wind, I lose focus.

The air is too dry and I can't find the strength to channel it.

I can feel my energy draining with every drop of blood.

"Use mine," Nox says suddenly.

He wraps his hand around mine in a vise grip.

Even through the fabric of my gloves, I feel him. The energy of him is like waves rolling across me. I can taste it on my tongue a little.

Salt and winter berries.

"Take it," Nox says, offering himself to me. "We don't have another choice."

When I realize he wants me to siphon his energy to heal myself, I panic. The last time I tried anything like that was with the man at the tavern who attacked us, and I nearly killed him.

I can't risk that again.

"I mean it," Nox presses, sensing my hesitation. "We need you to survive these trials, so you can earn whatever power is out here. Without that, we don't stand a chance against Seryth and your mother."

I know he's right, but I'm still scared.

I don't want to hurt him. I've been the cause of Nox's pain before and the weight of it is almost too much to bear.

"Selestra," he says.

His voice is soft and deep, and the way he looks at me tells me, impossibly, that he knows just what I'm thinking and he understands my doubts.

His hands tighten around mine.

"Take what you need from me. Please."

So I do.

I take all that he gives me, absorbing his strength, drinking it in like the finest honey juice until my whole body thrums.

I feel strong.

A simple blade cannot hurt me.

A single piece of metal cannot break me.

I am Selestra Somniatis, I tell myself. *I am descended from a goddess.*

I whisper it inside my mind, over and over like a prayer.

I look down at my torn shirt and the skin begins to stitch together.

I blink in disbelief. I've never healed so quickly before. A wound like this would usually take me hours—maybe even days, back when I was younger—and yet here I can see the threads of myself pulling together before my very eyes.

It takes only moments.

Nox is strong and that strength courses through me like lightning. I can feel every note of him inside me.

His hand grips tighter around mine.

The power funnels between us, everything he is slipping over me in a blanket. I sense the edge of it. Of him. I teeter beside it, letting the warmth fill me.

Then I pull back.

Nox's breath shudders against me and his hand hovers by my cheek. Thumb so close to the corner of my lip that if I close my eyes, I could almost trick myself into feeling him for real.

Into letting him feel me.

His eyes are such a deep, unyielding brown.

"Are you okay?"

His voice is thick and ragged.

He looks down at my shirt, still bloody. The fabric sticks unflatteringly to my stomach.

"I'm okay," I say. "Thanks to you."

I look at Nox, trying to spy any signs of injury or weakness. Something off in his eyes or an ashen color to his skin.

"How are *you*?" I ask.

"Dizzy," he admits. He runs a hand through the messy black of his hair. "But you didn't drain my soul, so I consider that a victory."

"You're welcome."

Nox stands, swaying a little, and I move to steady him.

He pauses at my touch, eyes shooting to my hand. The moment stills and I feel my heart begin to race.

Then Nox clears his throat and picks up his fallen sword, moving slowly away from me. My blood glistens on the blade, where it dripped from my wound.

"What's the score now?" he asks.

"The score," I repeat.

"For saving each other's lives." His lips quirk upward. "I'm guessing I'm in the lead."

I roll my eyes. "Not likely. You're as bad as a damsel."

Nox grins. "Guess that makes you my knight in shining armor."

I laugh at the sly tilt of his eyebrows, forgetting for a moment where we are and all the horrors around us.

Unfortunately, the forest doesn't let me forget for long.

I turn to the sound of footsteps, so many I almost mistake it for a rumble of thunder. Then I hear the crack of trees falling in their wake, see the tops perish to the ground and tumble over the cliff edge to make way for a small army.

A dozen dead warriors now stand at the foot of the bridge, swords drawn and bones jutting from their slashed armor.

We take off in a run, just as the dead slump onto the bridge. It staggers with the weight of them and Nox lags behind, weakened.

I grab ahold of his hand and pull him onward until we reach the edge of the bridge.

"Up ahead!" Nox says, still breathless. He gestures with the compass.

North.

It should be our safety. Or, knowing how sadistic my aunt can be, yet another doom.

When we come to a stop at the top of a great waterfall, I see it's the latter.

It gushes like a fierce, salivating beast, colliding into a pool of dark blue water below.

"We have to jump," Nox says.

"What is it with you wanting to jump off things all the time?" I ask. "First the Floating Mountain and now *this*. Can't you keep your feet on the ground?"

Nox takes his sword strap off. "Where's your sense of adventure?"

"Where's your sense of self-preservation?"

"I don't need it," he says, grabbing my hand. "I've got you to save me."

He pulls me off the edge and we hit the water below like knives, slicing through the blue.

I brace myself for it to be cold, but the lake is warm and welcoming.

I half expect there to be some kind of monster lurking beneath, or for flesh-eating fish to begin chasing us, or the weeds to tangle me up and drown me at the bottom.

Instead, my feet touch down on soft soil that springs me back to the surface.

Nox is already swimming back toward the waterfall and I follow him underneath to find a small ledge. He heaves himself up and holds out a hand for me, which I take gladly, but as soon as I'm out of the lake water, I feel the bitter cold of the forest gnawing at my skin.

I shiver, wrapping my arms around myself to keep warm.

Above us, the cavernous ceiling glistens with orbs of blue light, like hundreds of tiny tinted scars have embedded into the rocks. The ledge shimmers with a layer of thin water that looks like silk, sliding around the edges of my boots. It ripples in some sort of arrow.

I squint at it. The split curves up toward the star-freckled ceiling, dripping with water. I step forward to see an opening. It's wide enough to slip through.

"Is that some kind of cave?" Nox asks. "Tell me you're not thinking about going through there."

I am.

I can't explain it, but something about it draws me in, and the longer I stare at the jagged rocks, the more I inch forward. There is something in there, calling to me. I hear it on the echoes of the wind that whistle into the gap.

"I'm voting no," Nox says. "I'd rather head back out there and face off with the ghost army."

I hold out a hand, palm up to ask for the one lifeline Eldara left us. "Compass," I say, not taking my eyes off the cave opening.

Nox drops it into my hand with a sigh. "Really," he says, grimacing toward the cave. "We don't need to make it so easy for your aunt to kill us."

I look down at the compass, and when I do, I can't help but smile. The needle is resolute, unshaken, as it points toward the inscription.

Magic is never lost to be found.

"North," I say in a breath.

If Eldara wanted us to find something in this forest, then it's in there.

I know it. I feel it.

Nox groans, but I don't stand around to listen to him object.

I move forward, across the clear ripples of water and toward the thing that calls to me from the darkness.

38

NOX

We slip through the crack in the world and end up in a new world altogether.

The cavern is endless and filled with trees, with trunks a gray blue and leaves like crystals that shine against the spines of their branches.

It's a forest under the earth.

Only unlike the haunted trees above, this place doesn't look like it wants to kill us. I might even call it beautiful. The floor is a shallow pool of crystal water, tree roots swirling through it in a tangled maze. An array of silvery fish weave through them.

Above, light drips from the ceiling through a handful of tiny holes, pinpointed across the cavern like some kind of map. Water slips from the walls in tiny curtains.

"What is this place?" I ask.

"Magic," Selestra whispers. "I can feel its power, coursing from the ground and into me."

Though I don't say it, I can feel something too. It starts at my toes and then shoots straight into my heart like an arrow.

"Let's make camp," I tell her. "We need to gather our energy, for whatever the next trial is."

"Here?"

"It's not currently attacking us and I don't see any ghosts nearby, so it's as good a place as we're going to find for a while. Plus we're sheltered from any rainfall."

Selestra nods but doesn't say anything else.

She marvels at this place, taking in every ripple of the water with a sharp intake of breath. The power she feels must be invigorating, because when I tell her to gather firewood, she does so without a single quip or glare in my direction.

Whatever this place is, she looks like it was made for her.

We finish finding enough supplies to last us the night.

It's oddly warm here compared with the forest, barely a breeze coming from the few holes in the ceiling that let us glimpse the stars. Nearby where a bundle of bleached bones lie, there's a break where the damp ground turns dry. We settle there, and I try not to think too hard about what might have happened to the person those bones belonged to when they last ventured here. Selestra barely seems to notice. She's gathered enough soft branches and leaves to create a bed of sorts, cushioning our stay.

She's also found some crystals from the nearby trees for light and more of that fruit we'd discovered earlier. The shallow waters farther in are ripe with fish, and though it took nearly an hour, we managed to catch two of the smaller ones.

As they cook across the small twig fire, I can feel my stomach thanking us already.

Next time I'm sent on a mythical quest set by an ancient queen, I'm bringing cake and rum.

Selestra is silent as she pokes at the fish, suspended over the flames. I'm not used to her being so quiet and it sets me on edge.

I force myself to speak, to say anything.

"Why did my father turn against the king?"

Selestra removes the fish from the fire and places it on a large leaf in between us.

"He was loyal to the throne my whole life," I say. "Do you know what changed? I never got the chance to ask."

Selestra picks at her fish, like she's suddenly lost her appetite.

"I'm not sure he was loyal," Selestra says. "He trained me behind Seryth's back for years, preparing me to fight and be strong."

I still can't quite fathom the man I knew, who spouted such loyalty and trained me to be a part of the Last Army, doing all he could to ensure the king's heir could fight against him. How well did I truly know my father? Did he ever believe in Seryth, or did he always know the king needed to be stopped? Was he really training me to be a part of the Last Army, or was he training me to fight against them all that time?

"When the king last successfully attacked Polemistés two years ago, he managed to get prisoners," Selestra says softly. "There was a young family. I could hear their screams even from my bedroom."

"They were tortured?" I ask.

"The king was looking for something and he wanted their help in finding it," Selestra says.

"For the sword," I say.

For Lady Eldara.

Selestra nods. "Asden—your father—it didn't sit right with him that they were brutalized like that. He thought they were innocent."

I suck in a breath.

We both know the king would never think of anyone as innocent, let alone feel mercy for them if he did. My father should have known better.

"I think that's what made your father realize the king didn't care about anyone in the Six Isles if they stood in his way," Selestra says. "Seryth must have seen the shift in him. He made me look into your father's future and—"

She breaks off and her expression wilts in pain.

She looks ashamed, avoiding my eyes as she says it, like it's a sin she never wanted to admit.

"You were just a child," I say.

"I didn't feel like a child." The anguish on her face is enough to splinter me in two. "I felt like a monster. I felt like I betrayed him."

She looks at me, eyes threatening to spill over with tears. She swallows them down well enough.

"His last words were of you," Selestra says. "He asked my mother to promise to keep you safe and to not punish you for his mistakes."

It's a small comfort, but I'm grateful.

Selestra lets out another long sigh. "I haven't had someone care about me that way in a long time," she says. "My mother can't risk loving me."

She gets that look on her face again when she says it. The same helpless disappointment I saw when she spoke about not feeling worthy.

It's a look that makes me think she feels just as empty.

Selestra is a princess and, if Lady Eldara has her way, a future queen. She has some of the last magic in the world inside her, but even with a league of people so sure of her, she can't be sure of herself.

"I know you blame yourself," I say. "But if you're looking for me to blame you too, then you're looking in the wrong place. My father wouldn't have blamed you either."

I should have said it sooner.

I understand now why Selestra was so reluctant to look into my deaths. It wasn't just because she saw hers too, but because it reminded her of that day with my father.

I've always wondered why she didn't revel in death, despite being raised around it. Now I know.

I want to tell her that she's not the sum of her family's mistakes and that I know what it's like to be caught in the shadow of your parents' pasts. There's so much I want to say to her, but it's hard to find the right words.

"I was angry that you lied," I say. "But I never held you responsible."

"You'd be right to think I was."

I shake my head, but Selestra is insistent.

It's like she wants me to hate her.

Maybe she thinks she deserves it.

"You need to forgive yourself."

"You say that like it's easy."

The pain in her eyes is the same pain I've felt for years. I was wrong to think I was alone in it.

"Nothing worth fighting for comes easy," I say.

Selestra blinks up at me, a small smile on her lips.

The warmth of the moment fills the cavern, overtaking the fire. You don't always see beauty—sometimes you feel it too.

And I feel it when I'm with her.

I was stupid to try to push that away.

"I never would have gotten this far without you," I say.

"In an empty cave?" Selestra snorts a laugh.

"To the place my father always dreamed of. It's because of you that I'm going to be able to fulfill his dying wish."

Selestra isn't on some selfish quest for vengeance, too wrapped up in herself to see clearly. She cares, even if she tries not to, and she wants the world to be something I wasn't sure it ever could be: capable of redemption.

I think the only thing she's really afraid of is that she's not strong enough to help it.

I know better.

"I don't think Eldara is the weapon capable of killing the king." My heart pounds as she looks at me. "I think it's you, Selestra. You're what I've been searching for."

She swallows and I inch closer to her.

My pulse races and I can't tell whether it's from the adrenaline of near death, or from looking into her eyes.

"Thank you," I whisper. "For helping me find my way. And for being someone I can trust."

Selestra blinks. "You trust me?"

There's so much surprise in her voice that I feel ashamed.

"I always have," I admit.

Trust isn't just about letting go of doubt, it's about letting go of the past and looking to the future. When I look forward instead of back, she's all that I see.

I lean into her and Selestra's breath catches.

I move closer, letting the brush of her sigh hit my cheeks.

Despite what anyone might think, Selestra is strong. She's worthy. And with a lifetime of stars gathering in the sky above us, I don't need some trial to know exactly what she is.

A witch.

A princess.

A *queen*.

39
SELESTRA

Nox leans toward me.

I know he's going to kiss me and I want him to, more than I've ever wanted anything else before. But what I want has never mattered.

"We can't," I say.

I pull back, looking down at my gloves.

I can't touch Nox, or anybody else.

That's always been my curse. Locked away in my tower, alive but never living, watching as the people around me laugh and shake hands, or sling an arm over their friend's shoulder. Threading themselves together like it's nothing.

What if I have to relive the horror of Nox's death on that beach all over again? Or what if the curse of my touch triggers a new death somehow?

As much as I want Nox, I can't risk what touching him might do.

"It's okay," he says. "I know what my future holds. I'm not scared, Selestra."

The softness of his voice almost makes me believe it.

I let him slowly slip the gloves from my hand.

Left, then right.

The cool breeze from the cave slips through my fingers.

My heart pounds, punching against my chest like it's trying to break free.

Nox's fingers are so close to mine that I almost can't breathe.

One slip, one fracture of movement and we'll touch.

I keep my eyes on our hands.

Every inch of me is humming.

"I don't want to see you die again," I tell him.

It would break me.

"Don't focus on that," he says softly. "Just focus on this. On us. On something happy, instead of constant death. Your magic is more than that, Selestra, and so are you."

I bite my lip, nodding as the strength of his words shatters my fears.

I want this and him more than I've wanted anything in my whole life, and for once it is mine to have. I'm no longer locked in a tower and forced to push my magic away until it is convenient for someone else. This wish, this *want*, is mine to have and mine to keep.

There is nobody standing in my way but me.

Nox's hand drifts up my arm and to my cheek, slowly, to make sure I'm okay. I can feel a distinct tingling in my bones. The current of him passing through me, making me feel safe.

That's when it hits me.

A vision.

It doesn't hurt or rip through me like the others. As I focus on Nox and not death, just like he said to, the vision washes over me like a familiar river.

Nox and I are in a strange room, draped by ivy and wild daisies. Two thrones sit side by side in a mosaic of green glass, backed by a large stained-glass window that echoes their intricate shape. It lets the sun breathe into the room, radiating coils of color across the stone floor.

Above the thrones, a large chandelier sweeps downward, covered in crystals and entwined by the same deep ivy that circles the hall.

It's a room of beauty and nature.

Somehow, I know it's the old palace of Thavma. The once-home to my once-family and all the magic in the Six Isles.

I look down at my feet and see the stone twinkle beneath them like stars.

"Ready, princess?" Nox asks.

He's grinning, cheeks dimpling in the green light around him.

I reach up to adjust a crown of silver and vines on my head. It twists through my hair like the flowers surrounding us.

I know in that moment that for the first time, I'm not seeing death. It's something else: life.

Something happy.

Our goddess Asclepina's magic was rooted in life as much as it was in death: the power to heal and to protect. I've never considered that it could mean Somniatis witches can see any future, not just the awful ones.

What if we can see good too?

What if I'm not cursed?

I blink and stare back at Nox in the present.

"Selestra," he says.

For some reason just that word, just my name from his lips, makes me ache. It pulls something inside me, and I yearn to feel him.

All of him. To let him feel all of me.

When he kisses me, it sets the world on fire.

His lips brush against mine, softly at first, like he's afraid he might break me. Then when I don't pull away and the world doesn't end, I feel him smile against my lips.

One of his hands moves down my body, and gently grazes the small of my back where my shirt has ridden up. The other slides through my hair and finds its way to the base of my neck, pulling me farther into him so that every inch of us is touching.

My tongue feels numb as I drink him in, taste him on my lips. It's like something inside me breaks free and every touch makes me feel more electric than the next.

Then he says my name again, nothing more than breath on his mouth, and I think I implode.

I am a thousand tiny pieces floating high, higher, and I will never be put back together.

Nox presses harder against me and it all falls away.

Our families. The world. The war.

I'm breathless.

I don't know how much time passes before we break apart, but it is not enough. It will never be enough.

Nox pulls back, leaving the taste of him on my lips.

"See?" he says. "Nobody died."

He breaks into a smile, wide and toothy, like he's made some huge discovery. Like he didn't just split me into a million pieces and scatter them everywhere.

"Not bad for a runaway soldier," I say.

My voice is dry and winded.

"Such high praise."

He reaches out and cups my cheek, strokes his thumb along my jaw. I let my head fall into his palm, finding comfort in his touch. His skin, warm on mine, without any kind of fear or worry seeping into me.

"I saw a vision."

"My death?" he asks.

I shake my head, grinning. "Life."

All this time I've been worrying about my magic being caked in doom, but what if all along I only saw those things because I expected to? Because I was told that I would and let it be the only thing to plague my thoughts?

Years spent believing I couldn't touch anyone, and it was all lies.

I used to sneak out to look up at the moon and the stars, to whisper my secrets to the night for safekeeping, and hoping desperately it would whisper answers to any problems I had. Give me strength to overcome them. But the stars never held any answers, they were just lights. The strength was always inside me. And so was the light, brighter than any the stars could hold.

I won't ever let that be extinguished again.

We rest for only a couple of hours before I wake to hear the cavern humming.

I open my eyes and the air glitters with tiny yellow lights that I quickly realize are butterflies. Their wings flap in song, filling the cavern with a gentle hum.

I push myself from the floor and follow them.

"Selestra, wait a second."

Nox clambers to his feet to stop me, but I head onward, ignoring him. "They'll lead us to where we need to go," I say.

"They're *butterflies*," he protests. "They're not leading anyone anywhere."

I look at him. This tousled warrior wishing to change an entire world but unable to have a little faith first.

I'm still dizzy with the feel of his fingers in my hair and his lips brushing across mine. With the future of a life beyond war and locked towers that he opened for me. I wish I could have stayed in that moment with him forever, but we have a war to win first.

"Your butterfly led us somewhere," I remind him.

Nox's frown relaxes. He places his hands gently on my shoulders.

"I suppose if I've learned anything by now, then it's to trust you with my life," he says. "So lead the way, princess."

I grin. I would kiss him right here and now if I didn't think it would cause me to lose all focus.

We let the butterflies lead us through the trees, fluttering in and out of the branches.

Eventually they come to a stop by a single tree, unlike any of the others. It has leaves instead of crystals and a decaying trunk that opposes any beauty surrounding it.

Underneath its branches is a large wooden trunk, next to a pile of bones and a rusty sword.

"Over there!" I say, excited at the thought that I was right after all. "This must be what Eldara wanted us to find by heading north."

Nox raises his eyebrows. "A trunk in the middle of an underground forest?" He seems unconvinced.

"It's a special trunk," I say.

Nox gestures to the ground, where another set of bones lies beside it. "Bet the last guy thought so too." He shoves his hands into his pockets. "If it's not a ladder out of here, I'm just not sure how useful it's going to be for us."

Except I know I'm right. I can feel the magic reverberating off this thing, chorused by the hum of the butterflies.

I reach out a hand for the trunk.

"Selestra," Nox says in warning. "I don't think you should do that."

I pay no attention to him, flicking up the hook that seals the trunk.

Nox steps toward me. "Really," he says. "It could be a—"

I hear a brief whirl and then Nox is pushing me to the floor.

We splash into the water just as an arrow whips by my head and stabs into the tree trunk.

"What was that?" I ask, eyes wide.

Nox gets quickly to his feet and glares down at the box. "I bet that lock is rigged," he says. "It's a booby trap."

"A *what* trap?"

He turns to me, eyes alight in amusement. "What word is giving you trouble?"

I roll my eyes and get to my feet. Before I can think of a retort, the bones beside the trunk rattle.

We turn together to see the shattered pieces jumping from the ground. They crawl slowly toward each other and we can only watch as the bones slot into place and rise to a stand.

I stumble back a step as a disjointed skeleton raises its rusted sword.

"I told you that your aunt wanted to kill us," Nox says.

The skeleton juts its blade out to him and Nox manages to block it artfully. He swipes his own sword upward, then slashes it in an arc over his head and across the skeleton's neck.

The creature pauses and then reaches down to pick up its dislodged skull.

It places it back on its neck and stabs at Nox again.

Nox's eyes widen as he skitters backward.

"It didn't die!" I yell.

"Yes, princess," he says. He blocks another blow. "I noticed."

I cast my eyes over the skeleton, but I don't see a jewel like there was with the ghost who attacked us. There's no sign of an artifact to be smashed that could quell this magic.

"How do we kill it?" I ask desperately.

"I was hoping you could figure that out," Nox says.

He ducks down, narrowly avoiding the skeleton's blade, and I breathe a sigh of relief.

Forget bleeding out; one nick from that rusted thing and he'd probably die of infection.

Nox rolls forward and out of the skeleton's path, coming up behind it. He slices it across the back, but his sword simply clatters against its rigid bones.

Think, I tell myself. *How does one kill a dead thing?*

Not that I care to admit it, but killing a human is simple. They're fragile and easily broken. They bleed and they break, and even someone like me—with the ability to heal—isn't invincible.

Even I can't survive having my head chopped off.

"Whenever you're ready to lend a hand!" Nox calls out.

He slides out of the way of yet another blow, his feet splashing in the shallow water.

"I'm thinking!" I shout back.

I bite my lip.

Just like Nox to not give me a minute to come up with a plan. Never mind that I've been saving him day in and day out since we first met.

I pause, giving in to a smile as an idea crosses my mind.

The first time I helped Nox at the After Dusk Inn, I did so by nearly draining a man of his life force. Perhaps this skeleton can survive being chopped and dismantled, but that's only because something—some kind of energy—is animating it.

If I drain that away . . .

"Cut off its head again!" I yell to Nox.

He pauses, confused, but does as I ask, sweeping his blade across the skeleton's neck once more.

Its skull splashes to the ground.

"Pass it over to me!"

Nox wrinkles his nose and kicks the skeletal head toward me.

I kneel down as the skeleton's body skitters across the pool of water, searching for the missing part of itself.

"What are you doing?" Nox asks.

"What I always do," I say. I place my hands on the skull. "Saving your life."

I can feel the life force of the creature the moment I touch it. It's weak, like a fading song, or the last glimpse of sunlight before the dark descends.

I open myself up to let that essence funnel into me, dragging it from the creature's bones and into my heart.

Its life. Its energy.

It's not like what I did with Nox, where I tugged gently on his threads. He opened himself up to me, but this skeleton fights.

I have to pull and claw.

The headless skeleton pauses and shakes. Its bones rattle across the cavern. Then finally, it collapses into a heap on the floor.

"You okay?" Nox asks, coming to my side.

"Fine," I say, nodding. My heart races against my chest, like it's fit to burst. "I feel great, actually."

It's like I've just eaten from the grandest banquet and I can still taste every ounce of it on my tongue. I feel energized.

Full.

"You know, you're kind of scary sometimes," Nox says. "Remind me not to get on your bad side."

I shoot him a look. "You've always been on my bad side."

At that, he grins. A true smile that steals my breath.

Sometimes I think that Nox is like the wind, going from storm to breeze, from powerful to gentle. From a person I never wanted to know to someone I can't imagine not knowing.

As a team, we feel almost unstoppable.

Nox gestures toward the trunk. "Time to see if you were right," he says. "Go ahead."

I kneel beside it and take in a breath.

Whatever's inside this should be our way out. A pass for the tests and trials Eldara set us. This will prove that Nox and I are worthy, and we can be transported out of this place.

We've faced decayed forests, ground that has tried to swallow us whole, ghost warriors, perilous bridges, and skeleton attackers.

If Eldara wanted to see if we were ready, then she's seen enough.

My heart thumps like a war drum as I flip open the lid and lean to look inside.

A flash of blinding light bursts out from it, like a storm was contained inside.

Nox and I fall backward and I rub my eyes as my vision readjusts.

A furious hissing fills the cavern. When I blink the world back into existence, I see that the trunk is filled with snakes.

My eyes widen as the first of what looks like dozens begin to slither out.

Quickly, I scurry back over to the trunk. But before I can close the lid, I see the jewel. A tiny green thing in the center of the box.

It calls out to me, just like I felt when I first saw the cave. It feels so familiar, as though a piece of me is hidden inside it.

In awe, I reach out toward it.

The snakes curl around it.

One hisses up at me. Its forked tongue sways, yellow eyes meeting mine as it rises upward.

Eyes we share.

I stare at the creature and it stares straight back at me, like it's seeing into my soul.

"Watch out!"

Panicked, Nox shoves me backward and away from the box, drawing the ire of the creatures inside. I blink, snapping myself out of the daze as they lunge out at him.

Quickly, Nox slams the lid of the trunk closed, decapitating several of the snakes in the process. Their heads fall to the floor where Nox kneels.

My eyes widen.

"Selestra." Nox's voice is throaty and low.

"It's fine," I say, shaking my head to right myself from the trance-like state.

What was that?

"I'm okay," I tell him.

"Speak for yourself."

Nox turns to face me, clutching at his arm. Red welts rise up from his skin, dripping blood on the floor.

Snake bites. Too many to count.

"I think they might be venomous," Nox says.

And then he slumps to the ground.

I rush to Nox's side and drag him away from the trunk.

The puncture wounds on his arm are deep and the skin surrounding them is already turning gray. The venom must be setting in, searing inside his skin.

"What was that?" he asks.

"A box of snakes," I say. "But you trapped them back inside. Don't worry."

Nox blinks. "You just said *box of snakes* and I'm not supposed to worry?"

I tug a loose strand of hair furiously away from my face as I try to get a better look at his wounds.

"I need to heal you," I say. "Give me your arm."

I pull his arm forward and close my eyes. When nothing happens, I tighten my grip on his arm, pressing my lips tightly together.

I open my eyes.

Nothing.

The magic doesn't come when I call it. It's as though there's something blocking my connection to my own power.

"I can try again," I say, desperate as he begins to grow pale.

Nox pulls his arm back. "No."

"You don't want me to heal you?"

"Healing snake venom clearly isn't the same as healing a stab wound," he says. "And we can't risk weakening you. You need to be at full strength to complete the trials. I won't be the reason that wavers."

He tries to stand, but barely shuffles forward before collapsing back into my arms.

"You'll die if we don't do something," I say.

"That's been the theme of this month."

Nox's head rests against my chest, breath growing deep. His skin feels hot and sticky against me.

We don't have much time.

"The snakes were guarding some kind of jewel," I tell him, gesturing back to the trunk. "Like the one we smashed with that ghost."

I look over to the snake box and bite my lip, remembering how the snake's eyes met mine with such curiosity.

"I think it's a gift," I say. "Eldara said these trials would reward me with power. Maybe the jewel holds some kind of connection to the past queens."

I make to move out from under Nox, but he grabs my shirt-sleeve.

"Wait a second," he says, keeping me still. "Did you forget what was inside that box?"

I didn't forget, but I know that not everything is bad just because I expect it to be. I've spent too long fearing things. My powers and my family. Even myself.

"What if those snakes attack you too?"

He holds up his injured arm and I wince, seeing how the infection has taken hold, marring his skin. It looks like it takes all his energy just to do that single action.

"They won't hurt me," I say with certainty. "You had your sword and I think they sensed you were ready to attack, but when they saw me, I felt a connection. They're a part of my history, Nox. I told you once about how Asclepina fell into a pit of snakes and didn't harm them, so they gave her the powers of a goddess. This must be what the final trial is."

"What if you're wrong?" Nox asks. His voice is breathy as the venom takes hold. "I'm not strong enough to protect you. I can barely move."

"It's not up to you to save me," I tell him. I stroke the hair from his face, settling him down onto the cavern floor. "I'm the one who saves you, remember?"

Nox manages a weak smile, his hand slipping from my sleeve.

He may not have faith in a box of snakes, but I know now that he has faith in me, and that means more than I can say.

"Be careful," he warns.

His voice is breathy as the venom takes hold.

The last thing I want to do is move from his side, but for whatever reason, I can't heal the snake's venom. If whatever is in this box might give me the power to do so, then I have to try.

It's Nox's only chance.

I take in a steadying breath and then walk toward the trunk. I clear my mind of everything but Asclepina's tale, then I flip the lid open.

Instantly, the snakes slip out and then the trunk shakes, birthing more and more of them from its mouth. They come as if from nowhere.

The ground begins to rumble and then without warning, it folds in on itself. I shuffle quickly backward as it creates a pit that drags the serpents and the trunk itself down.

I peer over to see dozens of them swarming in the new hole.

The jewel is in the center.

It's just like Asclepina and the pit she fell into.

I turn back to Nox, who watches me with heavy eyes. His skin is damp with sweat and I can see the way he sways as he tries to hold his head up.

He doesn't have long and I won't lose him waiting around in fear of what could be.

I *can't* lose him.

"I'll be right back," I say.

I descend into the pit.

My fingernails dig into the dirt as I slide downward. The snakes rise when they see me, tilting their heads to get a good look. Their hisses are sharp and threatening, but they don't attack.

I spy the jewel I'm looking for and curse my luck when I see that the largest of the snakes is coiled around it in a vise.

I take a step toward it and it bares its teeth protectively. It is striped black and yellow, like the lines of night and day. The two sides of the world. Of the good magic my family once had and the dark magic we use now.

The snake sets its eyes on me, watching as I cautiously approach.

"I know you," I tell it, trying to keep my voice steady.

I don't blink, letting our twin eyes stay settled on each other.

I kneel down beside it, my heart pounding in fear at being so close to such a deadly creature.

I press my lips together.

The king made my family into deadly things too. I grew up thinking evil was simple and clear-cut, with no in-between, and that once the blood oath took hold of me, I would become a monster unable to feel or do good.

A part of me feared I'd never be capable of redemption.

But I'm not sworn to anyone and I should know myself better.

I have to learn to trust in my power and to not attack out of fear and callousness, like the king. Or to be scared of things I don't know or understand, like the people who flinched at my eyes.

The snake keeps watch on me, waiting.

"I'm going to change what we did," I promise the creature. "I'm going to make it right."

I reach over and pluck the jewel from beside the snake.

Its tongue forks out and when it hisses, I panic a little before I realize it is more a call than an attack. The remaining snakes slither toward their master, crawling in and out of my legs, pushing across the dirt. When they reach the snake that guarded the jewel, they merge into it.

Dozens of creatures, a rainbow of colors and sizes, morphing into something new.

The shape quickly begins to take hold, and in moments, born from the legion of snakes, a kneeling woman rises.

Her body is a mix of skin and brightly colored scales that glitter in the darkness of the cave. Her green hair tumbles down to her ankles, and her eyes, so wide and bright, are a mirror of my own, reflecting my awe.

"Selestra," she says, voice as light as wind.

The voice of a goddess.

Asclepina.

My family's patron goddess stands before me.

Asclepina, the first of the Somniatis witches. The Goddess of Snakes and Immortality. The Healer and the Protector.

She is more beautiful than I could have imagined.

I bow my head, unsure of what else to do.

A delicate hand lifts my chin back to rising.

"Queens need not bow or cower," she says. "Especially to the past."

Her voice is unlike anything I've ever heard before. It sounds like honey tastes and feels like silk against my skin, soft and warm as the setting sun.

"It's really you," I say, awestruck.

Asclepina nods, watching me with eyes like forest moss. The scales of her skin are iridescent.

"You have learned faith in yourself and your powers through these trials," she says. "You have proven your wisdom in embracing harmony. In knowing that sometimes enemies can be made allies, if only we let them. A true ruler understands that peace is the ultimate goal, far above power."

"My mother told me stories about you," I say.

"And people will one day tell stories of you."

My heart is like a butterfly, fluttering inside my chest.

There are so many things I want to ask her. Endless questions, so that I don't even know where to begin. About the blood oath and if my mother can ever be freed from the king's grasp. About the afterlife and if all the witches of Thavma are in a place of peace.

About Nox.

I hold out my palm to reveal the king's serpent.

Asclepina laughs and it's a beautiful sound, enveloping me whole.

"Two children, with the power to change worlds," she says. "I put it there so you would realize your shared destiny and we would have the opportunity to undo a grave mistake."

Isolda's mistake, I think. When she helped the king conquer Thavma and tied us to him.

Asclepina places a warm hand on my cheek. Touching her feels like touching the first breath of morning.

"I only hope destiny is not cut short."

I frown. "What do you mean by that?"

She doesn't answer, but she does look upward to the edge of the pit.

I follow her gaze.

Nox.

Panicked, I claw my nails into the dirt and climb back up and out of the snake pit. Nox is unmoving on the cave floor.

I rush to his side. His skin is gray-tinged, barely a whimper of breath escaping his pale lips. I touch a hand to his cheek.

"Nox," I say. "Wake up."

His eyes briefly flutter open. "Selestra?" he asks, squinting in the darkness of the cave. "I can't . . ."

He trails off and reaches out a hand for mine. I swallow as I press it tightly against me.

Nox's breathing begins to falter.

I feel him growing cold as his hand shakes in mine.

He blinks, eyes searching for me, rolling over and across the cave.

"There's nothing," he says. "Selestra, I can't see you."

I blanch. The venom is taking hold, erasing his sight and decaying his body. My heart collapses. "I'm here," I assure him, squeezing his hand tighter. "I'm here."

I grit my teeth as Nox stares over my shoulder and into the nothingness. I won't look on as he fades away, like I did with his father. I won't just sit here and have Nox die in my arms. I turn to Asclepina, who has risen from the pit and to my side.

"Heal him," I beg. "Please. He doesn't have long."

Asclepina shakes her head. "That is not for me to do," she says softly. Regretfully.

"I can't lose him!" I yell. "You don't understand. I need him. I—"

I love him, I realize.

"I can't watch him die again," I tell her, pleading.

"Then don't," she answers. "Magic is yours to command, dear one."

I steel my breath and turn back to Nox, angry that she refuses to use her powers to intervene in this.

It's up to me.

I'm not losing the first person to have faith in me.

I'm not losing the boy who showed me an entire world and the kind of person I could be in it.

I close my eyes, letting the tears slip down my face and onto Nox's ashen skin. His hand goes slack in mine.

Please, I plead. *Help me save him.* I call on every ounce of power I have in me and on all that surrounds me.

The wind that breezes through the holes in the cavern ceiling.

The river that puddles around us and the fish that slip through its waters.

The trees that breathe life and air into the world.

The goddess by my side.

I draw from all of them, reaching out and siphoning power from every inch of the world I can.

I pull it all into me and then let it wash over Nox like an ocean wave.

All that I am becomes all that he is. *Bring him back to me.*

Nox's hand tightens in mine.

I open my eyes and find he is staring up at me.

"Selestra?" he whispers, confused as he takes in my tear-streaked face.

I don't wait for more. I kiss him.

I taste the life and warmth on his lips. Nox sits up, pressing himself closer to me, not letting us break apart for a moment.

His hands knot in my hair and I'm breathless with the feel of him. The hunger for him, gnawing in my stomach and my heart.

Nox presses his forehead against mine. "You're a goddess," he whispers.

"Actually." I pull back from him and gesture to Asclepina. "She is."

Nox blinks, taken aback as if he hadn't realized we weren't alone in this cave any longer.

Nox's eyes widen and he scurries quickly to his feet. "Asclepina?"

I pull myself up to stand beside him. "One and the same."

Asclepina looks between us, a soft smile on the edge of her rose-petal lips. "It is time," she says. "Selestra is to be imbued with the magic of queens. All we need now is the final sacrifice."

I tense, my hand shooting to Nox's, in case she tries to approach us. "What are you talking about?" She cannot possibly think I would ever let her lay a hand on him.

"Do not worry, niece."

Eldara's voice fills the cave.

"It is my gift to give, not his."

I stare as my distant aunt glides toward us. Her feet barely leave a print and her dusty pink dress doesn't dampen as it kisses the watery ground. She has but one guard with her: Lucian.

"What are you doing here?" I ask my lost aunt.

"I'm here to do what must be done."

Eldara turns to Asclepina and bows deeply.

"My goddess," she says in reverence. "It has been an age since I saw you at my own trial."

"And now you must do what your past queen did for you."

Eldara dips her head in understanding, but I remain uncertain.

"What is she talking about?"

Eldara smiles when she looks at me. "I am so proud of you," she says. "You overcame the trials inside yourself, learning to be selfless and to trust each other and all you have inside you."

I don't like the way she looks at me, in a goodbye.

"What is the sacrifice?" I ask again.

"Me," Eldara says. "My power and all I once was. The goddess will share her magic with you as she once did with me, and in doing so remove the last sparks of it from my being."

"Will you die?" I ask.

"A part of me," she says. "And only so that you can live."

I shake my head, refusing to believe that.

"I won't ask you to do that."

"You don't need to ask me," Eldara says. "I do this because it belongs to you. I haven't deserved it since I abandoned my people in Thavma. I failed them, but I know you can succeed where I didn't. The Polemistés warriors don't need me, Selestra. They need you."

Nerves rise up in my stomach, but I know she's right.

"You must embrace your destiny," Eldara says, "rather than worry for mine. The past cannot decide the future. That is for you."

I started out so resigned to my future, only to realize I had the power to change it. Now I owe it to the Six Isles to help change their futures too.

To undo the wrongs my family has done.

To make the Six Isles a force of good once more.

Eldara isn't the weapon I was searching for, Nox told me. *It was you, Selestra.*

I bite my lip and nod.

Eldara takes my hand and joins it together with Asclepina's.

"And so it is," our goddess says.

Light radiates from her, warm and yellow. It flows from her hands and into mine. From Eldara's heart and across my skin until it touches my own chest.

I am alight.

I can't describe it, but it's as though something has awakened inside of me.

I can feel everything: the trees and the air and the earth. I can feel the sun, even though it has not yet appeared in the sky. I can feel the waters of the Endless Sea calling to me.

My breath sparks as I let the light of a goddess fill me, enchanting my blood and gifting me with the power to take on a king of souls and shadow.

"My power is yours, dear one," Asclepina finally says. "You are all that I am and I am all that lives in you."

I can feel her essence inside me, waiting for me to call on it.

I want to thank her, but I don't know how and I don't have time. She smiles at me and then she fades. In a blink. There and gone.

The cave seems dimmer somehow.

"You're ready," Eldara says.

The wrinkles on her face look newly deeper and her green hair has now mottled to white. She looks like she's aging in front of my eyes.

Suddenly I realize how much shorter she is than me, like a tiny pocket of a woman.

She collapses to the floor.

"No!" I scream, rushing to her side.

Eldara smiles up at me, the crisp waves of her hair sweeping across the cavern floor. She reaches a hand to touch my cheek.

I have taken every spark of magic from her and I can tell she isn't long for the world. Without our family's power to rejuvenate her, she will fade away.

"This is a beginning, niece, not an end," she says. Her voice is as soft and certain as ever. "I am glad for it."

"I don't want to lose you," I say.

Eldara is the one member of my family who believed I could be something more, encouraging me to be great where my mother always wanted me to keep my head down.

"Nothing is ever lost that can't be found again," she says. "I walk with goddesses now."

"Thank you," I say to her. "For believing in me."

Eldara threads her hand through mine like a needle and I feel the spark, the prick, of her magic within me.

"If Seryth wants a soul-eater," she says, "then when the time comes, you be sure to give him one."

Her hand goes slack in mine and the yellow of her eyes turns milky.

Then all at once, the butterflies that led us through the cavern surround her, landing on her still body. Their wings hum, singing her a lullaby goodbye. Then from those wings, they begin to glow and glitter. Their bodies are alight in magic, seeping from them and to Eldara.

When they depart, fluttering upward toward the very tip of the cavern, Eldara's body is gone.

I walk with goddesses now, she said, rekindling the stories my mother told me of the afterlife of our people. It doesn't fill me with mourning, but with hope.

Eldara is reunited with Asclepina and with the witches of Thavma who perished by the king's hand. She is at peace now and I will honor her by bringing that same peace to the Six Isles.

"Selestra?" Nox asks. He slips his hand through mine and the current returns, shooting up from my fingertips and through my entire body. "Are you okay?"

I nod.

His eyes flicker between me and Lucian, my aunt's most trusted guard. "What do we do now?"

"Now we get ready," I say. "We fight."

I look at him and his eyes glisten with a thousand futures. A thousand hopes and opportunities and *life*.

So much life, in place of the death I've always feared.

41

SELESTRA

I hoped a bath would get rid of the smell of the forest, but the damp seems almost permanent.

After Lucian escorted us from the cave and back to the safeguard of central Polemistés, he explained Eldara's sacrifice and my powers to the others, and then there was barely any chance for Nox and me to talk before we were whisked our separate ways.

Him, to be reunited with Micah and assess how close the king's ships were. Me, to be taken to get cleaned up and checked for any severe injuries. I was so desperate to bathe and wash away the dirt and mud that had gathered in every crevice of me, I didn't even bother to argue.

As I step from my room, dressed in an oversize hand-knitted sweater and the softest pair of moccasins I've ever worn, I wonder what my mother would think if she could see me now. No ballgowns or pretense, and no need to hide my power from scared men trying desperately to hold on to control.

I am blessed by a goddess, ready to wield the magic that will help us take back the islands.

I will make Eldara proud.

My feet creak against the floorboards as I approach Nox's room and I pause with a wince, arching my neck to peer around the thin corridor and make sure I haven't alerted any guards.

Though as I think it, Lucian saunters down the hall, his sword in hand and his patented armor shining in the dim torchlight. I wonder if he ever takes it off. Part of me thinks the warrior might very well sleep in steel.

"Majesty," he says with a bow.

I straighten.

"Evening, Lucian," I answer back.

"I hope you're feeling more rested now?" he asks.

If he knows where I'm heading, he doesn't let on.

"Yes." I nod. "Far more refreshed."

"I'm glad."

He smiles, like it's a struggle. I imagine Lucian is out of practice and that after so many years of serving Eldara, he's not used to what comes next.

He must miss her, as I do.

He must want to ensure her death was a worthwhile sacrifice.

"Well then," I say. "I better be going."

"Of course." Lucian steps to the side to let me past.

I give him a smile of thanks and continue on down the corridor, trying to remember which new room Nox was placed in after the trials.

"Oh, and, Majesty?" Lucian says.

I turn back to him, arching my eyebrows in question.

"Don't stay up too late with the soldier. The Red Moon is upon us and you have a long battle ahead."

I blink, mortified, and watch as Lucian saunters back down the hall with a chuckle.

I can feel my cheeks getting redder by the minute, and when I finally reach Nox's door, I almost don't want to knock.

My chest heaves as I do and wait anxiously for him to open it.

When it takes a moment, I bite my lip, wondering if maybe he's asleep. He must be tired. I know I am. Still, I couldn't resist wanting to see him.

After everything that happened in the forest, I haven't been able to clear my mind of him. Of our kiss—*kisses*—and how I've finally realized what he means to me.

The door opens and I breathe a sigh of relief, until I see that it's Micah who leans against its frame.

"Well," he says with a wink. "Little late-night visit?"

Souls, is there anyone else who's going to tease me tonight?

"I could ask you the same thing," I say to Micah. "Shouldn't you be in your own room? I heard it was rather new and fancy."

Micah shrugs. "I'm too energetic, thinking about battle."

"That's really sad," I tell him. "You should get a hobby."

"Not everyone can be the savior of the world," he says.

He throws the door open wider and takes a step back.

"Come on in and join the party."

To my surprise, it's not just Nox lounging on his bed by a deck of cards, but Irenya too. Her short blond hair falls across her face as she leans over to place her share of cards on the firm mattress.

Opposite her, Nox scoffs and throws his own hand in a messy pile at his crossed feet.

"You're conning me," he says.

"You conned me first," she answers back.

I smirk, glad that someone is finally beating Nox at his own game.

"Selestra!" Irenya jumps up from the bed with a grin when she sees me. "You're clean!"

"Don't sound so surprised," I say in a laugh. "It's known to happen every now and again."

I look back to Nox, feeling a little sad that everyone was together without me. As if she can read my mind, Irenya's eyes widen and she quickly says, "I was waiting for you earlier, but they wouldn't let me see you no matter how much I argued. That Lucian guy is a real piece of work when it comes to *the rules*."

She looks furious at the memory of it, wrinkling her nose.

"Damn Polemistés warriors," she says in a curse. "I was getting foot cramps standing there all evening. Micah found me hovering outside your doorway and dragged me back here to wait for you. He thought this might be your first stop."

Irenya looks knowingly between me and Nox, and I try not to redden again. I really hadn't planned on an audience.

"I'm so glad you're safe," Irenya says. She beams at me and places a hand on my arm. "I missed you."

I feel the same: I hated being apart from her while I was in the forest. It was the longest we've ever been separated and I've been longing to talk with her until the sun comes up about everything and nothing.

I'm glad to have not just an army in this place, but a true friend.

"I missed you as well," I tell Irenya.

Then for the first time in both of our lives, I truly hug her.

Irenya stiffens in surprise, not used to the contact. I'm not either. I've been so scared to touch anyone, even my best friend, for fear I'd see death. But now I know that it doesn't always have to be the case.

As long as I practice controlling my powers and don't let the fear of death plague my mind, I don't have to be cursed by it.

Irenya squeezes me back, her arms wrapping tightly around me. Years and years of wanting nothing more than to embrace my friend finally bubble to the surface.

Touch. Comfort. *Solace.*

It's more than a thirst being satisfied. It is as though a piece of myself I always knew was missing has finally been given back to me.

But I don't have full control yet. When Irenya's cheek grazes my own, a small flash of the future hits me.

Irenya, with fabric scissors between her teeth, adjusting the hem of the most beautiful dress I've ever seen. People line up outside a store with her name in cursive, waiting to place orders for elegant gowns and intricate lace.

I smile at my friend's future and the knowing that it's everything she deserves.

"Selestra," Irenya says, when I pull back. Tears fill her eyes at the shock of the embrace. "What happened in those trials?"

I wipe the tears from her cheeks. "I learned a lot," I tell her. "There is so much I need to tell you."

Irenya grins, wiping her nose with her sleeve. "I can't wait to hear it."

"We don't have to hug now too, do we?" Micah asks, looking between us. "I'm not sure I could handle the sentimentality. Or the possibility of you seeing my death. It would ruin the mystery."

Nox rolls his eyes. "Nobody wants to hug you anyway, Micah."

He approaches me with a tender smile.

His dark hair curls at the nape of his neck, longer and far more unruly than when we first met. The scar I first touched when I saw into his future still pinks across his cheek and for some reason it makes me swallow. The force of his stare nearly throws me off balance.

"You look really nice," Nox tells me.

I fiddle with the hem of my sweater, my fingers slipping over the thick woven fabric. I haven't worn my gloves since leaving the forest and it still feels strange. I want to practice and make sure I can keep control of my powers at all times, not just when I'm kissing Nox.

I blush at the memory and look up at him.

"Thank you," I tell him. "So do you."

At this, Micah snorts and I curse myself inwardly.

I'm not well practiced in this. Whatever *this* is.

"You look nice too," Micah mimics, jostling Nox with his elbow. "You both need to get a room."

"This *is* my room," Nox says. "And you're refusing to leave."

Micah shrugs and slumps onto the pillow beside Irenya. "You'll miss me when I'm gone."

"Not likely," Nox shoots back, and Micah presses a hand to his heart as if Nox's words are a bullet.

"Don't worry about him," Irenya says, giving Micah the side-eye. She gathers the cards up from the bed and reshuffles them. "Micah's just jealous because nobody has ever told him that *he* looks nice."

"Actually," Micah says. "I tell myself that every day."

I shake my head, unable to help but laugh. "How have you coped putting up with those two by yourself all night?" I ask.

Nox smiles and my heart tickles inside my chest. "It's been a struggle," he says. "But you're here now."

"Come on, Selestra." Irenya deals the cards out onto the mattress. "Let's show these boys how the professionals do it."

I smile broadly and fling myself beside her. "They won't know what's hit them."

We stay that way for hours, throwing cards and gibes, laughing our way through the night and forgetting all about the war that threatens to darken our doors.

The night feels eternal as I sit with my friends and I wish it was, forcing myself to stay awake even when my eyes begin to flicker shut.

Long after the candles dim, wax growing shallow in their holders, and after Micah and Irenya retire to bed, Nox and I stay.

"I guess I win," Nox says.

He looks down at the line of cards: a serpent's straight, just like the past three times.

"I guess you're cheating again," I declare.

Nox smirks and gathers the cards back up. "Sore loser."

"You forget that I was at the After Dusk Inn when you swindled the group of men who tried to kill us."

Nox waves his hand in the air. "A lifetime ago," he says. "I'm a changed man now. Honest, right to the core. *Noble*, even."

"I think you're confusing honor with idiocy."

Nox gasps dramatically and pretends to draw his sword. "I should run you through for questioning my integrity."

I flick a stray card at his chest. "It's your turn to deal."

"I think we've officially played every single game I know," he says.

We're sat by the fireplace in his room now, huddled on the shag carpet, bare toes tickling with warmth.

"Does that mean you surrender?" I ask. "I win?"

"You've lost the last six rounds," Nox says. "But sure. You win, princess."

I settle back into the carpet, leaning against the base of the dark green armchairs.

"Do you think we'll have just as good luck with victory when the king attacks?" I ask. "So many people have died because of me and my family already. I don't want any more blood on my hands."

"They're not dying for you, Selestra." The words shoot forcefully from Nox's tongue. "They're dying for an idea and a hope. Just like my father did."

He takes in a breath and his eyes hollow with a deep sadness. It makes my chest ache just to look at him and the way he has to keep his grief hidden away for fear it'll overtake him.

"My father died because he wanted something better for this world," Nox says. "It's our job to create that better thing. Everything you've done in the past is because you were taught it was the right way. You can't help the fact that you were brought up on a lie."

It's true, but somehow I still feel foolish.

I let the king fill my days with lies and I trusted my mother more than anything, because her judgment was all I ever knew.

"Our past is not our future," Nox says. "And though we can't change the past, together we can change our future."

He takes my hands in his and they ignite all the little fires inside me. Nox is right. I won't let my past determine my future forever and I won't let it hold me back with guilt.

The Six Isles need a leader who looks forward instead of back.

"I'm glad you came tonight," Nox says.

I rest against his shoulder, relaxing into him. "Me too."

"I'm glad I broke into your bedroom that night as well."

I chuckle a laugh. "Me too."

"And I'm glad that I have you by my side," he says.

He slides his finger under my chin, tilting my head up to press my lips to his in a tender kiss. Every inch of me tingles under his touch, the warmth of his words setting me alight.

"We should probably get some rest," Nox says. "We've got a kingdom to save."

"No," I tell him as our fingers press together. "We have one to create."

I settle into him, and as the night grows even darker and tiredness overtakes me, I stay wrapped in his arms. I let his breathing lull me to sleep, the sound of his heartbeat a steady constant in my ear.

"Your Highness!"

I jump awake, wincing as the sun screams through the windows.

A young warrior dressed in full armor bursts into Nox's room.

"Lucian sent me to find you," he announces, trying desperately to catch his breath. "They're approaching the whirlpools."

He must have run from one of the guard stations, because his entire face is flushed red and sweat paints his forehead.

I look to Nox and his hand goes to his sword.

"They," I repeat.

My voice shakes with the weight of what's to come.

The warrior nods. "They're finally here," he says. "Seryth and his witch."

42

SELESTRA

"They'll be on the beach at any moment," Nox says as we huddle around the forge, gathering our weapons. "We have to head there now."

He lifts up Asden's gleaming sword.

The sun beats down, warming the back of my neck.

Around us, the warriors fasten their swords and steel their breaths. The shine of their wartime metal blooms against a backdrop of fresh lavender and the smell of lemon juice dripping from the trees.

I wish Eldara was here for this final battle, but we will be fighting it in her honor. In the honor of everyone who has perished because of the king's evils.

"You have to stay away from the beach," I say to Irenya as she lingers by the rows of weapons. "No matter how good a fighter you might think you've become in our sparring, it won't compare to the Last Army or my mother's magic."

Irenya holds her hands up in surrender. "You won't hear any arguments from me. I've never been one for sword fights anyway."

Good, I think.

As long as I know Irenya is safe, I'll be able to concentrate on what really matters.

Destroying Seryth and putting an end to the terror my family has helped him create.

I look to Nox, the warmth of his eyes steadying my nerves.

"Promise me you'll follow my lead and be careful for once."

Nox smirks. "Kind of hard to be careful in war, princess."

I fix him with a firm glare. "I'm serious. I don't want to see you die again."

I couldn't stand it.

I want to grab Nox and hold him close to me, away from the clutches of death and my mother, but with the fiercest warriors in the land staring between us, I swallow down those desires for now.

"If you survive past the Red Moon tonight, then we win," I remind him. "The king's immortality will be yours and he'll lose all power. I know I can't convince you to stay here with Irenya, but you can't lead the charge with me."

"Selestra—"

"I want you to hang back," I say, not letting him try to debate it. "Direct the waves of soldiers where we need them. This battle is about protecting you. Promise me if you see Seryth, then you'll do nothing but run."

Nox looks hesitant, but I know I'm right about this.

It's the only way we can truly avenge Asden and save the Six Isles.

Nox threads his hands through mine. "Don't worry, princess. If there's one thing I'm good at, it's surviving," he promises. "We've conquered death before. This is no different, as long as we're in it together."

I nod and calm my nervous breath, forcing my pounding heart to quiet. Nox is right: We've survived everything that's been thrown at us so far by staying together.

This is no different.

Death won't take us today. I won't let it.

It's time we take back our destinies for ourselves.

My mother holds the whirlpools in her grasp, placating them as if they are scared children.

The king's ship is pure black, nothing but darkness cleaving through the waters, and at the helm of it my mother stands. She holds her arms wide and the waters of the Endless Sea spit and quake.

Her magic, our family's magic, bursts into the air. I can only watch as she siphons the power straight from the mouths of the whirlpools and back into herself.

The waters surrounding Polemistés calm, still for the first time in a century. Eldara's protections, gone.

I grip the knife Nox gave me back on Armonía before we stole a pirate ship.

I've always known my mother's power was great, but this is mighty, beyond what I could have imagined or been told. The reason the king has never tried to attack from the whirlpools before isn't because he thought she couldn't do it—it was because he was cautious and calculating.

I cannot risk losing you, he once told my mother. *Not when the heir isn't yet eighteen.*

Attacking from the whirlpools was a risk. But he's not afraid of losing her life or her power anymore.

He's afraid of losing his own.

If Nox survives tonight, Seryth dies.

If we win this battle, then we win the freedom of the Six Isles.

But if we lose . . .

Nox's hand threads through mine. "Asclepina chose you," Nox reminds me, his words pressing into my heart and clearing away any doubts like old cobwebs. "Her power lives inside of you. It's yours to wield."

My heart quiets in an instant, calmed by the reassurance of his words, as the king's ships dock.

There are three of them, but in the distance beyond the cove, I can see dozens more lying in wait, biding time until the Polemistés sea battalion arrives.

A third of the Polemistés army stands behind me, Nox, and Micah, the others still guarding the walls and boarding their own attack ships. There's barely a hundred of us on this beach and I know that there are at least double that on these three ships alone.

My hand edges closer to Nox's. I crave the comfort of his touch more than ever.

"Remember," I announce to our warriors. "We need to delay until the Red Moon. After that, the king loses. Protect Nox and know that you are fighting not just for your own lives, but the life of the Six Isles."

I watch as the ladder from the royal ship unfolds onto the beach.

Seryth and my mother descend.

It feels like eons since I've seen them, lifetimes ago when I last bowed before a man of souls and shadows.

Seryth's long black hair drips like squid ink down his bare chest, skin plagued by those same serpents that once marked me and Nox. They strike across his cheeks too, which are marred by black paint and ancient symbols, crisscrossing against his unblemished skin.

The immortal warrior. Ever young, ever brutal.

He holds my mother's hand, helping her descend the ship.

Like me, she doesn't wear gloves.

Like me, she is dressed for war.

A black suit chokes at her neck, cascading down her back in a cape threaded in gold and green. She looks older, somehow. And though she's standing right in front of me, she looks so far away.

A memory of another world.

When she sees me, her lips part.

I am not the little heir she remembers, dressed in fine gowns and clutching at my gloves. I look her straight in the eye, an army behind me and a knife in my bare hands.

"Daughter," Theola says.

"Traitor," Seryth drawls, louder.

It's the first time I've ever seen the slip of his measured cruelty. The anger that must simmer beneath him rises up to the surface so it's clear for me to see.

The gibe doesn't touch me.

Just weeks ago it would have pricked my skin like a hundred needles, making me feel worthless and inept. Not good enough to be his heir, let alone his witch.

Now it washes over me like the waves of the Endless Sea.

He's the one that's unworthy. That crown isn't his to have.

"So what is it then?" Seryth asks. His feet crush a wild lily flower. "Before I kill you, I'd like to know about the magic this island holds." He spreads his arms out, gesturing toward the hundred Polemistés warriors across the sand. "What keeps these cretins alive?"

There is a brief pause, where even the sun seems to flicker and hold its breath, before Seryth gets his centuries-awaited answer.

"I do," I say.

The sun beams down onto the beach.

Seryth smirks, the points of his lips curving upward, smudging the symbols painted in the creases of his cheekbones. "You're just an heir, Selestra."

At this, Nox inches closer to me. I think he wants to reassure me, give me some kind of comfort that his words don't matter.

It's not necessary.

I already know.

Seryth isn't my king anymore. He's just a man. I know better than to give him any power over me.

"That's true, I am an heir," I say, my confidence rising to the surface. "I'm the heir to goddesses and queens."

"You must stop this, Selestra," my mother says, scolding me like I'm a child. "Your place is at our side."

"That was never my place."

"Then you're nothing but a dead witch." Seryth spits on the sand.

"Your fleet can't match the Polemistés battalion," Nox says.

Seryth's laugh shakes the trees. "This isn't going to be settled with ships. Let your little boats destroy mine. Let them kill every soldier I have."

Nox's eyes narrow.

"I'm willing to sacrifice everybody," Seryth says. "Are you?"

He looks between us, seeing how closely we stand together. His eyes flicker as he notes my lack of gloves.

His smile widens.

"Who are you willing to let die tonight?" Seryth asks.

I glare. I want to kill him where he stands.

This man has imprisoned my family into servitude for generations, forcing us to be monsters at his whims. He's stolen souls and homes and now he thinks he can steal us from each other.

From his three ships, ladders drop down onto the sand.

Seryth's army begins to descend.

They are in the hundreds.

"Let's see how this ends," he says as they draw their swords. "Between the best of you and the best of us."

He glances at my mother and runs a hand down her cheek.

"Between mothers and daughters," he says.

Theola blinks. If I didn't know better, I'd say it was a flinch.

My hands shake as I watch my mother. Her chin is high and her hands are like daggers pointed at her sides.

I thought I was ready for this, but a seed of doubt grows in my mind at the solemn look on her face.

She's still my mother.

Maybe there is a way to save her from all this if only—

"Kill them all," Seryth says. "But leave the traitors until last."

His smile is ever ripe, eyes like pits that absorb any light.

"I want them to see the world burn before they die."

43

SELESTRA

I rush toward my mother, but her magic crashes into me before I even get close.

It is like hitting a brick wall. My head ricochets back and then I am being lifted, carried through the wind and straight into the waters of the Endless Sea.

Moments from shore, the shallows of water shackle me like chains.

My mother stands over me.

"It is your destiny to be by my side," she says.

I shake my head.

Destiny isn't about chance, it's about choice. Choosing to be who you want to be, because that's who you're supposed to be.

My mother has let herself become a monster and I won't choose to become one alongside her.

She slips to a crouch and slides her hands around my throat, digging her nails in deep. "Do not make me do this. Surrender."

My fingers tear into the sand that hides under the water.

"Never," I say.

I bring my head up, crashing it against hers.

My mother stumbles backward.

I don't wait before I push out my hands and siphon the power of the wind, thrusting it into my mother's chest.

"Foolish child," she croaks.

She curls her hands into fists and I'm brought to my knees. Her knuckles whiten as she clenches harder, and in an instant, I feel as though I'm being crushed.

Something pulls from inside me, trying to tear my insides out. Then a sudden wave of wind knocks into me and I careen across the beach.

I hit the sand hard.

The thud rattles through me, but I push myself back up, not thinking about the pain. The time for that will come, but it's not now.

My mother rushes to me and I flip myself back onto my feet. She reaches out a hand, her claws ready to tear me apart.

I don't give her the advantage.

Swiftly, I grab her by the hair and bring her face down hard on my knee.

"There it is," Theola says. She licks the blood that drips down from her nose and onto her lip. "The darkness inside that you have been fighting all this time."

"It isn't darkness," I tell her, thinking of Asden. Of Eldara and Asclepina. "Not all power, not all strength and magic, have to be so—so *cursed*."

Eldara died because she had faith in me and the light I could bring to the world. Our goddess blessed me with her strength because she believed I could right our family's wrongs.

Why can my mother not do the same?

"Why are you doing this?" I ask, breathless. "What happened to you?"

"To *me*?" she says, aghast. Her cloak sweeps behind her as she takes a step toward me. "All of this is your doing. You're the one who has chosen that boy over me."

She nods toward the battlefield, where armies fall in blood. The sound of their blades ricochets over to me, louder than the noise of any others that surround us.

My heart races.

Nox, I scream inside myself.

I can't see him at the edges of the battle where he is supposed to be.

"You would betray me for him," Theola says.

I whip my head back to her.

She's wrong.

This isn't about Nox or how much I care for him. It's about choice: needing it, demanding it. Finally having it for the first time.

It's about making amends for all the evil our family has helped inflict upon the world for so long.

"You'll never understand," I tell her. "The blood oath has corrupted you."

"I'm not corrupted, Selestra." My mother speaks in a sigh. "The blood oath keeps me loyal to the king, but it doesn't change who I am."

I swallow, and finally I ask the question I've been wanting to know since I was a child.

"Then who are you?"

"I'm a survivor," she says. "And I do what I must to live this life."

I cannot fathom the woman before me, talking of survival when all I have seen is her reveling in the glory of being by the king's side.

"You destroy enough lives and you become numb to it," she continues. "I don't have a choice, and so was I expected to be miserable forever? To cry and mourn for all those souls? I cannot live my life that way."

My mother hardens her jaw, shaking away any sign of mourning.

"*This* is who I am," she says firmly. "It's who we both must be."

I shake my head, because I know that's not true. Perhaps once I would have believed it, but now I've journeyed across the Six Isles and I've seen beauty in people and the world.

In myself.

I'm not a monster unless I let myself become one.

"I'm nothing like you," I tell my mother. "I could never be."

Theola nods like she knows this to be true.

"That's why I spent all these years trying to protect you. I knew you couldn't stomach what had to be done and that one day Seryth would find out and have me kill you and birth a new heir."

Her yellow eyes go dark.

"I didn't want it to come to this," she says. "I would have never chosen this for you."

She grits her teeth and her magic seeps through me like quick poison, stealing my very breath from the air.

I gasp and fall to the sand as she siphons it from me.

Every pant and sigh is ripped straight from my lungs. It whips across my lips and I clutch at my chest, willing my heart, my lungs, to work, fight, stop her.

Selestra, get up! I scream to myself.

But I can only heave as she chokes the breath from me.

"It is a terrible thing to kill one's daughter," my mother says mournfully. "Be glad you'll never have to."

44

NOX

Steel screams across the beach as the armies clash in a mess of blood and metal. Within minutes, the sand is riddled with bodies and blood, and I don't know which are enemies or allies.

The Last Army is brutal.

I know that from experience, but I've only ever fought alongside them before and watching my people fight against them is a different story.

They descend like wild animals, springing from the ground and ripping their swords through the air.

I'm pushed back, the maze of Polemistés warriors shielding me from the battle just as Selestra ordered. I quickly lose sight of her in the chaos and a panic sets through me.

I hate this.

I search the sands for her, my eyes roaming the beach to spot her green hair or sunlight eyes. But there is no sign. I want to lead the charge alongside her, fighting at her side rather than standing at the edge of battle like some kind of coward.

I can't just stand here and do nothing.

This is *my* fight, my father's fight, and I've been waiting years for it.

I know what I promised Selestra, but I'm not made to do nothing while people risk their lives for me. If I can't take on the king myself, then I can at least try to protect some of our warriors.

I grip my father's sword tightly.

I will avenge you tonight, I promise him.

I dart forward, weaving through the battle and blocking as many strikes as I can against our warriors. Blow after blow, I shield with my father's sword, before running to the next part of the battle.

I spot Lucian on the far side of the beach by the water, surrounded by at least five of the Last Army.

Quickly, I charge toward him.

I clutch my father's sword and bring it high into the air.

I don't hesitate as I attack each of them, slicing my blade across their stomachs and arms, blocking each blow with as much veracity as I can. Their swords shudder against mine.

I ram my blade into a chest. A heart.

"Get back, you fool!" Lucian yells. "We need you alive to end this."

"Where is Selestra?" I ask.

Where is Theola? I think.

Surely Selestra's mother will want to kill her first. I won't retreat until I see her and know she's safe.

"The future queen can handle this," Lucian says. "Eldara made sure of it. You must stay safe by the sidelines. You are meant to direct our warriors, not intervene in the battle."

I grit my teeth. "I know that."

Lucian and half a dozen Polemistés warriors surround me in a protective circle, fighting off any Last Army soldier who gets near, while I search the shores looking for my princess of magic.

Only instead of Selestra, I see something else.

Seryth stands at the edge of the beach, feet clipping the water as soldier after soldier falls to the ground by his feet. He lets them all die for him.

Even as an immortal, he doesn't want to risk scarring himself when he can watch the battle from afar like an amused puppeteer, searching for just the right victim.

His eyes connect with mine and my jaw hardens as a smile slips onto his hollow face at the sight of me in the battle.

I expect him to lunge forward and try to fight his way through the Polemistés warriors to get to me, but instead his eyes move left and over to a small group of palm trees.

Micah stands there, his sword plunging into the stomach of a Last Army soldier.

No, I think as the king tears his focus from me and puts it all on my best friend.

In a blink, he is at Micah's side, pulling my friend by the neck and throwing him to the ground.

Micah quickly recovers, standing and then charging him, but Seryth moves easily to avoid it and gives a hard kick to Micah's stomach that sends him stumbling backward.

When Micah doubles over in pain, Seryth whips a hand across his face, knocking him down once more.

His eyes find mine again.

He beckons me toward him with a finger. He's goading me with Micah's life.

I push Lucian out of my way and rush forward, ignoring his calls to stop.

I slip across the sand, diving out of the way of stray arrows that soar through the air.

"My little legacy," Seryth calls when I approach. "Let's see how much you've learned."

Without hesitation, I slice my father's sword through the air, but rather than meet bone, it meets nothingness. Seryth glides around my movements, skilled enough that even without a blade to defend himself, he won't let me get to him.

I throw a punch, but he bats my hand away easily, like I am more of an annoyance than a challenge.

"Weak," Seryth says. "You're all so *weak*."

He sounds disgusted by the word and its ashen taste in his mouth.

I can see on his face that just being in the presence of people like us—of mortals who live and die—revolts him.

He can't stand to be here. Not because he's afraid, but because he thinks it's unworthy of who he has become.

Seryth regards me with a disappointed shake of his head. "You're not going to survive this, Nox."

I twist my sword in the air, letting the sunlight radiate from it in a beam. "I've done pretty well so far."

"Your father thought the same," Seryth says, eyeing the blade apathetically. "You think as he did and live as he did. Now you'll die as he did."

"We'll see about that," Micah says, appearing from behind him.

But he barely raises his sword in the air before Seryth turns and pushes him to the ground, discarding Micah like he doesn't matter in this.

He was just a tool to get me here, face-to-face.

I hurtle toward him like a bolt of lightning. Seryth holds out a hand, as if to stop me, and I bring the blade straight through his palm.

He curses.

Now is my only chance.

Promise me if you see Seryth, then you'll run, Selestra begged.

I need to take Micah and get as far away from this king of shadows as I can. Then, when the Red Moon rises, I'll be able to kill him once and for all.

Seryth snarls over to me as I spring for Micah. "Not so fast," he says.

He raises his leg in a sharp kick to my knee. It connects straight to the joint, sending me reeling.

I yell out in pain.

Before I realize it, Seryth has heaved Micah from the sand. He brings a knife to his throat.

My blood goes cold.

"Don't," I say, lurching forward.

Seryth raises a dark brow and a cold, dry laugh escapes his throat. "Is that an order, soldier?" he asks, daring.

"Let him go."

Seryth's eyes narrow. "Now what fun would that be?"

He squeezes Micah by the neck.

"I said stop!" I yell, holding out my father's sword.

He knows I won't use it.

Not with Micah between us.

"Just run him through," Micah says, struggling under Seryth's grasp. "Stab him, Nox!"

"He can't do that," Seryth says.

His fingers tighten around Micah's throat, but his eyes never leave mine. Not even as the tip of the knife breaks the surface of Micah's neck.

"If he tries, you die," Seryth says callously to Micah. "And little Nox doesn't want to lose any more people he loves. Any more family."

He's right, of course.

Micah has been my only family for years. I've lost everyone close to me: My mother when I was born. My father to this demon king in front of me. But through everything there's been Micah.

So I stay still.

I watch as Seryth slides the knife slowly across Micah's throat, drawing a thin line of blood with the shallow cut.

It dribbles slowly down and Micah winces in pain.

"Let him go," I seethe.

My father's sword shakes in my hand.

"You should have stayed back," Seryth says. "But you can't help fighting, can you, Nox? Even with your life on the line, you can't resist the call of the sword. A true soldier. We're alike in that way."

"You can't win this with mind games," I say in a challenge.

"What do you truly want from your sad little life?" Seryth asks, ignoring me. "Vengeance? That is so *small*, Nox. So pitiful. You should think bigger. I wanted to be the greatest warrior to ever live. For people to know my power and not forsake me for an unworthy king. I wanted to rule the Six Isles and lead our lands to greatness. And look what I've achieved. Think of what you could accomplish if you joined me rather than fought against me."

"You've enslaved people," I say, voice wavering as his hold on Micah strengthens.

"Well, yes," Seryth says, with a small chuckle. "But that's beside the point."

Only there's no point to anything he's saying. It's all just words and a way to bide time and try to throw me off-kilter.

He wants to get inside my mind and I won't let him.

"What do you truly want, Nox?" Seryth asks again.

I narrow my eyes. "I want this to be over," I say. "I want you to suffer."

Seryth's eyes slip to Micah and the blade steadies against his shaking neck.

"Nox—" Micah starts.

I see the fear in his eyes as he realizes a beat before I do.

"We all must suffer," Seryth tells me. "You should know that by now."

He sinks the knife into Micah's neck.

I watch as my friend draws in a quiet gasp of pain.

The blood gushes down his shirt.

Then Seryth drops Micah's lifeless body to the ground.

"There now," he says with a cruel smile. "It's over."

45

NOX

The sound Micah's body makes as it falls to the ground is enough to send me stumbling backward.

His face presses into the sand. He doesn't blink or gasp for breath.

He stares at me, mouth agape and wordless.

The grief and fury rise inside me, burning away any chance of tears.

Micah is dead. My friend, my brother, my family.

No amount of healing is going to bring him back.

I will *kill* Seryth for this.

Forget waiting for the Red Moon and watching the battle from the outskirts. I will gut him from the inside out and sever his head from his limbs.

The death king steps over Micah's body and raises the knife to me.

"Now it's your turn."

"No," I tell him. "It's yours."

I charge and tackle him to the ground.

The sand spits up around us as we grapple with each other and my sword is flung from my hand. Seryth brings his head down hard against mine.

I roll away from him, not giving my vision a chance to blur.

I narrow my eyes back into focus, staring at the man my family has followed for generations.

I grab my sword from where it landed beside Micah's body. A line of his blood has stained the tip.

I try not to think about it.

I lunge forward and swing my blade at Seryth.

He moves not just like a soldier, but like a warrior too. He has spent centuries perfecting the art of battle and it shows. Every movement he makes is calculated and decisive.

"Have you learned nothing?" he asks, amused. "You cannot kill me."

"I'll do worse than that."

I reach into my belt loop and throw my dagger toward him.

He snatches it out of the air and throws it straight back into my leg.

The pain tears through me and nearly sends me toppling to the ground. I grit my teeth and pull the blade from my thigh.

I throw it to the sand and swallow down the agony.

I won't let it get the better of me. Not now.

Seryth regards me curiously. "I've made you strong."

"Strong enough to defeat you," I say.

He straightens, the skies darkening with his smile. "Not quite."

I spring up from the sand and slam my elbow into his nose.

Seryth's shock is the opening I need.

I waste no time. I press my blade to his throat and growl, "This ends now."

Seryth shakes his head when he looks at me, his hand caught around the blade's handle, stopping it from sinking deep.

"It will never end," he says. "There is no magic sword. No weapon hidden on this isle that will be my undoing."

My hands clench tighter around my blade in fury.

"There is only me," he says. "And eternity."

"You're wrong," I snarl, and press the edge of the sword a fraction closer to his throat. Enough to nip the skin. He doesn't blink as he bleeds. "Selestra has the power to destroy you. She'll save the Six Isles."

"Destroy me?" Seryth says in a laugh. "How do you expect her to do that when she can't even save herself?"

His smile slithers across his face and I turn, like I know he wants me to.

I see Selestra being thrown to the ground, her mother's magic whirling around her in a gust of gray wind, gathering the sand and leaves up from the beach.

Selestra gags, as though it's choking her.

My rage is overcome in an instant with worry.

Theola is going to kill her.

"There is your savior," the king says, but I am already rushing away from him and toward her.

"Nothing but a dead little girl!" he calls after me.

I run toward Selestra without glancing back.

I know it's what he wants. I know I'm playing right into his hands, but I don't care.

If Selestra dies, then all of this is for nothing.

My father. Micah. Their deaths are worthless without her magic to protect the Six Isles and help destroy the king.

I throw myself into Theola, breaking her hold on Selestra and sending us both hurtling into the sand.

I get up, quickly, and run to Selestra's side as she wheezes out a breath.

"It's okay," I promise her. "I'm here."

"Nox," she says, breathless.

She eyes my wound with a wince and I know it's bad. The blood is hot running down my leg, but I ignore it. I clench my teeth together and look firmly to her.

We have to finish this, I think.

Selestra nods, understanding that this injury means nothing in the face of all the Six Isles falling into Seryth's hands.

I grab her hand and press her close to me, shielding her against her mother.

Theola hisses as she eyes us both.

"Traitor," she says.

"That's no way to speak to the only person left in your family to be blessed by a goddess," I say, raising my eyebrows in a challenge.

"A goddess?" Theola glowers. "There is no such thing."

"You're wrong, Mother," Selestra says. "I faced the trials of our family with Eldara at my side. When I finished, Asclepina came to me and allowed me to inherit her powers."

"The trials," Theola says in realization.

Selestra's mother looks across at her, and her lips open in shock and awe.

"You're—"

"She's a queen," I say. "What the hell are you?"

I almost think the witch flinches, but then her jaw sets firm.

Theola squeezes her fists together. The wind picks up speed and before I know it, it's circling around us in some kind of cyclone, trying to pull us apart.

I grip on tight to Selestra's hand, but the wind lifts our feet from the sand and I can't stop Theola from tearing her daughter from me.

I'm thrown back and hit the ground.

Then suddenly I'm being yanked up by the collar. I see Seryth's darkening face and then his boot cracks against my ribs.

"Sentimental fool," he says.

I thrust my sword out toward him, but he grabs it from the air, his blood coating the blade as it cuts deep into his hand. He pulls the sword from me and pushes it back so the handle slams into my nose.

I tumble back to the ground, my vision blurring.

"You've sacrificed so much for her," Seryth says. "Your honor. Your friends."

Micah, I think.

His name tears me apart inside.

This wasn't even his battle. Micah has a family back in Vasiliádes and a life, yet he chose to risk it all for me.

He didn't have to die here.

He did it for me.

He died because of *me*.

I look up at the king with dark, dead eyes to rival his own.

"I'll give you what you crave," Seryth says, looming over me.

He holds my father's sword up to the light.

"I'll let you meet your father again."

"No!" Selestra screams.

The next few seconds happen fast.

Selestra's magic funnels out of her in threads of bright green light, reaching out to Seryth. The air grows warm and still as Selestra pulls it into a rope to lift Seryth up from the sand.

She holds the writhing king, letting her magic suffocate him.

I catch sight of her eyes and they are so bright, almost golden, like their own little fires. She looks aglow in miracles.

She is a wonder.

Not just a witch, but a goddess like the one from her stories.

I watch her and not Seryth, barely taking a breath as her body shakes with the force of her power.

I don't notice Theola, reaching out a hand for me, until it's too late.

Nor her magic, gathering into a ball of lightning. A storm in her hands.

It catches the light, blinding, as it shoots out toward me.

46

SELESTRA

My mother reaches out a hand and her magic plunges into Nox's chest, picking him up like he weighs less than paper.

She pins him to a nearby tree, squeezing his throat and tarnishing his skin. I drop my hold on the king, sending him plummeting back to the sand as Nox seizes.

Nox's mouth stretches open, convulsing.

His soul, I think. *She's trying to tear out his soul.*

My mother's magic snakes through the air and I feel like I'm reliving the day Asden died all over again, watching him be buried alive inside himself.

No, I think. *Not anymore.*

I'm not a scared heir, trembling at the sight of a shadow king.

"This is your last chance, Selestra," the king says in a breathy growl. The world darkens at the husk of his voice. "Bow to me and let Nox die peacefully. Or force him to suffer the same fate as his father."

My mother fixes her eyes on mine, warning me to obey like she has warned me for my entire life.

To smile. To bow. To be the perfect heir.

But I'm not a child anymore and I don't bow.

Nox once told me that I was descended from goddesses and queens. That only I had the power to choose who I want to be.

"I am Selestra Somniatis," I say.

I clench my fists at my sides.

"Witch of the Six Isles and ward to the warriors of Polemistés. My family are descended from queens and goddesses and their magic lives on in me."

"Selestra—"

"I bow to no one," I tell the king. "Not anymore."

"Then stand and die!" he growls.

"I don't think so."

For the first time in my life, I let go.

I know now that my magic is not just about death, but about life. About everything in balance.

So I take that balance and I knock it off-kilter.

I let the vines of my magic shoot out to my mother and curl around her neck. The wind and the air.

The breath of life, choking the life out of her. Using all of the magic Eldara gifted me with her final breaths. I grip tightly onto what is left of my mother's heart.

Nox drops from her grip, his soul safe as the brightness of Asclepina seeps out of me.

My mother brings her hands to her chest, clutching at the claws of my power.

Seryth turns at the sound of my mother gasping for breath and Nox seizes the advantage to elbow him in the face, reclaiming his father's sword.

I look up at the sky, darkening above us.

The Red Moon can't be more than a few minutes away.

My head whips back. It's as though I've been slapped across the cheek. The cold air of the beach hitting me as fiercely as a hand.

I look to see my mother glowering.

She presses her palms together and our family's magic pools inside them. It absorbs her hands in a flurry of crackling shadows. Pure death that ravages the wind, turning the air around us stale and putrid, disintegrating my magic.

"I've tried so hard to protect you," she says.

There are tears in her eyes as the smoke grows darker in her hands. The smell wrinkles my nostrils. She holds it in her palms, a capture of decay.

My fingers twitch by my sides. "You tried to make me a monster."

She looks tired and the dark magic in her hand recoils, weeping at her hesitation. "I tried to make you strong, Selestra."

"I am strong."

My power gathers in me, an opposition to the death she carries. The power of Asclepina and Eldara, and every one of my ancestors, thrums through me and my skin glows in light. In life.

Years and years, of immortality and infinity, pumping like blood.

I don't know if it's a last spark of magic from Eldara, or if it has been inside me all along, but I'm bathed in the true essence of our magic.

If I send it toward my mother, it will kill her.

She watches me. Her hands quiver with the darkness of her own magic, but she keeps it close and away from me.

"Let us end it," she says.

It almost sounds like a plea.

She looks over to Nox and a flash of something soft and delicate passes over her face as he defends a blow from Seryth's sword.

But the minute I turn to Seryth, I feel the snap of my mother's magic tighten around my wrist.

"I am your villain," she tells me. "Your fight must be with me first."

The words hit me hard, because it's then I realize there is nothing of my mother in her voice. I come to the awful realization that there never will be again.

For years I've been holding on to the hope that she could change, but I see now how wrong I was. Some people can't be saved unless they want to be, and my mother gave up on the notion of being saved years ago.

She is oathed and she can never be anything but.

Her magic tightens around me.

I struggle, but her grip is unwavering as ever.

A horrible sadness shoots through me.

I know what I have to do.

"Let me go, Mother," I beg.

Please don't make me do this, I think. *The Red Moon is so close.*

Her breath stutters and there's only a brief glimpse of my mother, a last glance at her shimmering eyes, before the darkness consumes her entirely.

Her voice drifts through the beach. "I'll let you go, if you let me go," she says.

Her shadows thrust over to me and I throw my hand up in response, sending every ounce of light and life I have back at it. Her magic dissipates, the power of the goddess alight and alive inside me.

I know I can't delay any longer.

This is the only way to truly free her.

"I'm sorry," I say.

My power explodes from me in a ray of light that coats the beach in pure, bright white. It surges toward her and then pierces into her heart.

My magic, Eldara's magic, Asclepina's magic.

It shatters inside of her, and my mother's arms shoot out like wings as she allows it to consume her. In a last breath, my mother smiles and then collapses onto the damp sand.

The sobs overtake me as I realize what I've lost. Not just my mother, not just Eldara, but more magic stolen from the world.

I walk toward my mother's body and kneel beside her, clenching my fists to stone.

This is what she wanted. Better to die than to be bound to Seryth for any longer.

I swallow as I take in my mother's lifeless body. I reach over and close her eyes, letting her finally find peace.

The light may have gone out inside her, but it only ignites in me.

"I will end this tonight," I promise her.

I stand.

And I let my fury rise.

If the king wants a soul-eater, then I'll give him one. Just as Eldara told me to.

Seryth circles Nox like a vulture, attempting to toy with him as Nox slashes his father's sword through the air.

This is a game to him: Our lives and our deaths. Asden. Eldara. My mother. They were all just dispensable chess pieces that got destroyed in his little game. The invincible king has never known anything of grief or loss.

It is time someone taught him.

"Seryth!" I call out.

The man turns to me, surprised at the use of his name. Just a month ago I'd have never dared to utter it out loud, fearing his reaction.

I'm not scared anymore.

Seryth looks over to me as I approach, then his eyes find my mother's body slack on the sand.

No more witch and no more ritual to gather his souls.

There is nothing that an immortal fears more than death. He has lived lifetimes, never having to worry about his time being up because my family made that clock eternal.

The moment he realizes it, I see the seed of fear grow in his eyes.

"Nox!" I scream. "Step back!"

Nox whirls around to face me, eyes wide. He jumps back just as I flick my arms out, sending a wave of light toward Seryth.

The tyrant throws himself to the ground, lunging from my magic.

"Do not be a fool, child," Seryth hisses, rising back to his feet. "I am made immortal."

"Then I'll unmake you," I say fiercely.

In the name of my mother and Eldara and Asden and every soul he has caused to vanish from this world.

My magic pulses at my fingertips as Seryth sprints toward me, his desperation stronger than his fear could ever be.

He is only moments from me when I send my family's power snapping into the air like a whip. The wind rips through his face, leaving a trail of blood across his cheek.

The king is undeterred.

He grabs a fist of my hair and yanks me toward him. His blood smears against my neck as he leans in to whisper in my ear.

I buck and kick against him, but his hold is firm.

"You could have been great," he says to me. "You could have ruled beside me."

"I'll rule without you just fine," I say.

I swing my head backward, my skull cracking into his nose. The moment he drops me Nox is there, slicing his father's blade clean across the king's neck.

"You're not worthy to touch her," he spits.

My breath shakes.

We are unstoppable.

Asden trained us to be fast, to be steady and determined. To be strong. Together, even an immortal does not stand a chance.

This is our destiny, set out by a goddess. Two sides of a coin uniting to destroy a great evil.

Seryth growls, the blood seeping faster and faster from him with every snarl.

I shoot my hands out like darts and my magic sinks into him, propelling him back to the sand before his skin can stitch itself fully back together.

The sky groans up ahead.

I lift my chin to see the moon slink from behind the clouds, radiating a fierce glow.

"Nox!" I call out. "The moon!"

Nox glances up at the brightening night. His eyes glisten with its reflection.

"No!" Seryth yells.

He charges toward Nox and cleaves his fist through the air.

At the last moment, Nox dodges his blow, swiping Seryth's legs out from under him.

He falls and Nox seizes the opportunity to bring his sword swiftly into the air and then stab it through Seryth's heart.

He drives the old king to the ground, pinning him in place.

"Now it ends," Nox growls. "Now *you* suffer."

And he's right: This is the end.

The king's eyes grow wide as the sky shifts above us. The Red Moon rises up through the clouds, with the sound of cracking thunder, staining the world in deep, dark red.

It reflects into the water below like a pool of blood.

The Endless Sea is no longer black, but awash with all the sins of my family.

Around us the soldiers' swords grow quiet, their blades falling slack to their sides as the month comes to an end.

"I cannot die," Seryth says, only it sounds more like a prayer. A wish. "I am your king."

"Kings can be replaced," I say. "Nobody is forever."

He is no longer protected by Isolda's spell and the Red Moon.

The ritual, the bargain, is void. Undone. The souls inside him are no longer bound.

I can hear the anger and fear in Seryth's breath. The sharp growl of a scared and bitter man.

His lips twitch and then stretch open in a guttural scream.

From his mouth the first gray shadow slithers.

47

NOX

"No," he begs in a whimper. "You cannot take them from me."

The man before us stutters. His face morphs to pleading.

The world, the magic, doesn't listen.

As the Red Moon grows stronger and Isolda's magic vanishes, it takes them all, letting the life funnel out of him like corked wine. The souls billow and curl from his parted lips, taking their years unlived with them.

Souls from weeks ago, years ago, a century ago.

Seryth, ancient warrior of Polemistés and self-proclaimed king of the Six Isles, ages before me. He withers like a rose.

I step forward, ripping my father's sword from his chest.

The old man growls in pain as I raise it into the air, his acid blood sizzling against the blade.

Around us, the armies are silent as they see their king, their enemy, become nothing before their eyes. They are frozen in time at the sight of us.

The chaos has turned to stillness.

I smirk. There is no loyalty to this man. There was only ever fear of what he might do if they didn't obey, and now, when he is on his knees, not a single person would come willingly to lift him back up.

"This is for my father," I say as the souls continue to flee from his lips. "This is for Asden Laederic. And for—" I break and swallow down a breath of grief. "And for Micah," I say. "This is for them all."

Seryth looks up at me, wrinkled by years of battle and darkness. Eyes no longer black, but a weeping blue.

He isn't an endless monster, warring against time. He is not a curse on this land or a keeper for Selestra's blood.

He is just a mortal.

I raise my father's sword higher.

"You cannot," the old man manages to choke out.

"I can."

I bring the sword down hard across his neck, every ounce of grief I have thrusting into the blow. I cleave through skin and bone, severing the once-king in two.

Seryth's head drops to the dirt and I release my father's blade, letting the sword fall by my feet. My breath steadies with the clang of the metal dropping from my hands.

The vengeance I have sought for years is done.

My father's soul can rest now. And so can Micah's.

I turn to Selestra, ready to breathe out the sigh of relief I have been holding for years, the weight of my father's death lifted from my shoulders.

She isn't smiling.

Her face contorts in horror and it's only a moment before I see why.

The souls that funneled from the king have not gone to a peaceful afterlife. Instead, they swarm, circling his body as if they're not sure where to go next. Prisoners, with no idea what freedom looks like.

They dart in and out of the king's open mouth, whipping through his bloody neck and then into the shards of his heart that lie inches from his severed head.

"What are they doing?" I yell out.

The sound of my voice causes them to stiffen. Under the light of the Red Moon, they set their sights on me.

I blanch as the gray wisps of souls shoot from the king's corpse and over to me. I feel the magic rippling inside them like a great sea.

It pulls me forward, into its current.

Selestra's magic. Her great-great-grandmother's magic.

Come, it beckons me. *Feed. Immortality awaits.*

The souls swirl around me, a whirlwind of death and chaos.

"Nox!" Selestra calls out, just as the whirlwind turns to an arrow.

And shoots straight into my heart.

48
SELESTRA

I watch in horror as Nox's eyes turn to shadow.

The souls pierce his heart like daggers and with each one Nox gasps out a desperate breath.

No, not desperate, *hungry*.

The deep brown of his eyes is lost to a merciless black. It is a void that erases anything soft and gentle that came before.

The bargain Isolda made for Seryth has found a new home in him, carving a king from the soldier who came before. An immortal from the boy who stole me from my tower.

Isolda's magic is corruptive. It is evil and chaos, and so far from Asclepina's legacy. So far from the magic Eldara gifted me before she slipped into the afterlife.

"Don't let them," Nox says to me. "Don't you let them make me into him."

I hear the words underneath what he says: *Kill me, before the power of these souls corrupts me.*

Kill me, before I become like Seryth.

"I won't!" I scream.

"Selestra," Nox says.

My name on his lips, the best and worst sound I have ever heard.

"I will not become him," he says. "Please."

I grit my teeth at his pleas. Even in death, Seryth and the dark magic that he cloaked himself in still seek to destroy everything I love.

I won't allow this to happen.

I won't let my great-great-grandmother's spell create any more monsters in this world.

Once, she was almighty. But now she is no more.

I am all that is left and I will not let this legacy continue.

I reach out and take Nox's hand in mine, wrapping myself around him. He frowns, shaking his head, adamant.

"What are you—?"

"We're in this together. Always," I say to him. "Remember the skeleton?"

Nox looks confused for a moment, but then a spark of recognition rises in his face. He nods.

I hold on tight to the magic of my goddess as Nox's knees threaten to buckle. He convulses, the souls shaking through him.

Let us undo it, I say to Asclepina. *The wrongs that came before.*

Then I pull each and every thread that lives inside of Nox. Threads I once felt in the king. I pull and pull until I feel them snap.

I call you out, I whisper, repeating my mother's words as I siphon out the souls. Her final lesson to me. *In the name of Asclepina, I free you.*

The souls shudder and tumble from Nox's heart as Isolda's spell finally breaks.

I pay no mind to the two armies, gasping around us as centuries of magic is erased. I don't regard the headless king by my feet.

I just look at Nox and at the power that swirls inside him as Asclepina's magic joins with my own.

Good magic, finally back in the Six Isles.

The souls rush from Nox's heart. Every single life stolen, newly freed and springing back into the world to find their peace. To see their gods and goddesses and find whatever afterlife they've so longed for.

I feel the Endless Sea shift around us and it turns from black to crystal blue, its cursed waters brightening under the moon's watchful glow.

I see it all in my mind too. A glorious vision of freedom as the Six Isles are unlocked to the world. To the kingdoms with the ice mountains and princes of gold Eldara spoke of. To sirens and all manner of mythical creatures as beautiful as the Lamperós bird Seryth held captive.

And the Six Isles, the beauty of them no longer imprisoned by a mad king and his mad dreams.

With every soul that escapes from Nox and back into the ether, I make a wish—a promise—to the Six Isles and all I'll do to rebuild them. To breathe life and magic back into their spirit.

I call you out.

I call you to freedom.

I squeeze Nox's hand in mine as the last lost soul funnels from him.

When he finally buckles to his knees, I slip gently beside him and let him fall into my arms, his heartbeat pressed against mine.

49

NOX

Slowly, carefully, Selestra draws closer to me.

The soldiers and the warriors around us are transfixed. There is no sign of battle in their eyes as they regard Selestra and her infinity.

"Are you okay?" she asks.

I gather my breath. "Sure," I say, though my hands are trembling.

It is not just because of the souls that threatened to rip through me, or the magic of Selestra's grandmother that sought to corrupt me. My hands tremble because they feel so light without the weight of my father's sword.

I've been carrying it for so long, I'm not sure what to do with my hands now.

As if sensing that, Selestra slips her fingers through mine, lacing us together.

My hands instantly stop shaking.

I look at her, remembering how she was bathed in light like some kind of goddess.

"You just set free thousands of souls," I say. "You saved the Six Isles."

"*We* set them free," she corrects. "We saved the Six Isles."

"I'm sorry about your mother," I say.

There is a pain in her eyes that nearly splits me in two.

Selestra's shoulders collapse and small tears break through to her eyes. "As am I," she says. "But at least she is at peace now. At least she belongs only to herself."

My father too, I think.

Lucian approaches us with a stained sword at his side.

"Is he dead?" the warrior asks, looking down at the headless body by our feet.

He means Seryth, of course, but the word *dead* brings only one face to mind.

Micah.

I whisper his name and Selestra goes rigid beside me. I don't wait for her to speak, because if I wait any longer, then I'll be drowned in grief.

I steel myself and walk to my friend's body.

He's lying on his side, eyes wide open and scared. I reach out to close them, hoping that wherever his soul is now, he was able to get a good look at the battle before he went.

"We did it," I tell him, just in case. "We saved everyone."

I lock a hand in his.

My friend. My brother. My *family*.

Selestra's jaw shakes as she clutches on to my shoulder, keeping me steady and grounded. Tears threaten to seep from her, but she keeps them hidden.

Perhaps she'll mourn for him later, but for now I know that she wants to be strong for me.

I sob at Micah's side, the world feeling out of focus without him there. I've never not had Micah with me. Every bad plan, every disastrous trick and scam I came up with on an afterthought, through Last Army training and nights in strange taverns.

"We'll bury his ashes here," Selestra says. "And erect a great tree in his honor. As we will do with all who died here today, Last

Army and Polemistés soldiers both. They deserve honors for their sacrifices."

I shake my head and swipe the tears from my swollen eyes. "No," I say. "Micah would want to go home to his family."

He wasn't an orphan like me, or a forsaken child like Selestra. He was loved and cherished, and his family will want to bury him themselves. I won't steal away their chance to mourn their son and to say a final goodbye to him. But when they do, I'll let them know that he died to save us all.

"They would be proud," Lucian says.

His voice is still gruff with battle, and though blood drips from his stomach, he keeps his head high, ignoring the depth of the wound.

It doesn't matter that around the beach everyone has stilled, most dropping their weapons to the ground as they await their new orders in eerie silence.

Lucian keeps his blade close, not yet trusting that things are over.

"Everyone who died for this war would be proud," he says. "Including Eldara."

I tense. "That's easy for the living to say."

"Nothing is easy for the living," Lucian says. "They have to remember."

His tone softens some. As much as a warrior with a voice as deep as a whale song can.

"We will always remember," Selestra announces, loudly enough for it to sound like an order to the entire beach and the two armies that still crowd it. "We will remember this day and every person who died here on this beach for eternity."

My shoulders loosen, the weight of the world sliding gratefully from them.

"Now what do we do?" I ask. "No more enemies to fight."

"There are enemies everywhere," Lucian says.

Spoken like a true warrior.

"But that will come later. For now, it's time we begin," he says.

Selestra groans. "I thought we just ended."

"We must begin the new order," Lucian clarifies.

Selestra's gaze cuts to him, a hard line casting across her brows. "We don't want to give any orders," she tells him. "The time for that is done."

"A new world order," Lucian corrects her.

He casts a hand across the beach and to the soldiers who eye us tentatively, waiting for proclamations or commands. Now that both of their leaders are dead, they're looking to us like we have any kind of certainty.

Lucian steps forward and clears his throat.

"Lucian—" Selestra begins, but he breathes in sharply, ready to address the crowd of Polemistés warriors and Last Army soldiers.

They watch him eagerly, waiting to hear the new plan for their futures with wild impatience.

For so long things have been uncertain, caught on the cusp of war, but now the threat of peace hangs and not a one of them seems to know what to do with it.

"Bow," Lucian calls out to them. To old enemies and allies both.

Selestra takes in a heavy breath and her eyes widen, like she senses exactly what's coming.

"Bow to your new queen of the Six Isles, Selestra Somniatis."

And they all do.

50

SELESTRA

Most of the bodies are lit on hastily built funeral pyres that line the southern shores of the island, by the sea battalion. It seems the most fitting for fallen soldiers, but the warriors of Polemistés prefer to be buried unburned, with their armor and their swords intact, and so the island is split.

Still, I make sure each and every soldier, no matter their birthplace, is given the same respect in the afterlife so they might find their River of Memory.

Each and every one of them is buried as an equal.

My mother's funeral is the only one that differs in custom. I lay her on a raft of daisies and forget-me-nots, her hands threaded together.

Lucian said that used to be the custom for witches in Thavma.

I think my mother would like it.

I think it will give her some kind of peace.

I cry as she's lowered into the earth and the soil cascades over her face like a current of fresh water. I'm not sure if it's for my mother or for me. For the last witch of the Six Isles.

I cry for days, eyes red and swollen, and it's only when Irenya reminds me of my mother's stories about Asclepina and the afterlife that waits for all witches, where Eldara is probably waiting too, that my tears still.

If those stories are true, then I hope our goddess welcomes my mother with open arms and that she finds forgiveness in her.

As for Seryth, forgiveness isn't an option.

His body is thrown to the water, far out in the depths of the Endless Sea, where it sinks straight to the bottom in a heap of nothingness. To be forgotten and lost to the wilds.

"All set?" Nox asks.

I nod as Lucian loads the last of our cases aboard Leo's butterfly.

We were offered a ship to make our way back to Vasiliádes, with Micah's body and the bodies of any Last Army soldiers who had family back home. But the butterfly brought us here and I think it's only right it's what carries us back across the Endless Sea.

It's the only thing I trust for this journey.

"Is *no* a good answer?" I say to Nox. "I'm not sure I'll ever be ready for all that's to come."

I was relieved when most of the Last Army that we captured from Seryth's attacking fleets agreed to join us willingly, grateful for the killing to finally be over and to not have to be snatched away to war for a wicked king. But not all of them were willing.

Nearly eighty refused to lay down their swords and had to be torn from the ships by force and held in the cells beside the warriors' training grounds.

I know it's the way it must be and that it will take people time to shift their loyalties, but still I feel a pang of guilt. A worry that they're going to start thinking I'm just like Seryth. Just like who my mother became for him.

I fear that when we set sail for Vasiliádes, the soldiers who remained there will feel the same, turning their backs on me, but I know with time I can convince them. It's part of the reason we're going back. I want them to know that when we promised a new world, we meant it.

We're heading to Vasiliádes, not just to return the dead, but to let them know what happened here and to show them my face, no longer locked behind the castle doors. With an entire fleet of Polemistés warriors coming with us, I'm anticipating it being quite the surprise when they learn that their king is dead and a new world is on the horizon.

A new queen.

"Don't look so worried," Nox says. "They need a new leader and you're a lot prettier than the last one."

"I'm not their leader yet," I remind him, ignoring that last part. "I haven't even been coronated and—"

"Relax, princess," Nox says, his voice soothing my worries a little. "It's going to be fine."

"You say that now, but we still have to lead an army, prepare a bunch of stubborn warriors, and persuade some even more stubborn soldiers," I remind him. "We have to motivate them to want to join hands when they've been at war for centuries and unite six islands under magic, when they've always been taught to fear witches."

"Not to mention letting them know there's no more Festival," Nox says, pondering this with a frown. "People are going to hate not having an excuse to drink until the early hours of the morning."

I scowl. "You're not helping."

Nox laughs and presses his hand over the top of mine. "I believe in you," he says, and I know he means it.

Perhaps more than anyone else, Nox has faith that I can unite our world.

"People want change," he promises me. "They want freedom from tyranny and to live their lives knowing they don't have to sacrifice their souls so they can wish for medicine for their children, or enough gold to feed themselves for a little longer. You won't hold their health and their lives to ransom. You'll rule with kindness," he says. "And I'll be right by your side the whole time."

"Promise?"

Nox squeezes my hand, the feel of his skin warm and rough on mine. I don't have to ache for it any longer: not just Nox's touch, but the feel of a hug from Irenya or a clap on the back from Lucian. I can reach out a hand for the world, without worry.

I still have my visions, but they're easier to command now. I know my powers and I will control them instead of letting them control me.

My magic doesn't make me scared anymore. It makes me fearless.

"We'll do this together," Nox says.

"Together," I repeat.

It's all I need.

With Nox by my side and the trust of the greatest warriors in the Six Isles, I feel strong and supported. I don't doubt myself or let my past plague me with guilt any longer. I know that what I was isn't important anymore, it's what I am and what I will do that matters.

Like Nox said, we can't change the past, but together we can change the future. We can forge a new world, filled with peace and hope, with magic and wonder.

So that's just what we do. Together.

51
SELESTRA

Epilogue

"Souls, Selestra, are you ever going to learn to keep *still*?" Irenya asks.

A pair of scissors are clenched between her teeth as she adjusts the fabric of my dress, trimming the ribbons that flow down my bare back.

"I thought escaping the castle meant I escaped your dress fittings," I say.

"You should be so lucky."

"Can't I fire you?" I ask.

"No," she says simply, stepping back to admire her handiwork.

"I'm pretty sure I have the power."

Irenya snorts and puts the scissors down on the small side table. "Not even you are that powerful," she says.

I let out a laugh and look in the mirror at the dress she's created.

Irenya has truly found her calling these last few months in Polemistés, creating the most wonderful gowns I could imagine. After seeing her designs paraded around on me, she has a waiting list of future clients over a mile long and it's easy to see why.

For tonight's celebrations she has created a masterpiece.

The gown is a pale lavender, embroidered with gold and silver falling leaves and flower petals. They dance down the corset and onto the sweeping train of the skirt, fitted with pockets deep enough to hold at least two daggers each. Then there are the soft ribbons, which tie at my shoulder and cascade down my arms and over the lines of my back. I can tell she drew inspiration from the rainbow of colors we saw in Armonía.

And unlike the gowns I was forced to wear back in Vasiliádes, I can actually *breathe* in this one.

"How is it?" Irenya asks, fanning out the skirt. "Does it look okay? Do you feel okay? Do you think the light hits it just right on the embroidery?"

She peppers me with enough questions that I nearly fall off the small square platform.

"Irenya, it's beautiful," I assure her. "Why do you sound so nervous?"

"It's a big day," she says. "What if you fall on the train? Trip, right in front of everyone."

"Thank you for putting that thought inside my mind."

Irenya grins and throws herself onto the plush yellow sofa at the corner of the small dressing room. "It would be interesting at least," she says, face relaxing. "Something to brighten up the event."

"Are you saying it's going to be dull?" a voice asks from the doorway. "Don't tell me I came all this way for a bad party."

Nox leans nonchalantly against the doorframe, his arms crossed against his broad chest. My heart races at the sight of him. It's been only hours since we last saw each other, but I've missed him more than I care to admit.

He adjusts his uniform as he straightens, the perfect blend of a Last Army soldier and a Polemistés warrior. It was Irenya's idea to create something new from the pieces of old, uniting the factions of our islands under one uniform.

It's the perfect outfit for today's celebrations, marking the official union of our people.

"You're late," I say, but I can't help but grin at him.

"Looks like you're the one who's late," Nox says, walking across the room to meet me. "At least *I'm* dressed."

He takes my hand, helping me step from the platform. The feel of his fingers laced in mine, without the barrier of my gloves, still feels strange and new, tingling across my skin.

Nox presses his lips to mine, soft and tender, but I can feel his ache for more in the way he lingers against me. It mirrors my own desire.

"You look beautiful," he says.

"Thank you," I say, at the same time Irenya says, "You're welcome."

I turn to laugh at her. "Don't you have somewhere to be?"

"Actually yes." She gathers up her bag. "I have to go and find my date for tonight."

I raise my brows, surprised. "You have a date?"

Irenya nods. "With that rather fetching new guard you have."

She wriggles her eyebrows.

"Does she know what she's in for, dating you?" Nox asks.

Irenya tosses a pillow at him and I laugh, about to step in between them when someone clears their throat.

"It's time, Majesty," Lucian says, appearing at the doorway in a blink.

I swear sometimes that man is like a ghost.

"Really, Lucian," I say, somewhat scolding. "I've told you not to call me that."

He bows in response and I shake my head.

After healing from his wounds, Lucian has taken over my training these last few months, and as one of the five reigning Polemistés champions, he's a worthy teacher. He'll never be a replacement for Asden, but I think my old mentor would have approved.

"You're not so formal when you're punching me in the face," I say to Lucian now.

"This is a big day, Majesty," Lucian says. His head stays bowed. "We must afford it the proper ceremony."

He's right.

Not just about the coronation, but our true plans for the future. Seryth stole a lot from the Six Isles, but most of all he stole their identity and their customs. We want to bring those back. To restore Vasiliádes, Armonía, Nekrós, Flóga, and even Thavma.

And now that the Endless Sea is no longer cursed into a boundary, we'll send expeditions to find whatever other kingdoms may be out there, waiting for us to join them.

We will spark magic and exploration back into the world.

I now know that if you think something is meant to be, then you have to find a way to make it happen. Destiny doesn't come to you.

You have to take it. Demand it. I plan to do just that.

"Ready, princess?" Nox asks.

I press my lips tightly together to mask my nervous heart.

"That's *queen* to you," I say.

Nox takes my hand and all the nerves slip quickly away with his warmth. "My queen," he says.

I smile at him.

Then the doors open and together we walk through.

ACKNOWLEDGMENTS

Writing a book always feels like the hardest thing in the world. No matter how many times you do it, how many tricks and tips, or how much wisdom (hah) you seem to gain, it never really gets easier. There are always sleepless nights, coffee-ridden and backaching as you hunch over your laptop, and there are times when you're sure nobody has ever written as many plot holes as you have before.

And yet there is also something else in the midst of it all: a world of *fun*. There is laughter and camaraderie and endless excitement.

Writing a book is hard, but it is made so much easier, so much more *joyous*, by all the people who help make it possible. My support systems: My friends, my family, my publishing teams who work so tirelessly, and you readers who continue to have faith in my stories and fall in love with my characters and the worlds they adventure through. Every person who leaves a wonderful review, or sends a kind message, or posts a beautiful picture of my books. You make this journey so incredible.

So thank you to my team at Feiwel & Friends, who always have my corner and whose passion and love for my stories is more than I could ever ask for. To Holly West, the most phenomenal editor who always knows exactly what story I'm trying to tell and how to get there. To Kat Kopit and Kelley Frodel and Jessica White for being my eagle eyes. To Dillon West and all the other readers who helped perfect this book. To Morgan Rath, who is hands down the greatest publicist in the world. To Celeste Cass, Liz Dresner, Teresa Ferraiolo, Brittany Pearlman, and of course Jean Feiwel and everyone else at Feiwel & Friends/Macmillan Children's who have supported and helped me, not just on this book but on all my others. You are the most wonderful team and I am so grateful.

Thank you also to Goñi Montes and Aurora Parlagreco for the most magical cover I have ever seen. It's surreal. You truly brought Selestra and Nox to life!

And to my UK publishing team at Hot Key Books, who are the most wonderful people to work with, and never fail to make me smile with the fun they bring to every new book! To the amazing Ruth Bennett, Molly Holt, Isobel Taylor, Tia Albert and every single other person who worked tirelessly behind the scenes to make this book everything it could be. I'm in awe. And of course Lisa Horton, Rengin Tumer and Dominica Clements for the stunning UK cover! I could not thank you all enough for everything.

Patrick Knowles, as always you have created a map beautiful enough to throw readers head first into this world.

Thank you to my agent, Emmanuelle Morgen, and the team at Stonesong, as well as Whitney Lee, for championing this story, as always, and helping to bring it to as many corners of the world as possible. You guys rock.

Thank you to BookTok and Bookstagram and all the bloggers out there who continue to blow me away with your passion and ability to keep my stories alive and help find new readers, even years later! What an awesome community.

To my wonderful friends in and out of the publishing world, who have been my shoulders to cry on and my biggest supporters, reading my stories from their very first iterations and screaming from the rooftops with support. Thank you to Sarah Glenn Marsh,

N.J. Simmonds, and Tricia Levenseller for being magical CPs.

Of course, I also have to thank my family for being so supportive and getting excited whenever I have a new book out. Plus, they bear with me when I attempt to explain the plot and end up rambling for an hour. And especially to Nick, for always believing in me, and for also believing I'll eventually name a character after him. Dream big!

To Daniel, for being my guiding light and making so many of my dreams come true. I love the life we've built together and could not imagine being a little weirdo with anyone else. Thank you for making me smile every day of our lives.

And, as always, lastly but never least: Thank you to you. To all the readers and adventurers who found Selestra and Nox's story. Writing *Princess of Souls* felt a bit like coming home, returning to a world of fairy tales, with a princess determined to fight for her own destiny in the face of the destiny others have carved out for her. I hope this book made you smile and brought as much fun into your lives as you have all brought into mine.

Also by Alexandra Christo

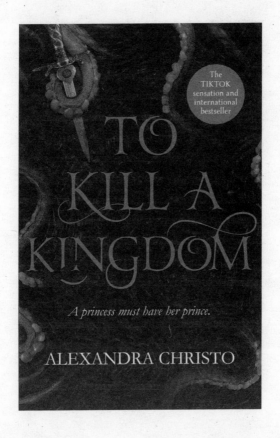

The TIKTOK sensation and international bestseller

TO KILL A KINGDOM

A princess must have her prince.

ALEXANDRA CHRISTO

Dark. Romantic. Unforgettable.

Also by Alexandra Christo

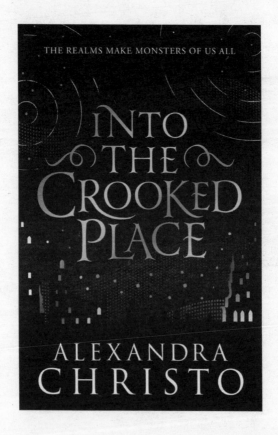

THE REALMS MAKE MONSTERS OF US ALL

INTO THE CROOKED PLACE

ALEXANDRA CHRISTO

The first book in a spectacular fantasy duology.

Also by Alexandra Christo

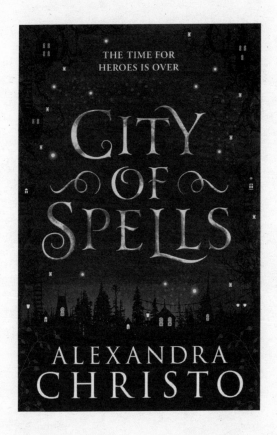

The thrilling sequel to INTO THE CROOKED PLACE.